RICHARD PRICE
LAZARUS MAN

Richard Price is the author of nine previous novels—including *Clockers, Freedomland, The Whites,* and *Lush Life*—all of which have won widespread praise for their vividly etched portrayals of urban America. His award-winning writing for television includes *The Wire, The Night Of, The Deuce,* and *The Outsider*. His feature film screenplays include *Sea of Love, New York Stories,* and *The Color of Money*. He lives in Manhattan with his wife, the novelist Lorraine Adams.

ALSO BY RICHARD PRICE

The Whites
Lush Life
Samaritan
Freedomland
Clockers
The Breaks
Ladies' Man
Bloodbrothers
The Wanderers

LAZARUS MAN

PICADOR
FARRAR, STRAUS AND GIROUX | NEW YORK

RICHARD PRICE

LAZARUS MAN

Picador
120 Broadway, New York 10271

EU Representative: Macmillan Publishers Ireland Ltd, 1st Floor,
The Liffey Trust Centre, 117–126 Sheriff Street Upper, Dublin 1, DO1 YC43

Copyright © 2024 by Richard Price
All rights reserved
Printed in the United States of America
Originally published in 2024 by Farrar, Straus and Giroux
First paperback edition, 2025

The Library of Congress has cataloged the Farrar, Straus and Giroux
hardcover edition as follows:
Names: Price, Richard, 1949– author.
Title: Lazarus man / Richard Price.
Description: First edition. | New York : Farrar, Straus and Giroux, 2024.
Identifiers: LCCN 2024016881 | ISBN 9780374168155 (hardcover)
Subjects: LCSH: New York (N.Y.)—Fiction. | LCGFT: Novels.
Classification: LCC PS3566.R544 L39 2024 | DDC 813/.54—
dc23/eng/20240418
LC record available at https://lccn.loc.gov/2024016881

Paperback ISBN: 978-1-250-39782-9

Designed by Gretchen Achilles

The publisher of this book does not authorize the use or reproduction of any
part of this book in any manner for the purpose of training artificial intelligence
technologies or systems. The publisher of this book expressly reserves this book
from the Text and Data Mining exception in accordance with Article 4(3)
of the European Union Digital Single Market Directive 2019/790.

Our books may be purchased in bulk for specialty retail/wholesale,
literacy, corporate/premium, educational, and subscription box use.
Please contact MacmillanSpecialMarkets@macmillan.com.

Picador® is a US registered trademark and is used by Macmillan Publishing Group, LLC,
under license from Pan Books Limited.

picadorusa.com • Follow us on social media at @picador or @picadorusa

10 9 8 7 6 5 4 3 2 1

This is a work of fiction. Names, characters, places, organizations, and incidents
either are products of the author's imagination or are used fictitiously. Any resemblance to
actual events, places, organizations, or persons, living or dead, is entirely coincidental.

For Lorraine Adams, my vivid, my raw-hearted twin
All I want, is what I have.

For the daughters who raised me—Anne Morgan Hudson-Price
and Genevieve Forrist Hudson-Price

For my brand-new granddaughter,
Willa Hudson Price-Polk

For Ben Polk and Stefan Marolachakis

To the memory of Calvin Hart (1948–2020)

And to the memory of Herbert Zucker (1920–2008)

"God is no thing but not nothing."
—HERBERT MCCABE

PART ONE

ANGELS

SPRING 2008

It was one of those nights for Anthony Carter, forty-two, two years unemployed, two years separated from his wife and stepdaughter, six months into cocaine sobriety and recently moved into his late parents' apartment on Frederick Douglass Boulevard, when to be alone with his thoughts, alone with his losses, was not survivable, so he did what he always did—hit the streets, meaning hit the bars on Lenox, one after the other, finding this one too ghetto, that one too Scandinavian-tourist, this one too loud, that one too quiet, on and on, taking just a few sips of his drink in each one, dropping dollars and heading out for the next establishment like an 80-proof Goldilocks, thinking maybe this next place, this next random conversation would be the trigger for some kind of epiphany that would show him a new way to be, but it was all part of a routine that never led him anywhere but back to the apartment, this he knew, this he had learned over and over, but *maybe-this-time* is a drug, *you-never-know* is a drug, so out the door he went.

One of the bars he gravitated to now and then was Beso, a small slightly grimy spot on Lenox off 123rd, the clientele a mixed bag of old-timers, younger arrivistes to the area both Black and white, and single straight women who felt at ease in here because of its vaguely gay vibe . . .
  On this night, the place was quiet; just two model-handsome young men talking to each other at the short end of the bar and a softly plump light-skinned younger woman, straw-sipping something peach-colored, who couldn't stop looking at them.

The men only had eyes for each other, and small-talking to the bartender, as he already knew, was like chatting up a vending machine.

One of the problems he had with living alone was all that talking to himself, talking without speaking and occasionally deluding himself into thinking that he was actually talking to someone else.

He ordered his drink then set himself up three stools away from her.

"I went there too," he said, chin-tilting to the Fordham Rams logo on her pullover.

"What?"

"Fordham. I went..."

"No, this is my cousin's sweater," she said looking past him.

"What year did he graduate?"

"She. Didn't."

"Me neither, I thought there were better things to do with my time." Anthony just saying it to say it.

"Like what?"

"What?" Momentarily unable to recall what he said last.

Then, "I wish I could remember." Then, "Anthony."

"Andrea." Saying her name as if she wasn't sure of it.

Either because she just didn't care, or was too naive to clock that they were a couple, she threw a smile to the men in the corner, one of them politely smiling back before returning to his conversation.

With the talk going nowhere, Anthony, as he sometimes wound up doing, concocted a more interesting history for himself.

"After Fordham, I went to a clown college down in Florida."

"For real?"

"For real. But I had to drop out because I was too claustrophobic to get into that mini-car with all the others."

"What others?"

"The, you know, clowns?"

Then, looking at him for the first time since he sat down, "Tell me a joke."

"Clowns don't tell jokes," he said, thinking, *I just did*. And gave up.

Columbia, not Fordham. Both the high point and the beginning of the end for him; full boat academic scholarship, freshman track, chess team, then kicked out three months into his second year for dealing in the dorms.

Why.

It wasn't because he needed the money; his Mobile, Alabama, grandparents had made sure of that.

So, *why.*

A therapist suggested that as a Black student he might have subconsciously felt pressure to act out the role expected of him by the white students but that was bullshit. First of all, there were two other guys in his year who were also booted for dealing in the dorms and both of them were white.

Second, there were more Asians than Caucasians.

Third, his parents were both professionals and solidly middle-class.

Fourth, he was raised in as integrated and urbane an environment as could be found in New York, relatively at ease in the private schools he attended, with his racial rainbow of friends and in the social circles of his parents. Columbia was just a seamless continuation of all that went before.

And while he was on the subject, he thought for the multimillionth time in his life—*Why does everything have to come down to race?*

But then, as always, he answered his own question—*Because it does.*

"As a Black student . . ." When the therapist referred to him as that as opposed to what he was, a half-and-half, it rattled him. It wasn't that he didn't know that an eyedropper of Black meant Black but . . .

He was light-skinned and Caucasian-featured enough that, if he wanted to, he could pass back and forth at will.

It seemed to him that nearly every day of life at least one person, intrigued by the mystery of his features, asked him, "What are you?"

Most people preferred to interpret his mixed-race face as Latino, Mediterranean or Arab, a few going so far as to specifically guess

Armenian, Israeli, Turkish but rarely the truth, because for the most part, either out of their own tribal discomfort or embarrassment or straight-up aversion to it they wanted him to be anything but.

Some even resisted that truth when he felt it necessary to share it in order to steer the conversation away from jokes starring Black people, or other shitty racial commentary.

Sometimes he preferred to present as white, other times as Black. Both were true, both were false. And both left him feeling like a spy in the world; a double agent inside a double agent. And both left him feeling psychically exhausted.

When the expulsion from Columbia came down, his mother, whose family owned a chain of funeral homes in Mobile and Birmingham, decided to let it be, but his father, an Italian Irish pugnacious race warrior who taught African American history and literature at various private high schools in Manhattan, tried, after Anthony had pleaded with him to drop it, to kick up dust by accusing Columbia of targeting minority students. But after going through the motions of an internal review, the school basically told the old man to tell his story walking and that was that.

In the end, after a few years of bouncing around from lesser college to lesser college while working here and there mostly as a men's shop retail salesman, he eventually received a BS in education. Over the years since, he had taught junior high school English in a few public schools until his last day three years ago when one of his ninth graders, not liking to be told to stop slow-dragging his chair every five minutes from one end of the room to the other, came up to his desk when he was grading papers and nearly brained him with his arm cast.

The lawsuit he filed against the board of ed was still pending.

But the worst thing that happened that same lousy year was when his stepdaughter had been accepted, minus any offer of financial aid, to the private school where his father taught at the time—there was no way he could have afforded the tuition—and he made the idiotic mistake of mentioning it to the Great Liberator himself who then promptly got into a war with his own administration, resulting in Grandpa losing his job.

The thing was, oddly or maybe obviously enough, when his mother, a passive and distant parent, died of a heart attack, he was shaken but not destroyed. But when his father, that bullying overlord of his life who gave him shit for choosing to marry a white woman, died in a wee-hours one-car crash some months after losing his own teaching gig, Anthony completely fell apart; back into the powder, loss of family, loss of job after job after job—see powder—and he was still falling apart, on this night, and in this bar.

"What do you want," he said, unaware that the words had actually come out of his mouth.

Then again, Beso was bar number three.

"What do *I* want?" she shot back, not liking his tone.

"What?" he said, then, "No. Sorry. I was talking to myself," then, talking to her, "I was in Garvey Park last Sunday with a sketch pad because I heard about a regular open-air outreach church service for homeless people and, yeah . . ."

Anthony drifting a little again, seeing that Sunday crazy man again in his orange wraparound ski glasses and soiled hoodie, his holey blanket-cape, his ballooning left hand bound to the point of bulging by dozens of rubber bands.

"And I wound up talking to this one guy there, he called himself Chronicles Two, he kept asking me, 'What do you want.' Just pressing me, 'What do you want. What do you want . . .'

"I asked why he wanted to know, he says, 'You got that pad and pencil you're holding so I imagine you came to draw pictures of us but you haven't made move one with that thing and I been watching you for forty-five minutes, so what do you want.'"

"Ok . . ." Andrea listening to him for real now.

"Then he said, 'Let me tell you something, you look at me and see what you want to see but know this . . . Yes, I am homeless, yes, I'm on medication but I didn't *lose* my home, I just walked away from it because I need to be here for the people who *need* for me to be here.

"'And I have a real hard time making this scene, sleeping inside my rock and hiding from my enemies, but the fact of the matter is, right now you look more burned out than me so, what do you want.'"

"'What do you want,'" she murmured.

The men in the corner slowed their talk in order to listen in, the standoffish bartender too, busying himself cleaning clean glasses. Without looking up from his nursed drink, he could sense their attention and it made him feel of momentary substance.

"He says, 'You and me, we are men of responsibilities, you to yours, me to mine, and we can't never rest neither of us. You want to survive all that weight? The trick is to think less but without surrendering your God-given intelligence. Can you manage that? Because it's hard and the thing about time is you got a little less of it than you did yesterday.' So . . ." Anthony trailing off, the tale at its end.

A few minutes later, when she got up to leave, Andrea startled him by sliding her fingers over the back of his hand.

He'd relive that touch for years, but it wasn't what he was after.

*   *   *

As she walked her fourteen-year-old son Brian across the Crawford Houses courtyard this evening towards the man who had shot him two days earlier, Anne Collins, wearing her USPS blue shirt and maroon-stripe slacks in order to project some kind of half-ass authority, kept the boy directly in front of her so that she could grab some part of his clothes in case he last-minute decided to bolt.

The kid had that angry/embarrassed look he sometimes wore—head lowered, eyes upraised as if he were about to attack—but she knew that that fuming expression was about all the attack he ever had to him.

At six-three, three hundred and twenty pounds, there was nothing junior about Junior White, one week back out on the street and intent on taking back his spots.

She could tell by the way Junior, through his goggle-thick glasses, barely took note of them as they came on, that he had no idea who her son was, even though he had put him in the hospital with a bullet graze that bloodied his calf.

As scared as he was that night, Brian knew enough not to talk to the detectives who eventually showed up in the ER, and when the female of the two turned to her for help—*Mama, can you do your mama thing?*—Anne played dumb too, thinking, *I'll handle this myself.*

"Hey, how are you, my name is Anne Collins and this is my son Brian Passmore," she said, striving for brisk.

Burning with humiliation, Brian glared at the ShopRite across the street as if he were trying to will it into flames.

"The reason I'm introducing myself to you this afternoon, is because Brian had got shot in his calf the other night right near here. Now, I don't know who did it, and don't want to know, but I've seen you out here and you might hear things and I would appreciate it if you do hear who was shooting the other night that maybe you could tell them for me that Brian is a good kid. I mean he tends to hang out with the wrong crowd, I can't control that from up in my apartment, but he himself, he's more of a go-along-to-get-along hanging in the back type of individual but he'll catch a bullet faster than the others just like he'll catch all the water when a bus goes through a rain puddle no matter how many other kids are standing around, he's just unlucky that way but he don't mean anyone any harm, and I just want you to know that about him so maybe you could pass it along to whoever was throwing shots the other night, you know, in case you ever run into them."

She had no idea if Junior, looking down at her with his lips slightly parted and his eyes unreadable behind his thick glasses, had heard a word of it.

And if he knew that she knew she was talking to the shooter himself—of course he knew—he didn't show any sign of it.

Now what.

"You live in building Six, right?" he finally said, his overweight lungs whistling through the words.

"That's right. My name is Anne Collins and my son here is Brian Passmore."

"What floor?"

"The fourteenth. It's really the thirteenth but they don't want to make anybody nervous with that number so they skip it altogether."

"I don't know anybody living on fourteen."

"Well, now you know me," Anne said, pretty much forcing him to shake her hand. "So maybe we can start saying hello to each other when we pass. You have a good night."

*, *, *,

Finally on his way home, half-smashed, Anthony found himself standing beneath an open second-floor window on Lenox, a microphone-amped voice, deep and female, blasting out into the empty street.

GOD, I HAVE BEEN . . .
GOD, I HAVE NEVER BEEN . . .
GOD, I AM . . .
GOD, I AM NOT . . .

Then, after a short microphone silence through which poured a raging aviary of disembodied howls and shouts . . .

GOD, WHAT I WANT . . .
GOD, WHAT I FEAR . . .

At first, he just stood there staring up, then, not ever ready to call it a night, he stepped through the propped open street door, climbed the cooked-diaper-smelling stairs and walked into a hotbox of chaos: a too-bright, too-small, airless room packed with too many people, some upright and juddering like jammed washing machines, others roaring, keening, yipping or rolling up and down the aisles like tumbleweeds, the mingled scents of body odor and bleach hitting him like a wall.

TELL THE PEOPLE ABOUT THE COMETS, GOD
WAKE 'EM UP IN TALLAHASSEE, GOD
WAKE 'EM UP IN ATLANTA, GOD
THOSE PEOPLE DIDN'T DO NOTHING TO DESERVE THOSE COMETS, GOD

And there she was, Prophetess Irene, as wide as a bus in a blue-and-white box-check pantsuit and matching newsboy cap, standing in the front of the room, mike to mouth, her eyes lightly shut behind great turtleback lids . . .

SO GIVE 'EM A HEAD START IN FLORIDA, GOD
GIVE 'EM A HEADS UP IN GEORGIA, GOD
GET THEM ALL OUT OF THERE, GOD

Before he could even begin to process the sight of her booming out her visitations, or to make any sense of all the people running in the aisles, snapping their hands at the wrists as if drying them off, or clutching their temples as if their brains were on fire, or to just square himself up, decide to bolt or to stay and see, the decision was made for him—big mannish hands steering him from behind into one of the folding chairs.

WE PRAY FOR THAT VIRUS COMING DOWN, GOD
ITS GONNA HIT US IN THE INTESTINES, GOD
KEEP AN EYE ON THAT VIRUS, GOD
DIVERT ITS MISSION, GOD

And even though she hadn't looked his way once since he came into the room, was yet to open her eyes as far as he could tell, he intuited that she was aware of his new-face presence, probably wondering whether he was friend or foe, and what to do about it either way.

GO TO CAMILLE THOMPSON IN PATERSON, NEW JERSEY, GOD
SHE'S HAVING A DIFFICULT PREGNANCY, GOD
RELAX HER FEMALE ORGANS, GOD
OPEN HER FEMALE PARTS, GOD
GO TO GINO LYONS IN YONKERS, GOD
HE DIDN'T MEAN TO HURT HIS WIFE LIKE THAT, GOD
HE WAS FRUSTRATED, GOD
HE WAS BESIDE HIMSELF, GOD
AND NOW HE'S SORRY FOR IT, GOD
SO, TELL HIM TO GO TO THE POLICE ON HIMSELF, GOD
BEFORE SOMEONE ELSE DOES, GOD

The man next to him began whirling his hands one over the other as if he were rolling up a skein of invisible yarn, whirling higher and higher with each rotation as if he were building a Jacob's Ladder, higher and higher until he had to rise up out of his chair to keep it climbing.

Misted with his neighbor's funk, Anthony sat head down trying to get a grip, wondering how people could just let go like this, come in off the street, hand their brains to the hatcheck girl in the lobby, step inside a room and immediately start whizzing around the walls like unknotted balloons.

He'd seen it before in some churches, understood that for some with hard lives the need to let it all out in a safe place for a few hours on a Sunday morning or a Thursday night was one way of fortifying yourself for the burdens of the coming week, but that ability to willfully vacate yourself, to disassemble your very being in pursuit of a fleeting release . . .

Carefully raising his eyes to the room, he saw that the only islands of composure were the dragged-along-by-grandma, seven, eight and nine-year-olds, the shirt and tie boys, the dress and hairbow wearing girls, sullenly flaccid in their folding chairs, their eyes as dull as nickels, one small boy looking back at him with embarrassed anger.

I PRAY FOR EVERY DOCTOR IN EVERY STATE, GOD
I PRAY FOR EVERY NURSE IN EVERY STATE, GOD
YOU GUIDE THEIR HANDS, GOD, YOU GUIDE THEIR SKILL, GOD
WE NEED THEM DESPERATELY, GOD
WILL NEED THEM DESPERATELY EVEN MORE IN TIMES TO COME, GOD

As the celestial teletype continued to stream he began to settle a little, drift a little, and experience a nugget of desire—not to bust loose but to burrow down—where he sensed there was some kind of thoughtless safety waiting for him.

AND KEEP AN EYE ON THE EIGHTH AVENUE LINE, GOD
DON'T LET THEM TERRORISTS DO WHAT THEY'RE PLANNING, GOD
THERE'S GOOD PEOPLE RIDING THAT A TRAIN, GOD
DON'T LET NOTHING HAPPEN TO THEM, GOD
THEY GOT TO GET TO WORK, GOD
THEY GOT TO TAKE CARE OF BUSINESS, GOD
EVERYBODY GOT TO TAKE CARE OF BUSINESS, GOD
THE BUSINESS OF LOVING YOU, GOD

He was getting there, feeling both above and beneath it all, floating and buried and slightly unable to form thoughts.

Then still unseeing behind those shuttered lids Prophetess Irene addressed his presence in her temple head-on . . .

THIS YOUNG MAN RIGHT HERE, GOD
HE CAME IN BECAUSE HE HEARD THE NOISE, GOD
WAS CURIOUS, THAT'S ALL, GOD
BUT NOW HE'S HERE, GOD
BECAUSE YOU BROUGHT HIM HERE, GOD
HE'S BEEN LIVING WITH SEVEN, EIGHT, TEN YEARS OF PAIN IN HIS HEART, GOD
HIS FAMILY HAS LEFT HIM
HIS FRIENDS HAS LEFT HIM
HE'S BEEN CRYING OUT TO YOU ALL THIS TIME, GOD, HE JUST DIDN'T KNOW IT
BUT NOW THAT HE'S FINALLY IN YOUR PRESENCE, HIS TABLES WILL BE TURNED,
AND HIS HEART WILL BE HEALED
HE WAS FIRST THEN LAST
AND HE WILL BE FIRST AGAIN, GOD

She was a hustler, he knew that, but it didn't stop him from viscerally experiencing a rush of hope. A hustler, no doubt about it, but he still felt grateful. To her.

I CALL OUT FOR AIDS, GOD
I CALL OUT FOR HYPERTENSION, GOD
I CALL OUT FOR DIABETES, GOD
I CALL OUT FOR OVEREATERS, GOD
I THANK YOU FOR MY HEART, GOD
I THANK YOU FOR MY LIVER, GOD
I THANK YOU FOR MY LUNGS, GOD
I THANK YOU FOR VITAMIN A
I THANK YOU FOR VITAMIN B COMPLEX
I THANK YOU FOR LEAFY GREENS, GOD
I THANK YOU FOR INSULIN, GOD

He closed his eyes and tried to return to that descending state of release but this time the small euphoria running through him he recognized as identical to the fleeting cut-cord elation he had felt right before deciding to swallow most of a bottle of aspirin a week after his wife and stepdaughter left.

AND GIVE US THE STRENGTH TO DEAL WITH OUR DAUGHTERS, GOD

WE CAN'T SAY NOTHING TO THEM THAT THEY DON'T GIVE US BACK TWO FOR ONE, GOD

HUMBLE THEM AND GIVE THEM BIGGER EARS TO LISTEN WITH, GOD.

NOBODY NEEDS MORE GRANDCHILDREN, GOD

BUT IF THEY'RE GONNA COME ANYHOW, GOD

GIVE US THE GRACE TO RECEIVE THEM AS THE BLESSINGS THAT YOU INTENDED THEM TO BE, GOD . . .

Spooked by his own deadly sense-memory, he impulsively raised his eyes to her for help.

And then he wished he hadn't.

I SEE YOUR ANGELS HOVERING AROUND THAT SPOT ON THAT YOUNG MAN'S BACK, GOD . . .

THEY SEE SOMETHING THERE, GOD

THEY'RE WORRIED ABOUT SOMETHING THERE, GOD

THEY KNOW LIKE YOU KNOW THERE'S SOMETHING INSIDE OF HIM RIGHT THERE, GOD

THEY KNOW LIKE YOU KNOW, GOD

THAT IF HE DON'T GET IT OUT, IT'S GOING TO KILL HIM, GOD

He had no idea what he'd done to make her flip the switch on him like that but those fretting angels of hers came off to him more like a threat than a divine insight; a menacing metaphor that he couldn't dissect right now, but one thing was clear—it was definitely time to go.

As he stood up to leave, the big hand that steered him into his seat once again came out of nowhere to slap a glob of cheap vanilla-scented lotion on his forehead and into his hair, Anthony knowing right off what the deal was—an effort to startle him into feeling like he had been hit by the spirit—it must have worked on some people in here but all he could think of was the shower he had to take to get that cloying crap out of his hair. It felt unworthy of her, but she still freaked him out.

Heading for the door, he could feel her eyes on his back.

SOME SET FOOT IN YOUR HOUSE, GOD
JUST BECAUSE THEY'RE CURIOUS, GOD
BUT THEY SHOULD KNOW THAT CURIOUS DON'T CUT IT WITH YOU, GOD
DOUBTERS DON'T CUT IT WITH YOU, GOD
SO SHOW THEM THE POWER OF YOUR TRUTH, GOD
LET THEM BE SLEEPLESS FOR YOUR VISITATION, GOD
LET THEIR COUNCIL OF REJECTION BE REJECTED, GOD
LET THEIR COUNSEL OF REJECTION BE SHUNNED, GOD

Out on the street, he could still hear her through that open window, as if she were chasing him home.

WE CAN'T HAVE NO MORE LONELINESS IN HERE, GOD
WE CAN'T HAVE NO MORE REJECTION, GOD
WE CAN'T LET REJECTION AND LONELINESS SET UP HOUSE IN US NO MORE, GOD
WE CAN'T DRINK NO MORE TEARS FOR WATER, GOD
SO, TEACH US TO GET TIGHT WITH YOU, GOD
TEACH US TO GET LOOSE WITH YOU, GOD

** * ***

When Anthony was five and his sister Bernadette was seven, their parents purchased a co-op apartment in the Renaissance Towers, a five-building privately owned mixed-income housing development; moderately upscale for the area.

After his father's death, the title was transferred to the children but neither one was anxious to live there given the childhood memories that they would have to deal with every time they turned a corner or walked into a room.

Bernadette was fine living in Riverdale with her dogs, but at least for the time being he just didn't have any choice.

Approaching his building entrance, Anthony saw that on this night, the super, Andre, a broad-shouldered near-mute, whose eyes set deep in his spade-shaped face projected all the warmth of a coal shovel, was covering for the regular doorman.

And so, as Anthony expected, when he passed the reception desk on his way to the elevators, Andre, as usual, looked up from his day-old *New York Post* just long enough to make eye contact but then, as usual, pointedly declined to even nod in greeting.

Whether out of personal pain or universal disdain, the man was that way with everyone; nonetheless, it was hard for Anthony, in his present state, not to feel judged.

His parents could have been dead for a century but the apartment still remained exactly as they had left it, because even after a half year of living there he needed to think of it as a mere stopover, and he was no more willing to modify it to his taste than he would a motel room.

And so it remained a visual tug-of-war between his mother's trim fastidiousness, her silver-framed multigenerational family portraits, her signed Jacob Lawrence lithograph and collection of home-stitched Sea Island quilts, and the artifacts of his father's burly social justice bent: his books, his Leon Golub prints and a framed photo of himself in cuffs at the tail end of some demonstration, grinning through his blood-rimmed teeth as if getting his ass beat by cops was a great victory in itself.

What Hubert Carter could never understand was how all of his righteous defiance, in the end, had cost him nothing, because he could come and go in his angry white skin as he pleased. Despite marrying a Black woman and having mixed-race kids, there was no such thing as an "honorary" brother, no matter how many times you raised your fist in solidarity, or how many prison writing workshops you conducted, or how many times you got up in some cop's face—because in the end, you were never stuck with the fact of your race or how the majority of people you encountered in the world chose to sum you up without knowing a single thing about you.

The only time Anthony could remember his father ever expressing any kind of rueful self-reflection on that score was on the one night when he came home stoned from a party and announced that at least when it came to law enforcement, Ellison had it backwards—Black people were all too visible, the invisible men were people like himself.

His hair stank and the lotion had spotted his shirt, so after first throwing back a shot of vodka straight from the freezer he went into the bathroom and stripped off his clothes. He'd been a sprinter in high school and college and retained his leanness, had his mother's delicate thin-featured face and skin (his grandmother once told him that her side of the family was part Choctaw and/or Cherokee but who knew).

He stepped into the shower, but then remembering Prophetess Irene's hovering cluster of angels, he stepped out again and examined his back in the bathroom mirror.

Nothing. Well, how about that.

And how about this—tomorrow morning he had his first job interview in a year; a low-impact gig, retail salesman in a big-and-tall men's shop. He'd done the work before, but he was more interested in just getting back into the working world, back into a routine that would help him regain his normal.

Post-shower he watched half of an old *Law & Order* episode before he realized he'd seen it before, said out loud, "Hello old friend," then got up to take one last slug of vodka to help out the sleeping pills and that was it.

Tomorrow, he hoped, would be a game changer.

PART TWO

BOOM

At 4:00 in the morning, Felix Pearl, who at twenty-four was still referred to as "the kid" by the family that adopted him, including his "real" younger brothers—couldn't, could not, sleep. The steel scream of the Metro North trains as they took the sharp track curve twenty-five yards from his third-floor bedroom window—normally a weird comfort to him on most nights—was, on this night, a screeching reminder of his bizarre encounter on the subway a few hours earlier.

The poetry slam that he had been hired to film at a Gowanus hookah bar had been over by eleven but the so-called guest curator made him wait around for another hour—which meant another hour of having to involuntarily inhale the floating wreaths of cigarette smoke into his sketchy lungs—before forking over Felix's one hundred and fifty buck fee.

Still feeling a little cloudy in the chest when he was finally able to board the 5 at Atlantic Avenue for the long ride home to Harlem, he immediately sized up the big man in the dark sunglasses sitting slump-shouldered across the car from him as some kind of Noddie, head-down motionless save for the way the rocking of the train made his chin rhythmically bob towards the newspaper spread across his lap.

But after traveling for forty minutes with this guy without him making even the slightest physical adjustment, Felix thought he might actually be dead, had died sitting upright on the train; no telling how many people had sat next to his corpse as it made its way up and down the line. He thought about taking the camera out of his backpack and squeezing off some shots, but then balked because if he posted it, it could be interpreted as heartless. Was heartless. But if he couldn't film the man he could at least imagine that he was, with the camera embedded in his head, his eyes the lens. And it was in this study of his subject that he noticed that the opened paper in the dead man's lap was the *New York Times*.

Not to say that it was impossible for that to be the corpse's paper of choice, but to Felix's eyes he was dressed way too street—a Homestead Grays hoodie, a pair of Jimmy Jazz ribbed and distressed jeans with too many pointless zippers, low-top bright red Superstar Pumas—for that to be likely.

One of the reasons why the *Daily News* and the *Post* were the commuter's choice was that they were easier to manage on a crowded train. Reading the *Times* on the subway was like trying to spread your arms in a phone booth.

And then Felix caught the movement—the slow steady tugging of an erect prick beneath the shadowed overhang of the paper.

No one else in the half-full car seemed to notice, most of them either playing games on their phones or at this late hour nodding off to the lullaby of the rails.

At first, the shock of discovery followed by the fear of a confrontation with a physically larger stranger kept him in his seat, Felix telling himself that the man wasn't hurting anybody.

But he was.

He was hurting Felix, straight-up freaking him out.

And he just kept at it.

He wasn't afraid of throwing or taking a punch if he had to, but there was too much X factor here, too many potentially grievously-stupid-in-retrospect outcomes to be any kind of confidence builder.

Nonetheless . . .

"Excuse me, *sir*," saying it louder than necessary as he leaned forward, "*Sir*. Do you know what time it is?"

When the not-dead individual realized that Felix was addressing him, he became even more corpse-like, borderline cryogenic, no telling what he would do when he thawed himself out.

"*Sir*," Felix kept at him, one hand now on the small can of bear spray in his jacket, "do you have the *time*."

For the next endless few minutes the man continued playing possum, but when the doors opened at the next stop he bailed like a bailiff, Felix having to press his palms together between his legs in order bring his shaky hands under control.

So, there was that . . .

And then there was this . . .

He lived in a former one-family brownstone broken up into ten kitchenettes, the majority of his co-tenants, all men, were freelance "entrepreneurs," grey market street vendors selling home-burned old-school soul CDs, bootleg movie DVDs and hot-off-the-presses memorial T-shirts of whoever iconic in the culture had just died the day before.

And when he finally approached his stoop at two in the morning, he saw that one of them, O-Line, a morbidly obese giant who had been an offensive guard with the 1985 New Jersey Generals of the USFL, making daylight for Herschel Walker until a broken leg retired him in the final game of the season and who now walked with two canes, was still out there, lightly toasted on Smirnoff Ice and in need of some assistance getting up to his third-floor flat, which of course Felix offered, shoulder-snugging himself up under O-Line's armpit as they hit the stairs, the climb infernally slow because O-Line had to stop every few steps to rest, muttering, "Monster, Monster," each time, which was what O-Line and the others had christened him within a week of his moving in.

Monster . . .

Fresh to the block after a lifetime of living upstate, and finding it constantly nerve wracking each time he had to weave his way through these older men and their hard-eyed assessment whenever he left or returned to the brownstone, he went to the Eat and Run corner store, aka the Clutch and Squat, and came back with a half-dozen cans of Monster, a high-octane energy drink, as a tension-breaker and peace offering; a reverse housewarming gift, the new homeowner handing out casserole dishes to the longtime residents of the block.

"No straws?"

When he started to go back, they laughed—just fucking with him—and raised their cans.

"Monster."

And then at six in the morning, just as he was finally dropping off, the gigantic neighborhood simpleton, Robert Cornish, aka Green Mile, aka the Rooster, took up his regular dawn patrol, Felix dragging himself to the window to watch him marching up and down the block wordlessly ululating like a titanic flute until his eighty-year-old aunt finally made it out of their walk-up building to bring him back upstairs, aunt and nephew as reliable in their early morning dance as two figurines emerging on the hour from a Swiss cuckoo clock.

Nobody around here liked to be woken up like that but no one blamed Green Mile for the way he was, either. Not to say that his neighbors were nonstop hearts and flowers toward each other, but no one ever passed judgment on you for just being who you naturally were. And that's what Felix cherished about his neighborhood more than anything else.

He was, by blood, probably some kind of Latin American or maybe North African or Amerindian, but raised Jewish by the family who adopted him in a small upstate town halfway to Canada. At first, his childhood was just boring, but by junior high school his classmates, a bunch of all-American snowballs if there ever were any, took a fresh gander at his squat, overly hairy self, his low forehead and broad-featured face with its small bunkered eyes, and christened him "Cro," short for Cro-Magnon, which is one of the reasons he left there as soon as he could save up and move to East Harlem—Spanish Harlem he had heard it was called at one time—in hopes of finding his true tribe.

And so, at eight in the morning, as he was finally drifting off and heard the abrupt harsh clatter and buckshot pop of shattered glass suddenly raining down on the street he was just too tired to get up, go to the window and check it out.

Oddly enough, what jerked him fully awake a minute later, what felt to him like the striking of some ancient chord in his gut, was the absolute silence that followed. It lasted no more than a few swollen seconds, just enough to establish itself as silence, before giving way to dozens of car alarms going off from one end of the block to the other, seemingly without cause as if in the grip of a mass timer malfunction.

Then, out of the corner of his eye he thought he saw one of his walls start to flutter. He thought he was still asleep, he thought he was dreaming, had to be, until a tremendous concussion of sound and invisible, everywhere, propulsion threw him out of bed and rolled him across the narrow floor until he until he came up face-first against the opposite wall, the impact bloodying his nose.

When he finally sat up, staring stupidly at the sky through his window, all that he could see of the outside world was a night-for-day roiling black cloud, which, by the time he was able to get to his feet, had turned a filthy white, but no less dense.

It had to be what he always imagined would happen one day: the Metro North train rounding that killer curve up there too fast, flying off the tracks like an arrow and burying itself into the side of a building.

Mastering the wobbles, he got himself into sweatpants and a pair of flip-flops and bolted for the building's stairway to scope out the damage on the street.

He was already two flights down, the smutty contents of that apocalyptic cloud already seeking out his lungs, when he stopped, wheeled and headed back up to the apartment in order to grab his Nikon.

* * *

Earlier that same morning, driving to the bank with Bobby Hazari, her partner du jour, Detective Mary Roe, a trim raw-faced woman of forty-two, her cropped red hair rapidly turning the color of steel, couldn't stop thinking about the Battle of Oriskany reenactment she had dragged her sons to over the weekend, and what a bust of a trip that was . . .

She thought they'd go for all the throwback redcoat uniforms, the musket fire, the whooping war-painted Iroquois and Mohawks swinging their war clubs and hatchets as the Loyalists and the Patriots closed on each other—*she* liked it well enough but the kids were so pissed/exhausted from being dragged for four and a half hours just to watch a fake fight that she had to up their allowances to even get them out of the car. Well what can she say, she still held the ancestral working-class conviction that a growing boy needed to learn how to take and give a punch or he'd never possess true confidence in himself and, by left-handed corollary, that there was nothing wrong with that same boy coming to a girl's door with a bunch of flowers.

The thing is, if you have a deep-seated fear of crossing state lines like she had, if in fact you refused to do so, sometimes you spent nearly half the day driving due north even though New Jersey was only twenty minutes away.

In any event, this crossing borders phobia of hers had never presented itself as any kind of problem when she was in patrol but once she made detective her inability to pick up a suspect in Connecticut or interview a witness in Pennsylvania nearly deep-sixed her career.

Her rabbi in the department, Jerry Reagan, a deputy inspector who knew her family, tried to help, hooking her up with an NYPD-contracted psychoanalyst, but after six months of talking and reflecting, talking and reflecting, she'd gotten deeply in touch with how much her mother resented her when she was little, but still couldn't bring herself to drive through the Holland Tunnel into Jersey City or over the GW Bridge into Fort Lee.

At that point, she had decided to go back to school to learn something else but the rabbi wouldn't hear of it.

He took her out for a number of beers and proceeded to run down a laundry list of her natural-born not-so-obvious talents—she knew how to talk to people, enjoyed it in fact, she had the patience of a guru, never escalated a bad situation or lost her cool, never took anything personally out there—all thanks to her either bulletproof or nonexistent ego.

"In a nutshell," he told her, "even the people that should hate you, like you."

The solution was to assign her to Community Affairs, where the overarching thrust of the job was basically to calm people down, whether it involved speaking at open-house Community Board meetings, greasing the way for street fair permits, stop-the-violence rallies, even anti-police rallies. Then there was coordinating the police presence at parades, at gang-connected funerals (at which there was always the danger of on-site payback), pulling together the unicorn-rare dignitary escort teams whenever some foreign politico/senator/celebrity was scheduled to make the local rounds, although given that her district was East Harlem these dignitary teams were called on about as much as it rained in the desert.

As they approached the intersection of Second and 116th, Hazari, fresh to the squad, nodded to the Banco Popular on the northeast corner.

"This the one?"

"This is the one," she said, then, taking in Bobby's mocha-toned complexion and coal-black hair, "You speak Spanish, right?"

"Who, me? I'm Syrian."

The street door that led into the ATM-banked vestibule was open but the interior door that led into the bank itself was locked.

The main floor appeared to be deserted, no one behind any of the tellers' windows or at any of the customer service desks.

"They're in there?"

"Police," Bobby blared, knuckle-rapping the glass, "NYPD."

It took three more shout-outs before the branch manager, a tall middle-aged Latina in a bronze pantsuit, appeared from around the bend, looking more pissed off than traumatized.

Mary pressed her police ID and shield up against the glass, but the manager—DORIS ACEVEDO her brass name tag read—waited until Bobby did the same before she finally let them in.

"This is the fifth time this year," she said, walking them back to her office. "Can you believe that?"

"How much did he get?" Bobby asked.

"Not a dime."

"Anyone hurt?"

"We didn't even know it happened," she said, then, "except for Charisma."

The tellers, three young women, were sitting together on a couch in the sizable but windowless room. No need to guess which one had been targeted, Charisma's shock-mottled face and death-gripped water bottle telling the tale. She was youngest and slightest of the three, Mary thinking she could pass for a ninth grader.

The other two, one on each side of her, came off as excited but holding it in out of respect for the victim.

"First thing," Mary said as Bobby stepped off to take a call from one of their myriad bosses, "is everybody ok? Anybody need anything, medical attention, more water?"

The other two murmured in the negative, but Charisma was in another world.

"How about you, honey?" Mary asked, perching herself on the magazine table in order to seek out her eyes. "Are you ok?"

When she remained mute, Mary turned to the branch manager.

"You see her," Ms. Acevedo said.

"Did he have a weapon?"

"She said no." One of the other tellers answering for her.

"Ok, good. Did he pass a note?"

Charisma nodded yes.

"Do you have it?"

"She said he took it back and just walked out," the same teller answered.

"That's what happened?" Mary touched the back of Charisma's hand.

"Yes," she finally said.

"Ok. Good. Can you describe him?"

Instead of answering, she rose from the couch and gesturing for Mary to follow, walked out of the office and across the main floor to one of the picture windows looking out on Second Avenue.

She pointed to a small group of bedraggled older street cats hanging in front of a bodega across the street.

"*Un flaco.*"

"I'm sorry?"

"The skinny one."

"Which skinny one."

"In the Yankees hat."

Mary took one look at the guy, a too-tall goateed wreck whose teetering body looked as if it were built out of collapsing shingles, and instantly knew his game. Nonetheless, this guy had them by the balls and there was nothing she and Bobby could do now but follow protocol.

"I have a gub," she muttered.

"*Maricón*," Charisma spat, turning away and walking back to the manager's office.

As Mary and Bobby left the bank, the first patrol car finally pulled up.

"Where the hell were you?"

"Banco de Ponce."

"Banco Popular," Bobby said, pointing to the name over the door.

"Stay close," Mary said.

As they crossed the avenue towards the guy in the Yankees hat, his buddies began to casually bail, disappearing around the corner or into the nearest buildings. But the man of the hour stayed put, playacting as if he were unaware of the two detectives closing in on him in order to lock his ass up.

When they got close enough though, he raised his arms in order to facilitate the coming frisk.

"Hey, how're you doing?" Bobby asked, patting him down as Mary kept an eye on his hands.

"I'm good, brother, how're you?"

Given his wrecked appearance, his deep voice was surprisingly radio-smooth.

"What's your name?" Mary asked.

"Tony G."

"Tony G, you tried to rob that bank?"

"Yeah, but I changed my mind."

"You gave the teller a note?"

"I did, yes, but I took it back."

"Well, you can't unpass a note," Bobby said, reaching for his cuffs.

"He knows that," Mary grunted, double-pissed and then some.

"That being said, I wasn't unpleasant to the young lady." Tony G offered, "You can ask her."

"Yeah, ok."

"So, what now?" he asked as the cuffs bit home.

"What do you think?" Mary asked.

"State or federal?"

"Fed crime, fed time." Mary again.

"How much time?"

"Two, three years, minimum."

"Ok."

"'Ok'?" Bobby sounded offended, but he was coming off four years in a more genteel district, so . . .

The majority of so-called bank robberies in this precinct were nothing more than a ploy to get off the streets. Sometimes Mary felt more like a homeless outreach worker for the DHS than a cop. Well, this is what some of these guys did in order to get a long-term roof over their heads.

She knew of one individual who had set fire to an abandoned building up here then waited around to be cuffed, another desperado who'd sucker punched a cop.

"Hey, guy," Bobby said, as he finally figured it out, "if all you wanted was three hots and a cot why didn't you just go to . . ."

Mary looked away, praying he wouldn't finish the sentence and come off like a tourist from Kokomo. And to his credit, he didn't, couldn't bring himself to get the words "homeless shelter" out of his mouth.

"Yeah, see?" Tony G crowed. "You can't even say it."

A moment later, as they were escorting him to the patrol car, a primordial volcanic roar wracked the air, its source too far away to be seen but Mary could feel its vibrations in her jawbone.

Looking to the west she saw a great billowing cloud begin its ascent above the rooftops, slowly morphing from black to white as it rose.

"Maybe one of you gentlemen should check that out," Tony G mildly suggested. "I'll be right here when you get back."

*　*　*

"We'll be safe in here," the young so-called actor said.

"*Safe? Safe?* There *is* no *safe*! How do you not *know* that by now!" the other one gasped, about as convincing in her panic as a recorded message.

The most interesting thing that Royal Davis discovered, as he lay face up in one of his own closed coffins listening to all this flat pap, was how distinctly he could hear everyone in the parlor.

On the other hand, the families that came to him, if they came at all, were mostly broke so he only showcased the cheapest models.

If they came at all . . .

The last person he had buried was his accountant, and that was two weeks ago, and only because she received an employee's discount and had paid in advance years ago, when his father was still running the show. A funeral home needed six burials a month to stay afloat; Royal, averaging more like four, sometimes three or two, was compelled to make his monthly nut by working as what was known in the industry as a tradesman, a freelance mortician contracted out to pick up bodies from homes or hospitals and deliver them to another funeral home which was, gallingly, so busy that they couldn't afford to expend the in-house manpower.

Well, what can you expect with the national funeral chains taking over. Shit, you could even buy your own coffin through Sam's Club or Target these days. And all the surviving independent parlors in his neck of the woods were run by directors with a little too much dog in them for it to be anything but a stone ulcer to compete for the same bodies.

If he wasn't in a tug-of-war over the building with his two brothers, both undertakers in Cali, he could easily get a refi mortgage in order to keep the business going, but they would never allow for it because, sensing the soaring real estate values in the area, they were just waiting until he went belly-up, broker than broke, to buy out his one-third stake and put the building up for sale.

But just knowing that that's what they wanted for him and his family was motivation enough for him to stay afloat by any means necessary until hopefully they both dropped dead.

"God, this place is disgusting," one of the other thespians said.

He hoped that last line was in the script, rather than improvised, but either way...

Some of the dropped-ceiling acoustic tiles in the parlor were so water-stained they looked like hanging spew. The plastic memorial candles with their fluttery flame-shaped bulbs and molded fake drips weren't what anyone would call elegant, and the flowers around the room needed to be dusted and given a fresh coat of Mop & Glo.

It wasn't always like this.

Back in the late 1980s, all through the '90s, and for a few years in the 2000s when between the crack-fueled violence, the cocaine turf wars and AIDS, a time when he could count on three to four bodies a day and sometimes even have to farm out the overflow to subcontractors, he had, relative to now at least, money to burn.

On the recommendation of his cousin, a funeral director in Mississippi, he hired a high-strung white kid from Tavares, Florida, a sign painter for Walmart by trade who'd never been north of Georgia, to come up to Harlem and, for five thousand dollars plus room and meals, paint an original *Last Supper* for the parlor, the only proviso being that it had to be twice as big as the two other *Last Supper*s that hung in the neighboring Carolina Chapel and the House of Solace.

It took the kid, Ellis Trimble was his name, two months to get it done. The result was pretty good except that Royal had wanted Jesus and the apostles to be Black, although in fairness to the artist he might have forgotten to mention that.

When he gave the late-breaking news to Ellis, the kid flipped out, bolted from the parlor and was never seen again, not even returning for his end money (which Royal would have given him a somewhat hard time about since in his eyes the *Last Supper* was still shy a few courses).

So, using the money that Ellis had left on the table, he hired one of his estranged brother's sons, a graffiti artist of some reputation, to redo the faces which also came out surprisingly well except that this superstar street artist had forgotten about the apostles' hands which remained white. In the end, Royal wound up selling the damned thing online for half what he'd paid for it.

A goddamn zombie flick. All these kids going to a high-end film school, their parents shelling out something like 60K a year and that's all they can imagine making?

They had first offered him five hundred a day to rent the parlor for a three-day shoot but, resenting how easy these kids had it in the world, how, due to the accidents of their births into relatively affluent and educated (he assumed) families, they had (he assumed) no fear of failure, he held out for six hundred, which he got, sort of.

They agreed to the six but only if he came on to play one of the zombies, which was why he was lying flat on his back in the dark with the right side of his face itching like crazy behind a rotted skin and exposed cranium prosthetic as the garbage dialogue continued to circle over his head.

One of Royal's two sons, Marquise, a seventh grader who damn well better have a fear of failure, was allowed to stay home from school today in order to watch his old man in action and—his wife Amina's idea, of course—maybe become inspired to be a filmmaker one day himself—but she wouldn't allow Patrice, Marquise's younger brother by a year, to be there because he had suffered from chronic nightmares since he was old enough to describe them and had probably had them even younger than that.

Amina wanted to find Patrice a child therapist but Royal told her, if for some fantastical reason she somehow wasn't aware of this already, they just didn't have the money.

"Besides," he added, "the kid's growing up in a funeral parlor, what do you expect?"

His wife was something else. Gambian-born and chronically happy to be here, she was perpetually on the community-oriented go, volunteering for this committee, chairing that event, hosting, canvassing, fundraising for whoever, whatever, and coming home at least twice a month carrying some kind of plaque or inexpensive statuette in recognition of her tireless service. Someone had once described her as a sunbeam in human form, although Royal in fact thought she might be depressed and in need of a mood regulator, but he never said as much because he also knew that that was just his bitterness talking, her star rising out there as his continued to fall.

And now this . . .

He was supposed to jump into action when he heard the lead actress, a good-looking big-eyed Nigerian girl with an irritating British accent, say, "There's got to be a back door!"

At which point he was to fling the coffin lid aside, pop up to a full seated position, grab her leg or arm as she tried to get past him, pull her down into the box and attempt to chew on her while the other actors struggled to yank her free and re-kill him.

As the crew and actors waited out yet another one of the endless sirens going off out there, Royal, swimming in his own sweat, started to doze off in his box . . .

The sudden tremendous window-rattling boom from somewhere out in the street was so strong that it made the wood of his coffin sing. Royal's instinctual reaction was to shove away the lid and bolt upright which is exactly what he did, his unexpected appearance scaring the shit out of everyone, some of them screaming, the cameraman running out of the parlor altogether, Royal trying not to laugh, thinking, *You wanted "scary," right?*

The lead actor, embarrassed now by his own nakedly Eek-a-Mouse yipping, pointed a shaky finger at Royal, bellowing, "Fuck you, man! Fuck you!" which made Royal's son, who, as instructed, had been quiet for hours, bust out laughing.

Through the window of the parlor, Royal, still sitting upright in his coffin, watched the black then dirty white cloud expand like a murderous balloon over the immediate skyline.

Rising up and stepping free of the box, free of the nonsense of this ridiculous side venture, he began to not-quite-gently tug at the prosthetic shit on his face.

"Marquise," turning to his kid, "go check your closet, if your black suit's in there, put it on." Royal thinking, *Time to get busy.*

,, ,, ,,

When Felix finally hit the street, the street hit him right back; the low-lying, near-impenetrable grey-white cloud, lousy with unknown particulates and reeking of what smelled to him like a mix of hot tar, cement dust and burning trash.

Given that he had made it to the street in the time it took to fall out of bed and fly down the stairs, he was amazed at how many people—a lot of them half grinning in their bewilderment—seemed to have beat him to it, with more streaming out of nearby buildings or coming around the bend from other blocks, some moving like sleepwalkers as they emerged from or disappeared into the filthy mist, others standing in clusters or wandering solo, a few shouting into their cells, many more—although no one seemed to know exactly where to focus—using them to record the scene, raising the phones over their heads at a high forward angle as if they were hailing cabs or saluting at a Hitler rally.

He began to shoot.

Maybe he could sell this you-are-there footage to a media outlet;

he'd done it before—three months ago capturing a fatal ATV versus SUV collision on Lenox then, two weeks after that, a straight-up bare-knuckle fistfight between a cop and some street-head who had tossed a beer bottle at his patrol car, but he was too young to really care about money and raised too middle-class to ever imagine himself as truly living in poverty.

For Felix, it was all about the Nikon. Just having it in his hands, let alone raising it up in order to capture an unprotected moment in the lives of others, served to bolster his own paltry sense of self, gifted him with a place-holding caption: *Man with a Camera*, and he would no sooner step out of his apartment without it than he would go into the street naked.

The train.

The curtained air was so thick, the visibility so low that he couldn't find it, couldn't even see above the second floor of his own building or as high as the el tracks.

But the metal moan of another unseen downtown express taking that Dead Man's Curve directly overhead meant that the rails were clear up there, so, not a train after all, so . . .

So, what was it?

Behind him, the front door of the brownstone cracked wide, one of his lone-wolf neighbors, Trip Dash, stepping out, as thin as a home-rolled reefer, all sunglasses and cigarettes and war stories about the street back in the day.

"Goddamn fool."

"Who, me?"

"Me," Trip said. "Whatever the fuck that big explosion was? It put a crack in my fish tank. I had to put the tetras in the toilet to save their lives. After, I'm runnin' around, getting dressed, forgot about the fish, took a leak and flushed. Get that shit out of my face." Putting his hand out to cover the lens.

When Felix lowered the camera, Trip took in his face and red-streaked T-shirt.

"Damn, Monster, what the fuck happened to you?"

"Bloody nose."

"Yeah, I can see that. It looks broke too. You should get that administered to. I'm gonna get some smokes," he said, Felix filming him as he disappeared into the fog.

As car alarms continued to chase each other up and down the street, Felix took the camera for a short walk, clocking endless broken windows stretching west as far as he could see, a black van driving into the low-hanging whiteness and coming out looking like powdered sugar, a cement stanchion with its bolted-metal No Parking sign whipped completely backwards by the force of the concussion, and the street itself, a glittering quilt of daggered glass topped here and there with scatters of mail and magazines.

When he reached the Eat and Run he stood with the remaining crew from the nearby halfway house, who, out of lingering prison habits, regularly showed up at 5:30 waiting for the Yemeni kid who slept on an air mattress behind the register to open up for their coffee and loosies.

At first, the sound of unseen multiple firetrucks wailing in the distance grew louder as they drew closer but then began to fade into the distance.

"Guess they found a better one," somebody said.

When he turned back towards the stoop, he saw that four of his building's originals were now congregated there to scope out the chaos: Trip, back with a fresh pack of Camels; O-Line; Billy Dupree, a freelance talent scout who claimed to be the illegitimate grandson of Sammy Davis Junior; and Eddie G, an auto mechanic who rented a car bay from a local garage when he had the money and the rent-free curb when he didn't.

"This is some terroristic shit," Dupree said. "Just remember, I'm the one who said it first."

"Terrorists around here?" Trip said.

"Terrorists around wherever they want to be. I call them Triple

Muslims, because they don't give a fuck about killing me, killing you, or killing themselves. And for what. How many virgins? A hundred?"

"Seventy-two," Awan, one of the new-breed grad student tenants, said evenly.

"Oh shit," Dupree said, wheeling around to see him standing in the doorway, "I didn't see you there, brother, no offense."

"No offense taken," Awan said slowly before heading back inside.

"What's he studying again?" Dupree asked no one in particular.

Feeling the sheer weight of the accumulated micro-debris piling like grain in his lungs, Felix reached for the inhaler in his sweatpants, but before he could take a hit someone shouted, *"Don't!"* as if Felix was about to pull the pin on a grenade.

"Don't!" The man bearing down on him now.

Felix reflexively raised his camera to both protect himself and capture the moment, seeing, through the lens, a man, like so many others, covered in that filthy snow and looking half out of his head as he raced towards him, then suddenly staggering backwards as Trip openhandedly popped him in the chest.

"Don't," he said again, massaging the spot where he was struck but otherwise ignoring Trip.

"Don't what?" Felix still filming him, having no fear of this guy and his shock-widened eyes.

"If it's not asthma that's making you tight but something else in your lungs, if you use your puffer you could wind up spreading it to your other organs. So please don't, ok? Please . . ."

He had a good point but despite the precision of his words, they had all come out of him in a chittering burble. And there were tears running down his face, although they could have just as easily come from all this smarting garbage air.

Felix put down the camera and pointedly looked away hoping the guy would leave. And he did, wandering like an ash-coated shaman through the chaos, repeatedly getting bumped and shoved by others but somehow staying on his feet.

"Hold up," Trip whispered, cocking his head. "You hear that?"

"Hear what?" Felix said, squinting into the ground cloud.

"Quiet, just listen."

From somewhere in the fog there came a steady high-pitched moaning in what seemed to Felix like a lost language. And then he realized that he had been hearing it from the moment he left his building but despite its unnerving pitch, it had gradually insinuated itself into his consciousness without ever really demanding to be heard. Others on the street seemed to absorb it in the same way; tuning in, tuning out, only marginally aware of the steady keening half-buried within the overall soundtrack of car alarms, callouts, chatter and the everywhere crunch of glass underfoot.

Moments later, as the fog began to grudgingly drift off, the wailing seemed to hit a higher pitch, but there was still so much else to process . . .

And then they all heard a loud voice somewhere in the crowd, "Hold on now, just hold on . . ."

Then someone else, "Wait wait wait . . ."

And then the block seemed to freeze, as if people needed to be perfectly still in order for their minds to meaningfully interpret what their eyes were taking in, Felix no different, thinking: it was the city that did that, tore it all down while he was sleeping, or some fuck-the-law property owner in the middle of the night or terrorists or . . .

Where a five-story building had stood directly across the street, there was now nothing but fuming low hills of rubble, the cars parked in front pancaked and coated in ash.

And when, a moment later, the first patrol car pulled up the two cops who got out just stood there, as gobsmacked as everyone else, one of them barely managing a monotone "Holy shit" before calling it in.

Another Metro North screaming on the curve had the people below crouching with their hands over their heads as if another building was about to collapse, but when they realized it was just the train they turned to each other and started to laugh, the whole experience turning into a hallucinating block party.

As the fog continued to dissipate, the source of that high-pitched wailing finally materialized, and it wasn't until Felix and everyone else turned to see, standing rigidly frozen between two crumpled cars, an ash-caked woman still gripping the leash of her equally ash-caked dog, that the horror of the collapse finally started to kick in, racing through the crowd like a virus, people crying now, running in every direction.

The woman was mute.

The human-like screams were coming from the dog.

Felix zoomed in on her as tight as the camera would allow and saw that her shoulders were minutely rising and falling and that she couldn't stop blinking—so not dead at least.

Ashamed of himself for hiding behind his lens instead of going to her aid, he stepped off the curb but as soon as he did, someone barreled into him, Felix instinctually bringing his camera up snug to his chest before landing on his back and looking up at the solidly built wild-eyed Latino who had sent him flying.

"I *said* I was sorry!" the guy barked back down at him before racing off as blindly as before.

When Felix got back on his feet, the woman and dog were gone.

As two more cruisers pulled up to the scene behind the first car and all six of the cops, after a quick barking discussion, began to gingerly wade into the rubble field, the vibe on the street shifted once again, dozens of people quick-stepping into the ruins after them and soon there was no separation, civilians and uniforms working together in search of bodies, living or dead, sliding away chunks of stone, lifting the half-smashed remains of beds, cabinets, porcelain tubs and sinks, doors and the shredded remains of plastered walls.

From their spot in front of the brownstone, Felix and the others, caught up in watching it all unfold, were still just standing around until O-Line, massively frustrated by his own two-cane immobility, exploded, "*Get the fuck over there!*" the force of his voice propelling them into the street.

And then he was in the middle of it all, the acrid intensity of the air rising up from the ground carrying with it an amorphous undercurrent of pure dread.

At first, he tried moving aside small chunks of stone with only one hand until a voice coming from somewhere behind barked, "*Put the fuckin' camera down like a man.*"

But before he could even think about that—*put it down where?*—he shot up straight at the sight of a huge older woman, another living lava cast, rising from the earth on her own, the red gash running in a straight line across her forehead vivid against the caked wheat-paste coating her face. Before he could react, the skinny young Yemeni who lived behind the cash register of the corner store deer-leapt over a shattered medicine chest to grab one of her flaccid arms, then, after squatting for leverage, quickly stood up to drape it over his bony shoulder, straining to keep his balance, wheezing, "I got you, Mommy . . ."

But it was a two-man job, so Felix finally slipped his camera into a small cleft in one of the debris mounds and got up under her other arm, small fragments of the grit and metal embedded in her loose skin chewing up the nape of his neck.

As they picked their way to the curb two newly arrived emergency services cops, both wearing breathing masks, rushed up to take her.

Turning back towards the collapse, Felix saw that the number of cops and now firemen in there had tripled and that they were all wearing breathing masks and when the locals started to pick up on that, someone shouted, "Nine-eleven!" then another voice, "Gonna get cancer!" and then one more of the endless small waves of mass panic kicked in, the locals both knee-deep in the debris and out in the street, either covering their lower faces with their shirts, hats or whatever else was at hand, or hightailing it out of there altogether.

Standing on the perimeter of the devastation, lost in a replay of bringing the woman out, Felix felt himself go cold.

Some small thing was not right, and the struggle to name it killed that amped-up reverie of his fast.

The camera. He left it in there.

Running back into the rubble, he reached into that hidden debris shelf where he had stashed it and came out holding a fistful of air.

Turning his head back to scan the street he caught sight of a long-legged kid race-walking away with the camera tucked under his arm like a football.

He shouted for him to stop which was stupid—he might as well have shouted for the kid to run faster, which is what he did.

Despite his stockiness, Felix, who had enough speed in him to have played linebacker in high school, took off in pursuit, the crowds making it more of a high slalom event than a footrace.

Two blocks, three, until the kid's flight path was abruptly blocked by both a UPS truck and a reticulated city double bus slowly gliding into its stop. With Felix coming down on him full bore and nowhere to run, the kid put the Nikon on top of a full trash bin, shifted gears and took off in another direction.

Struck by how carefully the thief had placed his pricey camera on top of some soft garbage instead of just dropping it on the street, Felix lost all desire to pursue.

On his way back to the block he saw a white-bearded man standing barefoot in the middle of Third Avenue like a raging prophet, gesticulating with a mop stick while screaming at the oncoming clueless cars to make way for the caravan of firetrucks, ambos, ESU and ConEd emergency vans that were still barreling toward the scene.

Which got Felix shooting again, first White Beard standing there, then, as he reached the edge of the block, filming an injured but conscious survivor being transported to an ambulance—reporters and cameramen from various media outlets circling the stretcher in a hunched sideways scuttle like a ring of floating surgeons.

By the time he made it to his building the cops, having finally set up an improvised perimeter, were now barking at people, "*Let's go! Out! Out!*" spreading their arms wide to hustle the remaining neighborhood volunteers still poking around back across the street.

And then he saw the four people laid out on the sidewalk, two being tended to by FDNY EMTs, and two motionless, black plastic sheets covering them from their heads to their shoes.

As he stood there, his camera momentarily at parade rest, two more bodies in basket stretchers came out to join the other four. One carried the massive Green Mile, four firemen needed to carefully lower his body to the sidewalk.

The other stretcher, needing only two bearers, carried his aunt.

And then Felix spotted Trip moving through the crowd, hawking improvised breathing masks fashioned out of underwear, socks, T-shirts and shoelaces, all loosely strung together and running up his left arm like a skein of pretzels.

Overhead, three helicopters hovered like small black spiders beneath the roiling sky.

*, *, *,

When Mary, wearing her Community Affairs windbreaker, finally left the NYPD's ad hoc command post which was set up inside a nearby vacant former head shop shuttered by the cops for selling synthetic marijuana joints a year earlier, she had been assigned to the team of detectives charged with interviewing witnesses or, less likely, survivors— shopkeepers, dog walkers, commuters; anyone whose regular morning routine on that block might have afforded them eyes on the building.

Given that her job was off-site it wasn't required of her to walk through the barricaded street of the collapse but she wanted to get a feel for what the people she'd be talking with had experienced.

At a street corner just outside the barricades there was a laundromat which the media had commandeered as their own command post, complete with a coffee station and a craft service table laid out with bagels, pastries and fruit, the reporters either on the phone dumping their stories to a rewrite man or sending off downloaded footage to the stations they worked for.

And mingling among them were the local West African and

Hispanic housewives doing their daily wash, the majority barely glancing up at the bank of TVs mounted over the machines showing live footage from just around the corner.

She slipped inside to grab a coffee for the long day to come, then came right back out before anyone could start pumping her for information which she didn't have anyway, and when she did, she saw that an Arabic vendor wearing a full-length *thobe* and a kufi had already set up shop, standing over a velvet-topped folding table displaying an assortment of rosaries, Jesus fish buttons and thin copper-plated cross necklaces, a square of cardboard taped to a lamppost over his head, announcing, 1 FOR 15, 2 FOR 30, 3 FOR 40, YOU PICK.

Her first sight of the collapse, that vast smoldering field, crawling now with ESU and FDNY search and rescue teams, with cadaver and rescue dogs, their trainers clambering behind, felt to her like something out of the Bible.

As she stood there, her heart roaring with awe, three pneumatic blasts wracked the air, followed by electronically amped commands for silence.

As the ambos, vans, emergency services trucks all shut down their engines and the locals on the opposite sidewalk started to more or less comply, a new wave of search and rescue firemen began to mount the rubble, this crew either wearing headphones or carrying ultrasonic resonance mikes, each man in his own way wirelessly linked to a variety of detection devices except for one fireman that caught her eye, belly-crawling over the debris with nothing but a medical stethoscope; his slow careful progress making her think of the demolished tenement now as a massive beached whale, dead to the naked eye but secretly harboring other forms of surviving life.

And then she saw the bodies still laid out on the sidewalk awaiting transfer to the coroner's van. The wind had picked up earlier and some of the plastic sheets now had rubble-stones placed at the corners to keep them from blowing away but some didn't, partially revealing faces and shoulders, including the one over Green Mile, lying there with his brow furrowed and his lips parted as if he had one last thing to say.

Bobby Cornish, aka Green Mile. She'd first made his acquaintance fifteen years ago when she was a rookie on patrol responding to a report of an ED in front of a walk-up on 116th, sent there without a partner or any backup, the guy twice her height and three times her weight. As he moved towards her, she stood her ground, speaking to him in as calm a voice as she could manage, "Hey, what's your name? Mine's Mary, are you alright? Do you need help? Tell me how to help you..." nothing she said slowing him down until he had her wrapped in his arms and two feet off the ground, at which point, from behind her, "Hey, Bobby, over here," Green Mile putting her back down in order to catch a Twix bar lofted his way.

Mary turned to see three senior patrolmen standing there having watched the whole thing from the shadows. They were laughing, but it wasn't just a practical joke, it was also a test to see how she'd handle herself in a panic scenario, see what kind of cop they might be partnering up with in the days/months/years to come.

Apparently, she'd passed.

They handed her another Twix bar to give to Bobby, so that he would always be happy to see her, but it made her skin crawl to do it, treating this oversized mental deficient like she was some anthropologist in the wild being filmed bonding with a big forest ape for a documentary. That being said, she did it anyway, had to in fact, because if she refused, they would brand her for all time as a bitch with a real attitude problem which would make her life miserable until she put in her papers.

A loud crash had her walking with her head turned back which made her nearly take a flyer over a crushed USPS mail cart lying in her path, its undelivered letters shredded and strewn in all directions.

And it was the sight of that cart, an everyday object so violently deformed, that hit Mary the hardest of all that she'd seen so far because for her it was always the unexpected smaller things she encountered within the confines of a larger horror—a charred doll, a family photo floating in a dirty pool of water, a ghostly palm print stippled with black powder on a bedroom door—that would trigger in her an unasked-for comprehension of the whole.

｡ ｡ ｡

Royal sat in his car with Marquise on the edge of the police tape, the kid taking off one of his shoes and rearranging the newspaper stuffing at the toe.

"What are you doing?"

"I think I got on your shoes."

"You what?"

"I was rushing," the kid said.

"You want, I can make you some little oars for them."

"Am I going to see dead bodies? I'm not afraid, I'm just curious."

"Maybe."

Royal didn't understand; the kid saw dead people all the time.

"But who you *need* to see is the relatives."

"How am I gonna know who's a relative?"

"They'll have a big neon sign, says *'Relative'* hanging over their chest."

"Dad. I'm serious."

"I don't know. Just hand out the cards, man."

Marquise inflated his cheeks then slowly expelled the air. For whatever reason, Royal mused, the kid really was anxious, which moved him to briefly massage the back of his son's neck.

"Why don't you do it instead?"

"I can't," Royal said.

"Why not?"

"Because it wouldn't look right."

Marquise reluctantly stepped out of the SUV.

"Little man."

"What." Marquise looking up from the sidewalk, hoping for a reprieve.

"You forgot the cards."

*　*　*

In the gym of a nearby parochial school converted into an ad hoc Red Cross shelter providing bottled water, oranges and Lipton Cup-a-Soup—"Just like in Riker's," someone drawled—twenty or so people from the area were sitting on the lower rungs of the roll-out bleachers as Ralph Esposito, a bit overweight and dressed a touch too dapper—pale blue French cuff shirt, gold links, and a silk-wool blend suit—stepped up to address them; Mary and three other detectives standing silently against one of the walls, eyeballing the assembled.

Esposito, as Mary knew, had a big voice, so there was no need for the mike in his hand.

"Everyone in this room has the potential to help us. If you saw something, if you heard something, even if you just smelled something, at this point what we're looking at, truth to God, it's all one big puzzle. Maybe you noticed an unfamiliar individual either hanging around or coming into or out of the building this morning before the collapse, maybe you saw someone running, or heard raised voices, any detail you can share with us, no such thing as too minor, it could be a small piece of the puzzle that'll help us start to put things together, ok? So what I'm going to do right now is have our people come around and if you could just give them a few minutes of your time . . ."

Immediately after that Mary along with the other detectives started to work the room, steering people one by one to higher rungs of the bleachers or into the school's hallways. A few of the locals she spoke to were able to offer minor bits of information that might or might not be helpful down the line—a long-standing feud between two apartments; the fact that the building super sometimes had liquor on his breath; that the man in 2A used to threaten to kill his wife—but a lot were pretty useless, like the woman with the cane and oversized glasses who waved up at her from the gym floor, Mary having to climb down and usher her into one of the hallways.

"First off, thank you for taking the time, can I get your name?"

"No, you don't need my name."

"No problem, so . . ."

"There was this man I saw, he looked kind of jumpy to me. Like he was up to something."

"Ok, can you describe him?"

"Tall and nervous."

"And what made you think he was up to something?"

"I just told you."

"Did you notice anything else about him? Maybe his clothes, or facial—"

"Yeah, his clothes. He was wearing a dark color puffy coat, like a winter coat."

"Ok."

"It's sixty-three degrees outside."

"Right. And where exactly did you see him?"

"Out my window."

"Out your window . . . And where do you live?"

"2234 Madison Avenue, third floor front."

"Ok then . . ." Mary closed her notebook.

The address was three blocks away from the collapse, and even if the woman had been looking through a high-powered telescope her low floor view would be blocked by dozens of high-rise buildings.

※ ※ ※

From somewhere in the sound-riot, Felix heard someone hoarsely reciting what he recognized from his father's funeral as the Kaddish.

Tracking the incantations through the din he came on a tall thin Black man wearing a skullcap and a prayer shawl, standing in front of the open back bay of a second coroner's van, rhythmically dipping his upper body toward the dead as he sang.

At first, he couldn't bring himself to take the shot but then he did.

When he turned away a young queasy-looking kid in a black suit was standing in front of him holding out a business card for a funeral home, which, given that all of this death and destruction he'd been documenting was starting to take its toll, made him think that the card was offered because the kid somehow knew that Felix's days were coming to an end.

He gave the card back but when the kid began to walk away

he called out to him. And when he turned around, Felix took his picture, too.

*, *, *,

Once the woman from Madison Avenue left, Mary remained in the hallway trying to get it up to call her almost-ex Jimmy Roe and ask him to come over to the house tonight and make dinner for the kids because she didn't know how long she'd be stuck here. Stalling for time, she walked over to a long bronze memorial plaque bolted into a wall listing the mostly Italian and a few Hispanic names of former students who'd died in the Second World War, and below that, the mostly Hispanic and a few Italian names of those who died in the Korean War. Finding no other distractions, she grudgingly rang him up. He was only too happy to do it, which put her on edge.

On her way back to the gym she ducked into a classroom where some detectives were sitting at a bank of screens running CCTV footage pulled from various street-facing security cameras on the block, a few capturing the front entrance of the building this morning, the cops pausing the tapes and blowing up the faces or profiles of people who were just leaving the building for work and probably safe, but also the faces of those just entering the building and who probably never came out.

Among those heading inside, Mary saw her mailman passing through the front door with his as-yet-undamaged cart.

Back in the gym the skinny Yemeni kid from the Eat and Run, his face and arms scraped raw, his hair powdered white, gave her the names of two tenants, the Braithwaite sisters, who before the collapse had come in to the store for their regular tea and pastry then headed off for work in their pink hospital scrubs just like they did every morning; Mary checking them off as accounted for, then getting a whiff of throwback Paco Rabanne, looked up to see Esposito coming her way.

"How you holding up?" Esposito asked without looking at her, the question coming out side-mouthed as if he were passing on a secret.

"I'm good."

"You're good?"

"Yeah, I just said that, Ralph. Thanks."

"Good. Just let me know if, you know . . ." Then walking away.

An hour later, crossing the floor on her way to the girls' room, she felt a feathery pressure on her arm, and turned to see an older woman in a housedress and slippers.

"I can't find my daughter," she murmured, her eyes jellied and red. "She was on the corner."

"Ok, come with me, we'll see if . . ." Mary steering her to one of the low rungs of the bleachers.

"Can you tell me your name?"

"Coral, her name is Coral."

"No, honey, your name."

"I'm Coral too."

"And your last name . . ."

"Hoover."

"Is that your daughter's last name?"

"No."

"What's her last name?"

"Simpson."

"And how old is she?"

"Twenty-five."

"Twenty-five . . ."

"Twenty-six."

". . . and you saw her on which corner?"

"By the corner store. She always hangs out there."

"Were you with her?"

"No, I was asleep in my bedroom, the helicopters woke me then I looked out the window."

"How did you know she was on that corner?"

"Because she always hangs out there."
"When did you last see her?"
"I don't know."
"Did you see her today?"
"No. I don't know."
"Ok, did you try to call her?"
"No."
"Why not?"
"She never answers."
"Do you want to try now?"

The woman looked off as if she hadn't heard the question.

"Do you want me to call her for you?" Mary taking out her cell phone. "Give me her number."

As she waited for Coral to respond, another younger woman approached. "Miss Coral." Taking her hand.

"It's ok, thank you," she said to Mary, "I got her," helping Coral to her feet and walking her out of the gym.

"Did I give you permission to take my picture?"

The bulky teenage girl sporting oversized hoop earrings that came to rest on her shoulders looked like she was about to come at the photographer, a short stocky kid in a dried blood–drizzled T-shirt.

"I wasn't shooting you, I was shooting the overall scene. You just happened to be in it. Like a lot of people."

"Don't you ever take my fucking picture again."

"I sure won't. Sorry."

At first the teen, thrown by the polite apology, didn't know how to take it or what to do with it.

Mary, out on a break, had seen that same teetering confusion in other stymied street encounters before; some someone, always wanting that last word, even if there was no need for one, even if it led to the morgue.

She braced to see if this young woman was about to up the stakes,

Mary clocking her constantly shifting expressions and the movement of her hands.

The photographer, young as he was, knew enough not to turn his back on her which would be seen as a sign of disrespect, and also to keep his mouth shut as the girl figured out a way to assert her existence.

"I want to see what you took of me," she finally said.

"No problem, give me your email and I'll send it to you," he said, taking a small memo pad and pen out of his back pocket and offering it to her.

And that was all the verbal parrying the teen could take; Mary almost feeling sorry for her as she stormed off flustered and finessed.

As Mary turned away, a boy, no more than thirteen and wearing a dusty too-small black suit, white shirt and tie, handed her a business card for the Royal Davis Funeral Home and Chapel.

The anything-but-royal Royal Davis.

"Is your dad here?" Mary tracking the boy's gaze to Royal sitting in his SUV.

Stepping to the car, Mary draped her arms over the open driver's-side window and locked into his eyes. "Are you serious?"

"Times are hard." He shrugged.

"Royal, he's a child."

"Around here, a child is nothing but a small adult."

"Oh bullshit. If you don't get him out of here right now, I'll take him off the street myself."

"You'll kidnap my child?"

"Just get him out of here, ok? Please? Thank you."

When she returned to the gym, the building's manager, looking like he'd just been Tased out of his bed, had finally shown up. The tenant log that he had brought with him was divided between the detectives, although Mary, along with the others, knew that it would only give them half the story because in that neighborhood many of the apartments tended to harbor ghost tenants: relatives, adult children with their own children going through hard times who'd had to move back in with their own parents, grandparents. Then there were the boyfriends, girlfriends, a best friend, half living there, an undocumented family member that no one was supposed to know about, legit tenants who might have died or moved back to the islands sometime in the past, their relatives or friends having taken over the apartment on the sly without telling the landlord.

Nonetheless, with the log in hand they could finally start tracking people down by name, social security number, cell phone number, workplace and emergency contact. But, as she expected, a lot of the listed numbers were out of service, some of the offices, factories and shops informed her that the person didn't work there anymore, and a few of the emergency contacts told her, "We broke up," or, "I haven't seen that guy in two years," or, "I don't know that name," etc. One emergency contact she reached had no information on the whereabouts of the tenant that had put her name down but took the opportunity to complain about all the nonstop ATVs and dirt bikes zooming up and down the block every night.

But she also got some names to add to the missing or to scratch off, sometimes both, like the woman on the rolls who no longer lived there, but her daughter did; Mary was able to reach the daughter at work.

Another call yielded the names of two people currently living in the building who had left for Florida the week before, so scratch them off, too.

And then a surviving tenant came in, a woman who was out of the building at the time of the collapse.

When Mary asked her who else lived in her apartment the woman's eyes became blank.

Mary sensed that she was worried that if she gave up the other names, she'd be in violation of her lease and might be evicted even though the apartment was gone, the fucking *building* was gone.

"We just need to know if there's any people we don't know about that we should be searching for."

Then, off the woman's vacant-eyed shrug . . .

"You're not in violation. It doesn't matter anymore. Nobody cares, ok? You *get* that, right?"

"Yes."

"So?"

So nothing—the woman walking away.

"Officer." It was the younger woman who escorted Coral out earlier. "I want to thank you for not challenging me when I took Miss Coral away and I'm sorry that I couldn't explain to you what was going on with her at the time."

"Is she alright?"

"Not . . ." Wincing, then, "She's getting on in her years and this building crash has got her all shook up and confused. The fact is, her daughter passed two years ago."

"Well, I appreciate it," Mary said, unsurprised by the explanation. She thought it had to be something like that, which was why she had let the woman take her away to begin with.

* * *

Since jumping out of his coffin and tearing off the prosthetics to stir up some business, Royal had forgotten about the zombie film being made in his parlor. But the filmmakers were still there shooting when he and his son returned.

"Sorry about that," he said to the room. "It was an emergency."

"No problem," the student director said unconvincingly.

Royal gestured to his still-flung-open coffin. "You want me to get back in?"

* * *

Towards the end of her twelve hours on, Mary could feel herself becoming borderline useless and was all too happy to pack it in.

Her only unfinished business was to locate the one tenant on her portion of the rent log she'd been unable to account for, a Christopher Diaz, forty-two, who was the husband of Rosa Maria Diaz, one of the DOAs.

He was either still buried in the rubble—which at this point she seriously doubted—or at the time of the collapse had been somewhere else, but he had no known family besides his wife, no known occupation, and if he had a cell phone it was nowhere in the files.

She was only responsible for finding him until the end of her tour after which the job of locating Diaz and all the other outstanding MIAs would transfer over to the local squads, but Mary had always been a compulsive completist, something that the therapist described to her as one of her childhood coping mechanisms which had outlived its purpose but she still enjoyed the internal sense of urgency that came with it, that is, unless she was thwarted, at which point urgency morphed into anxious obsession; and she could feel it coming on.

"So how are the kids doing?" Esposito asked her as they headed back out through the collapse site.

"Good."

"Who's got 'em tonight?"

Mary hesitated, then dodged. "I mean at their age? They have themselves," then added, as he waited for a straight answer, "Me."

"Got it. Alright then . . ."

And that should have been that but Esposito still took his time taking his leave, stubbornly refusing to entertain the possibility that after a day like today the last thing she might want to do was go to some anonymous just-off-the-thruway motel; which is to say that even after six months of them sporadically doing just that, Esposito being one of those highly compartmentalized individuals still had no real idea who she was. Which was fine with her.

The cumulative visions of the day having finally overtaken him, Felix stood in front of his building as if the street had become a meadow, his eyes dull as nickels.

"You ok?"

He would have described the woman asking the question as "petite" except for her mannish vibe and raw features, so Felix came up with *hard petite*, her Dockers chinos and NYPD windbreaker sealing the deal.

"Are you hurt?" Running her eyes over his body. She had a patient voice.

"No, I'm good."

"Are you sure? Because there's a first aid tent one block over. Do you want me to walk you there?" Searching his eyes for ghosts.

Felix meant to answer the question, but . . .

"What's your name?" Still trying to assess his state.

"Felix Pearl."

"Felix. How'd you get that blood on your shirt?"

"Fell out of bed this morning." Pointing up to his window, which, unlike all the others up and down the street, remained miraculously unshattered. In any event, she seemed to get the context.

"I'll leave you alone, Felix, but if something happens to you after I go, that makes me a fuckup."

That got him laughing; Mary was relieved, thinking that people in shock never get jokes.

* * *

"Ma, it's me. Did you hear about what happened up here?"

"I saw it on the news," she said. "Was that close to you?"

"Across the street."

"Jesus, why didn't you call me?"

"Too much cell traffic."

"Are you alright?"

"Yeah, I guess."

"What does 'I guess' mean."

"It means 'I guess.'" Felix unwilling to share with her any of what he'd seen or how the unwelcome afterimages were continuously coming through the door, taking up house in him like a second self.

Or how overwhelmingly alone he felt right now sitting on the edge of his bed with no one else to talk to but her.

"Anyways, I shot a lot film out there but I don't think I want to look at any of it for a while."

"You could sell it to one of the TV stations."

"Yeah, I know but . . ."

"You have to do it fast though, two days from now nobody'll care."

"Mom." Felix kept having to remind himself that she was the parent who wanted him.

"You sound low," she said. "Do you want to come home for a while?"

"I don't know," then, "No, I'm good."

After the call, he stepped to his window and took in the activity across the street, slow-moving American flag–draped cranes and backhoes now roaming the floodlit rubble field like grazing dinosaurs.

Despite all that, the street felt eerily hushed, as if it were buried in snow.

He also saw that O-Line and Trip were back out on the stoop. His first impulse was to go down and hang with them in order to avoid being trapped with himself but then an unasked-for wave of cold knowledge kept him where he was.

Monster.

Who was he kidding, they weren't his friends any more than he was theirs. He was just some suburban kid narcissistically flattered by their appearing to take him into the fold. A see-through ego clown whose every moment in their presence was buttered with self-congratulation.

Monster.

An in-house running joke that kept them from getting too bored out there.

And what were they to him?

With a shotgun-loud crack, his window suddenly and finally succumbed to this morning's explosive force, fragmenting before his eyes into a frozen mosaic of glass pellets which freakishly held fast in the frame.

It happened so instantaneously that at first he couldn't react.

But once that moment of unreality passed, he started to shake so uncontrollably that he thought his bones would snap.

*　*　*

Sitting by herself at the rail of a jazz bar on Adam Clayton Powell, Mary had a head stuffed with numbers.

Forty-six renters on the books with probably as many ghosts. Staying just with the legals for the moment, forty-six less six dead and twenty-eight located, was thirty-four, was twelve people, at the very least, that they still couldn't find, including her very own, Christopher Diaz.

More numbers: sixteen hospitalized, the injuries ranging from a shattered pelvis to a fractured skull to a grit-infected eye, but save for the two miracle tenants discovered still breathing and uncrushed in random air pockets inside the multiple tons of debris, the rest were all profoundly unlucky pedestrians just passing by when the building blew itself out.

One stool over from her, a neighborhood alley cat sporting heavy black-framed Bo Diddley glasses and a thin gold chain over a thin gold V-neck pullover abruptly leaned into her space, his breath three VSOP Henneys to the raw.

"Here's something you should know about me," he said. "I am the baddest motherfucker in this room."

"Ok." Mary barely registering the words.

"You know why?"

"Why what?"

"Because I am a man of God."

"Hey, there you go."

"Super Philip," he said, then, after she passed on giving him her name in return, "You police."

"All day long."

"How about at night?"

"Hey, Super Peter, do yourself a favor . . ."

But he'd already given her his back, his attention now on three women in skirt suits and office-appropriate makeup, drinking together farther down the wood.

"Ladies, please tell me you're all lesbians, so I can relax and enjoy my cocktail."

They stopped talking to stare him down, their unblinking sheet metal eyes making him swivel back to Mary.

"I will tell you one thing, though," he said, "it does feel good to be out."

"Good for you." Mary not needing to ask what "out" referred to.

"Just finished a nickel, armed robbery, or so they claimed."

"Oh yeah?" She just couldn't resist. "What did they claim you robbed?"

"A bar."

"A bar. A bar around here?"

"Yeah, this one," he said, then off Mary's half smile, "It's all good. They're under new management."

The three women left for the privacy of a small table, Super Philip watching them go with noncommittal eyes.

The kids.

She felt like she should at least call one of them, choosing the Little One, Terrence, who at nine hopefully was still too young to pass judgment on her.

Nonetheless, it took another cranberry vodka for her to do it.

"It's Ma."

"I know."

"What are you doing."

"Eating."

"How about your brother."

"Eating."

"Who made the dinner?"

"Dad."

Forgetting that she had called him earlier to do just that, Mary had to put a check on her anger: *It's my night with them.*

LAZARUS MAN

But here she still was, chatting up a felon.
"Is he there with you?"
"Dad?"
"Yes, your father."
"Yeah. Do you want to talk to him?"
"No." Then, "Tell him I'm just wrapping up work, I'll be home soon."

She had met Jimmy Roe thirteen years ago when as a speaker for DARE she dropped into his eighth-grade homeroom class to try and scare the students away from drugs. Afterwards, he asked her to have a coffee with him, but she could tell he was high and passed.

The second time was when she interviewed him in the hospital after he had been tuned up outside of a bar, where, despite his blood-blackened face and broken ribs, his wrists were in restraint cuffs attached to the bed rails.

Midway through the visit he suddenly recognized her from her class visit and as soon as he did the visceral shame and anguish which came so palpably into his eyes had her thinking—and she remembered thinking it word for word like a news bulletin—*This is a decent guy.*

A year after that he was a functioning dry drunk, who recognized her in the street, and appeared so overjoyed to see her again that he immediately took her hand in his as unconsciously as if he were already her boyfriend, her husband and the father of her kids.

No one had ever been so happy to lay eyes on her in all of her life and it made her feel—there was no other way to put it—*enfolded*.

At dinner that night, he told her in a guileless rush everything that he had imagined saying to her since that rock-bottom day in the hospital; the infinite apologies, the phantom conversations, all the ways that he imagined proving to her that he was so much better a person than who she saw that day, every word out of his mouth sounding honest and true. And then, for the first time in a long time, a man actually asked her about herself.

For the first few years of their marriage, fueled by a fear of falling off the earth again, he still had that edge to him. When she first met him, he was a Jekyll-and-Hyde drunk, a mild and personable guy just leaning into the rail until scotch number three had him blindly swinging at whoever was in range—ergo the hospital—which for all its danger gave him a subtly electrifying presence.

As long as he continued to feel haunted by his various past brushes with mortality—a heart attack, a car crash, another beating outside a bar that ended with a priest giving him Extreme Unction—there remained a bubbling beneath the skin that made him feel to her like a trapped animal.

But when enough time had passed for him to become confident of his own will to live, that electric edginess of his that so attracted her in the beginning had been replaced by a never-ending sense of "gratitude"—for the sun, the rain, the stars, for the kids, for the food on his plate, the water in his cup. And for her.

Grateful.

As soon as he decided in his heart that he truly wanted to live, like many people that come to that decision, he started to purge all that was jagged in himself. Moderate in everything. Patient, reasonable, a good listener. Addicted to puns.

Over the years as she became acclimated to this reborn individual she fell into a numb stability with him; even with the job and two kids, her life still felt as flat as a runway.

And then it was her turn—two years ago stepping into a crowded elevator car from the fifth floor of an old industrial building a moment before a cable snapped, the descent, soundtracked by a hammering rattle, turning into a plummet, the velocity such that she couldn't tell if the car was going down or shooting into space, then waking up in a hospital with a concussion and a broken leg and a vague memory of screaming people trying to climb the walls of the car. She was told that three of them died on impact, another a day later from multiple organ damage.

But unlike her husband's desire to play it close to the vest for the rest of his life, all Mary wanted to do after that was bust out of the stable, see what else was out there, although her imagination on that front was fairly limited; she had no desire to ride a hog across America, or live in a desert commune or learn how to barrel race in Wyoming;

in fact, all she could manage to do was ask for a divorce and now and then get a motel room with another man.

Coming out of her fugue, she saw that Super Philip, despite his next Hennessy having just landed on the bar, was no longer her neighbor.

She found him hovering like a claw over the three women at their table. With his voice just low enough to avoid drawing eyes, he was in the middle of a seething tirade calling them out in the freakiest most vicious cunt-this bitch-that language for thinking they were better than him.

She began to reluctantly push herself away from the bar intending to try and coax this debonair psycho away, but then, to her relief, she saw that all three women were unfazed by his ugly shit, two calmly videotaping his tirade on their cells while the third waved for another cocktail.

By the time Super P returned to the bar Mary was on her feet and tabbing out.

"You have a good night now," offering his fist for a bump then turning to a woman who had just sat down a few stools away. "Mommy, I humbly request that you immediately pack up and move to Saint Louis before you destroy my marriage."

Out on the street she got a text from Esposito.

If it had only been a Hail Mary appeal to hook up at some no-tell motel, this time she might have gone for it.

But instead he wrote this—

fyi

100+ yr old crap tenement v underground subway extension excavations vibrations

for months

A moment later, another text.

boom

※ ※ ※

When she and Jimmy finally agreed to divorce, in order to avoid being eaten alive by lawyers, given that their combined annual income was a little under 200K, they had opted for mediation, but as they quickly found out, going that route required an exquisitely torturous mindfulness; they had to agree on everything: money, kids, house, who takes possession of what, money, kids, house, money, because all it would take is one unresolved issue between them, any perceived unfairness on the part of the other, that, if not worked out right then and there at the table with zero chance of someone needing to "sleep on it" and possibly waking up red in the head, could lead to years of the-meter-is-running mostly bullshit mini-litigation, drained bank accounts, health problems, compounded kid trauma and fearsome drops in weight.

One of their close calls concerned a twenty-thousand-dollar windfall that had dropped into Mary's lap courtesy of her great-uncle's will. Jimmy assumed it was to be shared, but Mary considered it exempt. When she said as much at the mediator's table she saw Jimmy's face instantly tighten. Spooked by where that could lead, she was just about to reverse herself and agree to a 10K–10K split, but to her surprise he beat her to it, letting her have it all.

The relief she felt was tempered by an unasked-for sadness at how eager he was to keep things moving forward in order to be free himself. She felt the same way, but still . . .

At first, at the suggestion of the mediator, they tried sharing the house, living their separate lives under the same roof so that the kids wouldn't have to shuttle between homes and could continue going to the same schools, have the same friends, see the same therapists and basically have the same lives as before; Jimmy sleeping in the "media room," Mary in the bedroom. After that it got complicated. There were the occupation times to be worked out for all the common areas; kitchen rights, dinner-with-the-kids rights, living-room-with-the-good-TV rights, but they kept stumbling into each other's zones because they just did.

The first room to go was the living room, Mary insisting that she get to finish an episode of *Band of Brothers* past her allotted time. Jimmy shrugged it off, sat on the other end of the couch and took in the last fifteen minutes, the kids watching from the sidelines as their parents pretended that the other one wasn't really there.

Then came the breakdown of the dinner hour, the absurdity of only one of them getting to eat with the kids while the other foraged in the refrigerator and brought the food to another room. The hell with that they agreed, but when they returned to eating as a foursome it was actually worse, the chatter between the adults suffused with a strained cordiality, the boys having to sit there and pretend to not notice because they knew their parents were, quote unquote, doing it for them. Night after night, Mary and Jimmy like two talking marionettes, until it finally blew up in their faces.

It started one night with Jimmy asking her, "So how was work today?" Mary as usual lobbing back, "Good, you know, given the hot weather and the crazies out there," then after a bite of fish, adding, "And how were your classes?"

"And how were your classes?" Douglas, aka the Big One, mimicking her note for note.

"Sorry?"

Douglas rose out of his chair, shouting, "If you're going to fake everything's ok, *fake harder.*"

Meanwhile, Terrence, the younger one, just sat there staring at his plate, his head resting nearly horizontal against the palm of his hand.

Mary wanted to say, *We're trying as hard as we can*, but then stopped, realizing that that was her son's point.

As Jimmy lightly palmed Terrence's shoulder, Douglas dropped back in his chair, muttered, "You should just move out."

Mary, reduced to a child by that, said without thinking, "Who should."

"You can't ask me that!" Douglas screamed. "I don't care!"

So, it was back to the mediator who suggested renting a nearby apartment, a modest one-bedroom which they would take turns occupying in shifts, three nights, three nights so that the one at home could relax and the kids wouldn't be subjected to the nightly puppet show.

When Mary finally made it home, Jimmy was slouched on the couch watching news footage of the building collapse, his spine so banana-curled into itself that his chin was resting on a shirt button.

"Sorry about tonight," she said. "Thanks for covering."

"Happy to." His eyes still on the screen. "You're alright?"

"It was rough, but yeah." Mary dropping her keys on the dining table.

Even though she'd asked him to be here, his presence in the house when it wasn't his turn, as always, left her feeling both relieved and annoyed.

It wasn't like the guy was hard to look at; tall, decently put together, in his sobriety, a reborn runner with just a slight gut and a lazy posture, but he had a full head of brown almost black hair and kind eyes, although since the separation those eyes sometimes seemed to project a benign indifference towards her, or so she imagined.

"Not to tell you what to do"—Jimmy finally looked at her—"but you should get checked out."

"For what." Mary resisting the impulse to tell him to sit up straight.

"You were breathing that air."

"I was off-site," which was a kinda-sorta half-truth.

"Still." Jimmy's eyes returning to the TV.

She walked into the kitchen and opened the refrigerator, but nothing in there was calling to her.

"Kids ok?"

"They're good."

"They're what?" Her head was half into the fridge.

"*Good.*"

"Asleep?" Coming back into the living room.

"The Big One's probably still up," he said, then, "No, I'm just thinking back to how many rescuers got sick from the Towers."

"Got it." Mary thinking about Douglas, whether she should go up to him or let him be.

"Ok then," Jimmy said as he finally rose from the couch, Mary once again resisting the urge to tell him to pull back his shoulders and lead with his chest.

"I put it on Record for you," he said, gesturing to the screen.

"Thanks."

When he got to the door, he stopped and turned.

"You know who never got sick from that day? The ConEd workers. Why? Because their supervisor made them wear respirators."

"That guy, the supervisor? He used to live next door to my sister. He told her that both the NYPD and FDNY bosses came up and asked him to have his people lose the respirators because they were demoralizing their own people. Can you believe that?"

"Nobody had a crystal ball back then," she said.

After Jimmy left, Mary lingered downstairs doing this and that before finally going up to check in on the boys.

They were asleep, Mary both relieved and guilty, about to go back down the stairs when the nine-year-old called her name.

"What's up?"

"Douglas made me look in a mirror and say 'Candyman' five times."

Mary sat on the edge of his bed. "I'll kill him."

"I told Dad and he said Candyman's just a made-up person, but I don't believe him."

"Ok. So, did you see him?"

"Dad?"

"Candyman."

"No, but I think he's hiding somewhere in the house waiting for me to fall asleep so I have to stay awake. You should stay awake, too."

"Well, to tell you the truth," Mary touched by his concern for her, "I don't know if Candyman's real or fake but I do know this."

"What."

"Even if he is real, he can't leave Chicago."

"Why not."

"Because ghosts or whatever can't travel far from the place that they were killed. That's the law."

"How far away is Chicago?"

"Fifteen thousand miles, so there's no way he could come all the way to our house. We're totally safe."

Terrence stared at her for a beat. "How do you know that?"

"Because it's in the Bible."

Another beat, another stare, then a sigh of relief.

"Ok, but can you just stay with me until I fall asleep?"

"You bet," Mary said, easing herself flat on the narrow twin.

After accepting his mother's confident bullshit, Terrence went down fast, Mary lying there next to him thinking, *Well, that went pretty well . . .*

And this was another thing with her and the kids. When it came to having to really engage with them, she was like a person who hated going to parties, started to brood about them two days ahead of time, but whenever she actually got there more often than not she had a surprisingly good time.

When thinking to herself about the boys, she tended to adapt an arch interior tone like some '70s TV comedienne PG-13 bitching about her family. But every now and then she caught herself and cut it short, seeing all that practiced drollness for what it was: a defense against coming to terms with the fact that she never really wanted kids to begin with. They just came anyway.

She was fine with the chores; buying their clothes and organizing playdates when they were younger; driving them to school, to soccer games, to doctors; driving them wherever they had to go—give her a child-related job and she was relatively ok, but even in those moments, Mary was always splitting herself in two, one half self-consciously observing the other half in action, doing the things that a mother would do.

She took great pains to hide it from them but she knew all too well that kids read you like a comic book, so she doubted her secret heart was any kind of secret to them. And if her own childhood raised by a mother who felt the same way about her was any indicator, their judgment when looking back would be harsh.

When her rabbi the deputy inspector sent her to see the NYPD talk therapist, who was way better than she had to be, regarding her crippling phobia around crossing state lines, she suggested that, given Mary's parentage—a mother who was a human glacier when it came to her and her brother; her father, a former ranked welterweight who still thought with his hands out in the world but at home always fell apart in the face of his wife's ruthless silences—maybe those state lines she feared breaching were metaphorical stand-ins for the emotional boundaries she had to create for herself in order to survive childhood.

Her father was capable of killing a man with his fists, had almost done so in the ring, but he'd never laid a hand on her. Neither did her mother; but it was Jeannie Burns, with her distant clinical gaze and her taste for withholding affection from her kids as a means of bringing them to heel, who'd put the fear of annihilation into Mary on a daily basis.

After her mother's death, she met with her father at a bar and for the first time described to him some of the more chilling moments she recalled from her childhood. His response nearly knocked her off her seat. "That's all you remember? Sister, you have no idea how much you forgot."

Borders. Boundaries. Playing it safe by making life choices that would never again place her under the thumb of another emotional terrorizer, life choices she labeled *good enough*: a lover who was nothing more than a clap-on clap-off dick; a husband who, at least in the beginning, was a good enough companion and good enough in bed when she felt like it, good enough as an overall functioning intelligent and sympathetic human being; but the deal-clincher for her with Jimmy was that she never really lost her heart to him, which meant she was safe.

Same when it came to her work on the street.

One of the reasons why she was so talented at calming down red-hot people was that even though she might be curious about their grievances and what she could do to stabilize their situations, she knew they could never get inside her. They were the other, they were the job; and that too, despite the ever-present possibility of physical danger, meant she was safe.

But to give an emotional straight-arm to your own children? People did it all the time she knew; Jeannie sure had and Mary hated her for it until the day she died.

The big difference between them was that Mary constantly and exhaustively struggled with it, while Jeannie, like some animal out in the wild, had never given her own actions a second thought.

Easing herself out of Terrence's narrow bed, she went across the hall to the bathroom. Washing her face, she stared into the mirror and attempted to say "Candyman" the required five times, getting as far as number four, then stopped, unable to bring herself to say his name that one last time in order to send out the invitation.

* * *

Still in his bathrobe at nine the next morning, Royal looked out the kitchen window at the city-owned lot that sat between his funeral home and Lilies of the Field, the flower shop on its opposite side.

The florist, Benny David, a born-again ex-con, was out there right now on the buckling weed-poked macadam talking to his Greenthumb expeditor, the woman who had been helping him for months navigate the system, pushing his paperwork from one phlegmatic bureaucrat's desk to the next and the next, until the Parks Department finally got around to giving his proposal for a teaching garden the go-ahead.

A teaching garden. You want to grow vegetables? *Why.* There was a big ShopRite just up the block. Flowers? The Koreans have a stand on the corner of 124th and Fifth.

It wasn't that Royal didn't understand how know-nothing his argument sounded or couldn't appreciate the satisfaction it would give some city folk to learn how to grow their own food, it was more that the conversion of that cold sore of a space to *any* kind of garden would create big problems for him.

Royal stood there in a trance of agitation until the bang of a plate being set on the dining table turned him around to see Amina, dressed for the gym, holding his glass of OJ and glaring at him, Royal wondering if she was going to bang that down on the table too.

"What." Royal striving for bewildered.

"You know what."

He did.

"Oh c'mon, he was fine out there."

"That's not what *he* said."

"What do you mean? What did he say?" Royal not really wanting to hear it.

"Hustling bodies for you? Really?"

"That's going to make for one hell of a college application essay someday," Royal wondering if she was ever going to pass him the OJ. "Besides, that's how I learned. And that's how come there's always food on our table."

"Oh no, oh no, not that 'food on our table' bullshit."

"Ok, how about . . . 'And that's why we always have clothes to put on our backs,'" Royal wishing she would just sit her ass down instead of standing over him with her momma-bear death-ray eyes.

When he first laid eyes on her at her mother's funeral thirteen years ago, she was soft and roundish, which he kind of liked, but after giving birth to Patrice, the younger, and no longer liking what she saw in the mirror, she had thrown herself with her usual manic energy into working out until her arms, legs and torso rippled with definition.

Royal, on the other hand, having played Division One basketball for four years, followed by a few more as a pro in Europe and Asia, held a retired elite athlete's disdain for exercise.

"One last, then I give up, you ready?" Royal dabbing at his mouth. "'And that's why we always have a roof over our heads.'"

Amina held up her hands as if to fend him off, which he knew from experience meant she was cooling down. He started to eat.

"Marquise is not you," she said.

"He's half me. Far as I know."

"As far as you know," she bounced back.

They were ok.

❦ ❦ ❦

The next morning when Mary came down from her bedroom, Douglas was sitting cross-legged in front of the TV watching a rerun of *Big Brother*.

"Turn it off."

"Why?" Not looking at her.

"Just turn it off."

It must have dawned on him that he was in the shit because he did as he was told.

"Come over to the table."

"I already ate," he said weakly, then once again did as he was told, Mary taking note of how baby-faced he still was, even though, the same as Jimmy had been, he was the tallest kid in all of the seventh grade.

"Last night, you think what you pulled on Terrence was funny?"

"No, it was a joke."

"Did *he* think it was a joke?"

"I thought he did."

"Was he laughing?"

"No."

Eyes down, Douglas reached for a crumpled paper napkin, then began flattening it out over and over until it started to look ironed.

"I came home close to midnight, he was wide awake scared to death that Candyman was coming for him. I had to stay with him for an hour before he felt safe enough to close his eyes. This is what you consider a joke?"

"No." His voice going small.

Ok, he got the message, give him an out.

"If you saw someone else do that to your brother how would you react?"

"I'd *destroy* them," he said with heat, grateful for the question.

"Uh-huh, I believe you would."

"I *definitely* would," sounding almost happy now.

"Ok, so look, I'm letting Terrence sleep a little longer this morning, but when he comes down . . ."

"I'll apologize."

"Ok, that's good of you." Then worrying that "That's good of you" possibly sounded to him like sarcasm, she kissed the top of his head.

※ ※ ※

The community room of the Lieutenant Samuel J. Battle Houses with its glazed concrete walls and paint-chipped cement floor was an echo chamber, the high voices and sneaker skitter of the small kids randomly running in and out of the place sounding like screeching tires and small arms fire which would make the filming of the mitigation video a stop-start nightmare.

Nonetheless, Felix looked around for a good spot to set up his camera. There weren't many options in the mostly empty space except for a long vinyl-topped folding table set up and pushed flush to one wall, its surface littered with a few bunched-up cocktail napkins and a dinner-sized paper plate rimmed with rock-hard blue cake icing from a recent party.

He carried all of that to a garbage bin, then hand-swept the remaining crumbs onto the floor. When that was done, he dragged the table across the room to a spot out of the sunlight streaming through the windows.

And when that was done he carried a few folding chairs over from a standing stack leaning against a wall near a locked bathroom. And then he waited for his people to show up. Three heads were scheduled to speak on behalf of Micah Wade, seventeen, who, after getting his ass kicked by another kid, went upstairs to his mother's apartment and came back down with a bread knife with which he proceeded to punch a hole in that other kid's gut.

This was his third time shooting for the Aspira Group, a collection of legal activists and former public defenders, what was referred to as a mitigation video, a short visual doc of positive testimonies on behalf of their client who had already been found guilty and was now coming up for sentencing. This then would be folded into the overall "mitigation packet," a collection of school records, social work records, child services records, photos and occasionally old childhood videos, all of which would be sent to the sentencing judge as a humanizing biography of the perp in hopes of him (rarely her) receiving a more lenient sentence.

It was a simple enough gig, set up the camera opposite a family member, a priest, a social worker, a counselor, a teacher, et al., seated at a desk or a table, and shoot. Simple to film but afterwards tricky and dangerous. Given that in general, New York sentencing judges were notoriously tough sells, if they interpreted these packets as an effort to manipulate them—which of course they were—or felt insulted or in any way irritated by that; if they felt the effort smacked of sentimentality or ham-handedness or the subtlest of background violins, the whole effort could very well boomerang into a heavier sentence.

Considering all that, the mandate was to keep it all dry as a bone, straight-up faces talking about the client's pre-criminal life, the biography of mounting pain, of family trauma and bureaucratic misplacements.

That, and show to the judge the network of support waiting for the client when they came out in order to emphasize the diminished odds of recidivism; all in five to ten minutes per talking head, no artificial staging, no filming the client walking down the street holding his little daughter's hand (the one time they tried that the daughter's mother came charging out of a building screaming about what a wife-beating, child-support-dodging motherfucker their client was and how she hoped he'd get shanked in the showers).

And definitely no soundtrack; that was for Cali judges.

The building's custodian came through the door with a rolling bucket of ammonia-laced water and started to swab the floor, the rising fumes making Felix's eyes sting and tear.

There were three pre-screened testifiers today: Calvin Ray, an ex-con turned community activist; Micah's older brother JC; and Father Ekubo, a Malian priest from St. Rose of Lima who knew the kid from a church-run summer camp.

So where was everybody?

Christopher Diaz, Mary starting her search by running the name through the NYS DMV records. There were three drivers on file with that name; one was seventy-six years old and living in Buffalo; another twenty years old, a marine stationed in Kuwait; which left her with her MIA, Christopher Wilson Diaz, forty-two years old, his address, the building that was no more.

The driver's license that appeared on the screen had been suspended then revoked altogether for multiple DUIs and failure to attend the mandatory safety classes. There was no car registered to his name which given his track record behind the wheel was probably all for the best. But at least she got his photo, a heavy-faced Latino with a crop of richly curled hair, thick eyebrows in a permanently upward arch over dark fatalistic eyes, and what seemed like a permanent five o'clock shadow hanging like a feed bucket from his temples to his rounded jaw. It would be the face of a rustic peon in an opera or a minor villain in a cheap Western except for his mouth, a real rosebud, a ruddy petite oval, as disorienting in the middle of all that hairy male density as a flower growing out of a gun barrel.

But there was something more.

Diaz had an uncanny resemblance to a fighter that her father had almost killed in the ring thirty years ago, and who later on had almost killed her father in return.

Shaking it off, she went to the eJusticeNY site and discovered that her MIA had something of a sheet: a few minor arrests, one for misdemeanor assault in Staten Island, which to her sounded like a bar fight, and another for one of those DUIs, his sentence in each case, community service. He had no passport, and no social media presence.

So now what.

She thought of going to her boss and asking him if she could take it to the squad, maybe get the go-ahead to work with them, but she knew that if they were at all interested in finding Diaz, they'd do it themselves. But they wouldn't be because there were no warrants out on him and no criminal complaint unless she herself filed one, but for what? What had the guy done besides be unaccounted for?

Plus, this being above 96th Street, their caseloads were off the hook; Mary hearing them in her head—*Either he'll show up on his own or he won't.*

※ ※ ※

After sitting by himself for half an hour, the first of his testifiers finally came through the door, Calvin "Cal" Ray, a dark-skinned barrel-chested man in his early forties, Felix immediately taking a liking to him in that instinctual way where one finds oneself randomly sitting next to a stranger on some bench, or in a waiting room, or standing on a ticket line and somehow just knowing that you want that person in your life.

It had only happened once before, with Mr. Henry, his ninth-grade English teacher, Felix hanging on his every word and following him around the school like a baby duck, until someone told him Mr. Henry was gay.

"Young man," Calvin stopping to slide his bulging backpack to the concrete floor before coming forward with his hand out, "let's go make a movie."

"My name is Calvin Ray and I am both the founder and director of an anti-violence organization known as PGD which stands for Put the Guns Down and also a youth mentorship program known as YSF, which stands for Young Scholars for the Future."

Calvin's face was both broad and carved, the power in it enhanced by his habit of simultaneously lowering his head and raising his eyes from beneath the deep overhang of his brow which made him look like a bull contemplating a charge.

"I have known Micah . . ."

"Ok, wait, sorry . . ." Felix having to stop filming because someone outside had shouted, *"You think I'm fooling with you?"*

"No problem. You want me to take it from the top?"

"Just from 'I have known Micah.'"

"Say when."

"When."

"I have known Micah Wade since he was eleven years old, when his mother had brought him along to one of our YSF youth mentoring street parties, says to me, 'I have another child with special needs, which takes up all my time.'

"Over the next few years I got to know the boy well, going to his home, taking him with some of my other mentees on trips to Orchard Beach, some Mets games, Knicks games when I got someone to donate a few tickets, and in general just being there for him. But whatever we did, wherever we went, I have always found him to be appreciative and grateful. And here's another thing. Most of our Young Scholars need some kind of assistance with their schoolwork but not Micah. He was smart and intelligent. He had a future."

Calvin held up his hand to stop the filming, took a water bottle filled with what looked like tea out of his backpack, draining it in three gulps.

"How we doing?"

"Great," Felix said, keeping his *a little more of this, a bit less of that* suggestions to himself. "Let's keep going."

"The only thing, the only hint, or possible storm cloud or what have you that I ever noticed in regards to Micah was that whenever his father came back home after being away for a while, his personality got dark and incommunicative.

"I tried to get him to talk to me about what was going in that house between him and his father but I could never get him to say, because if in fact, this individual was violent or abusive towards him or his mother I wanted to talk to this man, see if he needed to be addressed in no uncertain terms."

Calvin paused here for effect then leaned forward into the lens.

"Now, this incident. I can tell you with confidence that it was an emotional mistake on his behalf, a tragic one-time outburst . . ."

Calvin stopped again, then slightly raised up from his seat to look past the camera. Tracking his gaze, Felix turned to see someone standing in the shadows against a far wall near the door, no telling how long they'd been there.

When he turned back, Calvin appeared to have retreated inside himself, Felix waiting until he came up from wherever he went, then cueing him up. "A tragic one-time outburst . . ."

"A tragic one-time outburst because right afterwards he came to me all shook like he couldn't believe that was himself had done that, handed me the knife and asked me to call his mother.

"Now, the thing to understand here is that that boy is no thug. I know this because a thug has got no truck with remorse like that, because the street, as such, just don't allow for it."

From behind them, the abrupt slamming of the community center door stopped the filming, Felix thinking gunshot, sitting frozen in his seat until Calvin said, "You good?"

"Yeah, of course," Felix fussing with the camera to camouflage his embarrassment.

There wasn't much left to say except for the punch line, Calvin serving it up with his penetrating charging bull face.

"I understand that Micah has got to pay the price for his actions, there's no argument there . . . But please know that whenever his time inside has been served, he'll be walking out into the arms of a loving family, a loving community and all the strength and support of the PGD and the YSF."

* * *

Before she left the house Mary dug up the thirty-year-old tape of the second Teddy Burns–Danny Rivera fight. She'd only seen it once, maybe half a lifetime ago, after which she vowed to never look at it again, but she had to see if Christopher Diaz and Danny Rivera bore as uncanny a resemblance as she thought, so she popped it into the VHS machine and braced herself for what she knew was to come.

For the first two rounds the fighters mostly danced, taking each other's measure, but in the third it turned into a war; these two naturally elusive counter-punchers uncharacteristically slugging it out until in the fifth, when her father caught Rivera with an uppercut that lifted him off his feet. He beat the count but when he got up off the canvas it was obvious he had no idea where he was. The fight should have been stopped right then, but it went on for three more rounds, Rivera landing mostly jabs and going into a clinch whenever they closed, Teddy sending him to the canvas again in the sixth. But in the seventh Rivera managed to rally and drop her father with a left hook which had more to do with him losing his footing than the power of the punch, Teddy right back up, then restlessly dancing in his corner through the mandatory eight count before wading back in, landing two blows for every one of Rivera's. At the end of the round, Rivera, increasingly disoriented, walked with her father halfway back to his corner before turning himself around and heading to his own.

With both fighters beginning to tire, the eighth round started off sluggish; two exhausted clinches for every thrown punch; the ringside commentator remarking, "So far, this round is pretty quiet compared to what we've seen before."

Almost immediately after those words went out over the air, Burns trapped Rivera against a corner post and with a tremendous barrage of punches knocked him out. But instead of hitting the mat, Rivera became entangled in the ropes which kept him upright.

And then came the next twenty-five seconds that destroyed both men's lives; Rivera unconscious at this point, but still on his feet, spastically raising his arms as if he were still defending himself, which made the referee slow to call it a fight, as her father kept pounding him—a flurry of fifteen unanswered punches to the head and midsection before Rivera finally slid down to the mat.

Immediately mobbed by his handlers who carried him back to his corner then raised his arms in victory, Mary's father didn't realize how seriously Rivera was hurt until he saw the stretcher carried into the ring. When he tried to go to him after that, he was blocked by Rivera's cornermen and pulled away by his own.

When the referee raised his hand in victory and the announcer called the result, Teddy Burns's gaze never left the medical scrum over Rivera's body.

It was that unanswered and undefended barrage of blows; those twenty-five seconds in which her father, lost in his own instincts, nearly beat a man to death, that gradually over time changed him into a person so different from the one Mary knew before that she never really saw that man again.

Neither of them ever fought again; her father, devastated by what he'd done, calling it a career; Rivera, afflicted with seizures, in and out of hospitals and brain trauma rehabilitation centers, drug rehabilitation centers, until his final disappearance four years later, on the night when Mary realized that she had finally lost her father for good.

So. Did Christopher Diaz really look like Danny Rivera? Some, but not as much as she'd first thought; nonetheless, in her mind, the association between the two men held fast, so where the hell was he.

*　*　*

On his way to the drugstore to pick up more eight-hour Tylenol for his banged-up basketball knees, Royal found himself walking past Lilies of the Field. *Don't you dare, just keep walking,* but he couldn't resist, so in he went to duke it out yet again among the flowers with Benny David.

At the front register Benny's uncle Maurice, his unshaved face silver with stubble, sat reading *My Grandfather's Son* as he waited for the rare walk-in customer. But when he looked up to see Royal standing before him, he sucked his teeth and went back to reading.

Gospel music fighting its way through crackling static on WLIB drew him towards a work area behind a counter where Benny's mother Pauline and her sister Martha were putting together sympathy sprays of white lily, white rose, and lavender.

Reaching a long arm over the counter, Royal adjusted the radio dial to at least kill some of the static, neither one of them acknowledging his presence.

"Where is he," Royal asked the women.

"Right here," Benny David said, appearing from behind a curtained area holding a vase filled with Madonna lilies.

"We're gonna go another round again? Let me just put these in the cooler first."

Royal stood there holding his breath against the sweet frosty air of the shop which everyone but himself seemed to find exhilarating.

"Ok, hit me." Benny turning from the cooler.

"You're gonna be making mulch?"

"You have to. You know what that is, right?"

"Yeah I know what that is. And I know how it stinks."

"Small price for helping out the planet."

"I tell you what, you want mulch? How about the next time someone stiffs me on a burial I sell you the body."

"Embalming fluid going to be a problem," Benny said, enjoying himself, always enjoying himself, which drove Royal up a wall.

"Then move the hell upstate. You Greenpeace that lot? I'm losing sixteen parking spaces. In *this* city? In *my* profession? Those spaces are like gold."

"I hear you, but Royal, I got to ask you, when was the last time you needed sixteen parking spaces?"

* * *

"My name is John Charles Wade, Private Second Class in the Tenth Mountain Division, First Brigade, Second Battalion, Twenty-Second Infantry, currently posted in Fort Drum New York and Micah Wade's older brother by four years."

JC was stiff; Felix thinking that maybe he was trying too hard to project the air of a military man. That, or maybe he was just camera-shy.

He hadn't been like that when he came into the room, animatedly embracing Calvin, who had stayed to see him, but the moment he saw that light under the lens turn green he shot back his shoulders and the words came out of his mouth as if each one were listed vertically.

One of the techniques Felix picked up from observing other Aspira shooters faced with a tightly wound individual like Private Wade was to keep up eye contact while constantly bobbing your head in affirmation, so bobbing he went.

"Micah has always been small for his age and in the Battles that meant he got tormented a lot by some out here."

Nodding like an overexcited oil rig, Felix gave him a thumbs-up and John Charles started to lose a little of his ramrod demeanor.

"Whenever I saw that happen my personal impulse was to step in, but Micah, he hated that, said it would only make things worse for him the next day." JC shot a quick look at Calvin, sitting elbows on knees in a folding chair off to the side.

"I remember one time when he got beat on in front of my eyes and it killed me not to step in." JC rolling his shoulders now as if his shirt and jacket were too tight. "But he wanted to sink or swim out there on his own, I would say sinking most of the time, that is, until he went through his shoot."

Felix stopped filming.

"What's his shoot?"

"His maturation burst."

"Can you use another word?"

"Hold on, hold . . ." then, ". . . Until his body matured. He was still on the small side, still got picked on but at least he could fight back with some muscle on his bones." Then leaning forward, speaking to Felix as if there were no camera between them, "Let me tell you something, everybody says the Battles is a jungle. The Bookers, the Jeffs, Duncan, Crawford, all of them, that's what you read in the papers, day in day out and I'm not saying it was a picnic growing up there, but sometimes the jungle in the apartment was worse than the one outside and that was the case for us. My father was a big individual and a mean drunk who when he got his load on, let his hands do the talking. I swear to God, that man turned our apartment into a minefield, everybody having to go around on tippy-toe like we did. We were scared to death of him," then turning to Calvin off camera, "You know what I'm saying?" then back to the camera, "And Micah?

Oh, did he have it out for Micah because he convinced himself that Micah wasn't his, and what made things worse was that as little as he was? Micah was the only one of us who would stand up to him but that just made that man madder and madder and then those hands went into action." JC held up his hand to stop the filming then leaned back in his chair.

"Taking five now," turning away to deal with what he had just conjured up for himself.

This interview, Felix already knew, was too meandering and anecdotal to be of any use—maybe something could be salvaged if the film editor used a machete instead of a splicer but he kept rolling in order to capture something new for him, a human being painting his own portrait with words and gestures.

This wasn't like shooting on the hoof out in the street, documenting spontaneous actions. This was controlled and framed video portraiture and it offered him the barest glimpse into what he could possibly make of himself in this life behind a camera.

It was a selfish thought given the circumstances, but an exhilarating one that brought with it a jolt of joy.

"When our moms kicked him out the last time, it was like the sun came out. We were all smiling again, especially Micah as you can imagine, telling jokes, watching TV together, being easy . . . Yeah, well, that lasted about six months before she took that man back. Again. I never understood why she always did that when we were doing so good without him, but . . . I guess she had her needs."

"Can you use another word besides 'needs'?"

"What's wrong with 'needs'?" Then off Felix's silence, he sighed, then . . . "She was lonely. But whenever she let him back in, Micah would go total dark-side, angry all the time, messing up in school, starting fights instead of catching them, he even got caught once in school with a Taser in his backpack. It was like his maturity went into reverse."

Felix glanced again at Calvin who was nodding his head in agreement, testifying for the testifier.

"See me in this uniform? I am not by nature a physical aggressor, but after the one time when I walked in on him hitting her, I finally lost my shit and took a bat to him. The judge gave me a choice, the signup or the lockup, so . . ."

JC took another breather, staring at the nearest wall as if it were a picture window, before coming back to wrap it up.

"That man is out of the picture again, but it's too late for Micah and that's the real tragedy here. But I love my little brother and I'll be right there for him on the inside and on the out. So will all the people here who truly know him. That's all."

As Felix was setting up for the priest, JC came back over to the table.

"Let me ask you something. You filmed my mother the other day? What did she have to say for herself? I need to see it."

He instinctually looked to Calvin to see if this was a good idea or not but the man was on the phone again so Felix was on his own.

"Micah was never any trouble to me, never any trouble to anybody," the mother began, her voice slow and heavy, her eyes avoiding the camera.

"Your moms looks beat," Calvin said.

"He had the biggest smile, Micah, except for when his father was around which was not often."

"Often enough." JC's voice starting to climb.

"That man, when it came to his youngest son, they were always at it tooth and claw. It just drove me . . ." Shaking her head in bewilderment. "I remember once I took Micah aside. 'He's your father, can't you just get along with him? Can't you just accept him the way he is?'"

"You asked *Micah* that? You don't ask *Micah* that, you ask *him*!" JC shouted, spittle flecking the screen.

Calvin turned to Felix. "Pause it." Then, "J, all your moms is doing here is trying to help."

"She should of asked *him*!" JC snapped, before wheeling and charging for the door.

"I'll talk to him," Calvin said more to himself than Felix, then stepped into the shadows to make yet another call.

Felix's cell started to vibrate, a text from Father Ekubo apologizing for having to cancel.

When Calvin returned, Felix was nearly through packing his gear.

"Young man, how good are you with that camera?"

"Depends for what."

"Shooting on the hoof."

"Like a cattle drive?"

"A what?" Calvin at first not getting it, then half laughing, like someone who doesn't have time for a full guffaw. "No, no, ok, what it is, is we're having a PGD YSF rally in the Crawford Houses on Sunday and I would like to very much invite you to be on hand and maybe shoot some footage for us."

"I can do that." Felix just wanting to keep hanging with him.

"Now"—Calvin reached deep into his backpack—"we can't pay you except for a free shirt and some burgers."

"No problem."

"Good." Handing over a rolled yellow tee. "Here's your advance."

* * *

The Community Affairs squad had only three police: Mary, a detective; Anna Quinones, a uniform, who at present was on vacation; and their boss Lieutenant Billy Ryan.

Ryan had an interesting history; he was an eight-year all-star in Brooklyn South Narcotics and the recipient of two departmental commendations and a Combat Cross until the day a car accident left him with a shattered pelvis. Stuck behind various administrative desks after that, he gradually morphed from a high-and-tight gym rat into an overweight bureaucrat with an unkempt air about him. But for all that, he was a reasonably decent boss to work for.

"So, this missing Diaz guy from the collapse." Mary standing in Ryan's doorway, "First I was thinking about going up to the squad with it but I know what they'll say."

"Right," Ryan lowering his head to look at her over the tops of his reading glasses, his ergonomic desk chair squealing in submission.

"And forget missing persons because . . ."

"Mary, what do you want."

"If it doesn't get in the way of my work I was wondering if I could go after him myself. Just, you know, canvass the area, call in some favors. Nothing heavy."

Ryan stared at her, Mary waiting for his counter.

"Are you still tight with Reagan?"

Her rabbi. And there it was.

"I don't know about tight." Then off his silence, "I mean, if something comes up, I guess."

Ryan looked down at his desk blotter, shuffled a few folders, Mary thinking, *Just spit it out.*

"So, my sister Lana's son is graduating the academy next month."

"Ok."

"She's divorced but when her ex-mother-in-law started in with dementia she took her in because that's what kind a human being she is."

"Wow."

"Believe me, it's a full-time job."

"I'll bet."

"The kid used to help her but who knows where they'll post him when he gets out."

"Sure."

"I mean if he landed in the One-Two-One, -Two, or -Three, it would be a godsend to his mother. This way if something ever happened, if she needed him, he could be over there like a shot."

"Right."

"Do you think you could maybe give your guy a ring?"

"Yeah, I mean I can put it to him, but I can't promise . . ."

"Try, that's all I ask."

"Understood."

Ryan went back to exploring his blotter for so long that Mary almost forgot why she was there in the first place.

"The first time you show up late for a Community Board meeting, or a street rally or some kind of Pride thing . . ."

"Absolutely. Thank you." Then at the door, turning back to him, "Your sister. Where's this ex of hers? It's his mother, right?"

"Her ex?" Ryan raised his eyes to her, a theatrically insinuating half smile on his face. "Nobody knows."

"Ok then," Mary said and left the office.

* * *

When Felix and Calvin finally came out of the community center, the mystery man who had been listening to Calvin's testimony from the shadows before stalking out of the room was now crouch-walking parallel to them from about fifty feet away, his eyes hot in his head.

"A *mistake*?" barking at them. "My cousin's shitting into a bag 'cause of that little motherfucker and all that was, was a *mistake*?"

Felix started to film, but Calvin put a hand on his arm and he stopped.

"You go out and forget to lock your door? *That's* a mistake. You go in a store and leave your car running with the keys in it? *That's* a mistake."

"Eric . . ." Calvin calmly calling out, "I would go to bat for you just the same as him."

"I hope that little faggot goes and gets killed in there!"

Eric came to a stop, Felix and Calvin moving on.

"I'll talk to him," Calvin murmured, the second time those words had come out of his mouth.

"*Mario Howell!*" Eric shouted after them. "You didn't even say his name!"

* * *

Returning to the block, Mary inhaled the acrid air, weaker than it was yesterday but still strong enough to make you want to hold your breath. A high plywood barrier had been put up around the collapse site, making it impossible to see anything but the tops of the bobbing cranes and the work crews stationed on the surrounding rooftops.

Mary looking around the block now; the laundromat and corner store were still open but not much else; the dry cleaner, the check-cashing place and a tax prep office were all shuttered, their damaged windows crisscrossed with heavy-duty electrical tape.

And then she saw, halfway down the block, a number of men sitting on the steps of an old brownstone, listening to what they couldn't see behind the barrier.

"Hey fellas, how are you all doing?" Mary looking up at them from the sidewalk.

A lot of nods in return but that was it, everybody waiting for more.

She took out a blowup of Diaz's driver's license photo and handed it to the nearest man, a huge hulk, two canes lying sideways across his lap.

"I'm trying to find someone who might have been in the building yesterday, hopefully not, but he is missing and I need to know if he's ok."

The photo made its way around the stoop but she was still waiting for someone to speak.

"He's not in any trouble."

"Well his wife died and he's homeless. I'd call that trouble in spades," the one on the highest step drawled, this guy hawk-thin and a snappy dresser, his eyes hidden behind wraparound shades.

"I just need to find him. Did anybody see him on the street yesterday?"

"Yesterday?"

More silence.

"Guys I'm not here to pull teeth, help me out or don't."

Waiting, waiting, then, ready to walk away . . .

"Nah, but normally he's always out there. He likes to work out on the cross pipes over there, you know, doing dips, pullups and the like."

Mary looked across the street to a tenement like the one that had collapsed, its facade veiled top to bottom in iron braces and support beams.

"Scaffolding," one of the others said, "the poor man's gymnasium."

"Ok," Mary said, "we got that covered. What else?"

"Hustling, hustling, all the time hustling."

"What kind of hustling?"

"Putting out people's garbage on pickup days, recycling and whatnot. Mover's helper. Driving people."

"Driving people where?"

"To work, or wherever. Upstate, Long Island, I heard he once took a dude to up to Canada."

"He used to take Green Mile's mother to pain management, cruise downtown for people stuck in rush hour."

"The guy doesn't have a driver's license," she said, "how does he drive?"

"Carefully."

"Very."

"You know his car?"

"He rents it from some guy but he don't bring it around."

"Do you know the guy?"

"He don't bring him around, either."

"How about his customers?"

"If he don't bring the car around, or the guy with the car around, then he don't bring them, either."

The front door of the brownstone opened and the stocky kid that Mary had thought might have needed medical attention the day before came out into the gritty light with some camera equipment. Picking his way down the stoop between the bodies, he took off down the street stopping only once to look back at Mary, as if wondering where he might have seen her before.

* * *

Felix's only paying gig was with the Parks Department, the city issuing him a tripod and a video camera to set up across the street from the Jordan Rampersand Memorial Playground and basketball courts, each separated from the other by a chain-link fence running straight down the middle.

All he had to do was lock the camera onto the tripod mount, which automatically swiveled in a never-ending 180 arc, and let it run from midafternoon to evening.

The tripod was key because it didn't draw attention to itself. The few times he tried shooting with a handheld it invariably led to some mother charging across the street, "Why are you taking pictures of my child? Let me see what you shot . . ." Which led to a long-winded explanation of what he was doing out here, which, more often than not, failed to chill anyone out.

The point of all this numbing footage was to help the Parks Department determine if there needed to be any new safety protocols put in place in regards to the shifting demographic traffic.

Are there male adults coming around on the early side with no kid in tow? Once it starts to get dark, are there dope fiends settling in for the night? Is there dealing, are they banging; the city allegedly scouring the footage to make safety decisions—sodium lights, curfews, surveillance cameras, police posts, etc.—although after three months of being out here, he'd seen no new security measures or installations put in play, and the human tide chart was exactly the same as it was in the beginning.

He caught a shooting once, the shooter, gun still in hand, bolting across the street with his head turned back towards the courts and tripping over the tripod, the camera smashing itself against a streetlight stanchion, Felix never to forget the guy regaining his balance and saying to him, "My bad," before continuing to book east.

He handed over the footage to the local squad, and sat for a witness interview but he never found out if there was an arrest and by the next week he could barely remember it happened.

It didn't take long to get to know the regulars; the kids and their tenders, the teenage ballers on the other side of the fence and the homeless cooping on the sidewalk benches directly outside the park, endlessly rearranging their Hefty bag suitcases and plastic backpacks, some of them sharp-eyed and industrious, sticking religiously to their hard-learned survival routines, others so untreated or so fucked up by whatever they were ingesting—even weed wasn't just weed anymore—and so oblivious to their surroundings that whenever one of them tried to cross to the other side of Fifth Avenue all the cars had to go into slalom mode.

The police would make their periodic sweeps, but it was like pushing a broom without a dustpan, the homeless, the helpless and the drugged quickly finding another spot a few blocks away, before returning when the local outcry zeroed in on some other encampment.

But even the craziest, the most drug-whacked never wandered into the playground area although they sometimes sat on the mostly empty benches on the basketball side, nodding out or talking to themselves.

This afternoon was like most other afternoons, toddlers and preschoolers swarming the climbing bars and slides, the mothers on the benches striking him as off-duty caregivers working for families downtown—brown mommies—finally getting to hang with their own kids for a hot minute.

All as per usual, until just before three, when an NYPD maintenance van dropped off two police sawhorse barricades on the corner next to his spot then another two barricades directly across the street, dividing 133rd into two sectors, Fifth Avenue lying like a DMZ between them.

A few minutes later two squad cars pulled up on the opposite corners, the uniforms assigned to man the checkpoints taking up their posts.

"What's going on?" Felix asking the cop nearest to him.

"Gang shit," one of them, his arms inked with twin dragons, answered without looking at him, the guy no older than Felix but coming off hard, as if he'd been asked for state secrets.

"What's with the camera," the other, slightly older cop said. "You a reporter?"

"Not me." Felix showing them his Parks ID, then, "What kind of gang shit?"

"The usual kind." Then, to a senior citizen approaching the post, "How are you doing sir. You live where?"

"3102 Madison, why?" the old man rearing back, pre-insulted.

He was tall, thin and long-necked, with a prominent Adam's apple as sharp as an arrowhead.

"You have proof of residence? Some ID?"

"Why?"

"Public safety . . ."

"I'm living here thirty-four years, maybe you officers should take the time to know the people you serve," as he fumbled for his wallet, the knuckles of his hands like bronze walnuts.

"Public safety," in a dull mutter, pulling out his New York State ID card. "Look at me. Last time I held a weapon I was with the Twenty-Fourth Infantry at the Pusan Perimeter. Ask your grandfathers what that was."

The uniforms exchanged a look, then stepped aside to let him through.

"Next time have your ID handy."

"You need to be educated," the old man snapped before continuing down East 133rd.

Soon after, lines started to form at both corners, everyone waiting to get through.

"Only people living east of Fifth! I need to see proof of residence, so IDs out!"

And the bounce-back chorus from across the street. "Only people living west of Fifth!"

Then, at a little past 3:00, "Ah, shit, here we go."

Felix turned to see that the junior high school up the block had just let out, some of the students approaching the barricades, then mobbing them, both cops going into Lost Platoon mode, yelling, "IDs out! The sooner we see 'em the sooner you get home!"

More interested in the action at his barricade than the action on the monkey bars, Felix foot-nudged the tripod so that the camera could capture the cops without them being aware. After that, he wouldn't even risk looking their way, worried that one of them would notice the repositioning, not knowing how they'd react to being taped on the sly.

"Unh-unh. You live thataways," the dragon-sleeved cop told a kid.

"I'm doing a project at my boy's house. It's for school, ask him!"

"We got paired," the other kid said.

"Oh yeah? What's the project?"

"Olden days Harlem with the Dutch. Mister Flannery paired us."

"You know what happened on this block last night?"

"They were talking about it in school."

"Then you know anybody from your side of Fifth is fair game over here."

"But I don't truck with them!"

"Sorry, somebody throws a shot your way that's on us. Just go to the library," then pointedly looking down at the repositioned camera before raising his eyes to Felix, "I hope you're getting my good side."

* * *

Still canvassing the block, Mary entered the Eat and Run with its endless racks of junk food, deli station and glassed-in refrigeration banks for beer, soda and canned rocket fuel.

The Yemeni kid who had come in yesterday to tell her about the two sisters in their hospital pinks was now busy restocking the Fritos and Cheetos, while his smudge-eyed uncle Malik, wearing a black Yankees cap over a black Kufiyah, stood behind the register occasionally glancing up at the blank six-screen CCTV security monitor mounted on the opposite wall.

Mary felt a lot of sympathy for corner store workers because they couldn't run and they couldn't hide, so if someone came in shy a quarter for a can of beer and took the no-sale personally, or wanted something for nothing, or was spotted pinching a candy bar, the man at the register always had to anticipate the consequences of not going along because if they pissed off the wrong person and that person returned with a friend or with something sharp, they were sitting ducks.

This guy behind the register, Uncle Malik . . .

Mary remembered first laying eyes on him fifteen years earlier when he had started to work in here for his own uncle, Faisal. Malik, at the time a frightened teenager just off the boat whom she encountered one morning sitting on the sidewalk stone drunk and getting yelled at by a neatly dressed woman with a walker telling him to get his ass up and zip his damn fly, Malik rising bleary-eyed then taking a step toward her and just staring into her face. At the time, Mary had thought he might be working himself up to push or hit her but no, it wasn't that at all. Homesick, he was simply pondering her, wondering if he'd just found his American mother.

And that woman was just getting started, hustling Malik back inside the store and demanding that the uncle give his nephew a cup of coffee. And when Faisal refused because it was Ramadan, she started in on him, too. "He already done broke his fast with the liquor so give him a piece of bread and a damn cup of coffee." And when Faisal continued to balk, she stepped closer to the counter, her voice lower than before but just as angry. "Faisal. Do you remember *you* fifteen years ago when *you* first come here? No family, your own people working you to death, I would see you cry your eyes out, you was so socially depressed and now it's *his* turn so give the boy a damn cup of coffee and *you*"—turning back to Malik—"go wash your face, eat something, and sleep it off."

"Hey how are you doing," Mary said.

"Good," Uncle Malik murmured, then looked away.

Because she had witnessed his earliest humiliations he always acted as if he'd never seen her before.

"Do you know this person?" Passing him Diaz's photo.

"He's in here sometime."

"Hamburguesa with mayo," the deli man called out.

"When last?"

"When last what."

"How recently was he in here."

"Maybe last week."

"Remember what day last week?" Asking both of them.

"Saturday." The sandwich man said, "Hamburguesa with mayo, every time."

"Does he ever talk to you about anything?" Mary asking Malik now.

"No."

"How about you?" asking the deli man.

Two college age kids wearing painful half smiles like apologetic intruders came into the store and started to quietly look about for something to buy that wouldn't kill them, ultimately disappearing behind a short wall of shelved food.

Then Watson, one of the sidewalk regulars, came inside, blade-thin six-foot-forever and bristling with so much scattershot energy he just about gave off sparks. "A salaam aleikum, my brother," to Malik, then one-eyeing Mary and making her just like everybody else around, here including the blind. "Gimme two loose."

Malik looked to Mary, just in case she was in a bad mood.

"Aw don't worry about her, she got bigger fish to fry."

The girl reappeared coming to the counter with a mottled banana.

Looking down at her from his too-tall height Watson laid a hand over hers, while reaching into his pocket. "A young lady such as yourself should never have to pay for her own banana."

The boy then reappeared, eyeing Watson's play and turning red with confusion.

"I got it, I got it, thank you so much," the kid said.

"You a team?" he asked easily. "Where you from?"

"Michigan," the girl said

"Detroit City, the motor city."

"Near there," the boy said.

"See, I don't mind you all starting to move in up here because more white people means more police protection." Turning to Mary, "Right, officer? Just don't get too blase-blase. Grow some eyes in the back of your head and you'll be ok."

"Thanks a lot," the boy said as they headed for the door.

"You're welcome a lot." Watson waving them on their way, then turning to Mary. "These kids nowadays, they see what they see, but you know how it was back in the day, a straight up Terrordome, bodies droppin', hookers poppin', old people walkin' around their own homes with umbrellas 'cause the pipeheads ripped out the pipes, everywhere you looked, drama, drama, drama. You all called it Crackistan, right?"

"Not me," Mary said. Back then the cops had called it Methadonia.

"Crack, huh?" Malik groused. "How many you smoke a day?"

"This?" Watson looked down at the two loose in his hand. "Shit."

"How many."

"Was I even talking to you?"

"A pack? Two packs?"

"Yeah, uh-huh. And who do I buy it from. Who takes the money?"

"Everybody hears you all day coughing out there."

"Yeah well, that's because I have childhood asthma. It ain't got nothing to do with smoking."

"You should be on TV, you know that?"

"Couldn't agree more," Watson said as he headed out the door.

"That guy," Malik said shaking his head.

Mary showed him the photo again. "Nothing else comes to mind?"

"He came in once asked me to cash a check. You go to a bank for that. I'm not a bank."

"What kind of check."

"A check."

"Was it printed out or handwritten?"

Malik shrugging then, "Hand."

"Do you remember how much?"

"A hundred and fifty, can you believe? I told him 'Hey guy, I'm not a bank.'"

"Did you catch the name on it?"

"His name?"

"No, the person who wrote it out."

"No."

"Do you have CCTV?"

"No more. Someone stole the camera."

When Mary stepped back out onto the street, the kid was hosing out plastic garbage cans, his sneakers and pants cuffs soaked through.

Mary watched him work for a bit. "Hey there, remember me from yesterday?"

"You were that lady cop, right?"

"I still am. What's your name?"

"Souleymane."

"Souleymane, let me ask you," tilting her head towards the shop, towards Malik, "does your uncle treat you good?"

"Of course," the kid said. "He's my uncle."

* * *

On his way home from his Parks Department gig, Felix thought back to the first time he had experienced the impulse to seize an image. He was eight or nine and his parents had taken him to an upstate Renaissance Faire, all lutes and jesters and acrobats and performers whose job it was to continuously stroll the grounds in full Elizabethan regalia, kings and queens, knights and damsels . . .

It was a hot and boring outing until he wandered off from his parents and caught sight of Queen Elizabeth on her break sitting at a picnic table behind the Porta Potties along with Sir Walter Raleigh and a bunch of nobles smoking cigarettes or weed, their crowns and veiled cone hats on the ground. He didn't have a camera and had no concept of irony but there was something in that tableau that was so inarticulately exciting to him that if he could, he would have found a way to stuff it all in his mouth.

Felix's shooting MO, as much as he had one, depended on the color of his mood ring. Some days like today it was just open the aperture to the max, crank up the shutter speed and shoot the hell out of everything, which never seemed to bear fruit.

As hard as it sometimes was for him, whenever he was able to master his natural-born impatience, the results were always better.

But even on the sloppiest of days, much like an FBI trainee in a pop-up friend-or-foe shooting drill, he was forever trying to master the art of thinking slow but acting fast. To master losing himself in the street without losing control.

Since he'd moved to the city six months ago there had been only one time that it had all come together in the way he wanted. It was on a day like today, coming home from work to see the usual crew draped like a languid pride of lions along the steps to the brownstone. He went up to his apartment, grabbed the camera that he wanted, then came back down and asked them if he could take a group portrait. Posed shots weren't considered street photography but he had a notion of how he could make it so, even if his subjects were more or less immobile. First, he told them it was a video portrait so they would relax and not break his balls for the long pose.

Then, after setting up, he waited until they lost interest in the camera, then waited some more with no idea of what exactly he was waiting for.

At one point O-Line looked away and yawned like a lion, *not that*, then Trip lowered his shades, his eyebrows rising high over the frames as he watched a girl walk by, *almost*, but street guys ogling the ladies as they go past was too old hat.

And then Awan, the Paki grad student, came out of the building, a small grimace playing on his face as he braced himself to weave his way down through the bodies to the sidewalk. That twist of the lips from above said so much about so much, Felix taking the shot so instinctually that he wasn't sure if he had taken it or was still thinking about taking it.

To lose yourself but stay in control.

And patience, patience.

He just didn't have any today, Felix shooting blind, block after block. And then he saw the woman in a T-shirt and gym shorts running up and down the subway entrance stairs on 125th Street, dropping out of sight then reappearing headfirst like a rising sun, turning and disappearing again, over and over like a slow-motion magic act. Loving the rhythm of her, Felix shifted to video and filmed her through two climbs until her trainer, whom he hadn't noticed before, got up in his face, the guy a towering shirtless exhibitionist with an impossible body, all mountain-range shoulders, screaming veins, and bulging calves.

"Did you get her permission to do that? Did you get *my* permission?" hanging over him like a streetlamp.

"No, I didn't," Felix said. "I'm sorry I just got carried away watching her. I mean I wouldn't last two minutes on those steps. I didn't mean any disrespect."

Respect/disrespect/respect, the words urban anti-inflammatories.

"That's an invasion of her person, do you understand that?"

"I do, and I apologize. I'll apologize to her too if you think it's the right thing to do." Felix getting off on his own coolness under fire.

As a street shooter, if there was one natural trait he possessed that worked in his favor, it was that.

"If it was me you were filming I'd be way more aggressive with you."

"I understand."

"I'm not being aggressive with you now, am I?"

"Nope. You are not."

When the trainer finally walked away, Felix furtively started to play back the video, but then the guy turned and approached him again, Felix quick-checking his remaining inventory of "no disrespects."

"Explain something to me. Why do you think people assume they have the right to take pictures of anybody they want," this time sounding like he wanted to have a real conversation on the subject.

"I can't speak for others," Felix began, one eye on the woman still rising and sinking behind her trainer's humpy left shoulder, "but when I take a picture like that it's to remind me where I've been in my life."

Enjoying his own openness, he was too buzzed to be intimidated.

"And also, to—"

"How do I know what you're going to do with it?"

"I'm not going to do anything with it. It's just a hobby."

So much for a conversation.

"Do you know how hard I worked to develop my program?"

"I can imagine."

The trainer stared at him as if trying to decide how far to take this, Felix bracing himself, wondering if he should offer to delete the footage—*Nah, fuck that*—and when the big man ultimately chose to turn and walk back to his client, he started shooting him too.

※ ※ ※

When Jimmy let himself into the house after spending three nights in the apartment, Mary was in the bedroom packing.

A few minutes later when she came downstairs with her go bag he was in the kitchen trying to bully a decent cup of espresso out of their ten-year-old machine.

"You want some?"

"I'm good."

"Good."

She hadn't noticed it the night before, but he looked like he'd put on a few pounds, although she wasn't sure.

"How are the kids?"

"Funny you should ask," Mary said. "I found a Penthouse under the Big One's bed. I tried to pick it up, the thing weighs about twenty pounds. You should talk to him."

"And say what, 'we know what you're up to'?"

"You don't have to say it like that, exactly."

"When I was in school," Jimmy dumping out his cup in the sink, "the priest told us that every time we yank on that thing we're slapping Jesus in the face. So after, I was like"—turning his head from side to side—*"Take that! And that! And that!"*

"You're going to hell," she said, turning away so that he wouldn't catch her smiling.

"If he can't get it *out*"—Jimmy pounded the counter—"then it's going to back up and clog his *brain*."

"Maybe he could just use his imagination."

"Thing is Mare, if you toss the magazine he'll know that you know and he'll die."

"What if I throw it out and get him a fresh one? Or better, switch it out for a Reader's Digest?"

"No, the Farmer's Almanac."

"No. Christian Living Magazine!"

She couldn't think of anything else after that, but no matter, Mary taken by how capable they were of getting along since they split the house.

And then the Big One, Douglas, came into the kitchen, saw them laughing together and not knowing what to make of it, just stood there, as red-faced as if he just walked in on them having sex. His confusion at seeing them so at ease with each other was so palpable that it became their own, neither Mary or Jimmy knowing what to say to him that wouldn't make things worse.

"Hey. How you been, brother-man?" Jimmy greeting him with forced brightness.

"Good," Douglas said, then turned to go back to his room.

They waited until they heard his door shut then turned to each other.

"Shit . . ."

"We were just talking." Mary pleading her case in a high whisper, "What were we supposed to say to him, 'Don't get your hopes up'?"

"I know," Jimmy said, then, "I don't know, it's their age."

"It's our separating."

"Yeah, of course." Jimmy blushed. "I meant to say that too."

"Look, we're doing what we can. I mean, under the circumstances."

"We are."

Mary looked down at her packed bag, but made no move to pick it up.

"Can I ask you something?"

"Sure."

"Off the record, what do they say about me?"

"Who."

"The kids." Mary right away sensing that she never should have asked.

"I don't know, these days, they're very careful, talking about us."

"That's not an answer."

"You're their mom."

Again, not an answer, Jimmy's evasiveness making her angry now.

She stared at him until he spit it out.

"Ok, the one thing, the Little One said sometimes he thinks that you're scared of them."

"Of *them*?" Mary flushing down to her feet. "What does that even *mean*?"

"I'm just telling you what he said." Jimmy looking away from her.

"The Little One said that? What do *you* think?"

"I think this whole deal's got everybody walking on eggshells."

"Is that a fact." Mary wanting to punch him.

"I don't know," he sighed, "no one wants to screw up, everybody's on their best behavior, it's fucking nerve wracking."

"Well shit, they like *you* enough!"

"He didn't say anything about not liking you."

He's their spokesman now? Mary started walking in hot circles.

"Mare, I'm sorry, you asked."

"I'm sorry I asked too."

"I should have kept my mouth shut."

She stared down at her bag as if willing it to levitate into her hand.

When she finally looked up she saw that he was watching her in her pain, and the sight of her in that state was painful for him too.

"I'm sorry," he said.

"For what? I asked, you answered," she said, picking up her bag and walking out the door.

¤ ¤ ¤

At nine in the evening, Royal heard voices coming up from the prep room below the main floor. It sounded like a bunch of not-quite-adolescent boys talking in hissy whispers and nervous blurts. Had to be Marquise and his friends down there, Marquise up to some Marquise shit. Let's see what.

Royal quietly took the stairs down to what he called the body shop, stopping at the shadowy landing and peering around the corner unobserved. Yup, it was Marquise who had slid Ervin Moore, forty-two, aka Uncle Permafrost, halfway out of the body cooler for his three buddies to gawk at.

Uncle P had been in there for four weeks and counting because the family's check to Royal had bounced, thus his own check to Mount Resurrection had bounced and so the cemetery had put the interment on hold until he made good on the money.

Well he couldn't do that until the family made good on the money owed to him, so . . .

"He's dead?" one of the boys whispered, his mouth a frozen O.

"No, he's pretending."

"What he die of?"

"He didn't die," Marquise pausing for effect, "he was murdered."

It was a stroke, but on the other hand it depended on how you looked at it; Royal recalling Ervin's sister at the viewing, screaming at his wife, "You made a man with three ninety cholesterol stop taking his Lipitor just so you can have a stiff dick around the house any time you want it? Bitch, you're a goddamn murderer."

"Can I touch him?" another boy asked.

"Go ahead, he won't care."

Royal waited until the kid had his hand on Ervin's iced forehead then let out a soft moan, the three kids screaming, running blind this way and that until one of them ran face-first into the edge of a door, then staggering back, his nose a bloody tomato.

Shit . . .

Royal retreated halfway up the stairs, then noisily came back down and charged into the room.

"What the hell's going on down here! Marquise!"

His son shrugged as he slid Uncle Permafrost back into the body cooler and shut the door. Royal would have given anything for his wife to have witnessed this, to see her tender impressionable boy in action.

❦ ❦ ❦

When Mary first opened the door of the apartment, the vaguely camphor-scented air along with the sight of the as-is furniture, the

Sam's Club pastoral art on the walls, the exhausted-looking nubby rugs and the lifeless silence, all of it, as usual, made her feel like she had been sent there in exile.

It was all they could afford but even if they had been able to spring for a nicer setup, its purpose would have been the same, as would that feeling of her having done something that had mandated some kind of incarceration.

She had no idea of how Jimmy felt when it was his turn to isolate in here, but her hunch was that, like everything else in his life these days, he took it in stride.

Because it was alternately occupied in three-day shifts by two people on the verge of divorce, the apartment had its rules for survival, mostly regarding sex. No one can walk in and see any evidence of a third person. There was to *be* no third person. Any relationships developed with the opposite sex had to remain outside.

Even though their sex life was well over by mutual agreement you could never predict what kind of havoc sexual jealousy could wreak on an otherwise placid human brain.

Did Jimmy know about Esposito? She seriously doubted it. Did Jimmy have some lady friend of his own? She seriously doubted that, too, although there was that one incident with his new moustache six months ago that had given her pause.

Another hot tip for survival:

Don't ask, don't tell and keep them divorce dogies movin'.

They were pretty respectful of each other in here, not only because they were still on amicable terms but also because they had heard some of the horror stories about what could happen in shared apartments like this one when the mediation process started to deteriorate.

If a couple really hated each other the place could become ground zero for their creative bile; used condoms on the pillows, depilatory injected in the other one's shampoo, Krazy-Glued keyholes and drawer pulls, thermostats rigged so that it's ninety degrees in the summer, or forty degrees in the winter, obscene messages written in Magic Marker on the walls, bogus 911 calls to the fire department and the police.

If you wanted things to work out in here it was all about the small gesture; the outgoing party showing some consideration for the incoming as in: no dishes left in the sink, all surfaces wiped down, garbage bins emptied, leaving enough toilet paper on the roll, etc.

But in fact, what added to the overall dreariness of the place was how careful they were not to offend the other.

Remembering the vodka left in the freezer from her last stay, she stepped into the narrow kitchen and saw the flowers, Korean market daisies, the petals food-dyed sky blue, sitting in a plastic vase set on the counter.

Jimmy probably left them there to give this tomb a little color but their sheer crappiness just accentuated the stifle.

If she didn't know him better she might think he left them there just to mess with her, but that wasn't his nature.

Grabbing them by their pulpy waterlogged stems she tossed the whole bunch in the garbage then started to go off in her head: first he just had to tell her what the Little One said, making her want to crawl under a rock, and then looking at her so pityingly while she tried to process the blow and then he goes and does this.

Working herself up, she grabbed the phone to call him, but killed it on the first ring, knowing that whatever he had to say for himself—*Mare, c'mon, they're just flowers*, or whatever soothing response that might come out of his mouth—would not only piss her off further but make her feel like she was being "handled."

Suddenly she had a glimmer of understanding why all those bitter couples turned their nesting apartments into battle zones; the galling frustration of not knowing how to soothe their outraged hearts other than through petty gestures of annihilation.

But that wasn't Jimmy and that wasn't her.

Well, she couldn't go home, but she didn't have to stay here either.

She thought about hitting the bars, but then re-remembering the vodka, she opted for watching a movie in bed.

But the cable was out—of course it was.

She picked up the phone again.

"Hey."

"Hey yourself."
"Kids with him?"
"Yup. Yours?"
"With her."
"So . . ."
"So, yeah."

	*	*	*

Royal sat with Marquise's young friends around the dining table while icing that one boy's swollen nose, not wanting him or any of them to go home with a story and get his own kid in trouble.

"You all know what's going to happen if you tell your parents what you were doing, right?"

Or himself sued.

"Maybe I should call them right now."

"Don't, don't."

"I don't know, they're probably wondering why you're not in the house, maybe already called the cops. If they find you were trespassing . . ."

"It's not trespassing if I invited them in." Marquise for the defense.

"He invited us in!" like a chorus.

"Besides it's your fault," Marquise again. "You scared us."

"I *what*?" Royal then, holding up his hand. "Wait a minute, wait a minute . . . You know how many bodies we had down there over the years? Hundreds. Maybe thousands." Royal thinking, *If only* . . . "And every once in a blue moon we get one has got just a little bit of life still in them. Mostly they're just moving their arms or legs until it passes, sometimes the eyes open, I saw one sit up and turn her head to me. It happens."

Marquise, of course, knew he was full of shit, but let him run with it nonetheless, probably because he enjoyed his father's stories.

"Do they ever talk?"

"Well, there was the time I finished prepping an old lady for her viewing so I closed the casket and went upstairs had some dinner and watched a Knicks game on TV. But then sometime later in the night, when I was lying in bed, I had a thought that maybe I could have done a better job with that woman's makeup so I went back down and worked on her a little more until I was satisfied then closed up the coffin again. And when I turned to go back up the stairs I heard a soft female voice say, 'Thank you.'"

"You're welcome," one boy whispered.

That one really happened, or at least he remembered thinking so at the time.

What was he doing with these kids? Enjoying himself, that's what.

"Then there was the time I had a child prepared down there and a little bit later I was sitting right at this table when I heard her crying for her mother." Royal reaching back to a story his funeral director grandfather had told him when he was a kid. "So, I went down and opened the casket. Oh, she was dead, her mouth shut and nothing moving, but I could still hear her. Well, that crying went on for so long I had to call her mother and ask that poor woman to come in and talk to her daughter. I thought she'd be surprised, upset or what have you but no, she was calm about it, said she'd been hearing her girl crying too, but thought it was her imagination.

"So, the next morning, she came in, pulled a chair up alongside the coffin and talked to her daughter for hours, telling her not to be scared and that it was ok for her to let go. Can you imagine how hard it was on that woman? But you know, once she did that, the crying stopped."

Looking around the table, Royal saw that one of the boys had tears at the corners of his eyes and another's mouth was starting to quiver. Even Marquise, who'd heard this one so many times before, was looking at him with something like soft awe, Royal remembering him as a little boy hanging on his every word and how good that felt.

The memory filled him with regret; Royal having wanted to be so much more than he was in this life.

"Do you believe in God?" It was the kid with the bloody nose.

Royal took a long beat before answering.

"Why wouldn't I?" he said. Then, rising from the table, "Let's go. I'm driving you all home."

Royal herded Marquise's friends from the parlor to the broken lot where he held one of the rear doors of the SUV open for them to pile in back.

He hesitated before getting in the car himself, something bugging him. He hunched down to study the faces under the roof light.

"Did he charge you to see that body?"

When no one would answer the question, he straightened up and gave Marquise the eye.

"Give it back."

* * *

At ten in the evening, Mary walked across the lobby of a generic chain hotel in lower Westchester then down a purple-and-mauve carpeted corridor, knocked on an ajar door and stepped inside to find Ralph Esposito making the drinks, V&T for her, Jameson rocks for him.

The good thing about hooking up in a chain hotel as opposed to a one-off was that once you got over the sterile layout of the appointments, you weren't as preoccupied with catching something that would permanently alter your biology.

The first place they had chosen to meet six months earlier, a motel near Citi Field in Queens, looked so sketchy that they never took their clothes off or sat on the furniture.

After that, wherever they went, Esposito brought along a UV flashlight and a spray bottle of Luminol that he'd pilfered from the Crime Scene Unit to highlight any traces of blood or other body fluids not visible to the naked eye. In one motel, the purple beam had picked up so much unknown DNA off the pillowcases, blankets and sheets that the bed turned psychedelic.

———

"They don't *have* to like you," Esposito announced as they sat on the small couch that divided the room and allowed the hotel to charge for an "executive suite."

"That's not important. What *is* important is that they *respect* you."

Mary nodded noncommittally, wishing she had never brought it up.

"I didn't say he said they didn't *like* me, what I said—"

"Mary, Mary . . . Do you think my kids like me? But they *respect* me and therefore they do what I say. How else am I going to teach them anything?"

Mary swallowed half her drink. "Jesus, Esposito, what I *said* was my kid thought that *I* was afraid of *them*."

"Nothing wrong with that."

"Come again?"

"My point being, a parent is like being on patrol. If you don't show people who's who in the zoo, if you don't get them to understand the consequences of ever defying you, well then you just lost the war and they'll eat you alive."

"Jesus Christ, open your ears. He said that *I* was afraid of *them*."

"What?"

Finally.

"I think he was right."

"Fuck. What are they, demon seeds?"

"You have to understand, when I was their age, my mother treated me . . ."

"So, don't be like her."

"I just don't want them to judge me like I judged her, so, I keep my distance."

It was the story that she told herself about herself, afraid as she was to dig deeper.

"Again," he said, one finger in the air, "they're not the judges. *You* are."

Reminding herself that she wasn't here for the scintillating repartee she threw back the rest of her drink then took a backup nip straight from the bottle.

Taking that as his cue, Esposito threw back the rest of his own drink, rested his hand on her thigh.

"Shall we?"

When it came to the field strip, Mary, not into that kind of fore-foreplay, preferred to undress herself.

It wasn't as if she was shy about her body although that had been the case for many years. In fact, for most of her younger life she felt miserable about her lack of curves.

But these days, as long as there were no horns coming out of her forehead or forked tail coming out of her ass, she was good with herself. As far as all the rest of her, it was what it was.

The best lover she had ever known—Jerry something (it was a long time ago)—had had a concave chest and a face like a frying pan, but he was physically confident, up for anything, and wasn't shy about letting her know how much pleasure she gave him. Free of that performance-oriented preening anxiety most men in her experience carried like luggage into the bedroom, what she saw when she looked at Jerry was the *all* of him looking right back at her, none of that eyes-over-the-shoulder-looking-for-the-exit-sign vibe (which she was often guilty of herself), and that kind of locked-in no-rush attentiveness, letting time go its own way, allowed her to take a breath and discover a variety of new mostly small pleasures.

For her, when she was in that slowed-down state, the first rush with him was the first clinch, the belly-to-belly folding into each other, her arm wrapping tightly around his ribs as his fingertips strolled down the buttons of her spine to the soft delta at the base and made small light circles there.

She also liked to hard-burrow her face into the side of his neck so she could hear his heart beating in his throat, sounding to her like one of those plush toy animals you'd put in the crib of a newborn that imitated the swashing sound of a womb.

And another thing: she was never much into giving head, but that man brought something out in her, a kind of lascivious tenderness, that made her reconsider, announcing to him right before, "I can't believe I'm doing this." Every time, right before she put him in her mouth she would say it again, "I can't believe I'm doing this." As if she had never said it before.

And then Jimmy came into the picture. The first time they slept together she told him how her body—the very one that he seemed unable to stop caressing—had been the bane of her school days. He didn't say much at the time, mainly just shrugged it off, but the next day he showed up at her apartment with a tissue-wrapped gift—a white sleeveless tee, *tits are for kids* scripted in sparkles across the chest, which at first in her confusion, she took as an insult, but then she got both the joke and the message behind the joke, Jimmy later saying that her laughter sounded to his ears like an escaped flock of butterflies.

Jimmy. At times like that, Mary thought of him, in the words of her grandmother, as *a good piece of cake*.

She never wore the tee of course, but never threw it out either.

Jimmy Roe—he could be like that.

But this guy here with her now, Esposito.

Like most men, he always seemed to be focused on the wrong things when it came to his own appeal; his gut, his softening torso, his not-quite-double chin, and no matter how many times she tried to straighten him out on that score, as soon as he was naked he went right back to sucking it in and tensing his pecs.

Plus, he must have read the wrong magazine article because despite her repeated attempts to get it into his head that that wasn't her thing (she didn't like men doing stuff to her that she couldn't see—it was like someone talking behind her back), he always insisted on going down on her until she finally gave up and just let him, because he was a fragile boy who sulked at the drop of a hat and she'd submit to just about anything in order to avoid that.

On this night as he went about getting busy down there with all the finesse of a pool vacuum, she went off brooding about her kids again, then jettisoned that subject fast and switched over to thinking about the next steps she could take to find Christopher Diaz.

The morgue for starters.

That's where his wife would be, but more importantly her possessions; wallet, credit cards, ATM cards, her cell phone and whatever else.

The ME's office would require a subpoena, but if Jaynie Perez was the supervisor on duty she'd be ok with leaving Mary alone for a few minutes to take photos of whatever she found.

That check-cashing attempt at the corner store. One hundred and fifty dollars handwritten from a personal account. It could be in payment for one of his long-haul chauffeuring jobs and if that's what it was, she doubted he accepted Amex but given the amount, maybe he accepted checks. But why wouldn't he just go to his bank with it? Or maybe he didn't have an account anywhere, or . . .

When she got as far as she could run with it, she reached down and pulled Esposito up by his ears until his head—along with the rest of him—went to work where she could keep an eye on things. He wasn't the great Casanova that he imagined himself to be but his bulk was comforting, the sexual equivalent of a square meal—hearty and filling—and these days that was good enough.

"I was thinking," Esposito said as they started to dress on opposite sides of the bed, "what if the next time we get together we actually went out. Take in a movie, go to a restaurant, you know, like a date."

"I don't think that's a good idea," Mary said as calmly as she could. They had an agreement.

Esposito stopped buttoning his shirt. "Why not? You afraid somebody's going to see us?"

Yes.

"No I just think it's playing with fire."

"Really," he said. "Ok, well how about this . . . we go out like I said, movie, restaurant, the whole . . . But! We do it dressed head to foot in giant fucking panda costumes. This way nobody'll know it's us."

"We could go to a better hotel, that I wouldn't mind."

Esposito shrugged and resumed dressing in silence, his humpy disappointment making her nervous.

As far as he knew, she was still dividing the house with Jimmy and the kids so she never had to explain where she was headed after they were done with each other. If he ever got wind of the nesting apartment and started to pressure her into hooking up there instead of spending all this money, the results could be catastrophic. Besides, unlike a hotel room she couldn't very well leave her own place, and her ability to control her time with him was key.

※ ※ ※

After reviewing this day's shots—one or two good enough to keep, the others like a bunch of bum lottery tickets—Felix found Calvin's rolled T-shirt at the bottom of his backpack. The front featured PGD imprinted across the chest, but it was what was written on the back that brought it all home: a list of every ER in the Bronx and upper Manhattan along with their addresses, and beneath that, the locations of the two county morgues, Bellevue in Manhattan and Albert Einstein in the Bronx.

PART THREE

RISEN

Before he felt the skin of his calf being zippered open against jagged stone and heard the high nasal snarl of someone struggling with a weight they couldn't manage, Anthony Carter had been treading water with his six-year-old stepdaughter in a rough sea. He was trying to save her from the frightening chop by holding her close to his chest while cycling his legs in order to keep their heads above water but she wasn't having it, wriggling out of his arms and then, without looking back, dog-paddling to a boat far in the distance, Anthony watching her go, wondering where she'd got all that self-confidence.

"Hey *you*. Step off and step away." The voice male and full of authority.

"He ain't coming out of there"—another voice, cracked, crazy, and raw—"You can try, but . . ."

"Did you hear me? All the way. To the *curb*," then muttering to someone else, "Christ, if the building didn't kill him . . ."

There were other hands on him now, higher up his body, the fingers probing his person as delicately as a pickpocket.

His body felt loosely encased; he could move around a little if he wanted to, but even with the dull, persistent pain in his lower back and his lungs crackling like radio static, he felt safe where he was, felt, in some way, comforted, so why should he?

Those same hands now carefully slid a soft collar behind his neck, then bringing the ends around to join so tightly beneath his chin that his face started to swell.

"Sir, can you open your eyes for me?" Voice number three, husky and female.

He could, but vaguely knew that if he did, it would only lead to a world of trouble.

"You want to know why?" That raw voice calling out from a distance now. "Because he's a helicopter and helicopters have to fly on a dot matrix. Dot to dot to dot. They go anywhere else on the grid up there they crash. He just figured ok I'll crash just so to take a break from those dots, because that shit is exhausting."

"Come on, let me see your eyes." The female voice again.

Reluctantly doing as he was told, he found himself in a narrow haphazard recess in the rubble looking up at the underside of a suspended dresser, its four legs hovering a few feet over his head, a housedress or a robe half hanging out of a splintered drawer just inches above his face.

To his left was a tumbled wall of stones, to his right an airy mangle of brick and wood with just enough of a gap at the base to offer access.

And kneeling busy-handed alongside him was an EMT, her head shaved, her temples tattooed with lightning bolts.

"Can you tell me your name?"

I was there, I was . . .

"Tell me your name."

"Anthony Carter." His voice like caked dirt.

"Anthony, my name's Inez, my partner, the guy yelling at the guy that found you? He's Hassan and we're gonna take care of you, ok? Do you know where you are?"

"No. I don't know."

"Do you know what happened to you?" Slipping a BP cuff around his left arm, another encasement.

"I was asleep."

I was asleep.

"Samuels One!" That gravel voice still at it. "'And Samuel said to Saul, Why hast thou woked me, and brung me up?'"

"Fuckin' guy," Hassan muttered, clipping a pulse-ox monitor to one of Anthony's fingers.

I didn't want this.

"Anthony, where do you live," Inez asked, the BP cuff pulsing now, strangling his upper arm. "Do you know where you live?"

I didn't ask for this.

"At home."

"Wise guy, huh?" Hassan said without an edge.

"My parents' apartment," wanting to explain his situation to them but it was too much work. "They're dead."

"My condolences, can you tell me where it hurts?"

He tried to bring one hand around to the small of his back, but she stopped him.

"Don't move, we got you," as she gingerly probed for the source, coming up against resistance then slowly withdrawing her hand. "No bleeding, that's something," then moving back in, a flashlight in her mouth. "Looks like you're laying on a chunk of rock or cement but I don't want to remove it in case . . ."

"136 over 85," Hassan said.

I don't remember. I don't know.

A stethoscope was pressed to one side of his chest then to the other.

"Bilateral wheezing." Hassan again. "That's about it."

Every good-news announcement out of Hassan's mouth hit him like an indictment.

"Anthony, do you have any history with asthma?"

"My stepdaughter does." Seeing her swimming away from him again.

"Not you though, huh?"

He began to fight off the O2 mask the moment he saw it closing in on his face—encasement after encasement.

"Relax, relax, it'll make you feel better, ok? Just leave it on." Then, "Where else does it hurt?"

"What?" The mask like a squatting lobster.

"Does it hurt anywhere else."

"Water."

"Yeah, I can imagine but you just got to hang tough with that for a little bit, can you do that?"

"I didn't ask for this." Saying it out loud this time.

"Who would?" she answered.

The earth-rumble of a heavy truck pulling up close by rattled his bones.

LAZARUS MAN

A moment later, a fireman from search and rescue stuck his head in, eyed the stability of the ad-libbed walls, the gauge of the opening.

"He's good to go?"

"All things considered."

"Ok then, we'll bring him out."

Anthony started to panic.

I don't remember.

Inez took his hand. "Just take your breaths, deep in deep out. We'll be right outside waiting for you."

After they left, a second fireman came in.

"How the hell . . ." he murmured to his partner. "Thirty-six hours, the dogs couldn't find him? The resonance mikes?"

As if he couldn't hear him, every word.

I don't remember I don't remember.

And then they were gone.

Alone for the moment, he prayed to be retroactively struck with a true blackout memory loss and the safety that it would provide him, but it was too late for that and flashes of what he couldn't forget played like a flip-book reel behind his eyelids.

Just leave me here.

And then they were back.

A long basket was slipped under his body, straps were secured across his chest and thighs, wrapping him up like a gift.

He was briefly jostled sideways then slid out of the rubble and into the fresh night, where his appearance triggered cheers and whistles from the lined sidewalk and overhanging windows, which spooked him but also nudged him towards feeling less like an exhumed mummy and more like a newborn in swaddling cloth, as if his life was being playing out in reverse, from buried to delivered.

On his way to the open-backed ambo, he was finally able to lay eyes on the shirtless and shoeless man who first found him.

"I told you before and I'll tell you again," he called out from the sidewalk. "You should've left him be!"

Hassan tossed him a spray dispenser of antiseptic, the guy twisting and ducking to avoid it.

※ ※ ※

"You're a lucky man, Anthony."

The ice-bright ceiling lights directly over his head reduced the ER doctor/trauma nurses/monitor techs to globular silhouettes.

A narrower beam of light trained on his eyes made him blind.

Then came the disembodied requests . . .

"Can you smile for me?"

"Puff out your cheeks?"

"Stick out your tongue?"

"The president of the United States is George Bush," he volunteered.

"Oh yeah?" one of them said. "Which one?"

The room felt like a refrigerator to begin with but when the cold conductivity gel for the cardiac monitor was applied to his bare chest he started to shake.

"So, Anthony, are you married?" The question meant to distract him.

"Yes."

"Uh-oh, she's hitting on you, brother."

And then came the trauma shears. When the last ribbon of his clothes hit the floor, he began to tremble so uncontrollably that two pairs of hands were needed to keep him from flying off the table.

"Yeah, I know," someone said, "we'll be quick."

"Can you move your legs for me?"

Lost in his own unbearable exposure, in his inability to defend himself from the flat scrutiny of others . . .

YOU put me there.

"Anthony, are you with me? Just try."

And then his father, balding, ponytailed and chesty, barged into the room, lunge-walking towards him, his head thrust forward like the prow of a ship, his knees bent as if he was about to spring or attack.

"Anthony, try and move your legs, last chance . . ."

A latexed finger suddenly inserted into his rectum brought him back into the room front and center.

"Good sphincter reflex," someone said. Then, "Sorry. That's how we check for lower extremity paralysis."

"Hey, Anthony. Here's a hot tip. Next time someone asks you to move your legs and you can? You should do it."

They rolled him on his side, more fingers navigating his spine from nape to coccyx before focusing on the raw and tender spot in his lower back, a forget-me-not from that torturing chunk of debris.

Pressing on it made him arc like a sailfish.

"Just tissue trauma but damn," someone said, "that must've hurt like hell."

It was YOU

"Hug yourself, please?"

A portable X-ray machine was wheeled into position above his curled back.

YOU put me there

"Try not to move."

YOU lifted me out

"Deep breath . . . Hold it . . ."

YOU raised me up

"Perfect," someone said.

At some point, there was a CAT scan; Anthony on the hard, sliding table experiencing a new level of cold. And when they funneled him inside the ringed barrel, for a second he thought he was back in his rubble-bed.

When they transferred him to a curtained cubicle in the trauma wing for overnight observation, he caught a glimpse of uniformed and plainclothes cops clustering outside in the hallway and at first, he was sure that they were there for him.

Laid out on his gurney in curtained darkness, he couldn't help but hear the conversation coming from behind the nearest cubicle.

"Did you see a gun?"

"I thought so."

"You thought so."

"I don't know. It happened so fast."

"And how many times do you think you fired?"

"Twice, maybe three times? Like I said . . ."

"The shooting team says nine. You fired nine times."

"God." Then, "I need to call my wife."

"Did you call for an ambulance?"

"Of course."

"Did you give him first aid?"

"I tried."

"Well that's something at least."

"*Hey*. Are you my fucking lawyer or the vic's?"

"You mean the perp's," the lawyer coached.

When the curtain on that cubicle was swept aside by a nurse, Anthony caught sight of the lawyer, wearing, in the wee hours of the night, a three-piece suit, a silk tie flowing like butter over a snow-white French-cuffed shirt.

The cop he was apparently representing/grilling was sitting hunched over and shirtless on the edge of his own gurney, his torso compressed into a series of fleshy rolls, his eyes sweaty and half popped out of his head.

They held off talking until the nurse finished up, the silence continuing until the curtain was redrawn.

"What are you not telling me," the lawyer said.

"What do you mean?"

"What, if I ever have to go to court for you, will the prosecution spring on me that you could have told me about right now."

"Nothing," Anthony whispered before the cop said the same.

"No dark past, no domestic violence, no DUIs, gang affiliations, mob affiliations, civilian complaints . . ."

"Anybody can file a complaint," the cop said.

"Meaning?"

"They were all dismissed."

When Anthony finally decided to tune out on the drama next door and attempt sleep, a new unseen voice, urgent and greedy, had him back on high alert.

"That's him? He's in there? You sure?"

And then his own curtain was yanked aside, a wiry man in green hospital scrubs rushing in like he was being chased.

"Hey, Anthony, wake up dude, how are you feeling? You ok?"

Then blinding him with a cell phone camera flash, "Just one more. Can you give me a thumbs up?" A second blast, then "Beautiful," before nearly tearing down the curtain in his rush to leave.

"Hey, I'm sending it to you right now," he heard the shooter say to someone on his cell, his voice diminishing with distance. "As we speak."

Anthony stared into the darkness.

Then scrambling, scrambling . . .

YOU put me there and YOU lifted me out.

YOU raised me up.

Stick to that, begging himself.

Stay with that.

※ ※ ※

On 9/11, in the open-air morgue tent abutting Bellevue Hospital, Mary had been part of an assembly line of detectives set up to collect whatever IDs they could from wallets and phones, jewelry and watches, the constant sharp snap of fingers being broken in order to remove rings still with her after all these years.

On her break that day, she walked over to the nearest East River pier—the same pier used to lay out the victims of the Triangle Shirtwaist fire for identification nearly a century earlier—and saw one of the overwhelmed DNA extractors sitting with her legs dangling over the edge and smoking two cigarettes at the same time, one hanging from her lips, the other smoldering between her fingers.

Needing the same relief, Mary sat down next to her, a young pregnant Latina, and after a few minutes of mutual quiet, one of them started crying and the other took them into her arms. To this day, they still argue over who was the crier and who was the hugger.

* * *

As usual, the stringent aroma of ammonia-based disinfectants in the morgue whacked her sinuses from the door on in, but today the air also carried a sweet malty undertone that put her in mind of a wee-hours saloon.

Only three out of the sea of stainless steel tables were occupied, the rest in the process of being scoured.

As she waited for Jaynie Perez to come back from her break, Mary tried to avoid looking at the bodies on display, but there was one that felt like it was calling to her: a slim elderly woman lying naked, her skin youthfully unblemished, her half-open Irish-blue eyes calmly staring off as if trying to recall a fading dream.

To Mary, the woman was a twin to her mother, the resemblance shocking her to the core.

"They say she fell down the stairs at her assisted living center but who knows?" Jaynie Perez sidling up to Mary. "How you been, sis?" Then, "Are you cold?"

"What?"

"You're shaking."

"Rosa Diaz, do you want to see her? She's not that bad." Jaynie asked, reaching for the handle on one of the body slots set into the long bank of coolers.

"That's ok."

"Seriously, given what happened? She looks good."

Mary took Jaynie's arm and stepped in closer.

"I'm trying to find her husband, he's either dead too or missing, and if you can help me out, I need to take a peek at her personal property."

"I can't do that, sis."

"You can't?" Mary surprised at the turndown.

"All her stuff was sent over to the Two-Five last night. You sure you don't want to see her?"

"No, I'm good," Mary said, thinking, *The Two-Five, who do I know there* . . .

"So did you hear about the guy they pulled out of the building collapse last night?"

"Dead?"

"Still kickin'," Jaynie said.

"How hard?"

"Hard enough. My cousin over at Sinai, the transfusionist? She said she heard they might even send him home today."

Last night was at least thirty-six hours after the building went down, maybe more.

"How'd they not find him before?"

"Maybe he's bionic."

As Mary turned to leave, she nearly collided with one of the techs carrying the top half of a skull sloshing with scotch to a sink.

"I should bring this to my next AA meeting," the tech said, rinsing it out.

When she came out onto First Avenue, the comparatively fresh air of the street made her dizzy.

The Two-Five. Mary putting in a call to find out when Terry Mackie had the desk.

*, *, *,

Anthony opened his eyes in the darkness like someone waking up with a murderous hangover; his brain a cocktail of adrenaline and haze as he struggled to remember the exact circumstances and actions of the night before.

"How we feeling today?" It was one of the trauma room doctors moving at speed into the room and right away pulling back the curtains—the sunlight a shock—then perching himself on the edge of the bed—D. LAZANSKY the name on the badge—and starting to examine eyes, ears, nose and throat with the speed and brio of a three-card monte dealer.

"Complain to me."

"My lungs are pretty raw."

"Are you hawking up anything?"

"Some. It feels like sand."

"How long were you underground again?"

"I don't know."

"Well, you inhaled a lot of crap down there." Lazansky pressed his stethoscope to Anthony's chest, then lowered his head as he listened to the pulmonary soundtrack. "Better than when you came in. Take a deep breath? Hold it, hold it . . . Ok blow it out."

"*Shit!*" Anthony clutching his burning chest.

Lazansky laughed. "Feels like two Brillo pads in there, right? You smoke?"

"Not for two years."

"Well, if you ever feel the urge to go back just remember what that felt like. Stand up please?"

At first, Anthony resisted, but did what he was told, the sudden up-rush of blood knocking him buzzy.

Pulling up the back of Anthony's gown, Lazansky gently probed the swollen flesh on the left side of his lower back.

"It's going to turn some pretty colors back there for about a week, ten days. Do you want to see?"

"Not right now. Thanks."

"Walk with me?" Offering Anthony his arm.

They made one circuit from door to window and then it was Anthony on his own, at first feeling like he was on stilts, but then quickly enough, he started to walk as if he'd been doing it all his life.

"Like a natural-born man." Lazansky lurched himself off the wall where he'd been observing. "Ready to go home?"

"Home?" Anthony feeling like someone at the tail end of an interminable flight who nonetheless finds himself balking when the final landing announcement comes over the PA. "Yeah, I guess."

"Ok, think RICE—rest, ice, compression, elevation. Ice packs or a bag of frozen peas applied every two to three hours, ten minutes and out. Tylenol. Are you getting all of this?"

"Yes."

"Ok, good. Sit tight, somebody'll come around with the release forms and bon voyage," Lazansky said, flying out of there as fast as he came in.

An hour later, a nurse came by with the forms for him to sign.

And an hour after that, an aide came in with some clothes that he'd never seen before; a pair of paint-spotted grey sweatpants, a maroon sweatshirt advertising Catania Carting—*Did you call your Mother today?* printed across the chest—and a pair of thin argyle socks.

"Where's mine?"

"You mean the clothes you were buried in?"

There was no underwear.

"We ran out. Do you need any help?"

"I'm ok, thank you."

Waiting for her to give him some privacy, he sat with the clothes in his lap, but she continued to stand there, blatantly taking his measure. Worried that she was preparing to call him out, he was about to say something, anything, but she beat him to it. "God must love you to hell and back."

Next up was a wiry crew-cut aide from Transportation pushing a wheelchair. "Release time," she said, squatting to lock the wheels then rising up and offering her hand.

The idea of being rolled out of the room to face whatever was waiting for him out in the world was too much.

"I don't need it."

"It's the rules."

"Seriously. I can walk. I'm fine." Almost begging her.

The aide blew out her cheeks.

"Let me tell you something."

"Look I know you must hear that all the time, it's just . . ."

"Let me *tell* you something," cutting him short. "Last month a patient talked some Transpo idiot into letting him walk out of here on his own. He gets to the lobby, people everywhere, and passes out, hits his head on the floor so hard it bounced. Blood all over. He gets rushed into surgery, the aide gets canned and the hospital gets sued. So, do me a huge favor and take a seat."

As she wheeled him out into the corridor, he caught a few tentatively smiling faces from people who apparently recognized him, Anthony hoping that they'd all forget this moment soon enough. But then as he was being rolled through the hospital's central atrium he picked up more half-smiling faces and a woman working in the gift shop came trotting out to hand him an oversized Hershey's bar and a small bear doll with heart stickers for eyes.

Out on the street there was more applause, mostly from some hospital staff; Anthony, despite his tension, finding himself raising a hand in meek acknowledgment. Then, as the aide rolled him towards a line of taxis, two video shooters came out of nowhere, their hip-mounted cameras perched like infants as they circled him all the way to his ride.

"Anthony, how are you feeling?"

"Anthony, what was it like down there?"

"Talk to me, brother."

"Look at me, bro."

"C'mon, man, people are happy for you, just give them something."

Happy for you . . .

"I'm grateful to be alive."

It wasn't much, but it was true.

※ ※ ※

Terry Mackie had been Mary's patrol partner for a year in the late nineties and her friend after that, she and Jimmy often breaking bread with him and his wife Ilona and twice going on a ski weekend with them upstate.

They were a tight couple with no children, Terry one of the few cops she knew who almost never looked at other women.

So understandably, when Ilona was killed in a car crash, he fell apart.

A week after the funeral, Mary went to his house to sit with him, Terry still so devastated that he could barely get to the end of a sentence without sobbing.

But when she laid a sympathetic hand on his shoulder, he startled her by recoiling in shock. And then he lunged, grabbing at her body, anywhere he could get purchase, Mary having to punch him in the throat to get free, bolting up from the couch as he gasped for breath.

Standing in the middle of the room, she was shaken by what happened but not enraged, the lucid part of her brain struggling to give her a context as he continued to sit there, staring straight ahead, staring past her, through her, as if he were alone, his eyes boggled with disbelief.

This was not Terry, this was grief—Mary drawing on her mother's near-amphibious detachment to insulate herself until he finally saw her again, his face red with apology.

She didn't want to hear a word of it, so before he could commence barraging her with frantic repetitive pleas for forgiveness she cut him off.

"I'm going." Then out the door.

Holding on to her Jeannie brain in the car, she sat there marveling at how calm she felt, even though she knew that it wouldn't last, and that there would be aftershocks coming her way in the not-too-distant future.

But for now, while still in the grips of that weird lucidity, she thought that it was a mistake not to let Terry apologize; who knew what that throttled outburst would do to him.

She still didn't want to hear a word out of his mouth, so she did what she could handle, coming back into the house to yell at him. "Don't you *ever* put a fucking hand on me again!"

Then back out the door, Mary's reasoning being, if he can't apologize, then maybe being chastised would keep him from imploding.

After that day, they never spoke of it again and remained friends, sort of, but it was hard work.

Surprisingly (or unsurprisingly), he remarried (badly) within a year and became a father six months after that.

When she walked into the precinct lobby he spotted her right away. "Hey, there she is . . ." But as she approached the elevated duty desk, he made no effort to come out from behind the barrier.

"Hey, it's himself," Mary said. "How's the family?"

"How's yours?"

"I asked you first."

"Good," he said.

"Same here. How's the kid?"

"His mother says he's back home and doing better."

"She took him back?"

"Says he's been getting random piss-tested and so far, so good."

"Good."

"They're in Florida and I'm here, so who knows."

"A mother's love."

"A mother's stupidity. What do you need?"

He brought her down to the basement, a long and dank runway of a space where the property safe, a tall dented grey locker, once used for cleaning supplies, stood against a wall.

"You don't happen to have a subpoena on you, do you?"

Mary looked at him.

He sighed. "This goes anywhere you're dropping paper, right?"

"Absolutely."

"I'm going for coffee," he said, handing her the key, then headed back in the direction of the stairs.

It took her more than a minute to haggle with the cheap lock, but when she finally got it to yield, she checked the surroundings to make sure no one was eyeballing her and saw him still standing there at the foot of the stairs.

The four deep shelves of the locker held name-labeled cardboard boxes, each one containing personal items either in envelopes or plastic self-sealing Ziploc bags.

Mary pulled out Rosa Diaz's box which contained her purse, her cell phone, a stamped return envelope addressed to ConEd, unsealed, inside of it the bill statement and a check, signed by her, from a joint account with her husband (*Jerry Daly the man to see*). Another return envelope addressed to Verizon (*Ray Scanlon for that*), her ATM card (*Jerry Daly again*), three twenty-dollar bills and a small photo of Rosa as a kid standing with an older woman against a seawall.

The cell phone was dead so Mary plugged it into her own portable charger and while she waited for it to power up started taking photos of everything else.

When the screen came back to life she scrolled through Rosa's contacts until she found Diaz's number, took that and some others, then listened to her voice messages; two automated spam calls, a message confirming a dentist's appointment and a message from her husband at ten p.m. the evening before the collapse—"I got stopped up here, so I might be a little late."

What does "stopped" mean? Where is "up here"?

Using Rosa's phone, Mary started to call Diaz but quit mid-dial.

If he knew about his wife's death, she didn't want to give him a heart attack when her number popped up.

Calling from her own phone she got a recording informing her that his phone was no longer in service.

*　*　*

Getting out of the cab in front of his building, Anthony saw through the lobby's picture window that Andre the super was once again covering for the doorman. Bracing for the sullen silence to come, he stepped to the entrance, but Andre, coming out from behind the reception desk, got there first and actually opened the door for him.

Surprised, Anthony just stood there until Andre backstepped into the lobby.

"I saw you on the TV," he said, standing almost too close to him once they were both inside. "And I just want to say that I'm glad you're ok."

And then he offered Anthony his hand.

Andre did.

Anthony was so moved by this—*People are so much more*—that he could barely get out his thanks.

*　*　*

He hadn't used or even charged his phone since the collapse; at first, he had forgotten about it altogether and then when he finally thought of it in the hospital and could have powered it up, he opted to leave it drained.

But the startling warmth he experienced in the lobby was still with him and now he wanted to know who might have been trying to reach out.

As it was charging, he turned on the TV to a local news station, sat through a street fair, a demonstration, a follow-up report on the building and then there he was, being wheeled out of the hospital, his survival playing like a healing coda at the end of a dark narrative: *"I'm grateful to be alive."*

The messages: His sister Bernadette, near tears wanting to know how he was. His wife Clare in California, no tears but wanting to know the same; a cousin in Mobile that he didn't remember; two of his neighbors in the building, one of the teachers from the last junior high school where he had taught, a Robo message in Chinese, and then one from his now nearly thirteen-year-old stepdaughter, Willa.

"Hi Tony, how are you, I really want to know. Ok." *Really want to know*, as if she needed to convince herself of her concern.

Well she probably did, and who could blame her; coming into his life as a six-year-old, she was eleven when her mother took her away to live in California and his depressive lack of resistance to the move hit her like the death of a parent, which in a way it was. For the first few months their talks on the phone were full of tears, both hers and his own, followed by his apologies and sloppy explanations for his non-actions that never seemed to do any good and sometimes made things worse. Gradually over time, her phone voice became calmer, then flat, cool, and then straight-up distracted as if he were keeping her from something or someone more interesting, each transformation in her tone ripping him up because, in his mind, it was all his own doing.

Towards the end, he thought they started dreading each other's calls.

He did at least.

But what bullshit.

He called her number but no one picked up.

Just hold on to this feeling and try again tomorrow.

He went into the bathroom and stripped. In the mirror, he caught sight of the massive bruise shaping up on his lower back. In the shower, the grit came off him in runnels, and when he dried himself the towel came away streaked with grey.

Dressed, he came back out into the living room and saw that there were two new messages, both from journalists wanting to set up interviews, but the requests evoked in him a sense of jeopardy, so, no.

R.I.C.E.

Rest. Ice. Compression. Elevation.

He knew he wouldn't follow through with any of that, because the pain and discoloration were his validation and if it came to that, his evidence.

Someone rang the doorbell, the sound making him jump because no one rings anyone's doorbell anymore, and at night? Anthony stepped to the peephole thinking, police, process servers, a death.

Toting a bottle of Rémy Martin VSOP, George Early came into the apartment like he owned it.

"Tony Carter, people want to come by, see how you're doing but they don't know if you're up to a visit. Myself, on the other hand, think you should have some company . . ."

And he was right—Anthony unexpectedly thrilled to see him. George and his late wife were his parents' first friends in the building. He had to be pushing eighty by now, a smallish round man, bald as a Buddha, his heavy-lidded eyes, downturned at the outside corners, and his pursed, sympathetic mouth had always made Anthony, who had known him since he was a child, feel safe.

Stepping into the kitchen, George took two snifters from where he knew his parents kept them then came back out, sat on the couch, cracked the bottle and poured each of them three fingers.

"The doctor told me to lay off drinking for a while," Anthony lied.

"Then let's not tell him. Cheers."

He took a sip, then decided right there that he was done with drinking for all time.

"So." George leaned forward, his arms resting on his thighs.

"It's . . . I don't know what to say. The whole thing, it was like a dream."

"What kind."

"A long one."

"My wife would say God was looking out for you. Like Daniel in the lion's den, like Shadrach, Meshach and the other guy. I, however, would say that if he was looking out for you he never would have let a building fall on top of you to begin with."

The mention of those Bible men momentarily threw Anthony back into the pit.

The building didn't trap him. He trapped the building.

"You look like you just seen a ghost."

But it wasn't a lie. He never said . . .

"Hope it wasn't your father's."

"What?"

"I said . . ."

"No, I already saw his in the hospital."

"Did I ever tell you about the first time I laid eyes on Hubert?" George asked, hunkering forward. "I didn't know your parents when this happened, because they just moved into the building . . .

"Seems there was some kind of holdup at one of the gate entrances, people waiting to get inside, and I see this forty-something white guy with a ponytail and a backpack, he's pointing at this white woman standing next to him and yelling at this young Black security guard we had back then . . .

"'Where the hell do you get the nerve to speak to her like that! You need to show some respect or I'll get your ass canned in a heartbeat . . .'

"And this kid, like I said, he's young but he's huge and when he hears that, his eyes go big. *'You threatening my job? You threatening my job?'* looking like he's going to kill someone and so what does your father do? He slips off his backpack, like he's ready to rumble. *'You think I'm afraid of you?'*

"And that white woman, she's kind of blasé about it all. 'Oh for Christ's sake, just cut it out, everybody. Jesus.'

"But those two look like they're about go at it, so I step in front of your father and start chest-bumping him backwards. 'What are you doing, you want to fight him? He'll leave parts of you all over the street. What's going on?'

"Your father points back at the gate. 'You see her? She goes to get inside, he says, "You ain't gettin' in, Grandma." Piece of shit . . .'

"I say to him, 'Just relax, you live here?' He says, 'We just moved in and we're not taking any crap from anybody anymore,' and he starts making a move to go back to the gate, so now I have to step in front of him again. 'Hold on, hold on, I'm telling you as your new neighbor, you're not going back there.' I think it was me saying, 'as your new neighbor' that cooled him out a little.

"'Then you go get her, she's got a heart condition!' he says. 'We didn't move here to put up with this shit again. This place was supposed to be different.'

"Now, I wasn't sure what he was talking about but no way am I letting him go. 'Don't move, you hear me?' and I walk back to the white woman at the gate. 'C'mon back, your husband's worried about you.'

"She looks at me. 'He's not my husband. I never saw him before in my life!'

"So, I look back at your father and now I see he's pointing to a *Black* woman, standing a little off to the side. 'Ok, that's interesting.' And as I'm walking your mother away, I hear the white lady saying, 'Everybody in here calls me "Grandma." The kid was just telling me the gate was broken. Who asked for that idiot to butt in like that!'"

That idiot—Anthony thinking of himself back then as his father's stalking horse for righteous confrontations. As was his sister and his mother; they all should have been housed in a paddock.

"I don't understand how you could be friends with a man like that."

George took a moment, then, "I guess I just felt for him."

"Felt *what* for him."

"Your father was a wounded man whose pain came from not knowing that he was a wounded man. My brother Eric was like that, striking out at everything because he didn't understand anything. I guess Hubert reminded me of Eric."

"He understood plenty."

"Did he, though?" George Early smiling gently as he pressed his case.

It was a mess of a question, stirring up in Anthony a grudging compassion for the man, raised in a home with a physically abusive father, another fight-the-good-fight civil rights warrior who also enjoyed public confrontations. At least Hubert Carter, who possibly out of a need to protect himself by slavishly imitating his own tyrant, had never put his hands on his wife or kids.

"What was my mother like that day?"

"Embarrassed, but quiet about it. I got the impression she was used to him acting like this."

"She was and she wasn't. I think after a while, he just wore her down."

"Or maybe she was tougher than you think, Tony. She's got two kids, what was she supposed to do?"

"Go back to Mobile," Anthony said. "Her parents had money."

"Oh, no, no, no. No one wants to go home like that. It makes a person feel defeated. I mean, do *you* really want to be living here?"

"No."

"You've had a hard time of it these last few years, haven't you."

Closing his eyes, Anthony tried to fend off the worst moments of that time.

"I didn't say that to make you feel bad."

"No, I know."

And then he heard the prophetess again—the one who predicted the raw scoring of his back, the one who saw angels there . . .

He's been crying out to you all this time, God, he just didn't know it. But now that he's finally in your presence . . .

"I feel a change coming on."

"That's good, that's good," George saying it like he wasn't so sure.

"I would've been around five then. Do you remember if I was there too?"

"I do not, but for your sake I'd like to think you weren't."

George Early, Anthony back with his grateful-to-be-alive heart, newly born and finding newness in everything.

"Mister Early . . ."

"George, please . . ."

"George, when I was a kid, my parents' friends, my friends' parents, other adults, Mister This, Miss That, they weren't quite real people to me. They were just there. But you and Misses Early, you would come into the apartment and there'd been some nonsense going on and you'd always look at me like, 'I see you, Tony, I got you, Tony,' like we had this secret understanding, and I don't know if you were even aware of doing that or remember doing that, but it was . . . And whenever the doorbell rang I always hoped it was you with your wife." Anthony felt his face growing hot. "And, I am so goddamn glad to see you again."

At first, George looked taken aback, then deeply touched, the old man reaching across to shake Anthony's hand.

All night, Anthony had been swinging wildly between his fear of exposure and this sense of blooming rejuvenation, but the feel of Mr. Early's warm dry hand in his, the palm and fingers as smooth as ceramic, had finally tipped the scales.

His tables will be turned . . .

This whole thing—it was a gift.

*   *   *

It was pushing ten in the evening when someone rang the funeral home bell. It was now three days since the collapse and Royal had come up empty.

However, given that people died every day, building collapse or no, he threw on a sports jacket before coming to the door.

"Mister Royal Davis, do you remember me?"

"I'm sorry?"

Thick in the chest and shoulders with a buffalo-sized head, the guy looked like some kind of trouble.

"Remind me," Royal said, gripping the edge of the door in case he needed to slam it shut.

"Cal Ray." Extending his hand.

At first, the name meant nothing.

"Back in '89 I paid your father in full for a funeral."

"Uh-huh." Royal bracing himself for some kind of shakedown. "And whose funeral was that?"

"Mine."

"Right."

"Calvin Ray. 1989. You really don't remember me?"

Royal was unable to tell if he was amused or offended.

"How about *Chaser*, you remember him?"

"Chaser . . . That's you?"

"Was me."

"Yeah, ok, yeah." Royal nodding as he finally saw the teenager's features in the middle-aged man standing before him.

Cal Ray, aka "Chaser" back then, a lieutenant in the Lincoln Gotti crew that ran out of the Booker Houses; nineteen years old, and like a lot of the gang stars who took pride in the fact that they weren't destined to live long lives, coming into the parlor and dropping a couple thousand in cash on Royal's father's desk for his own future send-off.

Well, look who forgot to get killed; Royal thinking, *He wants his money back*. Shit.

"Well, if you think of it, you didn't get your money's worth, but you're alive."

"You still have it though, right?"

Hell no. "The money? Of course. Two K, was it?"

"Five. You'll forgive me if I lost the receipt."

"Maybe you want to keep it as is. We're all going to die someday."

"No, no, that's ok. I'm not asking for it. All's I want you to do is reroute it."

"Reroute it."

"There's a boy named Reginald White, a good kid, was killed trying to break up a fight in the Jeffs, and his family, they don't have any money, but a lot of people want to give him a good sendoff so I offered them mine with you."

"You have to understand, five K bought a lot more funeral back then than it does now."

"May I come in?"

"Of course. Sorry." Royal stepping back.

Calvin came into the parlor, looked up at the stain-streaked drop-tile ceiling, looked down at the ratty carpets, the old couches and chairs.

"No disrespect but I see you might not have it at the ready right now. How much time do you think you need?"

Royal hadn't agreed to take on the body; in fact he'd be within his legal rights to pass, but there was something about this evolved Chaser—back then that was a kid you just didn't cross—but this older version, this *Cal* version, made you want to do what he asked because you wanted him to think well of you.

Money, money, money . . .

"I'll need a few days."

"I understand."

"Where's the body now?"

"With the coroner."

Calvin shook his hand. "I appreciate you doing this. I'll talk to the family tomorrow, then come back on you."

He started to leave, hand on the door, then stopped and turned.

"This Saturday coming, my organization, we're having a anti-violence rally over at the Crawford Houses. You should come. People get to know you, it could be good for your business. You got kids? A family? It's as much a street fair as it's a rally. We got games, music, dance contests, they can have some fun."

"Cal!" Amina called out to him as she came flying into the room before abruptly slamming on the brakes midflight. "Oh, my God, what happened."

"No, no, no, it's all good. Your husband just . . ."

Royal stared at his wife. "You know him?"

"Everybody knows Cal."

Everybody knows Cal.

He really had to get out more.

He was back in his rubble-nest, but this time without the fogginess, keenly aware as he was of the body's distress; his rattling lungs, the dull endless pain from the hard chunk pressing into his lower back, his nostrils and mouth caked with cement dust.

When he woke up, he was standing in the middle of the room having no memory of leaving the bed.

Shadrach, Meshach, Abednego. Daniel.

Even if they were forced into the furnace and the lion's den by others, they were in charge of themselves, they were in control because they knew it was God's doing.

What was he thinking at the time? He wasn't. He just did it, lying there senseless beneath all that debris. He had no will, reasoning, or endgame. It was as if someone else had taken him over.

Well, someone had.

People are happy for you, just give them something.

Listening to his messages again, he called back one of the reporters, who picked up on the first ring, "Jeannie, what the fuck, where *are* you?" His voice nearly drowned out by a thumping bass line in the background.

He hung up and called the other one, left a message, then started pacing, itching to go back out like always but not to any bar.

Why did God put them in the shit only to have them waltz out unscathed? To deliver a message.

Lying there in all that debris, like a rake of oysters that has to be buried for a time in order to come to its full flavor.

He was given a message, too, he just didn't know what it was.

*   *   *

Back in Mary's patrol days Jerry Daly had been one of her partners. But whenever she recalled their time together she automatically returned to that one day, when driving back uptown on Park Avenue from an Italian place on their lunch break, they spotted a five-year-old girl on the downtown side of Park trying to cross the street on her own. Mary was already out of the cruiser and running through the hedgerow that separated the lanes, when the girl was sideswiped by a Volkswagen, the impact sending her spinning backwards like a mad ballerina to the sidewalk.

Somehow Jerry got to her first, giving her CPR while Mary called it in then dealt with the driver and the girl's distraught mother.

When the ambo arrived, he had already gotten her breathing on her own but when the first EMT knelt down to check her vitals he turned to his partner. "I think she's been drinking."

The second EMT knelt down. "Smells like Sambuca." Then turning to the cops standing nearby, "Who did the CPR?"

Jerry looked away, but the EMT read him like a billboard, throwing him a hard look but in the end saying nothing and a few weeks later she and the newly christened "Sambuca Boy" both received commendations from the district commander.

Citibank's investigative team was off-site in an anonymous office building with an elevator so creaky and juddering that it sent her into sweaty flashbacks of her near-death plummet.

Mary rode it up to the sixth floor with a reedy goateed young dude dressed all in black who turned to her midway through the slow ride and without a word pulled a live sparrow out of his ear, Mary jumping back as he held it in his palm then brought his other hand down in a hard clap on its head as if to squash it.

"*Jesus!*" Mary ready to shoot him but when his hands parted the sparrow was gone. If it was ever there to begin with.

"What's *wrong* with you?" Mary said, the birdman blinking at her in faux bewilderment.

They both got off on six, Mary, not knowing if he was following her, holding a slim cigarette lighter–sized pepper spray dispenser behind her back.

There were two long corridors, extending from the elevator banks in opposite directions, Mary walking backwards down the one to the right, the birdman heading down the one to the left.

She passed Star Time Talent Management, Champion Stamp and Coin, and Aziz the Tailor, before getting to the untitled office door at the end.

A security camera was mounted above the door frame and she was buzzed in before she could reach for the bell.

Inside, there were a dozen desks in two rows of six, all unoccupied except for the one nearest to the front door where a retired detective from Computer Crimes—she couldn't remember his name—sat texting, not even looking up at her when she came in, and in the farthest back desk by the lone window sat Jerry Daly, a beef-eating, beer-and-a-shot kind of guy, now looking leaner and more fit than she had ever seen him.

"Hey, there she is," rising to embrace her, some kind of a vaguely herbal scent coming off his clothes. "How you been, Mare . . ."

"The same. You?"

"I'm good, I'm good." Saying it like he meant it.

And then she noticed the prayer beads, a string of milky white balls around his left wrist.

"What's with?"

"My new girlfriend got me into it."

"What's 'it'?"

"A little meditation, some yoga. I follow this guy on YouTube, he's kind of whack but he knows his stuff."

"Do you chant?" Mary struggling to keep the edge out of her tone.

"Sometimes. But not—"

"Well, you look great, I got to admit." Sounding like she was trying to be gracious in defeat.

"You too."

"No, I mean it. You stop drinking?"

"Just about."

"Who's your girlfriend?"

"Janna McCann. She used to be an ER nurse at Lincoln."

"I remember her." Mary recalling Janna, high-strung, chatty, nice figure, too much makeup.

"Yeah, she was going through a rough divorce a few years ago and swallowed some pills."

"She was a drinker too, right?"

"Used to be. After she got out of the hospital a girlfriend started taking her to her meditation group and it took. She quit Lincoln, took some classes and now she's a massage therapist."

"Like a licensed therapist?"

"You don't have to be for what she does. It's Eastern."

"Eastern."

"You know . . ."

"Actually, I don't," Mary said tightly.

Why was she getting angry?

"Breath release, energy flow, Chakra unblocking, some movement stuff but she puts her own western spin on it too. Being a nurse and all."

"Of course."

"Look, it sounds like whatever it sounds like, but it works because I never felt so good in my life. I mean not like every day, but more than I ever did."

"I don't know, Jerry. East, west, could be she just makes you happy."

"Well, there's that too. So, what can I do for you, Mare."

Daly pulled up the Diaz joint account on his monitor screen, a chronological track of all deposits and withdrawals.

"What are you looking for?"

"He tried to cash a check in a corner store last week for a hundred and fifty dollars. I want to know who wrote it."

Daly scanned the deposits. "Not here. Maybe he didn't get around to it, or he cashed it somewhere else."

"Why would he go out of his way like that? He's got the account right here."

"Well," Jerry began, "it could be that . . ."

"Maybe he didn't want her to know about it," Mary said.

"It could be that."

"How about the other deposits?"

"Paycheck from Estilos de Rosa for her, another paycheck two weeks before that, let's go back two, another and another, all for her."

"Nothing coming in for him?"

"Nothing I can see."

"What about ATM withdrawals."

"There's a bunch."

"Just on the day of the collapse or after."

"The last withdrawal I have is the day before, a hundred dollars from Banco Popular, two-thirty in the p.m."

Banco Popular, Mary just there the morning of the collapse in response to that bogus bank job.

"There's video too."

Daly pulled up the CCTV footage of Christopher Diaz inserting his card into a sidewalk ATM outside of an African food shop/boutique/handicraft emporium, then cupping his hand around the screen as he put in his PIN, went through the bank's query prompts and then, as the machine went through its information retrieval, he casually glanced to his left and then to his right for any freelance carnivores that might be lingering nearby. When his card popped out and the cash dropped, he pressed himself against the ATM, counted out the five twenties, slipped them into his front pants pocket, checked the street again, then left the frame.

There was nothing in his actions or facial expressions that was helpful in tracking him down. He was a burly somewhat good-looking street-alert individual, seemingly unstressed as he went about an everyday task, but just to see him in motion for the first time, while meaningless regarding anything that may have happened to him after the collapse, somehow further convinced her that he was still alive.

"How about the withdrawal before that?"

Daly pulled up the previous ATM video from the day before, this one featuring Rosa Diaz withdrawing sixty dollars from a cash machine inside a ShopRite. She looked to be in her midforties, a small solid woman with puffy-lidded eyes and short feather-cut hair, neatly dressed, the gold cross that hung from her throat nearly lost in the foliage of a floral-patterned blouse.

To all appearances, she seemed like a pretty squared-away individual but that puffiness around the eyes which reduced them nearly to slits made her hard to read.

Well one thing was for sure; two days before her violent end and she hadn't a clue.

That was always the thing that got to Mary, watching people who had died, still alive on some recording device going about their day oblivious to their impending doom. It smacked of cosmic unfairness, making even the worst players seem painfully innocent.

Without her asking, Daly took it upon himself to pull up photocopies of the account's outgoing checks; among them, monthly rent payments of six hundred and fifty dollars to Bright Management, monthly payouts to ConEd, AT&T and Cablevision, weeklies to Mujer Mágica, a beauty parlor, and one made out to Prophetess Irene Mayfield LLC for a prayer towel, three hundred dollars.

"Three bills for a towel," Jerry said.

"Must be made out of platinum," Mary said.

"Some people," Daly said, "it just makes you sad."

She wanted to make a crack about his bracelet, but . . .

Business done, Daly introduced her to the retired detective from Computer Crimes: Wallace Brown, that was his name, the guy pretending he didn't know her from his days on the job—Mary not bothering to wonder what the hell that was all about, then continued on her way into the hallway, Daly at her side.

When the elevator doors opened, that reedy guy dressed like a cat burglar popped out, Mary waiting until he disappeared down the hallway before turning to Daly for an explanation.

"Antoine. He owns a magic shop down at the end there. It's a real destination. You wouldn't believe some of the characters going in and out."

"Coming up he scared the shit out of me."

"Yeah, I'm here five years, and still whenever I see him or one of his customers waiting for the elevator I take the stairs."

He handed her a card for his girlfriend's massage studio.

"You should give her a shot."

"Why, do I look that bad?"

"I'm just saying it couldn't hurt."

* * *

When Mary got home, the Little One was waiting for her in the kitchen; the contents of his book bag—some spiral notebooks, a science text and the dregs of his half-eaten lunch—splayed across the dining table.

"You have to go to my school tomorrow," he announced.

"Why?"

"You or Dad."

"*Why*, Terrence."

"Because I hit a kid."

"You did? Why'd you do that?"

"Because he hit me first."

"Why did he hit you?"

"Because a girl he likes, likes me better."

"This other kid, he's in trouble, too?"

"We both are."

"Oh for Christ's sake."

"I told the teacher I don't start fights, I finish them."

"Where'd you get that from?"

"From you. You told me once that Grandpa always used to say that."

"As long as you don't start them."

That's not right.

"Next time that happens go to your teacher first."

There, that's better.

"So who's coming you or Dad?"

"Better him because he's a teacher too."
"But you're a policeman. You could scare her."

※ ※ ※

The journalist Anthony had left a message for the night before turned out to be one of the producers of a local cable show, *Around the Town with Blue Williams*.

One of the young staff writers FaceTimed him early that morning, asking after him, of course, then making general small talk in order to assess his lucidity and composure, then asking him, in a roundabout way, to relate a personal story, constantly bobbing his head in encouragement as Anthony told him about his surprising encounter with Andre the super, how that hulking churl offering his hand to him when he returned from the hospital had so filled him with revelation that he nearly wept.

"My God," the kid said, "I feel like I was right there with you, thank you for that, but it's too interior."

"Too interior . . ."

"For us."

"Do you want a more exterior story? I have a few in my car."

"You're quick," he said. "Blue likes quick. Let me talk to some people and I'll call you back."

※ ※ ※

Given that Citibank had no record of the husband ever making any deposits, Mary decided to canvas the check-cashing businesses in his immediate area: a tax prep outfit that only cashed checks for their customers, a Western Union office that only cashed government-issued checks, and a currency exchange center where she had to sit it out in the waiting area while the sole cashier, who apparently only spoke English, dealt with three customers, none of whom were fluent except in the languages of their respective countries. And when it was finally her turn, the same cashier pointed to a small sign that had been staring her in the face all the time that she'd been in the waiting area: NO PERSONAL CHECKS.

※ ※ ※

"So," the staff writer said, "everybody likes you, but here's the thing. We all understand . . . No, wrong word . . . We all have an *inkling* of what you've been through and, if you at all feel like this is maybe too soon and you need more time to emotionally process before you commit to going on the show, we could try to book you for later in the week."

"But not after that."

"Not after that."

He didn't need any time to process; what he needed was to embrace his buoyancy in order to keep his other, darker thoughts at bay.

"No, I'm good. Let's do it."

The studio was in a former nineteenth-century piano factory along the waterfront on the Bronx side of the East River.

The loftlike space on the top floor was evenly split between the shadowy camera zone and the aggressive brightness of the stage. Anthony, escorted up by a production assistant who then stepped away, stood around not knowing what to do with himself until another aide came by to steer him to hair and makeup.

On the way, the friendliness of whoever crossed his path, the quick smiles of recognition coming his way, had him alternating between feeling blessed and feeling like he was being set up.

In the mirror-lined room, the stylists lounged in their respective swivel chairs; one tricked out in neo-punk was smoking an e-cig, the other, a caffe latte half-and-half like himself, sat hunched over herself reading a beat-up paperback of *On the Road*.

Makeup had him first. "I'm Sasha, close your eyes?" spritzing his face with a thin coat of foundation then cupping his cheeks with her palms and slowly drawing them down to his chin to smooth it out evenly.

"Are you excited?"

He thought she asked him if he was excitable. "Not really."

"Close them again?" Sasha dabbing his lids with eye cream then fingertip stroking his brows and on and on, a featherlight sequence of soft wedges, brushes and caresses, the tenderness of her touch working on him like a sweet sedative. Even though she was just doing her job, he couldn't remember the last time a woman had caressed him like that. Couldn't remember because the answer was never.

Just doing her job, got it, but that gentling touch of hers, both reassuring and sensual, offered him a blind taste of what his life could become if he surrendered to his new heart's commitment.

"I'm Libya," the hairstylist murmured as she ran her hand through his hair to get a sense of texture.

"I'm Anthony."

"Congratulations," she said. "I mean, not per se."

"No, I know what you mean. Thank you."

He was making her nervous but he didn't know why.

Covering his eyes with a makeup wedge she trimmed his brows then began running a large-toothed comb through his not-quite wiry hair.

"So, how's your day been so far?" he asked her through the mirror.

"Good," she said brightly without meeting his eyes then stepped off as Blue Williams, still wearing his makeup bib over a light blue shirt, came strolling into the room to stand behind Anthony's chair.

"Are you good?" Blue looking at himself in the mirror over Anthony's head.

He was thin and tall with a short neatly cropped Afro and stylishly oversized horn-rims, his voice trained and deep, full of confidence.

"I think I am."

"Good." Laying a hand on Anthony's shoulder. "Just be yourself."

"Which one?"

But Blue was no longer there.

Libya returned to business, dipping her fingertips into a small jar of gel then massaging it into his hair, but then abruptly stopped midscalp, her sticky fingers coming away studded with minute crumbs of debris. She went in again and brought up more; stared at her fingertips and then at him, big-eyed and aghast as if he were death itself.

* * *

When Mary came into the break room on the second floor of the precinct to take her name-labeled personal pizza out of the communal refrigerator and pop it into the microwave, a detective from the Robbery Squad was eating his lunch while watching a talk show on the room's portable TV.

She hated talk shows but the other detective was there first, so unless she wanted her office to smell like pizza all day she had no choice but to eat in here.

* * *

"Anthony Carter," Blue began, addressing the camera, "I'm very glad you're here."

"I'm glad to be anywhere."

He was in a too-high director's chair on an otherwise bare stage with nowhere to anchor his shoes.

"Shit, that's that guy they dug out," the robbery squad detective said.

"How are you feeling?" Blue finally turning to him.

"Good enough."

"That day, those days . . ."

Anthony waited for the rest.

"What do you remember?"

"Smells, voices, trying to breathe." Anthony closed his eyes. "Being lifted. The sky. The hospital."

"Thirty-six hours."

"If that's what they said."

"What got you through it?"

"Oblivion." Which was true.

Oblivion . . . Mary believing him because otherwise he would have come out insane.

Blue waited for more.

So give him more, let it rip.

"When they first started to pull me out, I didn't want to leave. I felt . . . I felt that I had had it with myself, and I was through."

"Through . . ."

"I was tired of all the mistakes I've made in my life. And they kept coming, every day, every day . . . I just wanted to . . . Stop."

"But now?" Blue wanting him to say something positive.

"Now? Now I'm scared. I wasn't before."

Scared. He didn't mean to say that.

"You're reliving it all," Blue said.

No, I'm worried about the future . . .

Anthony momentarily slipped back into his dread but then began to will it away, the effort speedy but exhausting. And so it would always be, he realized; the underbelly of his propulsive sense of joy forever needing to be blasted away by the force of his will.

But you have a message, embrace your gratitude and you'll find it.

"Do you think that might be because now that you're out of danger it's finally safe to experience the fear? I would imagine . . ."

"But on a deeper level, I also feel . . ." Anthony tuning Blue out as he began interviewing himself, raising his hand like a stop sign until he could find the words.

"You know, you look back at your life, the things that you did or failed to do and you wish, if you could only be given a chance to return and repair the damage . . ." Anthony paused again, letting it come.

"And, I feel like I've been given that chance and I'm not going to waste it and I am *never* going to take it for granted."

"*Good for you*," Mary said out loud as the other detective tossed the remains of his lunch in the garbage.

"I'm not one to talk about religion but it's like God buried me under that earth, wiped my slate clean, then brought me back up to be who I never thought I could be before . . . And all I want, all I want now, is to be worthy of that gift and . . . and to be . . ."

The applause startled him, Anthony, until that moment, forgetting that there was an audience, and their approval, like so many of the positive reactions from others he'd received since first being carried out of the rubble, made him feel *seen*. With so much of his life lived in the insignificance of failure, the gratitude he felt was overwhelming and he began to tear up, Blue more or less ceding him the floor.

"Sometimes, I have this joy in my heart, I have," palming his chest, "I have so much in me to offer and all I want, is to be of *service*."

"Of service," Blue quietly repeated, both a statement and a question.

"I feel like . . ." And then he paused, allowing this yearning to do good to continue to rise in him. "I feel like I have so much to say to people now. Things I'd never known or felt before and it's all good news."

More applause.

"You know, when I was a kid," Blue began, addressing him in a more intimate, conversational voice, "I had a Sunday school teacher who talked about the martyrs, that sometimes you have to lose your life in order to find your life."

"I'm no martyr," Anthony said. "I am very alive and just bursting to be."

"*Good for you*," Mary said again, this time to an empty room.

At the end of his segment he was guided offstage, many of the people working on the show beaming at him again although a few others looked at him with pity.

Someone handed him a fistful of downloaded messages that had come in during his segment.

Sasha stood outside of hair and makeup, silently applauding. "Come on in, let me clean you up."

Back in the chair again, he started riffling through the pile, a few *God love you*s, a photocopied painting of Lazarus, an invitation to invest in some moneymaking scheme, and one from someone named Calvin Ray from PGD YSF. "We are a grass-roots anti-gun violence organization. Here is my number please call me, I think I have what you're looking for."

*, *, *,

Due to the financial standoff with his brothers, Royal had no choice but to reopen his tradesman's app, which had apparently expired, pony up the re-registration fee and wait for the phone to start ringing, most likely when he was dead asleep.

There was a communal mortuary prep house for freelancers like himself who needed the space and equipment to do the embalming—which would have doubled his fee—but most of the high-end funeral homes preferred to use their own people so the job was mainly pick up and drop off, pretty much akin to working for a dry cleaner.

*, *, *,

"Last time I was in the Jeffs I was in high school," Royal said. "Came up here to buy weed and wound up getting robbed and my ass beat by twin brothers."

Calvin smiled. "Back then that'd been the Judkins, Jason and Mike."

They were in the elevator of 8 Building heading to the fourteenth floor to sit down with Tutti Speedwell, Reginald White's mother, and discuss the funeral arrangements.

The front door of the apartment had a sign—LITTLE SUNSHINE DAY CARE—spelled out in uneven multicolored letter magnets dancing beneath the peephole.

The bell produced an anemic tinkle which Royal couldn't imagine anyone hearing, but a small boy came to the door in no time at all then disappeared, leaving them to walk down a storage bag–lined hallway, family photos covering the close walls, past a bathroom and number of bedrooms on either side.

Through an ajar door, Royal caught a glimpse of a small elderly woman gripping a fistful of tissues and staring at the ceiling as she lay fully dressed on the bed.

Tutti was waiting for them at the table in a small dining alcove that opened out into a darkened living room dense with potted plants.

She was a heavyset woman with a motionless face that looked half-erased as if some great hand had smeared its features; her eyes bunkered into slits, her blanched skin the color of sand, her hairline commencing so far back on her head that it looked shaved.

But when she saw Calvin, she got up so fast that the two plastic glasses of water that were laid out for them jumped off the table and hit the floor. Her sister Rose, who was in the kitchen washing dishes, came out with a roll of paper towels and started to swipe at the floor, Calvin squatting down to help her out.

"Rose . . ."

He was inches from her face but she wouldn't even look at him, and when they were done she went back without a word and resumed washing the dishes so loudly that it sounded like she wanted to murder each plate.

At the table, Royal sat quietly awaiting his cue alongside Calvin who reached out to take Tutti's hand. "How's Mommy?"

"She's trying to sleep."

"You need to check on her?"

"No, I just want her to get some rest."

Calvin turned to Royal: go.

"My sincere condolences, Ms. Speedwell." Royal using his funeral planning voice, solemn but not sepulchral, "I understand that Reginald was a very good kid."

"He is."

"*Was*," Aunt Rose said from the kitchen.

The mother didn't seem to register her sister's angry correction but Calvin sure did, staring balefully at the half wall that separated the two rooms like he wanted to put a hole through it.

Royal forged on, "If you feel like you're ready, I'd like to go over some burial options with you."

"I don't have money for any of this."

"Tutti," Calvin taking her hand again, "I told you, we got this."

We.

"Since we're working with a small budget . . ."

A grim-faced, thickly built teenager wearing a T-shirt and sweatpants, a tattooed spiderweb rising and spreading from his gullet to his jawline, came shuffling shoeless into the dinette and sat down next to Tutti who clutched his forearm.

"Petey," Calvin said, "I'm sorry about your brother."

The kid barely nodded at that, his eyes trained on the table.

Royal knew that look from a number of young men's funerals; a brother, or a cousin, or a friend, whether they ultimately did anything about it or not, mulling over how to even the score. On the other hand, this kid's leaden silence could come purely from the weight of his grief.

He started over.

"Since we're working with a small budget . . . What I would first suggest to you is cremation."

Tutti shook her head.

"Uh-uh, no," Rose called out from the kitchen.

Petey had no reaction.

"I respect that," Royal said.

He would have been surprised if they had agreed; in his experience, most low-income families hardly ever opted for destroying the body.

"Petey, you good?" Calvin reaching across the table to tap the back of his hand.

"Another option is a service called a direct burial."

The phrase wasn't exactly self-explanatory, Tutti looking at Calvin then at him.

"The body is buried without embalming in a non-pine coffin, which goes directly into the ground."

He had her attention at least, Royal bracing himself to deliver the downside.

"But without the embalming, due to the nature of nature taking its course, there's no viewing and no ceremony."

"No, I want a ceremony," Tutti said.

"You can always have a memorial service after the burial."

"No. I want people to see him."

"I understand," Royal struggling to keep his voice from losing its equanimity as the overall cost continued to rise with each rejection.

"Now I would be happy to offer you the use of our private chapel . . ."

"No. I want a church."

Shit. Royal speed-tabulating—church fee, 500; sexton, 100; organist, 200; florist, 250 for a casket spray; transpo to cemetery, 500; casket, even a cloth-covered non-pine, 1800. The burial had to be in New Jersey where it was cheaper, non-plot, non-title, maybe a plaque, 400, with no stone.

"Do you attend one?"

"No and this is what I get for that."

"Tutti, it's not your fault," Calvin said.

"No, it's fuckin' not," Rose said, back to banging the dishes.

"Petey, get them some water," Tutti said.

Petey eyed the half wall that separated him from his aunt, then reluctantly got up to do what he was asked.

Rose started right in on him.

"My sister's baby gets killed, now she has to deal with all this shit." Her voice like a slash. "This is how you looked out for your brother? Where were *you* that night? Huh?"

All they could hear after that was Petey sounding like he was choking on a bone, sounding like he was strangling himself.

"Pete," Calvin called out, "come on back out here."

Tutti, her sunken eyes turned to a window, seemed oblivious to her sister tormenting her son.

Royal was familiar with this, too: families suddenly tearing each other's guts out at some point during the funeral arrangements.

And this is how I chose to make a living.

Petey came back out but not to the table. A moment later they heard the slam of a bedroom door.

"Excuse me," Calvin said, rising and going into the kitchen.

"Why do you want to go and gas up his head like that?" Calvin's disembodied voice carrying into the dinette. "You want your sister to have to bury him, too? You want your mother to go through this again?"

"He should have been there," Rose said.

Royal sat alone with Tutti. Where were they at? Churches . . .

"How about anyone else in your family. Do they attend somewhere?"

"Mommy used to go to Rose of Lima. But I don't like that priest they have, Father Ekubo. I can't understand anything he says."

Calvin left the kitchen and headed down the hallway to find Petey's room.

"Is there someone else you'd like?"

"I don't know anybody right off."

"I might know a few good pastors," Royal said.

There was just one, a part-time preacher whose father he had buried a few years back, which hopefully made it a freebie.

"We can have the service here, but the burial is going to have to be in New Jersey."

"Mount Nebo," Tutti said, "with his father."

"Right," Royal said, relieved that he didn't have to break down the comparative costs or itemize what she could and couldn't get over the state line.

When Calvin finally came back to the table the business for the day had pretty much concluded.

As they headed back down the hallway towards the front door, Royal glanced into a bedroom and saw Petey sitting hunched on the edge of his twin bed glaring at a TV screen not a foot from his face.

※ ※ ※

In the narrow maze of crisscrossed streets at the far western end of Harlem, there was a low anonymous building that housed, on its ground floor, a Depression-era union hall that had been converted into a small church, Blessed Redeemer, although not much had been actually converted. The interior was long and narrow, a damp-smelling rectangle with two aisles of folding chairs on either side of the nave's central aisle, which ran up to the apse with its lectern and pulpit beneath a crude cross allegedly made out of twisted 9/11 steel beams.

Beneath a vinyl-tiled ceiling the walls were painted sky blue which only served to highlight the numerous cracks and peels.

When Anthony got there, the church door was locked but the building super who had been playing dominoes with his friends on the sidewalk out front let Anthony inside for a five-dollar gratuity and now he had the place to himself.

So, what was he doing here, sitting with one arm stretched across the back of an adjoining folding chair?

He was waiting.

For a message, physical or cognitive, a small infilling or epiphany that would validate his freewheeling God justification.

Growing up, his father declared himself a Quaker as a kind of political statement but never went to a meeting and his mother just went through the motions, attending on Good Friday, Easter and Christmas Eve, so the church was never really part of his life.

The last time he tried to make the connection he did it only to keep the peace with his grandparents, going with them to their church in Mobile, but his heart had been elsewhere so it never took.

After the service, at their urging, he went to a men's prayer circle in the church basement's music room, which was tougher because it was harder for him to mask his detachment from six believers than from six hundred and so he just, all due respect, came clean to them about where he was at, then left.

But here he was again, this time of his own free will, hoping for some kind of permission for the continued use of God's name.

He wasn't so naive that he expected any kind of tangible sign—maybe if he was lucky he'd have some kind of minor commotion of the soul or an inspired insight, but he might as well have been sitting there waiting for a bus.

* * *

Bracing himself for the agitation to come, Royal stepped inside Lilies of the Field, the fragrant refrigerated air as always making him grit his teeth.

Benny David was behind the front counter eating short ribs and fried yellow rice off a silver foil plate.

"Uh-oh," Benny said without raising his eyes from his food, "watch out Mama, that man's here again."

"That crap's gonna kill you."

"Well, good thing there's a funeral parlor close by."

"I once picked up a shotgun homicide from the morgue, I get the body on the prep table, and I see what I thought was small maggots between the shoulder blades . . ."

"The scapula, you mean."

". . . but they weren't moving. You know what they were?" Royal determined to throw him off his feed, "The kid was eating Chinese right before he was shot and the pellets blew the white rice right out through his back."

"Well this here is yellow rice."

"I need a floral spray for a casket."

"Anybody I know?"

"Some kid from the Jeffs trying to break up a fight between two crews. I guess he should have minded his own business."

"Some people can't help it because it's in their nature," Benny said, dumping the silver foil dish into a small trash bag then tying it off.

"Yeah well, everybody says he was a good kid."

"That's a shame," Benny said, wiping his mouth. "You're having the service at your place?"

"Blessed Redeemer."

"When?"

"In a few days."

"I'll put together something nice."

"How much?"

"Fifty."

It was a fraction of what Royal had expected.

"Who's doing the service?"

"I'm still looking."

The half-a-preacher that he was counting on had moved down to Florida.

"You say he was a good kid?"

"I just said that."

"Then look no more."

"You?"

"Why not?"

"You're ordained?"

"Sort of."

Royal stood there, stumped by all this generosity. There had to be an angle.

"I'm still going to fight you on that garden."

"No kidding," Benny said.

Or maybe he was just a good guy.

※ ※ ※

Towards dusk, Anthony returned to the site of the collapse with a camera crew from a local news station and immediately realized that coming here so soon after his rescue was a terrible mistake because as soon as he stepped out of the van he felt himself propelled back into his two-day grave: mouth, throat and eyelashes thick with cement dust and the scent of his cold urine-soaked pants rising to his nostrils.

The sound man sidled up next to him.

"You alright?"

"What?"

"Are you . . ."

"I am."

"Don't wander off, ok?"

The reporter, dressed in jeans and a smart black jacket, her deep brown eyes made bottomless with heavily applied mascara, quickly looked down at her printed-out notes then up at him.

"Anthony, I know it must be difficult for you to be back here. But if you can tell me, what do you remember about that day?"

That again.

"Sorry. Give me a minute." Turning away to get a grip, he quickly became transfixed by the sight of an excavator dumping a load of stone and brick chunks, chaotically mingled with more fragile remains of life as lived in the building, into the open back of a Sanitation Department truck.

Directly across the narrow street, he saw a group of men draped like music notes up and down the front steps of a brownstone. He couldn't tell if they were staring directly at him or just looking in his direction.

"Bro, we're losing the light . . ." the cameraman called out, making him finally turn their way.

The reporter gave it another shot.

"Anthony, what can you recall about that day?"

The remembered stench of his entombment—however that came about, it didn't matter right now—was becoming unbearable.

"Anthony, on that day . . ."

"I don't think I can do this . . ." he said.

She continued to stand fast, mike in hand, waiting him out.

Then, down low, off mike, "Anthony, c'mon, you got us out here . . ."

"*I* did?"

This was her idea, not his, but right now all he wanted to do was leave this place, so he let it be.

"Maybe we could just shoot him walking around," the cameraman said.

❋ ❋ ❋

"Royal Davis? Sorry for the late call, this is Ron Killins from Freeman's Chapel."

"Yeah Ron, what's up?" Royal rolling out of bed without opening his eyes.

"We have a pickup, if you're available."

"Yeah, go ahead." Feeling for the chain of the bedside lamp, the sudden light making Amina flinch in her sleep. Royal turned it off again, then made his way out of the bedroom with his hands out in front of him into the moonlit living room. "Yeah, sorry, go ahead," reaching for pen and paper.

"2124 A. C. Powell, George Banks, male, sixty-six." Then, "It was expected."

"House or apartment?"

"Apartment. 3-F."

"Which room?" Royal asked, praying it wasn't the bathroom.

"Bedroom. On the bed."

"Elevator?"

"If it's working."

"What if it's not?"

"Then maybe you should bring a helper."

He didn't have one but kept that to himself.

"Big man?"

"The grandson guesses around two, two twenty."

Royal thinking, *Let's say, two forty.*

From the third floor, using the stretcher trolley, he could negotiate that.

"How long has he been there?"

"Died in his sleep sometime yesterday, but nobody knew about it until tonight so, thirty-six hours? Probably a little more."

So, ripe . . .

"No super-staph?"

"His GP said no, but don't take chances."

Not for the money you're paying me.

"Family there?"

"Some."

"How are they dealing with it?"

"That you'll have to see for yourself. Ask for the grandson, Jason Beatty."

As it had been drilled into him by his father and his father's father before him, Royal picked out one of his three black suits, a white shirt, a dark tie and a pair of thick-soled hiking shoes, the leather dyed black, so as to avoid slipping on body fluids. His wedding ring was ok but he removed his neck chain and watch and left them behind.

Heading down into the basement work area, he began putting together his go kit: a Tyvek bodysuit for himself, a fiber-vinyl body bag, plastic sheets, slide sheets, cotton sheets, a packet of nitrile gloves, another of breathing masks, a roll of surgical tape, a small jar of Vicks VapoRub—which wasn't as effective as peppermint oil or Tiger Balm but the oil gave him a rash and the balm made him tear-blind—protective goggles, and a pair of nostril plugs to prevent any reek from clinging to his nose hairs. Putting everything in an oversized Nike sports bag (its logo blacked out), he stepped out of the house. When he pulled the car cover off the old limo which was parked behind his SUV in the lot that he shared with the florist—*maybe a pocket garden wouldn't be the end of the world*—he was surprised/not surprised to see that he could finger-write his name in the accumulated dust and grit anywhere along the chassis from the front grill to the taillights.

Can't have the family coming outside and seeing Dad loaded into something looking more like a tricked-out garbage truck than a limo.

But even after twenty minutes of close-range spraying with a garden hose the hearse looked pretty much the same except a little shinier due to the glint of water beads catching the beams from a streetlight.

Well, it was night anyhow; he just wouldn't park under another streetlight and hope for the best.

The interior of the limo was as musty as a cellar, the fuel gauge needle on the dash all the way down to Feed Me, the brass-coated casket rollers and bier pins in the back worn away in places to their nickel core, but otherwise, if you were a grieving relative last-minute peering inside through the tinted windows, what you saw wouldn't seem unduly disrespectful.

As he was about to key the ignition he realized he'd forgot a few more things and went back inside the house down to the basement again and grabbed a neatly folded oversized American flag and a similarly oversized relatively clean purple quilt blanket. Which one he used would be up to the family, but no one wanted to see one of theirs coming out the door wrapped in a body bag.

*   *   *

The body was in 10-F, not 3-F as he was told, but the cloying odor emanating from the high-rise had already made it down to the street, lying thick in the air for the better part of a city block.

Pulling up as close to the building entrance as he could, he sat in the limo, checked his notes for the name of the deceased and the name of the grandson, smeared the Vicks under his nose, and put his DMV funeral director's parking permit on top of the dash.

Hoisting the Nike bag to his shoulder, he stepped out, went around to the back, popped the lock on the rear loading door, slid out the stretcher trolley and commenced to roll it before him into the building.

The sweetish stench, trapped in the scantily furnished too-bright too-big lobby, seemed to both expand and condense, the elderly Hispanic doorman, swimming in his oversized uniform behind the reception desk, grinning sheepishly as if he were the source.

There were a few silently morose family members down here sitting on a couch and staring at air.

Shifting into his death-handling personality: patient, humble, unflappable—"*People are all over the place,*" his father had told him more than once, "*don't contribute to their scatter*"—he made his way over.

"Sorry for your loss," he said, not too damp, not too crisp. "How are you all doing?"

They stared at him like he was an intruder, which in a sense he was.

"I'm here to take care of Mister Banks."

As if they didn't know, all eyes on the stretcher trolley leaning against the opposite wall.

"You're gonna take him with that?"

"When everybody's comfortable with letting him go."

"What is he, an Amazon package?"

At least they weren't attacking or screaming at him like a time or two before.

"I was told by the funeral director to talk with Jason Beatty. Do you know where I can find him?"

The elevator door opened and two pissed-off looking detectives, both smoking cigars, stepped out into the lobby.

There was no need for them to have gone up there: the cause of death had already been signed off as unsuspicious, Royal guessing that they never got the update, ergo the faces.

"Show some respect," one of the relatives snapped.

"You mean this?" one of the detectives said, looking at his cigar like he had just noticed it. "It's for the smell."

"No disrespect," the other detective added making it sound like a fuck-you in sheep's clothing.

Royal stepped in front of them.

"Can you guys help me out up there?"

"Can't, we just got another call," the first detective lied.

"Lot of family up there?"

"Half a dozen maybe?" the other one said.

"In the apartment?"

"Hallway."

"How are they head-wise?"

"Not too bad."

The elevator was a crawler, Royal able to clock its ascent with a calendar. No problem going up, but going down this slow with a body on board could be another story altogether.

The five silent relatives who were keeping vigil in the darkened hallway had fired up a number of incense sticks along the walls which masked nothing and in fact, mingling with the odor of decomp emanating from inside the apartment, made the air so woozily noxious that Royal wanted to apply a second layer of Vicks using a spatula.

Before he could say anything to the relatives, a young man rose from the floor, his big-eyed, clear-skinned baby face at odds with his full beard.

"You're here for him?" he said looking up dull-eyed as if Royal was keeping him from a long-overdue nap.

"I am. Are you Jason?"

"I am."

"Royal Davis, Freeman's Chapel," extending his hand. "I'm sorry about your grandfather."

"Right."

"How's everybody dealing?"

"They're dealing."

"He's inside?"

"He is."

"May I go in and see him?"

"That's what you're here for."

"Can you let me in?"

"It's unlocked."

Normally Royal didn't like to invite a family member to assist because sometimes they just freaked on you when they had to deal with the body up close; more than one volunteer wound up puking, another came in just to reach up inside his dead grandmother's support hose to grab the roll of twenties she always kept stashed there, and in one case, he was fairly certain that the family member who came in to help with the shrouding had murdered the woman on the bed and had just volunteered to gloat.

But this kid seemed pretty good to go.

"If you'd like to, you're welcome to assist."

"Yeah, no, I don't think so," Jason said, stepping aside, "He's in the bedroom with the French doors off the kitchen. You can't miss him."

His first view of the body lying face up on the bed—hands crossed over the chest, belly swollen with fluids—was through the glass panes of the bedroom door, making Royal think of a preserved saint on display in a European church, the entire bedroom its transparent sarcophagus.

Once inside the doors, Royal's first surprise was that the reek was not as heavy as it was in the rest of the apartment or even in the hallway.

Then he saw the small open tub of Room Shocker on top of the dresser, felt the crunch of the crushed DOA crystals sprinkled on the floor. Both had to be left by the two detectives who had come here on a bullshit call; an act of consideration for the next visitor which in no way jibed with their sour sarcasm down in the lobby.

The moment he slipped the Tyvek suit over his clothes the sweat began to sprout in earnest, trickling down from his neck to his calves.

Be quick.

He used butterfly tape to close the eyes, stuffed cotton balls in the nostrils, and covered the slightly parted lips with nonstick surgical tape to stopper any contagion.

The hands were already crossed so all he had to do before rolling the body up on its left side was to bend one leg at the kneecap, tuck half of the slide sheet against the contours of the exposed back, unroll the sheet flat, then bring the body back down. Then do the same on the right, roll it up, pull the remaining slide sheet flat and bring that side down until the body was fully on the sheet.

Raising the horizontal of the trolley until it was the same height as the mattress, he laid out the cotton sheet on the stretcher bed then, pressing his groin against the far side of the trolley for more stability, reached across to the bed, grabbed the slide sheet and carefully pulled the body onto the trolley. He repeated the two-sided body roll, this time to remove the slide sheet, then began to bind George Banks like a chrysalis into his cotton shroud.

When Jason Beatty entered the bedroom, Royal was in the process of Velcro-strapping his grandfather to the stretcher. He was hoping to avoid any of the family seeing him in his work suit but the kid didn't seem to notice.

"Were you close to him?" Royal asked in a sweaty murmur, his hands in constant motion.

"When I was little he used to take me with him everywhere but then he met someone and bailed on us overnight for like twenty years."

"That's too bad," Royal said, half listening.

"I'm over it, though."

"Sure." Royal securing the legs now.

Jason walked over to his grandfather's dresser, briefly opened the top drawer, then shut it without touching anything inside.

"He took me to a Mets game once when I was eight, we're in a bar by the stadium beforehand and I told him I was worried we were going to miss the start. So, what does he do? He orders himself another beer, says to me, 'Look down there,' and I see three Mets sitting at the short end of the wood throwing back cocktails.

"He says, 'When *they* leave, *we* leave.'"

That one had Royal smiling for real. He wanted to ask who were the Mets but refrained.

"He only came back to us because he had cancer," Jason said, "and knew we'd take care of him."

"And you did," Royal said automatically as he stripped out of his jumpsuit to his sweat-soaked shirt and suit.

"That shows character. The family ok with me bringing him out now? Anyone you know won't be able to handle it?"

"What?"

"Is there anyone . . ."

"No, we're good."

Since the grandson was right here he offered him up the choice of American flag—*was he a vet?*—or the purple quilt for a body wrapper.

"You choose," Jason said, leaving the apartment.

The ride back down to the lobby, as he knew it would be, was as slow as creeping Jesus, the flag-wrapped body standing upright on the trolley like a patriotic mummy.

The car stopped on the eighth floor, a sleepy-looking woman with a shopping cart full of laundry stepping into the car then, "Oh," as if embarrassed and reversing back out into the hallway.

On the fifth floor another woman, older and wearing glasses the size of coasters, got on and stayed on, facing forward as the car continued downward.

He wasn't sure she even registered the presence of her neighbor until they were almost to the lobby. "The dead don't scare me none," she said staring at the elevator door as if it were a television. "It's the living you got to watch out for."

Normally, the drive to Freeman's should have taken thirty minutes but with the body on board it took double that because he couldn't go over twenty mph for fear of having to suddenly hit brakes and hear the casket go flying off its rails.

When he finally arrived at Freeman's delivery bay, at 4:30 in the a.m., there were two other limos ahead of him waiting to offload their own pickups, Royal fuming as he waited. *Three hundred dollars for this shit.*

Well, only four more bodies, and he's got his non-pine casket.

* * *

"Let me lay it out for you then you tell me if you want to get involved."

Why a chain restaurant in the middle of Harlem would be blasting Hawaiian music over their PA system was both a mystery and an annoyance, Anthony having to lean in to hear Calvin's every word.

"My organization, PGD YSF whenever there's a shooting in the area, we arrange for a street demonstration right where it happened, kind of a half block party, half anti-violence rally for the people, all expenses coming out our own pockets. Eat a hot dog, hear from one of my CMs tell his story, dance to the music, hear from another of my CMs, and so on."

"What's a CM?"

Calvin answered the question as if he were addressing a crowd.

"A Credible Messenger. A man who's been through hell and back because of gun violence. A man who had blood on his hands and served time for it. A man who has come out the other side of his journey and has got things to say to the youths of the future."

The hostess floated by but didn't look their way, Anthony desperate to ask her to seriously lower the volume. Calvin, sensing his discomfort, got up, had a word with her then returned to the table.

"Mostly the people who show up are females, mothers, grandmothers and what have you and their kids. The older boys, if they show up at all, just grab a free hamburger and bail. I mean so be it but they're not our target."

The music suddenly dropped to a whisper, Anthony feeling like he could breathe again.

"We want those young ones. We want to get a hold of them while they're still soft enough for us to make a dent in their mind sets."

"Ok." Anthony hoping this wasn't a pitch for money.

"Now, why I'm telling you all this is that sometimes we get guest speakers at these things, police captains, local politicians, mothers who lost their own kids."

"Ok . . ."

"This rally, I want them to hear from you."

"Hear what from me."

"Whatever you're moved to say."

"I'm no Credible Messenger."

"Oh, I think you are. You said you want to be of service? Here's your opportunity."

"Ok." Anthony agreeing without really understanding what was being asked of him.

"You sure?" Calvin lowering his head and raising his eyes.

"Yes."

"Beautiful." Calvin shook his hand, then ducked under the table to dig a T-shirt out of the backpack resting on the floor. "This is for you." Then dropping dollars to cover the check and rising from the table. "I'll hit you with the details tonight."

He watched Calvin make it as far as the front door, then stop and return to the table.

"Last year our cutoff age for young boys was twelve. This year it's eleven although I've come to think that it should be ten."

*, *, *,

Verizon's investigative unit was housed in an austere frosty suite on a high floor in the Verizon Tower, the investigators, mostly retired law enforcement, not much more colorful themselves.

"I got stopped up here, so I might be a little late."

It was a recording of Diaz's last message to his wife, Mary playing it for Ray Scanlon, a former detective who retired out of the NYPD Intelligence Bureau and was the former husband of Mary's former best friend.

"'Up here' so, I'm thinking 'upstate'?" she said handing him Diaz's phone number.

"Better be," he said. "Too many cell towers down here, you'd go out of your mind trying to pinpoint the location." Then, "You can't give me more to go on?"

"Sorry."

"I'm going to need some time."

"Gotta make some calls?"

The joke bombed, Mary wondering if her lame quip technically qualified as a pun.

"I'll call you in a few days, no guarantees."

*, *, *,

Because there was a 911 complaint about some grown man across the street from the Rampersand playground taking pictures of little kids for hours on end, a patrol car rolled up on Felix while he was working, one of the cops taking his Parks Department ID, his various other IDs, his video camera and his tripod back to the patrol car for what felt like forever, to run his name through the system looking for outstanding warrants, arrests, convictions, lists of registered sex offenders and what have you, while the other cop kept an eye on him, Felix standing there with his thumb up his ass, trying to ignore all the passersby stopping to gawk at him before getting bored and moving on.

One of the playground mothers, seeing what was happening, left her kid in the care of another woman and went to the corner with the intent to cross over Fifth and vouch for him. This he knew because he had dealings with her from before. A heavyset Latina with a heart-shaped face, she was the first mother to confront him some months ago when he began this work, coming over to ask him why he was taking pictures of the children, but she did it without getting hysterical or enraged, asking to see his Parks ID, then calmly listening to his explanation of the job, which she not only accepted but became curious enough to ask him how to get a job like that.

She had even waved to him that day as she made it back across Fifth, which of course left him with a crush on her.

And here she was again, waiting for traffic to pass, Felix waving her off—*I got this*—while, and not for the first time, imagining them together in some alternate universe.

※ ※ ※

The next morning, Anthony met with John Filly, the ironically small-boned and razor-trim New York–New Jersey personnel director for the High and Mighty Men's chain of stores in the coffee lounge of a straining-to-be-edgy boutique hotel off Times Square, the walls hung with enormous black-and-white photo portraits of cows and steers staring directly into the lens, the small lounge table tops featuring collaged cut-up portraits of rock stars preserved under thick coatings of amber-tinted varnish.

"So, I read your personnel file," Filly said, looking over the same in his lap. "It seems like you were quite the closer back then."

"I wasn't bad."

"Your manager described you as 'highly creative.' I'm not sure what that means. Can you give me an example?" Despite the mildness of the request, Anthony picked up a slightly prosecutorial undertone which made him think that the question was a trap. On the other hand, he was occasionally so wary these days of making the wrong move, saying the wrong thing, that he probably would have had the same reaction if the waitress had asked him if he wanted more coffee. It was in these moments when he most needed to embrace his sense of being reborn in order to do some good in the world.

Filly was still waiting for him.

"Well one thing I did was try to get a read on the customer the minute they came through the door, see how they carried themselves, the look in their eyes, and, I could pretty much tell right away how they felt about being bigger than most men out in the world. A lot of them came in, they're just looking for something loose enough to hide in, but when I saw a man who seemed to really enjoy being the size he was, you know, what I thought of as a Big Daddy, I'd come up, 'Hey, did you see who just left here?'

"And they'd be like, 'What? Who?'" Anthony deciding at that moment to do all the voices. "I'd say, 'Lawrence Taylor!' or, I don't know, 'Joe Klecko! Jumbo Elliott!'

"Or for the taller guys I'd bring up one of the old Knicks.

"'Oh yeah,' I'd say, 'he came in for a couple of suits, but I guess he didn't realize how much weight he put on since he retired so . . . You know how it is, some of these guys when they hang it up they just keep eating like they did when they were still hitting the gym, doing half-day drills . . .' Then I'd give the guy the once over. 'So, where'd *you* play?'

"And they'd come back with a high school somewhere, maybe a small college or nowhere at all, but they always appreciated the question. 'You know, you're actually closer to the size that so and so thought he was, can I show you what caught his eye?'

"And unless I overplayed my hand or underestimated the guy's sharpness, more often than not he'd wind up buying a couple of suits, leave them for the alterations, and that was that. Other times, I would—"

"It's ok. I get the picture," Filly cutting him off in a way that told him that the New York–New Jersey personnel director for the High and Mighty Men's chain of stores had found the tale offensive.

And Anthony, for the first time since those days, realized that that's exactly was what it was. Offensive.

He was so unknowing of himself back then, barely in touch with how much anger and resentment he had carried with him every day into that store, the helplessness he felt trying to get a handle on how his life, once so limitless in possibilities, seemed to continuously slip instead of soar, until he found himself a shop clerk with a drug habit, and how all that angry bewilderment manifested itself in a slick contempt for the customer.

As Filly excused himself to make a call, Anthony thought back to a day when he came on to one of his so-called Big Daddies, the man looking like he was trying not to laugh in Anthony's face as he listened to the whole of his bullshit retired-athlete spiel, then mimed tweaking his nostrils as if he had just done a line before turning away to find a salesman who wasn't high.

But Anthony knew that John Filly was here under orders to rehire the famous-for-the-moment Lazarus man, a former employee who, in the moments before his world caved in, had been intent on rejoining the High and Mighty team.

As it turned out, the H&M stores closest to the one that had to be demolished in Harlem were in Buffalo and Atlantic City, so those were practical no-gos, but even if there was a new H&M going up a block from where they were now sitting, after hearing himself crowing, Anthony couldn't ever imagine setting foot in one again.

Calvin's rally. He still didn't have any idea of what he was going to say but in his present state of mortification he knew that whatever it was, he'd give it his all.

* * *

They had Felix standing on that corner so long that three more patrol units, independent of each other, had pulled up to the first one, then reluctantly left when they saw that the stop was a bust.

When the first cop finally emerged from his cruiser to return all of his gear, he advised him to keep his Parks ID hanging from a neck chain, so that time-wasting incidents like this one would be avoided.

Felix accepted the apology.

Calling it quits after that, Felix packed up and began walking east on 128th Street towards home.

As he approached the corner of Madison Avenue, he heard her before he saw her. "*Excuse me, excuse me . . .*" the woman almost race-walking towards him from across the narrow width of 128th; light-skinned, bony and tall with the restless over-alert eyes of a soldier on point in a village full of hostiles.

"Excuse me, excuse me, can you help me?"

Enough with people rushing up on me, Felix taking a big step back from her urgent presence. "What's up?"

"My boyfriend locked me out of my apartment," half turning and pointing to a top floor window in a five-story walk-up across the street. "He's got my keys, my cell, my purse, my dog, *my* dog, he don't even like him and I got to get to my mother's because . . ." Crying a little and whirling like a top, "He wants to be with that other bitch? She can have him, I mean, but what did *I* do? I work so hard and he's in there sitting around all day with her . . . I do not deserve this from him or anybody else but I don't care, I just want my dog, I just got to get to my mother's house, I need to take the train, but he's got . . ."

Off-balance, Felix handed her two singles from his front pants pocket. "Here you go, no problem." Feeling good about himself, feeling like a kind person.

She gave him a swift hug before stepping away, doing that nervy dervish thing of hers then crisply walking back to him with the money still in her hand.

"I'm so sorry, I should have said, she's in Milford," then off his blankness, "It's Connecticut, it's a Metro North train."

"How much is that?"

"Eight dollars. Just a one way 'cause I'm not coming back. All my family's there, my mother, my aunts, my cousins, they told me not to go with him and they were right, they were right . . . He's got all my stuff, I can't even call my mother to tell her I'm coming . . ."

Felix fished out a ten without even thinking about it.

At first her eyes widened in disbelief.

Then taking the bill with one hand, she offered back the two singles with the other.

"Keep it," he said like a king.

"You're such a good person."

Rushing towards him again, she wrapped her arms tight around his ribs like she'd never let go and burrowed her head hard into the side of his throat, a ripe waft of dried sweat and a lingering attar of cigarettes rising up, stoning his senses.

With the flat of his palm now on her back he felt a birdcage tracery of bones, felt slim muscles lightly burbling beneath the skin as if she were standing on a nerve—"*Terror keeps you slender*," he remembered someone once saying—all of her unprotected essence, the sheer frankness of the unguarded chemical information, this onrush of her, made him wish that she'd never let him go.

But she did.

Attempting to mask the crazy-blood in his veins, he pointed up to her window.

"Why don't you call the cops on this guy?"

"Because he is one."

Felix dropped his arm, needing to think this through.

"I just want my dog he can have everything else I don't care . . ."

"What kind of dog?" Just wanting to keep her there a little bit longer.

"Pitbull greyhound rescue, I got him after his owner was locked up for raising fight dogs. They had to put all his other dogs down except for my baby because he was only a pup."

"What's his name?"

"I call him Nutty."

"What's your name?"

"Me? Crystal. But listen to this . . . When I first took my baby home he started throwing up all over the apartment like for three days just wouldn't couldn't stop. First I thought it was nervousness because he had such a bad life but when I took him to the vet, the guy said his puke had traces of gunpowder in it. That's what those bastards fed them. Gunpowder. I saved his life."

"You surely did." Then bracing for her to go, "Ok then . . ."

But she didn't, she didn't.

"I got up this morning," she said, "feeling like everything bad's going to happen to me today, but there's always something good in a day too. And that's you. *You're* my good."

"Your boyfriend?" he offered. "Men are like that."

"Not all!" Finger-stabbing his chest. "*You're* not!"

"Call your mother." Offering his phone.

"I can't believe you . . ." in a husky whisper, then stepping a few feet away from him, dialing, waiting. "Mommy? It's me. I'm coming home . . ." Pausing to listen then lowering her head, a hand to her brow. "I know, I know. You were right. You were right . . . About an hour, two . . . Can you pick me up at the . . . Why not? . . . I don't have any money for a cab." Waving Felix off as he reflexively dug into his pocket. "How about Ray-Ray, can he pick . . . Ok please just ask him, ok? I can't wait to see you. I love you." Ending the call and handing back the phone.

"I'll never forget you . . ." A last nerve-bubbling embrace then walking away.

It was only after he had gone another block or so that it dawned on him that she had split west back towards Fifth which was in the opposite direction of the Metro North station, east on Park.

Stopping to quick-check his phone log he saw that the last outgoing call made was two days ago to his own mother upstate.

He didn't understand why that made him smile.

He walked south two blocks to 127th, then west towards Lenox then up Lenox to 129th then east towards Fifth in order to block her retreat, catching sight of her as she came out of a corner store peeling the foil off of a fresh pack of cigarettes.

It couldn't have been more than fifteen minutes or so after she conned him but when they came face-to-face, he could tell that she didn't recognize him.

And then she did.

"The train's not for another—"

"Stop, stop, I don't want the money back."

"Ok then, what . . ." Dropping her role, but coiled for anything. Good question.

"I don't know," he said. "Wait a sec . . ."

"I have to be someplace."

"Ok, wait, it's like . . . You already had my money but you just kept it going, telling me all those stories with the boyfriend, the gunpowder dog, talking to your mother, you faked that so well, with the pauses when it was her turn to talk . . ."

She looked at him as if every word out of his mouth was a trap.

"I'm just saying, you were really into it. Shit, *I* was into it . . . Just one question, that's all. Why a dog? Why not a child?"

No way would she answer that, sideways confess like that, so he answered the question for her, "Because a child would freak people out too much. They'd go all 911 on it. And nobody doesn't like dogs, but they're dogs, so . . ." He shrugged. "I get it."

"I have to be someplace," she said again, starting to walk away.

"I'm just saying, if I were you . . . No, well, alright, maybe we'll run into each other again someday." And then stepping off himself.

"You'd what . . ." she said.

"What?"

"You said if I were you . . ."

He came halfway back to her. "I'd look into some kind of acting. I don't know how you go about it, but you're good."

Walking away again, he made it halfway down the block then turned to see her where he left her, watching him go.

※ ※ ※

When Anthony returned to his building, he had a copy of today's *New York Post* for Andre the super because the guy was always reading day-old editions and because after that humiliating job interview he needed to extend himself in order to get his heart back in the game.

But Mario, the regular doorman, after being out with the flu for a week, was back at the reception desk.

According to him, Andre had been fired after getting locked up for assault the night before.

"Guys like that?" Mario said. "If they're going to drink, they should drink at home."

* * *

Royal's second body pickup, relative to the first, was a piece of cake; the call from the Our Savior Home Chapel in Yonkers coming at a decent hour of the evening, ninety-five-year-old Henry Cotton (natural causes) already prepped for transport at the Daughters of Rachel Assisted Living Center in Riverdale.

The name of the deceased meant nothing to him until he saw his photo on the memorial pegboard propped on a side table in the main lobby with its ever-changing mini-obits of whoever went off to the Long Home in the last few days.

Henry Cotton—finally and hallelujah.

Royal knew him all too well from past pickups over the years, always sitting in his wheelchair by the lobby elevators, two of his left-hand fingers lost to a chain saw in a turpentine camp sixty-five years earlier in Florida.

Henry Motherfucking Cotton, just sitting there as if he was waiting for Royal to show up, each time calling out, "Uh-oh, run for the hills everybody! Here come the Death Pimp!"

And the one time Royal brought his son Marquise with him for some reason that he couldn't recall, Henry took one look at the big-eyed kid and asked Royal if he "brung him to fix his hair."

He once asked a few of the other tradesmen who picked up bodies at Daughters of Rachel if the old man was like that with any of them too. Nope. Not a one. Just Royal, the Death Pimp, and so when Royal finally secured Henry Cotton's bundled frame to the rails in the back of the limo and took off for Our Savior Home Chapel in Yonkers he made a wee stop at Serenade, a bar on the border of the Bronx and Westchester, leaving the limo with the body in it in the parking lot while he enjoyed his scotch and soda.

* * *

"Young man." Calvin calling Anthony as promised on the night before the rally.

"Calvin."

"Just checking in. And it's Cal. How's it going?"

"It's not."

"Just think about all these young boys in the street. About what they're learning out there from the older ones."

"I wouldn't know. I wasn't a projects kid."

"No matter, bro, eleven's eleven. Just think about something stupid you did back then because you were too young and too dumb and what you'd tell that boy now."

* * *

Felix got to Calvin's rally spot at 10:30 the next morning, an hour and a half before anyone else made the scene, so with time to kill he went on another photo safari, wandering through the Crawfords and the immediate surrounding area until he found himself on the roadway beneath the el, its exposed tracks casting slanted bars of light on the cobblestones beneath. At first, Felix was tempted to shoot but it felt like something he'd seen endless times before, both in a number of photography books and in socially conscious grainy black-and-white docs from the first half of the last century; usually silent except for a simple piano track underlining the shifts in scenery. But the roadway itself, made with Belgian paving blocks that had to be over a century old with steel trolley tracks cutting through the heart of the stone . . . Ignoring the car traffic, Felix got on his knees in the middle of the road and attempted to capture the granular details, but the resulting photos wound up looking like a whole lot of nothing.

By the time he made it back to the playground, everything was going full boil; the equipment nearly all set up and dozens of tenants milling about, waiting for the show.

Calvin was too overwhelmed to give him any instruction as to what he was supposed to shoot so he shot what he wanted; a sea of folding tables, one stacked with PGD T-shirts and cheap vinyl children's backpacks; at others, kids playing chess, adults playing whist; another one piled with paper napkins, plastic plates and forks and next to that, by an unfired barbecue grill, a hill of bagged buns and wax-papered bricks of raw meat, burgers and dogs.

Then there were those tall shaved-headed twin boys off in a shady corner, dancing side by side, their eyes closed, their chins tilted to the sky as if they were in a state of shared bliss, a few of the younger kids giggling as they attempted to imitate their syncopated moves.

And this guy here—a scratch-bearded older dude in a PGD tee, Felix thinking that he had to be one of Calvin's Credible Messengers, perched on the top slat of a bench, watching a basketball game on his cell phone, ignoring the little kids that were climbing all over him as if he were playground equipment.

"Family! Let me see what you got!"

Calvin, mike in hand, was emceeing a dance contest, the song blasting scratchy from a pig-nosed amp as a dozen or so kids busted out with variations of the same moves, a few of the mothers dancing on the sidelines.

One solemn-faced girl, older than the rest, was throwing down some polished steps but she looked embarrassed to be doing so as if she suddenly realized for the first time that she wasn't a little kid anymore.

It bothered Felix just a little to zero in on her face, but it didn't stop him from shooting.

❊ ❊ ❊

Coming into the playground, jittery and desperate to do well, Anthony mostly avoided people's eyes, but peripherally picked up that some of the tenants, mostly women, recognized him from TV. He didn't know how to deal with that kind of attention right now so he gravitated to the sound of Calvin's voice, which brought him to the dance contest as it was wrapping up, Judge Cal going from kid to kid, his hand hovering over each head and letting the volume of the cheering on the sidelines pick the winners: a three-year-old boy and a nearly adolescent girl, her stony flat-eyed face reddening by the second.

Calvin handed each of them a five-dollar bill, the boy waving it in the air as he ran to his mother; the girl pocketing the cash then quickly walking into the nearest building without glancing to her right or left, Anthony getting the sense that she might not come back out until this was all over.

A few of the tenants were still eyeing him, Anthony at first turning away from them then turning back around to see her again. The woman, not young, not old, not thin, not fat, had a wry intelligent face with rivetingly bright silver eyes, eyes that looked like they had their own power source. And, and, and she was looking right back at him, throwing him a half smile, *Yeah, I see you too.*

She was wearing a wordless blue T-shirt, old jeans and beaded moccasins like you'd find in some dude ranch trading post. Her hair was in two long braids which she wore draped forward over her collarbones.

"Young man," Calvin said, "you good?"

Not old, but something about her suggested to him that she had lived a number of lives before this one.

"Young man . . ." Calvin again.

"Yes!" Anthony finally turned to him. "I'm good. I'm good."

"You got something to say today?"

"I do."

"Then just have a good time until it's time for you to say it."

"Cal, what do you want me to shoot?" Felix asked, as he came up alongside Anthony.

"Just the people having fun. Positivity. You got this."

"Still or video?"

"If it's video keep it on the short side so maybe we can get it on the news. Other than that, do your thing." Then, to both of them, "You get your T-shirts? Dogs be up in a few."

Anthony noticed that the kid with the camera seemed to be studying him, most likely another fan of his queen-for-a-day celebrity. He was starting to get used to that kind of open-faced scrutiny from strangers, so he didn't really think any of it.

But that woman . . .

When he turned back to drink her in again, she was gone, Anthony immediately going into who-was-that-lady overdrive, scanning the grounds until he finally caught sight of her as she entered one of the buildings.

Felix wandered over to watch a chunky rumpled middle-aged photographer—his hair sprouting in wiry stalks from his balding head—as he took a group photo of some kids in Crawford Hellfighters basketball jerseys.

"Guys, one more," he said, snapping off another shot. Then another. And another.

♩ ♩ ♩

"How y'all doin' Fam?" Calvin, mike in hand, called out from the bench that he was standing on.

"Because that's what we are. *Family.* You to me, me to you. Now, I'm not going to be long, but I promise to be strong." Waving to a mommy here, a mommy there as some but not all of the people started to collect in front of him.

"You know, people talk about their life-style, everybody's got their life-style . . ."

Anthony, on the edge of the crowd, was half listening, more focused on finding her again.

"But what we're dealing with in these times, in these streets, is what I call our *Death*-style."

"That's *right*," the woman standing next to him called out.

Someone yelled for someone to kill the music.

And then there she was again, Anthony seeing her coming out of that building, the half smile on her face when she caught him looking her way making him feel like she was looking for him too. She had swapped her T-shirt for a crisp white button-down. Her lips were a shade redder than before and her braids were rearranged into a swirling twist on top of her head to show more of her face. She had gone into her building and done that. For him? If so . . .

Then, standing fifty or so feet apart in separate clusters of people, they turned away from each other, like the rule book of whatever game they were playing said to do, Anthony embracing the slow swell of anticipation that was taking him over.

"We are out here today . . ." Calvin's voice echoing off the bricks. ". . . we are out here today to try and reverse the negative trend of violence in our community. We are PGD YSF, and who I have with me," gesturing to three men standing near the bench, "are my Credible Messengers, who are also my brothers. These men, like myself, are men who lived in these streets, devastated this community, and paid for it. Between us, we have served over seventy-five years incarcerated." Some in the crowd applauding at that. "But now we're home, rehabilitated, and paying it forward by doing what we're doing right now.

"We are all about our youth because our youth of today are the future of tomorrow."

More applause and a few shout-outs; people reacting like they'd never heard that said before.

When Anthony turned to look across the crowd to see her again, she was already looking back at him before he got there, as if waiting for him to do just that.

"We're tired of losing our children to the cemetery, we're tired of losing our children to the penal system. There's a pipeline from the schools to the prisons and we want to change that, we want to reverse that so what you have in us is men you can count on to be positive role models, examples and mentors to your boys. So, what we want to do, is we have a sign-up book over there by the food tables where you can come and register your son or you can just bring him over with you and we'll start working *with* you and *for* you, *with* him and *for* him. We will protect him, guide him and be his staff.

"We'll become their surrogate fathers because that's what they need because in my experience and no disrespect to you ladies, but in my experience, it takes a man to raise a man."

This time Anthony was waiting for her, his eyebrows raised in a *say what?* arch which had her laughing, the ease of their wordless conversation making him feel like whatever was to be, had already happened.

"See, a responsible male has got to understand that just because you can make a baby, that don't make you a father because a father is one who *fathers*, who will provide knowledge and wisdom and understanding of a child *to* that child and that's what we want to provide. We want to teach them all the positive values, honesty, integrity, self-control and how to resolve their conflicts without resorting to violence."

Good luck with that, Mary Roe thought, standing apart from the crowd in her Community Affairs windbreaker.

"We will teach them the art of de-escalation, we will teach them strategies that they can use to downgrade a confrontation they might be in, so that no one dies and no one has to spend twenty years in jail. We will get them to arrive at a place in their mentality where throwing shots is not their first instinct."

"Yeah, but what if that's the other kid's first instinct?" she overheard one of the few older teenagers say to a friend.

"I don't know man, these new kids comin' up now?" The friend shaking his head like the world's youngest geezer.

"And I'm not leaving out the young girls," Calvin continued, "oh no. We also have females in our organization who will work directly with the young girls to teach them mannerisms, etiquette and how to be classy young ladies."

This time Anthony and the silver-eyed woman didn't even have to catch each other's eye to continue their silent conversation.

"This is what we're all about. We're not animals, we're not savages, we're human beings and human beings take responsibility. And that's what we're doing today.

"As I said in the beginning, I wasn't going to be long but I promised to be strong so let's have some fun, and as we go along you're going to hear a little bit from our CMs and a very special guest because they have stories that if you listen to them I think you'll appreciate it. So, *DJ*!" Calvin pointing to someone on the sidelines. "Drop that music and let's give our youths a good time!"

Very special guest.

When the crowd broke, Anthony started walking in her direction, but Calvin's hand on his arm stopped him.

"I want you to meet my Messengers."

*   *   *

Felix took his camera over to the mesh fence along the basketball courts where a boys' fifteen-and-under four-team mini-tournament was in full effect, Felix shooting through the mesh as the first two teams ran up and down the full court, the ball handlers flashy and smooth until they found themselves in traffic under the boards and were unable to finish, a kid on the other team grabbing the rebound then showboating his way down to the other hoop before last-minute losing the ball under the same circumstances.

"How're you doing these days?"

"Sorry?" Felix turned to see Mary standing next to him. He felt like he should know her but . . .

"I talked to you a little at the building collapse," she said. "You were in pretty rough shape."

"We talked?"

"Yeah, I didn't think you'd remember me."

"I'm sorry."

"Don't be. But you're good?"

"I am."

"Good."

"Thank you." Offering his hand to this individual now. "I'm Felix."

"Mary." Then moving her hand in arc to take in the whole show. "And this is what I do."

"What is."

"Help out. Get the permits, bring in whatever they need. And make sure nothing pops off."

"You can do that?" Felix asked, finally registering that she was a cop.

"Do which?"

"The nothing pops off part."

"Not really, but I can slim the odds," Mary taking an intuitive liking to this kid and his wide-open face, sizing him up as half streetwise, half hick. She gave him her card. "In case you ever need it."

"I used to have a card, but all it said was 'My card,'" he blurted then added in his embarrassment at his own lame repartee, "Did you ever notice how you look back every year and all you can remember is what a jerk you were the year before?"

"Every year?" Mary shrugged. "How about every day."

"Why you not watching the game, bro? You think you're a star? 'Cause you're *not*, so you best watch and learn something, 'cause you ain't shit."

Mary and Felix turned to the harassing voice coming through the mesh to see a tall kid wearing a red St. Louis Cardinals cap pulled down low on his brow, a kid too old to play in the fifteen-and-under bracket, standing with his friends near one end of a team bench and ragging on a younger boy, twelve or thirteen, suited up to play sitting alone at the opposite end.

Felix knew he'd seen this younger boy before but he couldn't remember when or where.

"How old are you?" the tall kid snapped, taking a seat next to him on the bench.

There was no response, the younger boy stiff as a board as he stared straight ahead at the court.

"I ast how old are you."

His friends weren't joining in but they were smiling.

"Why you lookin' away from me? My making you nervous? You scared of me? I think you scared of me. Least I think so. No, yeah, you ain't denying it so I'm sure you are."

Felix felt like smashing this older kid in the mouth.

"Where'd you get that haircut bro, the lawnmower store? It's hard to look you, bro. It's really sad. You know why coach put you in before? Because he felt sorry for you. You know why he took you out? Because he wants to win."

"Is this where you stop the pop?" Felix said to Mary.

"Better if I have Calvin do it," Mary said, then walked off, ostensibly to find him.

Being police it was problematic for her to interfere; it was just some bully breaking balls on a younger kid. Stepping into it in uniform would be an overreaction and even if it wasn't, any kind of adult interference would just provoke him to double down on the torture the moment she was out of earshot.

And she also knew this: if anyone was in serious danger on those courts it was the bully—the younger boy wasn't saying anything, but his frozen physicality told her that he was internalizing every jab.

After the game he could go home then come back out here in a few hours, tonight, tomorrow with something in his hand and then Calvin's got himself another stop-the-violence rally.

One of the volunteer coaches sent a player to the bench and waved the stone-faced boy in, posting him at the foul line for a free throw.

"You best *do* something superstar."

And then Felix made the connection—the boy that was about to shoot was the one he had photographed handing out funeral home business cards on the day of the collapse.

"Look how scared he is, see it? Why you so nervous, bro? What are you so nervous about? Why you got your tongue sticking out? You think you're Michael Jordan? 'Cause you're *not*."

The free throw bounced off the rim.

"See that? What I tell you!"

Felix whipped himself around the mesh. "Why don't you leave him alone? He didn't do anything to you."

"Who the fuck are *you*?" The tall kid reared back.

"You don't need to know who I am. Just leave him alone."

"Or *what*."

"Or nothing. I'm asking you because it's painful to hear you. He's just a kid, so cut the shit, ok?" Then, "You think you can do that?"

The tall kid's friends stood there, eyes eagerly ping-ponging between their boy and Felix, happy with any outcome.

"You look like a gorilla."

"I am a gorilla."

"Ook-ook."

"Yeah, ook-ook. Just stop." Felix leaving the court without looking back after that.

"Wish you wouldn't have done that."

"Done what." Felix turning to look up, up, at Royal Davis.

"Defend him like that. He needs to learn how to defend himself."

"I'm sorry, I got teased a lot. Nobody stood up for me, so . . ."

"Nonetheless." Royal shrugged.

"He's your son?"

A woman came over with a hamburger plate in each hand.

"Where is he?"

Royal gestured to the courts. "Let him play."

"Hi," she said, smiling at Felix, "I'm Amina."

"Yeah, this is . . ." Royal waving a lazy hand at Felix. "I'm sorry, what's your name?"

"Felix."

"Like the cat," Amina said brightly, offering him one of the burgers.

"Thank you." But she had already gone off to meet and greet someone else.

"She's got a lot of energy," Felix said, feeling comfortable enough in Royal's presence to mention it to her husband.

"Tell me about it," Royal said, then, noticing the camera, "Who are you taking pictures for?"

"Cal. He asked me to."

"What's he paying you?"

"He's not."

"Nothing?"

"I don't mind. That's how I learn."

Royal passed him his cell phone.

"Put your contact information in there. I might have a learning experience for you in a few days."

Passing by the basketball courts again without looking to see what was going on, Felix overheard that tall kid, "I don't care about nobody man, because I don't *like* nobody, I don't *love* nobody and that's the way it is with me. In fact, I prefer it."

He couldn't tell if he was talking to his friends or himself.

* * *

Calvin steered Anthony to a folding table inside the darkened community room where three of his CMs sat, one of them reading the *Post*, the other two leaning into each other as they watched a Knicks game on a cell phone screen.

"Martin, Gerard, Raymond." Knighting each man with a pointed finger.

Martin and Gerard, wearing PGD tees and jeans, their faces deeply lined beneath indifferent facial hair, looked to be in their late forties, early fifties; Raymond, the reader, was older than the other two but came off crisper. Wearing a vaguely institutional-looking but fresh-pressed olive shirt and pants—probably not so different from what he wore in prison—he was whip-lean, with a shaved head that looked waxed, a goatee to compensate and a reserved air.

None of them gave him more than a cursory nod.

"Martin over there, watching the game with Gerard, is a part-time anger management counselor at the Bronx Probation Office," Calvin said. "Gerard's a security guard at a ShopRite, and Raymond reading the newspaper is writing his biography."

"Autobiography," Raymond corrected.

Calvin's cell rang.

"Yeah. Yeah. Ok hold on, hold on . . ." Pressing his cell to his shoulder. "So, you good?" laying a hand on Anthony's shoulder.

"I'm good."

Calvin left the room to resume the call, and the three CMs went back to what they were doing before the intros. And if Anthony hadn't been still thinking about that woman out there he would have felt a lot more uptight.

Lost in his personal cloudland, he had no idea how long he'd been sitting there when Raymond finally put down his newspaper.

"What was it like down there, what was it, two days?" he said.

"Two days? I was in the hole for two months once," Martin said.

"Well it looks like you both got out," Calvin said returning to the table.

"You nervous about speaking out there?" Raymond again.

"I was born nervous. Today's just another day."

"Do you want to give us a taste of what you're going to say?" Calvin asked.

"I don't think so," Anthony said. "I'm better off going out cold."

"That's fine, that's fine," Calvin said, checking his watch. "Alright then, let's go do it."

Anthony was the first to stand up, just wanting to see her again.

❡ ❡ ❡

Felix caught up with the other photographer while the guy was shooting young kids playing chess.

"Who are you working for?" Felix asked.

"Bronx Home News," he said, taking off his glasses for a spit-clean, his exposed eyes pink and small. "What you got there?" Eyeing Felix's camera.

"Nikon D3."

"Are you a pro or a buff?"

Buff, as in hobby, as in pastime.

"Pro."

"Then you should upgrade to the 5G."

"So I've been told. I'm Felix." Offering his hand.

"Marvin or Marv. Let me tell you something, Felix. Things like this, big dos, I always take a group shot, that's my fallback in case I can't capture anything on the hoof."

Capture—Felix's go-to word.

"You have to." Felix trying to sound *pro*. Then, "You make a living like this?"

"Oh hell no. I make my nut doing graduation parties, birthday parties, a wedding or two. How about you?"

"I shoot for the Parks Department, mostly. But for me? It's all about the street."

"Same here," Marv said, looking around for signs of photographable happiness. "I like the guys who shoot for the tabloids, every now and then they really nail something."

"Like Weegee," Felix said.

"Like who?"

❡ ❡ ❡

As Anthony stepped up onto the speaker's bench, Mary recognized him from that talk show in the break room the day before.

"I've been told that I had been buried for thirty-six hours or more. I have no memory of it because for most of that time I was either in some kind of dream-state or straight out unconscious. I was unaware of my own existence which is to say that for all intents and purposes, I had died. I had experienced the nothingness of death. But thanks to God it turned out that I was just a visitor to that black land."

I was just a visitor to that black land. The phrase threw her off, and she found herself writing it down.

"And so when they finally lifted me out it was like being reborn. I *was* reborn, and all I wanted to do as soon as I could breathe air that wasn't packed with dirt, all I wanted to do, was to live and live and live. I wanted to embrace the preciousness of what it means to be alive and to cherish it as the everyday absolute miracle and gift that it was.

"You all, as life-givers, as the life-guardians of your children, you have a full-time job on your hands with your kids because the street is a mother too. And not a good one. You have to know that once that child leaves your home . . ."

And then he saw her in the crowd and his words took flight.

"A young boy is like soft clay. And the street can be a brutal sculptor."

Mary turned to Felix. "'Brutal sculptor.' Did he just say that?"

"I feel like I've seen him before," Felix said.

"He was on TV."

"I don't watch TV."

"A young boy only knows what he wants in the here and now, which is to be accepted in the eyes of others . . . They're so full of life as lived in the moment, so full of, of, immediate *wanting*, of immediate *need*, to belong, to be seen, to be admired, respected, feared, to be a man among men as defined and dictated by Mother Street, and all of it going on inside of them minute by minute, no thought to the cost . . . that, that . . ." Anthony faltered, drinking her in as she raised those eyes to him.

". . . that life in full, in the years and years to come, to experience ten kinds of joy, ten kinds of sadness . . ." Saying this to her, for her. ". . . to learn who you really are, who you were meant to be, to learn what the world has to offer you and what you have to offer it in return. To find love . . ." Anthony felt himself getting teary. "To know what it feels like to give it and to receive it . . . all of it, to these vulnerable children, the long game of existence? . . . It means nothing."

The long game of existence.

Moved by his sincere and poignant listing of life's potential joys Mary refrained from writing the phrase down.

"Now, these men, as Calvin has said already, they started out as victims, grew into victimizers, paid the price and came back out into the world intent on putting their hearts and minds, their pain and experience, to work for you."

"That's *right*," Calvin called out, needing no mike to be heard.

"They need you as much as you might need them, they need to make their amends, they need to be of *service* to you.

"And who here couldn't use a helping hand? Who here, not just in these houses, but anywhere in the world young hearts need to be nurtured and protected, couldn't use a helping hand . . ."

Young hearts need to be nurtured. Mary snapping out of it, writing it down.

When he finally came down from the bench and handed the mike back to Calvin, some of the people who had been listening to his speech began to move towards him, thanking him for his words, one or two patting his back, someone else briefly taking his arm.

He was gracious and grateful, joyful even, but he also felt slightly out of focus, slightly *not me*.

And then there she was, at the back of the small scrum, patiently waiting for the others to finish up, giving him that half smile which left Anthony once again feeling that whatever was to be had already happened.

That they already were.

"What do you think of him?" Mary asked Felix.

"He's good."

"Good, meaning . . ."

"He's heartfelt."

"Sure sounded like it," she said, refraining from sharing her vague misgivings. "Anyways, here's my card."

Felix showed her the card that she laid on him before.

"Now I have doubles."

* * *

Sensing eyes on him, Royal looked around until he saw Tutti Speedwell standing alone by the T-shirt table, staring at him as if she should know who that man was, but couldn't place his face.

"Ms. Speedwell." Royal coming over to her. "Royal Davis."

"*Oh.*" A puff of a word, Tutti both relieved and saddened.

She was wearing a PGD tee and a pair of baggy shorts, Royal surprised to find a long-tailed peacock tattoo that began above one knee and ended at her ankle in a delicate sweep of feathers.

It took him a second or two to get back into the conversation.

"How are you holding up?"

"Not . . . Oh, you're a funeral man so I imagine you know. Nothing special about me."

She didn't mean anything by it, but "funeral man," to his ears, sounded like a variation of Henry Cotton's "Death Pimp."

"Well. I'll be giving your son a proper homegoing, I can guarantee you that." Royal just saying it to say it, having no idea if he could or couldn't.

Tutti pointed to Anthony down by the speaker's bench, standing in a loose horseshoe of people.

"I like what that man said, it made me feel inspirational."

The guy was pretty good up there, but as he spoke, Royal found himself vacillating between going with him full-on and feeling that there was something almost *too* earnest in his delivery.

"You think he can come to the funeral and talk about my son like that?"

"I can ask," Royal said, thinking it might not be a bad idea.

What did Calvin call him? *A very special guest.*

※ ※ ※

When the last of the tenants finally drifted off, that silver-eyed woman, pointedly not looking his way as if she was just, you know, *walking around*, began strolling in his direction. She was more solidly built than he first thought but carried it lightly, Anthony getting into how she moved, her stride, even in wander mode lazily powerful and core-deep, making him think of an athlete on her day off, all of which left him torn between wanting her to pick up the pace and just enjoying her calculated linger.

And when they were finally, if not exactly, face-to-face, both looking slightly off angle as if they had to get their heads screwed on properly before looking at each other full-on, one of the CMs took his turn on the mike, so they held off on talking, dragging out the anticipation of hearing each other's first words.

"Listen up." It was Martin, the scratch-bearded anger management CM, pacing on top of the playground bench.

"I didn't have no father to raise me. First, he was here, then when I was six, he wasn't.

"Every time after, I was looking in the street for him. If I saw some guy wearing his style of eyeglass frames or how he styled his hair, my heart would jump, I'd run up and see that it was someone else. Went on for years like that until one day I was so frustrated and angry I stabbed a man who I thought was him. And, I swear to God, to this very day I don't know if I stabbed him because I *thought* he was my father? Or because he *wasn't*.

"I went inside for that, came out with the same anger and wound up going right back in. After that, they needed to build a revolving door for me.

"One year I saw an individual splash gas on another individual who was locked in his cell then throw in a burning roll of toilet paper . . . That individual, *both* those individuals was me, the killer me on one end, and the lost soul me on the other . . .

"I watched that man like a running torch slamming himself into one wall then the other, and I felt nothing.

"The smell made me sick but I felt nothing. Why? Because I was living below waters in the lake of Dis. That is the darkest most frozen place in hell. Oh yeah, hell is cold, darkness is cold, people say it's hot but it's ice cold, like when you touch something frozen too long? It's like a burn, your skin turns as black as charcoal just like in fire . . ."

"He needs to work on his delivery," she said without turning to face him yet.

"I'll say."

I'll say. Anthony playing it back in his head, embarrassed by its nothingness.

"I swear, living here?" she said, finally turning to him. "I've been to so many of these stop-the-violence barbecues over the years, my blood's half Match Light."

"You can't be that old," he said, loosening up a little.

They kept turning to look at each other full-on, then partially turning away, as if fascinated by something in the distance.

"I'm forty-four," she said.

"I'm in my forties too."

"In your forties . . . I read that as you being younger than forty-four and you don't want to hurt my vanity. If you were older than, you'd just say the number."

"I'm forty-two."

"There you go." Then looking at him straight on again, "May I be blunt with you? You're a celebrity around here now but that doesn't impress me. In fact, you didn't do anything but be in the wrong place at the wrong time and kept breathing through it."

"No argument there." Anthony taking it in stride.

"I don't mean that to offend you, I just needed for you hear it from me, because, and strap in your seatbelt, we've been making sneaky eyes at each other since the door on in, and so if you have any interest in seeing me after today? I would be interested in seeing you, too. But I didn't want you to get the wrong impression as to why. First, I just liked looking at you, I liked your eyes . . ."

"*My* eyes?" Anthony almost laughing.

". . . and then I liked what you said up there and how you said it. You seem like a sensitive individual with a good head on your shoulders. And that's it." Then after gauging his reaction to that, "See? You're smiling, that's a good sign that I just didn't make a fool of myself as I'm known to do in these houses whenever I open my big mouth."

"I'm smiling because . . ." Anthony cut himself short, not capable of putting into words how her crisp and smart delivery had his heart going up and up like an elevator.

"I'm just smiling . . ."

"Like I said, I'm forty-four and around here if you want to find that special certain someone at my age? Your competition has just graduated high school. But I don't care about that nonsense anymore, it's a waste of time and it shrinks whatever self-respect you have left.

"In fact, I haven't had a man in my bed for two years but to be honest? I can't say I miss it all that much."

She was feeling him out with that, and they both knew it.

"But if you're a man," he said, "you can be eighty and as long as you have some kibble in your pocket the world is yours."

"And a feminist too, what do you know about that."

"I don't know what I am," Anthony said, thinking, *Easy on the humility*.

Was he looking *into* her eyes or *at* them, wanting to ask her about those eerily riveting irises of hers but then imagining that every man, *scratch that*, every person she ever knew at some point asked her about her eyes and, wanting her to think of him as *different from all those others*, he kept his mouth shut.

"Can I tell you a little about myself without sounding like a egomaniac?"

"Please." Anthony just wanting to hear anything she had say.

"First off, my name is Anne Collins. I've been with the US Post Office for eighteen years, last five as a station manager in the Bronx.

"On paper, I'm married but it's more accurate to say that I'm just technically undivorced because I haven't seen that individual in ten years.

"I have a son Brian who's fourteen, see him over there?"

Anthony followed her finger to a skinny kid with heavy-framed glasses, a short Afro and a long sullen face, who was folding dozens of PGD T-shirts as if the chore was akin to doing house laundry in Rikers.

"He's not a bad kid, but he's drawn to the wrong crowd. I know that's what every mother is supposed to say when their child gets in trouble but it happens to be true. In fact, he's a bit of a nerd. When he was younger in sixth grade? The other boys started calling him Urkel until I talked to their parents. He still hates me for doing that, but I don't give a damn. In fact, you know how that crazy female governor in Alaska likes to call herself a Mama Bear? Well I'm a Mama Grizzly Bear, Polar Bear or what have you." Then, "Your turn. Or do you want to wait until later?"

Wait nothing; Anthony jumping right in: "I've been a teacher and a salesman but for the last year plus I've been on my ass and barely looking for something. The thing is, since they pulled me out of there last week, with all the publicity, a few places reached out with job offers but I'm kind of embarrassed about that. Like you said, all I did was not die."

"I think I overspoke about that."

"No, yeah, it's fine, it is what it is," Anthony said.

"Give me more," she said, moving a step closer to him.

He wanted to continue matching her electrifying candidness with his own but knew he could never fully do that, with her or anyone else.

But there was so much more to him than that, more of him to offer up to her that was legit and truthful and since he desperately wanted to do so, he willed himself once again to disremember that day and that night.

"It's been a bad last two years for me all around. First, my parents died one after the other then I found an old cocaine habit that I thought I lost, which in terms of getting myself together was . . .

"Then I lost two jobs one after the other because I just couldn't . . ."

"Go on . . ." she said.

"My wife tried to pull me up out of myself but after a while she'd just had it with me so she took her daughter and left."

"Do you love her?" she asked in that tone of hers that he was coming to think of as *"Blunt Lite."*

"My wife?" Anthony hesitated.

"Yes, no, maybe . . ."

"No. That's over."

"Her daughter you said. Not yours?"

"Not by blood, but . . ."

"You love *her*, though, right?"

"Of course," he murmured, going off to relive the two, maybe three times he showed up wildly late to pick Willa up from school when she was little because he was busy chasing down powder, that sad scenario common enough fare in any NA or AA meeting, but what murdered him then and what murdered him now was the fact that she had never complained when he was late, just seemed to take it as her lot and back then he was not in any kind of shape to let her blue quietness get through to him.

And then in a flush of panic he realized that he still hadn't called her.

He could tell that this Anne Collins was reading him clean because she refrained from saying something comfortingly stupid.

"Are you still getting high?"

Finally, a softball.

"If I was, I wouldn't be here talking to you. You or anyone else."

"I'm not judging you," she said. "I had my time with it as well." Then looking across the playground at her son, she added, "Last time for me was when the rabbit died." Then, turning back to him, "So how'd you quit?"

"I went to the meetings, but I didn't quit from following the steps. I think, no, I know, that I stopped because it was so goddamn exhausting, all that twenty-four seven thinking about, scoring it, not scoring it, and all for what," he said, leaving out the overwhelming everyday shame of it all.

"Whatever it takes it takes as long as it takes for real," she said. "For me, all it ever did was take my nobody and made it feel like somebody but for only as long as it lasts and then come the wee hours. I imagine you know about the wee hours."

"Of course."

"In the end," she said, "cocaine is all about loss."

He had never heard such a compact summary of cocaine despair like that, and the precision of her words, in her voice, filled him joy.

"I need to tell you," he said, "the way I described myself to you just now? I swear, there's something going on inside me these days, that . . . I feel like I'm about to come into myself in a way that I couldn't have done before . . ."

"Before . . ." The word hanging there.

Before what, she meant. Before the building collapse she meant.

Again, the magician faltered, needing to divert both himself and his audience.

"It's like . . . the night before it happened, I was walking on Lenox, and I wound up in a storefront prophecy church. Prophetess Irene."

"Prophetess Irene, huh?"

"Yeah, I know. When I walked into the room, she immediately starts to size me up probably wondering if I'm friend or foe, then goes back to speaking in tongues, predicting this and that, comets, terror attacks, subway delays, some kind of mass virus, and then she singles me out."

Then, channeling her voice that night—

This man has pain, God
Has seven-eight years pain in his heart, God
But his tables have turned, God
His heart is healing, God
He was first then last, God
He will be first again, God . . .

"So now you believe in prophecy?"

"Not really."

"Well, that's good." Then, after thinking about it a little more, she added, "'Not really' isn't the same as 'no.'"

"Do you want to hear the rest of what she said? Because . . ."

"I do."

Once again, inhabiting the prophetess—

I see your angels hovering around that spot on that man's back, God . . .

They see something there, God

They're worried about something there, God

They know like you know, God, there's something right there inside of him that if he don't get it out, it's going to kill him, God . . .

"You're good," she said without any edge. "I could listen to you all night long."

And then, to his amazement, she blushed.

"When I got home"—Anthony looking away from her but still seeing the color come into her cheeks and throat—"I stripped down and checked myself in the mirror, but I didn't see anything. But then look . . ." Lifting his shirt halfway and twisting his hips so that she could see the purple-and-blue mottle.

"When they pulled me out they said I'd been lying on a sharp chunk of stone the whole time I was down there. It didn't hurt then but now it takes me twenty minutes to roll out of bed. Right where she said she saw those angels."

She took the liberty of lightly exploring the wound, her fingertips rough and vivid on his skin.

Swept away by her touch, he found himself elatedly reciting again, "'His heart is healing,' she said . . ."

"That's a good thing," she murmured, her fingers slowly sliding away.

"'His tables have turned,' she said . . ."

"Well maybe they have," something like a guarantee in her electric eyes before she was called away.

※ ※ ※

Towards the end of the day, when the street rally began to die down and the CMs and some of the tenants started folding up the collapsible tables while others were plastic-wrapping the uneaten food then packing it into Styrofoam picnic coolers, Felix continued to shoot what he hoped might be worth it—although he knew that none of these images would make the cut because he was tired and losing his eye.

"Hey, Felix . . ."

When he turned, Marvin, the Bronx Home News guy, took a shot of him. It was something that, for all of Felix's everyday stealing images of the other, had never happened to him before. It felt uncomfortable to say the least, more like a mugging of his essence than a simple snap of his surface. But he did that to others so . . .

Holding his camera pressed to his chest like a miniature pet, Marvin sidled up to him.

"Let me tell you what this is all about for me," he said. "You take a picture, you make a memory and you have created something. You have done something with your day. And if you do that every day? Then you have done something with your life."

*, *, *,

"See, I wasn't like Martin growing up because I never knew my father to miss his absence like that."

It was Raymond up there on the bench now, speaking to the last stragglers. "I was my own man full born. But when I got locked up the last time, I left behind a young son fatherless. Didn't think about that too much, either. Well I should have because right now that boy is living in the same facility I had been in before I got paroled.

"I temporarily stopped trying to visit him because he refuses to see me but even if he had a change of heart, I wouldn't know what to say to him except, 'Son, I'm so sorry for not being there for you.' It isn't much, but right now that's all I got."

*, *, *,

As Jimmy started to pack for his shift at the apartment, Mary read out loud some of what she had written down from Anthony's talk.

"'I had died. I had experienced the nothingness of death. But I was just a visitor to that black land.' And this: 'To be a man among men as defined and dictated by Mother Street.'"

"Ok." Jimmy reaching for his shirts. "And that bugs you, why."

"Because it's too eloquent. It's like, most people after they've been through something bad, some trauma, whenever you ask them to describe what it was like, they can start off ok, but then it's 'I need a minute,' 'Hang on,' or, 'I'm sorry, I can't do this,' because now you got them reliving it and every detail they give you feels like it's being yanked out of their guts."

"Makes sense."

"But this guy, when he talked about his ordeal he never hesitated, not so much as a twitch. It was like it happened to someone else," Mary said, momentarily discarding how Anthony's words had also moved her deeply because one thing had nothing to do with the other.

"Maybe to get through it he had to compartmentalize himself," Jimmy said.

"Maybe."

"Or maybe he's just happy to be alive."

"Maybe."

"Plus, it was a speech, right? So he probably knew what he was going to say beforehand."

"Could be."

And that was that.

When Mary started to leave the room, Jimmy took a step in her direction and cleared his throat.

"Can I talk to you about something?"

"What."

Mary hating the suddenly lilting tentativeness in his voice because it made her feel like he was about to delicately hit her with some kind of horrible news.

"Jimmy, *what*."

"I just want to say that after we had that, you know, not argument exactly, the last time we talked? I was thinking about the kids today and, I don't know, I think I was more into them when they were younger. I'm not saying I'm not into them I'm just, they're just different people now. They used to talk a lot more, ask questions, want to do things . . . I mean that's just the way it goes, I get it, but . . ."

"Oh cut the crap. You're just trying to make me feel better after what you said to me."

He gave it a moment before answering.

"Look, that night I wasn't talking to you so much as I was trying to handle you."

"Just like you're doing now?"

"Mare, for whatever it's worth, after you walked out, I felt like shit for talking to you like that."

"You just said you were handling me not talking to me, so make up your mind." Mary enjoying/not enjoying this little bit of payback.

"Mare, I'm trying to apologize to you."

And he was, she knew, even though she was just as guilty for boxing him in like that, pressing him for more of what she didn't want to hear about her and the kids in the first place.

"Mare." Her name like a plea.

And what if he *was* trying to make her feel better, what was so bad about that? Too many people in her life would have reacted to her distress by doubling down on what they had done to create it.

Jimmy Roe. Like she remembered feeling about him at his most degraded, cuffed to his bed in the hospital: *This is a decent guy.*

Without thinking too hard about it, Mary took a step toward him, not knowing what she was going to do when she got there.

"Oh!" Jimmy's sudden outburst checking her progress. "I have to tell you something. The school had me subbing for the regular teacher in an Earth Science class this morning?"

"Oh yeah?"

"They were in the middle of the astronomy packet, one of the kids got up to read his report on dwarf stars, you know the difference between white dwarfs, red, yellow, brown and I think orange, and after he finishes, this sleepy-looking girl raises her hand." Jimmy imitating the gesture, languidly lifting his arm, his wrist curled limply at the top. "Mister Roe? Where do *stahs* go on a *stahless* night?"

Good question, Mary thought.

"And you said . . ."

"'They're behind the clouds, Lilian.'"

"Right."

A good piece of cake, Mary hearing her grandmother's voice when she said it.

"So, I have to tell you something," he said for the second time. "This woman from the school asked me out for dinner."

"Ok," Mary said, then, "Asked *you* out."

"I'm not sure I want to go, but if I do, I don't want any secrets between us and I don't want it to fuck up what we're trying to get done."

"She's a teacher?"

"Just be honest with me," Jimmy said, "because I can wait."

"What does she teach?"

"Fifth grade."

"What do you like about her? I'm just curious."

"Honestly? She thinks I'm all that."

"No. I said what do *you* like about *her*."

"I don't know, she's funny."

"Funny. Funny like how. Like witty-funny? Whoopee-cushion funny? Like a keen observer of human nature funny?" Mary's face felt like red ice.

Jimmy stared at her, then stared at her some more.

"Seriously, I'm just curious."

"She's . . . forget it."

Esposito. *How the fuck does he not know?*

"So, hold on a second, I'm just curious. She doesn't have a face? A body? No legs, tits, no ass?"

"*Christ*, I said I could *wait*."

"*Then wait!*" She didn't mean to bark at him like that, but that's what she did, leaving her feeling stripped to her core.

"You got it," he said, turning away from her.

She stood there staring at the back of his head.

"Listen," she said, "I forgot some stuff at the apartment, so I need to go back. Actually, you know what? I'll just stay there another night. You can give me an extra night here sometime down the line."

"You sure?"

"Absolutely," she said.

※ ※ ※

"How would you feel if your wife came to you and said, 'Oh by the way, this guy asked me out'?"

"She wouldn't," Esposito said.

"But if she did."

"She wouldn't."

"But what if she . . ."

"She wouldn't . . ."

"Got it."

The room they had rented tonight was too small and smelled like cherry air freshener.

"Are you sure your husband never stepped out on you? I find that hard to believe." Then added, "Nothing personal."

"Well if he did, he was really good at it."

And maybe he was—Mary speed-combing through their years together for anything he'd ever done that gave her pause: a see-through lie, or coming home crazy late, or coming into the house and going straight into the shower—anything he'd ever done that gave her pause.

"Actually, there was this one time about a half a year ago, he comes home, I'm in the kitchen, and I get a whiff of something when he passes me. Smells like, I want to say turned over earth, or mushrooms, but . . ."

Mary took five to try and bring back that scent but the fruity room freshener got in the way.

"He had a moustache back then, and I thought maybe it was coming from that, so I tell him he's got some stuff on his face, reach out and brush it, give my fingers the sniff test, and I couldn't swear to it, but they pretty much smelled like lady-juice."

"The balls on him," Esposito said dryly.

"I mean, who am I to complain."

"Exactly."

"I don't mean us. I mean at the time I hadn't given him any reason not to. Hadn't touched him, kissed him, it felt like since forever, so why shouldn't he get some in his life? He's not a bad guy."

"This is not nothing," he said.

"What's not nothing," she asked, then, *Oh*. "No, this is not nothing. But it is what it is."

"Which is what."

"Oh, come on, Ralph."

"I think we're very good together," he said.

"I agree."

And as far as she was concerned that was the end of it.

"You know what I like about you?" Esposito asked, trying to make an end run around the slammed door.

Mary waited. And waited, but he never said what.

After that she shifted the conversation to voice her doubts about Anthony Carter, but she couldn't tell if Esposito's noncommittal reaction was a function of him being reluctant to pass judgment on someone he was hearing about secondhand, or him just being withholding in order to get back at her for slighting their relationship. Or maybe he just didn't hear a word that came out of her mouth. And she certainly wouldn't mention how moving she had found some of Anthony Carter's words, because knowing Esposito, she'd only come across as a weak sister.

"Alright, look," he sighed. "Maybe I could make some calls for you."

Make some calls for you—Esposito-ese for enough with the talking.

She wasn't in the mood anymore, if she ever had been to begin with this night, but she didn't want to be trapped with him in high-sulk mode because it would shrink the room to the size of a shoebox.

"So, not my idea, but we had our first couples therapy session the other day, you know, weep, shout, weep, shout . . ." Esposito speaking to her afterward as they dressed on their respective sides of the bed.

"And when it was finally over, the shrink asked me to stay behind. We're alone, she says to me, 'After the first session I always make a bet with myself—how many times is this guy going to keep showing up?' Looks me in the eye. 'Got any hot tips for me, Ralph?'"

"She's smart then," Mary said neutrally, thinking, if in fact Jimmy did hook up with this fifth-grade teacher she would never again make a fool of herself by grilling him about it. Besides, there were a thousand ways to check this bitch out without him ever knowing.

Not that she ever would.

* * *

Anne Collins; Anthony sitting in the living room by himself on this night. Anne Collins, Anne Collins; Anthony grinding his teeth in happiness.

* * *

The next day Royal parked his limo-hearse in front of the brownstone and tapped the horn.

Felix rose up from the top step and hoisting his camera bag over a shoulder began sidling his way down through the regulars to the sidewalk.

"Monster," Trip called after him, "you're not supposed to get in that thing until *after* you're dead."

Before he got to the passenger-side door, Royal came out on the driver side. Felix assumed that he was about to help him with his other gear, but the funeral man walked right past him to the men on the stoop, zeroing in on O-Line.

"Butch Carver."

"Who's calling?" O-Line barely looking at him.

"Royal Davis, we were in Alpha House together at LC."

"Ok . . ."

Felix could tell that Royal was making an effort not to notice O-Line's two canes.

"When you were with the Generals I watched every game. I was proud to know you."

"Ok."

"It's good to see you again." Offering his hand.

"You too." O-Line barely grazing Royal's palm.

Royal stood in front of the stoop for a few seconds more, everyone's eyes on him except the guy he'd come over to see.

"He didn't remember you?" Felix asked from the shotgun seat as they rolled west towards the river.

"He did."

"Why was he throwing shade then? Was he mad about something between you?"

"No, he was just embarrassed to be seen like that. You got to understand, when that dude was playing OG for us back then, the QB had time to read a book before he threw a pass. You're making an end run out of the backfield? You wanted that man right in front of you clearing the way. He was the most brickhouse dude on the team. Fast feet, fast reflexes and smarts. Horizon League Conference first team three years running then the USFL. Why not the NFL? Because the Generals offered him twice as much. Fucking canes. If I was thinking straight back there? I never would have gotten out of the car."

"You played football there too?"

"Basketball."

"Really."

"That's a story for another time," Royal said, "and it ain't a good one."

After clocking out for the day Mary decided to take a shot at more check-cashing spots, this time hitting businesses farther away from her first canvass: two more money exchanges that only took government-issued checks, a cashier at the last telling her about a laundromat owned by a guy named Pep, who was known on the street for providing that service.

When she entered the long and humid laundromat, Pep was hard to miss. Bald and fat as a zeppelin, he sat perched on top of a medium-height ladder, just high enough that the women needing to pay for their drop-off loads or get change for the machines had to lift their chins and raise their arms to him as if they were appealing to a God.

"How you doing?" Mary said, having to raise her eyes to him like everyone else. "Can I talk to you for a sec?"

When they sat down alongside an empty folding table, he had no problem answering any of her questions because he was "bonded." Mary had no idea if that meant he was paying off the cops or passing on a percentage to someone higher up the family ladder.

It turned out that unlike most other street bankers, Pep accepted all checks, private or second party, kept no records of the transactions and had no file on his customers because he pretty much knew everyone by sight. To Mary it sounded like he was just begging to be ripped off by any number of hustlers coming in with bogus checks but he didn't have that problem because after word of how violent his "recouping" encounters were, nobody in their right head would knowingly pass him bad paper.

"He came in once," Pep said, looking at Diaz's photo.

"When was that?"

"Maybe two months back?"

"Just that once?"

"Yeah, he never came back."

"Do you have a record of the check?"

"I told you, I don't keep records like that."

"That's right because you have a memory like a camera."

"I said like a computer."

"Like a computer. So you remember the bank, the amount, the name of the person who signed . . ."

"Nope. You know why? Because he never cashed it here. The guy just walked in with it, we talked a little and then he left."

"Why would he do that?"

"Because whoever told him about me, forgot to also tell him that I only pay out seventy-five percent of the amount because the other twenty-five, that's the price of my trust."

* * *

"Where are we going?' Felix asked as the limo-hearse took the GW Bridge exit off the Henry Hudson Parkway. "I thought your place was in Harlem."

"It is," Royal said. "This is an associate parlor."

"A branch?"

"Something like that."

Mid-bridge, Royal gestured towards the Jersey-side Palisades. "Every time I drive past I try to imagine what those cliffs looked like before the white man came on the scene."

"They probably more or less looked the same," Felix said. "I mean they're cliffs. What can you do to a cliff?"

A half hour later Royal pulled into the rear parking lot of Homegoings, a funeral parlor on the outskirts of East Orange that he had rented for the day from a funeral director he met and actually got along with at a convention of African American undertakers in Atlantic City.

The key to the parlor was hidden inside a plastic stone under a real bush alongside one of the four faux-marble pillars flanking the front door.

Stepping inside, Royal flipped a light switch to reveal the sizable reception room, as bland in layout and decor as the lobby of a Best Western. That being said, compared to his own place it was at least shipshape with nothing visually amiss; no spittoon-stained ceiling tiles or balding couches, and no telltale waft of mildew coming up from the basement carpet.

As far as Felix was concerned, never having been inside Royal's parlor, he didn't understand why they had to cross a state line to shoot the promo in a place that looked more like a suburban tax prep office than a house of the dead. Nonetheless, a house of the dead is what it was, which, despite or maybe because of its blank vibe, gave it, at least in his own mind, a certain charisma.

"You know," Royal said looking around, "at first, I was thinking I could just get away with using the standard voice-over slideshow of flowers, praying hands, chapel and whatnot, but I always prefer the human touch."

Entering the director's sizable office, Royal began to remove all personal items, family photos mainly, from the desk, then came around to where Felix had set up the camera.

"Show me how to look through this thing."

"You just look," Felix said, which Royal proceeded to do, hunching over squint-eyed. "Do me a favor, go sit at the desk."

Royal peered through the lens to see what else could be an embarrassing giveaway, for example all the name-writ-large certificates, diplomas and award plaques behind Felix's head. Stepping around the camera, he went back behind the desk intending to take down anything that had the other director's name.

"Wait, wait." Felix waving him away, then taking a photo of the wall as they found it.

"Just so afterwards we know where everything goes."

"Too late for the desk though, right?"

"Right."

After Felix had finally cracked the mystery of how to properly light the room, Royal settled in at the desk. "We good?"

"I think so."

"Then let's do it," Royal said, reaching into a shopping bag at his feet and bringing out a large clock and an elaborate fake crown, which he placed on opposite ends of the desk.

"Ready."

"Hold on," Felix said, "what's with the props?"

"You'll see. Go."

"It's your funeral," Felix said, unaware of his own pun.

"My name is Royal Davis, and I am the owner and director of the

Royal Davis Funeral Home and Chapel, a multi-generational family-owned institution in the heart of Harlem. And like my father and grandfather before me, I take it as my personal mission to attend to the final needs of our great community and beyond, because . . ." Royal paused to slide the oversized clock front and center on the desk, ". . . when it's your time, it's your time, but before that time, one of the most important things you can do is to prepare for when that time comes."

"Stop, stop . . ." Felix called out, rising from the camera.

"What?"

"You have to lose the clock. It's . . ."

"Yeah, you're right." Royal laughed. "I'm just trying to have some fun with this whole thing, because . . ."

"And I have to tell you, whatever you're thinking about doing with that crown . . ."

"Let's just see. Go." Royal waited until Felix was hunkered over the viewfinder again, then got back into it.

"Our pre-planning package will ensure that when you pass on you will pass on with an untroubled mind. No matter what your financial reality might be, rich, indisposed or in between, we'll find a way to work with you including all paperwork, outside institutional coordination, transportation and a free visual record of the memorial service and burial courtesy of our in-house master documentarian.

"So, let us take care of it all for you and you'll have the time and space to process your emotions without any material distractions. My name is Royal Davis," reaching for the crown, "and I will treat you royally."

But instead of crowning himself, Royal exploded in laughter then tossed the thing across the room.

"You know what all this stupidness is about?" he said to Felix, still behind the camera. "It's about me hating my fucking job. Sorry for wasting your time, you're a good kid."

"Why don't we take a break then do it again but without the props," said the director of the promo and to his surprise the adult in the room agreed.

"Just shut the door behind you," Royal said.

Back out in the reception area, Felix, starting out at the farthest wall, began shooting while slow-walking towards the closed door as if taking people on a journey to see the great man himself.

* * *

It had all started in Union, South Carolina, with Royal's great-great-grandfather's death. At the time, his son, Royal's great-grandfather Elgin, was eight years old. For the boy, it was a day of revelations; although he was scared to death of death in the abstract, he discovered, sitting by his father's inert body lying atop a bedspread on the living room couch, that he wasn't scared of it in the flesh, which thrilled him to the core.

Elgin's second revelation came about with the arrival of the funeral director, Beverly Harris. He'd never seen anyone in Union, white or Black, as splendidly dressed as that striking man, coming into the house with his black two-piece suit with satin peak lapels and satin-covered buttons, a gold brocade vest over white wing-collar shirt and a matching gold foulard tie. And he was handsome too, although in an outfit like that you could have a face like a hatchet and still wind up in the movies.

Mr. Harris, or Bev as he preferred Elgin to call him, took a liking to this kid, who announced right off the bat, "I'm not afraid!" and allowed him to watch as he bound up the body, transferred it to a flatbed cart, and rolled it out the door to his open-backed carriage, inviting Elgin to sit up front with him for the short trip back to the funeral parlor, where he stayed for dinner with Bev, his wife, and three sons, Elgin resenting those boys although he never let it show at the table.

When he returned to his house that night he announced that he was going to be a funeral man someday and that's what he became. Followed by his sons and his sons' sons and his sons' sons' sons, Royal and his two brothers, whether they liked it or not.

Royal did not like it.

As a small forward and sometimes shooting guard playing for Loyola Christian, a midsized Jesuit-run college back in the 1980s, he had been a three-year first-team all-star in the Horizon League

Conference hoping to get picked up in the NBA draft, but that didn't happen. He could have blamed his coach for not bringing scouts to watch him play, or the sex scandal his senior year that painted the whole team with a toxic brush even though only one player was indicted, but in fact, the truth of it was that he just didn't have the size or skill set needed to compete at the professional level.

After graduation, his father insisted that he come into the family business, but Hell no, said the young man, who chose to extend his basketball life by playing overseas; first in Israel for one season with a team sponsored by a supermarket chain, after which he played one season for a team in Budapest—or more specifically Pest—which turned out to be the loneliest year of his life, Royal hating the language, the politics, the food, and the way they stared at him on the street. There was one other Black player out of Baylor on that team, each of them known as the "other Black guy," as in, Sam and Dave, Kid 'n Play, Buck and Bubbles, can't tell one from the other; so they avoided each other's company as much as they could. And those goddamn fans, animals, making low monkey sounds and throwing food on the court.

And these were *their* fans.

In his last game, someone threw a hamburger at him. Before the referee could blow his whistle, Royal scooped it off the hardwood, climbed into the stands and mashed the slobby meat in the man's face.

He probably could have kept bouncing around after that, but it would have been for one Eastern European Podunk team after another, with nobody to talk to and no money, so he came home, but didn't tell his father that he was back for close to two years in which he tried a couple of things—real estate, a restaurant, another restaurant—but nothing took and so in debt up to his neck, broke to the broke . . .

*, *, *,

"I'm just going to look around," Felix announced to the empty reception hall then took off on another photo safari, shooting the chapel, the conference room, the family room, all as impersonal as airport lounges.

But then he discovered the showroom for coffins, each one as sleek as a high-end sports car, their names either sounding like summer retreats—The Azurest, The Glory Rest, The Riverside—or historical players—The Pharoah, The King David, The Cleopatra, The Samson and even The Pocahontas—the remainder evoking the starry vault—The Aurora, The Celestial and The North Star; Felix having some fun in here, capturing both the collective gleam and the singular luxury of each ride until he lost his eye and left.

On his way back to the reception area, he passed an unmarked door that he hadn't noticed before, so . . .

Inside was dark, close and smelling of chemicals, so at first, he thought it was a storage room for cleaning supplies. But as his eyes adjusted to the gloom he first made out the gurneys, parked at haphazard angles to each other, and then the bodies, three men, one naked, the other two barefoot but otherwise dressed in suit and tie.

He had never been so physically close to a corpse before, let alone three in such a cramped space. Feeling both drawn and horror-stricken he stood there as motionless as if he had just stepped on the pressure cap of a booby-trapped mine.

The concreteness of death was unknown to him, so he kept expecting some kind of mitigating small movement or sound but the absolute stillness and the absolute silence were even more of a shock to his senses than the bodies themselves.

The hand, coming from behind to rest on his shoulder, had him shouting in terror.

"I wondered where you went to," Royal said then, glancing at the bodies. "Shit, I wish I had three."

* * *

Mary was at home when she got the call from Ray Scanlon at Verizon. The cell tower that caught the pings off Christopher Diaz's phone on the night that he called his wife was in upstate Chatham in Columbia County.

"I got stopped up here..."

The Chatham PD had only a dozen or so officers, so she wasn't too surprised that the one who answered the phone was the chief, George Gutterman, a garrulous retired detective out of Brooklyn.

After a few back-and-forth niceties, he told her he could hear the Bronx in her voice which, he quickly added, was meant as a compliment because it made him homesick.

"Where are you posted?"

"East Harlem. I'm in Community Affairs."

"Community Affairs. So you have the temperament of a saint, right?"

"Depends who you ask."

"I retired out of the Eight-Three squad, then got this gig up here which was great because I was sick of all the stupidity. So, what happens? I'm here three days, walking out of a supermarket, some kid on a bike, on the sidewalk mind you, runs into me full speed and I'm two months in a body cast. This is after twenty years in a war zone without a scratch."

"Jesus..."

She liked the sound of his voice, furred and amiable with just a touch of broken glass in it.

"Irony squared, right? Did you ever read Appointment in Sumeria?"

"Can't say I have, Chief."

"Well, if you ever do, it was just like that."

"I'll have to buy it."

"Or you could probably download the e-book. So what do you need?"

At first, sedated by all the small talk, she thought he was still talking about books.

"Do you know about the building collapse in Harlem last week?"

"I do."

"I'm trying to find someone who lived in the building still unaccounted for. Name is Christopher Diaz. Last we heard of him was from the night previous, a phone message to his wife that came from around your area saying he was being held up, so I was wondering if he maybe might have gotten jammed up in a traffic stop. I can shoot you everything I have on him except the make, model and plate of the car."

"Well one thing I can tell right now is that there's been some kind of bug going around this last week that's got us down to three police, so if he did get pulled over it wasn't by us. Do you know what he was doing here?"

"I'm pretty sure driving someone up from the city. That's how he makes his money."

"But you don't know who."

"Nope. If I did . . ."

"Ok, shoot me what you got and I'll call around. Oh, while I have you, did you ever run into Iris Colon from the Two-Three squad?"

"Sure, I know Iris."

"What do you think of her?"

"That sounds like a trick question. She's your ex or something?"

"You're good."

"Then no comment."

"No comment, she says." Mary picking up a touch of rue in his tone. "Ok, Mary, give me your number, I'll call you back on this one way or the other."

* * *

"Look at this shit." Royal cursing the multi-mile creep of cars heading to the GWB.

"Can I ask you something? When you said on the video that you had a free in-house master documentarian, was that supposed to be me?"

"Only if you want to be."

"Yeah, ok . . ." Felix laughed, then, "I filmed a funeral once. Well, actually a memorial."

"Oh yeah?" Royal barely listening.

"It was for my father."

"Must have been hard on you."

Was it? "Yes and no."

"Tell me about it." Royal meant it as a generic expression of commiseration but Felix took it as a literal command.

"It started when he was dying in the hospital, and he called me up to come visit him, but he said I should come alone which was surprising because in my whole life I could count the times we spent alone on the fingers of one hand."

"Unh."

"I always had the feeling that adopting me was my mother's idea, not his. In fact if it was left up to him . . ."

"You're adopted?" Royal started to listen.

"And it didn't help that right after they took me in, my mom, who they assumed couldn't have kids, goes and gives birth to two real children over the next three years."

"'Real' children."

"I was being ironic." Felix's face turning colors.

"Ok." Royal knowing better than to challenge that. "So you go to the hospital . . ."

"So, I go to the hospital and, I'm nervous because he always made me nervous, and he tells me that he wants to make, what he calls, a farewell video for the family.

"And that he wants me to do the filming . . . And, I'm, 'Dad, I don't know the first thing about cameras, I don't even know which end to look through . . .' At which point I see that there's a Nikon D300 still in its box on the windowsill.

"'Then take this home and learn. Come back when you're ready and we'll go for it.'"

"There you go." Royal still stuck on "adopted" as in, "unwanted?" As in, "orphan?"

"When I get back to the house I'm hiding it from my mother and brothers, go up to my room and that's what I did. It took me all the next day to get the basics down and then I'm back at the hospital. This time, I see he's out of bed, in his street clothes, sitting in one of the two chairs in his room.

"I had to ask him to switch to the other chair because the sunlight coming over his shoulder where he was sitting, all I could make out of him was his silhouette.

"It wasn't easy for him to do that, given the shape he was in, but when I tried to help him get up he waved me off.

"When he's finally settled in and I'm all squared away on my end, he takes a speech that he wrote out of his pocket, puts on his reading glasses and . . . we're off.

"It went on for maybe a half hour, but the thing is, I was so worried about doing this right that I didn't hear one word of what he said. Next thing I know he's got his hand up. 'We're done, Felix, you can turn that off now. Thank you.'"

"Baptism by fire, huh?"

He didn't think Felix had heard him and it wasn't worth repeating.

"And it wasn't until two weeks later, after he died, that I finally played the video for my brothers and my mother. And even though he specified that I wasn't to show it to them until after his death, I was still braced for them to be furious that I did this without telling anyone. In fact, I was so knotted up that once again, I didn't hear a word that he said.

"But when it was over, they all got up sobbing like babies, came around and hugged me, everybody. 'I can't believe you did that for us, Felix. It must have been so hard for you, Felix. We love you for this, Felix, bladdie-blah.'"

"Must have been something of an eye-opener for you."

"For me? No, I was just relieved that the video went off without a hitch. The thing is I never cried, not once, not about the video, or about him dying. I don't know why."

"To me, it sounds like you still feel . . ."

"I didn't use the camera after that for a few weeks," Felix said, "but I carried it around everywhere I went. And I mean, everywhere, to the point that I forget about having it in my hand. My mother has the video now, and I can see it whenever, but I never do and I still don't know what he said on it. I think I'm afraid that he might not have mentioned my name."

"I bet he did." Another bland comment that went straight out the window. Despite that, Royal felt himself getting a feel for how isolated Felix must have been in that family home. And now he chose to live in a brownstone cut up into kitchenettes with a bunch of men that he didn't understand the first thing about.

"Before the memorial service my mother asked me to give one of the eulogies but I begged out, because I didn't know how I felt about him and I didn't want to say the wrong thing."

"You told her that?"

"No, of course not. I just said I'd rather keep my feelings to myself. But since I had the camera with me I started to film the others who got up there, and since then I shoot something just about every day of my life."

"Well, making you the cameraman that day?" Royal said, wanting to give him something for his pains. "Of all his sons, maybe he knew you needed to do this the most. Maybe that was his parting gift to you. I mean, look what came out of it for you."

Rattled, Felix armed himself with drollery. "I'd rather he'd of just gifted me with money."

* * *

Her cell rang while she was once again unpacking—or was it packing? All of this endless house shuffling sometimes made her lose track of whether she was going to, or coming from, occasionally to the point where she caught herself packing her bag in the middle of unpacking it.

The phone. Despite her last too-close encounter at the motel, Mary half hoped it was Esposito, but it was George Gutterman, the Chatham chief.

"So, I checked with the troopers and the county sheriffs, and there were two DUI collars that night, one in Coxsackie, one in Kinderhook, both known locals, and a rabbi who blew a light in Copake. Doesn't sound like your guy."

"Ok, Chief, thanks for trying."

"Hold on. You never really answered. Iris Colon. What do you think of her?"

"I think she's a good person. I like her."

"Yeah, she was," then correcting himself, "Is."

"Well, I owe you one," Mary said, "so reach out if you need anything."

The chief took a moment before responding, Mary wondering if he had hung up. "Thanks," he finally said, "I'll keep that in mind."

* * *

When Royal finally pulled up in front of Felix's brownstone, Trip and Dupree were still out on the stoop, but thankfully not O-Line.

"I buried someone out of here last year," Royal said. "Charles White. Elderly guy, he used to run a Harlem memorabilia business out of his car. I couldn't understand why he would do that until I went up to his apartment to take the body. That place, you had to walk sideways for all the crap he kept in there. Just junk, old newspapers, busted chairs, a busted-up cello . . . The man had three pairs of brass andirons but no fireplace. His people told me he was an Ivy League graduate, too."

Felix had never heard of Charles White, but he knew this: all these men out here day and night; the brownstone was their kingdom right now, but in regards to them continuing to live here, their time was running out.

Whenever one of them left, for whatever reason, they were immediately replaced by mostly white and Asian grad students going to CCNY or Columbia or entry-level Wall Streeters, out-of-town young people like himself, living on the cheap, staying six months or so before disappearing and being replaced by their doppelgangers.

People like himself, a reality that Felix contemplated for a few hot moments every day before invariably retreating into a willed unknowingness.

"I should get to work on what we shot," Felix said, once again reaching for the door handle.

"Oh, forget that nonsense."

"Just let me fool with it." Felix wanting to offer him some consolation but without the pressure of having to come up with any insightful commentary. "You might be surprised."

"*Pest*," Royal said. "Can you imagine living in a place called that?"

In the kitchen that afternoon, Mary, on the phone with Ed Murray, the precinct commander of the 2-9, regarding the upcoming Community Board meeting later in the week, was only marginally aware of the TV playing in the living room. Because of some overzealous arrests made recently by a few of the younger, situationally tone-deaf cops in the Battle and Crawford Houses—the most egregious being collaring male teenagers for loitering with intent in front of the buildings they lived in—this next bi-monthly open house promised to be a humdinger.

As always, the trickiest part of the night for the precinct commander who ran the meeting—and when he needed to hand off a question to her in Community Affairs or the sergeant running the anti-crime unit—was to somehow apologize to the community without actually apologizing, and to defend the actions of these cops without seeming to defend them. Wrong was wrong, but there was only so much backing down any of them could get away with, because they were police addressing criticisms directed toward the actions of police, and their job, in the end, was to hold the fort for all police.

Once the call had ended and her hearing became more attuned to the sounds of the house, she realized that the muffled drone from around the bend was not coming from a TV show but from the tape of the Burns-Rivera fight which she had apparently forgotten to take out of the VHS player.

Coming into the living room she saw that Douglas, slouched on the couch, had made it through to the end of the seventh round, Rivera in his battered confusion walking with her father halfway across the ring to the wrong corner before catching himself and turning towards his own. Mary stepped in front of the TV, blocking Douglas's view, and tried to pop the tape before her son, who'd never seen the fight before, could watch his grandfather beat a man into a coma halfway through the next round.

"What are you doing!" the kid squawked.

But the old tape had somehow gotten jammed in the teeth of the old machine, so she had to yank the damned thing out by its thin acetate intestines in order to get it free.

"I was watching that!"

"You were," she said, gathering the gutted tape into a ball. "And now you're not."

Hearing *that tone* in her voice he knew better than to keep protesting.

However, as Mary began to leave the room, he thought it was safe to say one last thing.

"I never knew Grandpa was such a good fighter. I thought he was going to kill that guy."

Mary took that with her into the kitchen, sat with it for a few minutes then returned to the living room where Douglas was now playing a game on his phone.

"What was the other fighter's name, do you remember?"

Douglas, still hearing *that tone*, shut his phone off.

"Do you remember?"

"Danny Rivers?"

"Rivera. Let me tell what happened to him. In the next round after what you saw, your grandfather knocked him out but instead of hitting the mat he fell back against the ropes which kept him upright and seeing he's still on his feet and the referee wasn't calling it, your grandfather kept pounding him until he finally slid down to the mat unconscious."

"Whoa."

"*Whoa?*" Mary disappointed in his reaction. "Let me tell you about '*Whoa*' . . . That man was so badly concussed that by the time they brought in a stretcher he already had his first seizure. He was in the hospital for a month then in and out of rehabilitation centers for over a year. And even after all of that, the brain damage was so extensive that he could barely speak and whatever he did manage to say was borderline gibberish. He also lost the ability to recognize people including his wife and kids, and sometimes he got so lost out on the streets that it could take over a day to find him."

"Did Grandpa feel bad?"

"Bad doesn't even come close to what he felt. He reached out to Danny's wife and asked what he could do to help."

"And did he?"

"Help? Oh you bet. Money, for one thing, whatever he could spare which was never much, and whenever Danny would go AWOL for more than a few hours, especially at night, she'd call and my father would go out to find him."

"*Good.*"

"One night when I was eleven he had to take me with him because my mother was working the late shift at the hospital and he didn't want to leave me alone in the apartment, and oh my God the places we had to go."

"But you were a child."

Child. The word sounding oddly formal coming out of his mouth, as if he were striving for an adult tone, Mary experiencing a rush of tenderness towards him, which in turn morphed into a rush of remorse, so on with the story.

"So, I wind up going with him all over the Bronx. I didn't know this, I mean how would I, but apparently Danny had been struggling with drugs all his life, even when he was fighting, so at the time I didn't understand why we went to the places we did."

"Like where?"

"I remember going to an apartment in some projects, a park, a playground, stopping by a couple of street corners. And wherever we went, whoever he talked to, no one had seen Danny, or so they said, but they were all a little too friendly about it, which even to me, a kid, sounded like they were lying. And I'm sure it sounded the same way to him. And believe me, everybody knew your grandfather, knew who he was and what he was, but his reputation meant nothing to these people. I remember this one crew hanging out on the stoop of an old walk-up that probably had a dope apartment inside, my father goes up to them, they're like, 'Hey Champ, how you doing?'

"'I'm looking for Danny Rivera, did any of you . . .'

"'Danny? Oh man, I haven't seen him since forever.' 'Me neither.' 'I heard he stopped using,' lying to his face like that. He looks at the house. 'I'm going to go check inside, ok?'

"'Sure Champ, go ahead.'"

"But he didn't because at the last minute, he remembered that I was with him.

"'If you do see him, tell him I'm looking for him.'

"'You got it, Champ . . .' *Champ.* The contempt in how they called him that."

"Did he fight them?"

"Why would he?"

"Because maybe they killed Danny."

"Nobody knew what happened to Danny back then and nobody knows now."

"Then what did he do?"

"Who's 'he.'"

"Your father. Grandpa. After that when he couldn't find him."

"He dragged me to the Four-Two to file a missing persons. Like they were going to drop everything to find some ex-punchie dope addict. Then we went home and he called Danny's wife with the bad news and that was it. It's going on thirty years now and your grandfather still hasn't gotten over it."

"What happened to Danny's family? Did he still help them out?"

"As much as he could," she said and left it at that, leaving out of the story that whether it was out of pity, grief, loneliness or passion, Danny's widow/wife and her father eventually became lovers, meeting up at various hotels and motels around the outer boroughs for the better part of the next two years.

"Anyways, the good news is that Danny's kids made it through and his wife remarried. Ok I'm done."

* * *

Taking his parents' Volvo out of the building's garage, Anthony got to the restaurant too early and rather than grab a table and not order anything, he stood outside and waited for her.

Across the street was a housing project named for a president whose crudely painted face on the welcome sign made him look scared to death. A tall mobile brace of NYPD floodlights lock-wheeled on the pavement and trained on the nearest buildings made the tenants coming and going look like solar-powered zombies.

Next to it was a firehouse, two firemen on the sidewalk slap-boxing in front of the gleaming grille of a massive truck with two rear-mounted aerial ladders. And a few doors down from that was the ER entrance to the hospital where he had been held overnight for observation.

There was nothing out of the usual in all that he took in, but on this night, when he could feel his pulse beating in his fingertips, everything around him seemed flammable.

Where is she.

An outgoing ambulance abruptly charging up the subterranean ramp beneath the hospital hit the street on the scream, which sent him right back underground in his half sleep, inhaling the razored air, then reliving the helplessness of being strapped and braced, lowered and lifted.

"Every fucking ten minutes, like clockwork on the hour," some street-whack muttered as he speed-shuffled by.

Where is she.

Anthony tracked the man's bent frame steaming its way uptown until he saw her passing through a cone of streetlight, coming his way, but not seeing him yet.

At first he wasn't sure it was her because she was wearing tinted glasses and dressed for a *date*: dry-cleaned slacks, low heels and a pearl-button silk blouse. But there it was, her private and true face, so he held off on meeting her midway in order to continue to take her in like that.

*, *, *,

Back to avoiding each other's eyes, they watched the waitress fill the water glasses as if she were performing a miracle.

"This is nice," he managed to say.

"It's ok."

She was still wearing those tinted glasses indoors, Anthony guessing it was to hide those startling eyes of hers from the double-takers.

"I like it because they give you a lot more shrimp than Crab du Jour, plus I like these small table lights, sconces or whatever," she said, then added after a moment of fluttery silence, "I mean, most chains around here, the light's so ugly bright I feel like I'm eating in a terrarium."

"That's funny," he said, breathing through his mouth.

"Are you nervous?"

"Oh yeah."

"Me too," she said. "I might not eat a lot."

Anthony stared at her hands, resting on their sides, palm facing palm, the fingertips of each gently curled toward each other to make a split heart.

"I think I've been thinking about you so much," he said, "now that we're alone, I don't know what to say."

"The same," she said, reaching into her shoulder bag to bring out a large manila envelope. "So I brought some things to show you," taking out an old runny-colored Polaroid of a little girl and a woman who looked to be in her sixties.

"That's me and my Granna when I was about five. She died ten years ago but I still talk to her every day."

Before he could say anything, or even begin to understand what she was doing, she offered him next an envelope with three folded sheets of stationery.

"That's a letter she wrote to me on the day I was born. You don't have to read it."

"But if I wanted to . . ."

"You can read it later," she said, going back into her shoulder bag, this time bringing out something wrapped in tissue paper which she carefully unfolded on the table, revealing an Asian-featured doll: a young girl wearing a multicolored ceremonial gown, her synthetic hair piled high and studded with gold foil flowers.

"She's called a Hanbok doll. My father bought it for me when his unit was stationed in Korea. I couldn't sleep with it because it was too fragile so I had it right next to me on my night table for years. And last one . . ." Handing him a Saran-Wrapped heart made out of beige construction paper and folded in half. She flattened it out to display the childish writing inside, the haphazardly shaped letters written in undulating lines, the words, the ones he could make out at least, spelled phonetically.

"This is a Valentine's Day card that my son made for me when he was in first grade."

Still trying to process the intimacy of what she was sharing with him, he stared at her son's misshapen letters until they started to dance.

"Tell me what you're thinking," she said.

"I can't, because I'm still trying to think it."

"Then tell me something I don't know."

"About me?"

"About you. Anything."

"Ok, wait . . ."

"I'm waiting."

Her jump-on-it responses to his hesitation could have come across as pressuring but he knew better because he felt it too—this hunger for *what else, more, give me more*—questions, answers, stories, or, when words fail, like now, a little show-and-tell, all of it fueled by a fear of time running out.

"Talk to me," she said.

His first instinct was to tell her something charming and entertaining but he knew that if he did that it would be like telling her nothing.

"I've been thinking a lot about God since, you know. But it's a battle for me. My father was an atheist and loud about it, my mother, she'd go but I don't really know what she thought about things like God."

"Ok."

"I remember going to a men's prayer group in my grandparents' church after the service, and I was honest with them about my doubts. The leader says to me, 'Oh, have no doubt, He is here, He is in this room, and He wants you to open your heart to Him so that you can feel His presence.'

"'Well how do I do that?' I said.

"He says, 'Nothing to it. All you have to do is let go.'

"'Let go,' I said. 'Ok, I'll try.'

"'No don't try,' he says. 'Don't ask why, just let go.'

"'I'm trying.'

"He says, 'No, *don't* try. Just step back from yourself and watch what happens. It's the most amazing thing you'll ever feel.'

"'Ok, so "step back."' I'm telling myself, 'Ok, I'm stepping back . . .'

"'Just let go,' he says.

"'It's not easy . . .'

"'It is . . .'

"'Ok, I'll try.'"

Anthony came out of his reenactment, whirling his hands one over the other.

"But since the thing that happened to me I've been trying again because now I need to believe like I never did before but whenever I try to let go, like the man said, it just feels like an argument between me, myself, and I."

"The man said don't try."

"I don't know, I mean, what if it's just us out here, and that's it."

"Well, you know what they say, if you don't believe in God you damn well better be right."

She was smiling at him as she said it and without even thinking about it he reached out and brushed a lock of her hair away from her forehead, immediately after which they pretended that it didn't happen, her looking towards the front window, him at the swinging kitchen door.

When they turned to each other again, wherever she had gone in her head in that brief time came back with her, Anne looking like she was either trying to forget or remember something.

"After my son's father—I prefer to call him his sperm donor—left us, I told myself I am never going to be dependent on a man for survival ever again," she said.

"You have to be making decent money at the PO," he said, rolling with the transition.

"With my years in, I make seventy K plus overtime, job security, pension plan, paid time off, flexible spending account, income tax breaks, health, vision, dental, life insurance, fuel discounts, tuition assistance and free gym membership not that I ever used that one."

"I topped out at sixty-five."

"That's it? Public school teacher? Is that with or without the ten percent combat differential?"

"Without." Then, "How did we get talking about this?"

"We're just talking," she said.

"What's it like living in the Crawfords these days?" he asked.

"It used to be worse, then it was better, now it's worse again. But it still feels like home."

Her turn. "Of your parents, who was the white one?"

"My father. He was an Irish Italian Catholic who converted to Quaker. My mother had some Choctaw blood in her or so my grandparents claimed but no one would mistake her for Pocahontas."

"And what did they do?"

"To me?"

"For a living."

"My father taught high school. African American literature and history."

"The white parent."

"And as long as I can remember my mother was writing a history of her family going back to before the Civil War but as far as I know she never got around to finishing it."

"Is that right," she said, sounding impressed but he didn't tell her that in order to impress her; in fact, her reaction made him uneasy, as if he had fucked up in some way.

"My father lived in the projects when he was a kid. When they started turning color most of the whiteys took off but his parents wouldn't budge. He was a tough old lefty, my grandfather, worked as a labor organizer for the AFL-CIO for twenty-five years. My father used to say 'If you gave Pop a bag of clothespins in the morning he'd have them picketing the wet laundry that night.'

"He always walked around the projects wearing a beret. People thought he was some kind of beatnik but it was his shout-out to the Abraham Lincoln Brigade. When he was teenager he tried to join up but they wouldn't take him because was too young. He was in the Army during World War Two and he could've gone to college on the G.I. Bill but he considered himself a working man."

"What's the Abraham Lincoln Brigade?"

"Volunteers from all over who went to Spain to fight against fascism in the 1930s."

"Oh, ok."

"He made my father go to a red diaper camp."

"A what?" she asked, her voice tightening a little. Anthony told himself to answer the fucking question, be done with the did-you-know history lessons and get her back.

"Socialist kiddie camp, or Communist, I forget which, all I know is he hated it."

"Just so you know I have an associate's degree from Manhattan Community College," she said.

Not knowing how else to respond to that complicated declaration, he asked the obvious question.

"What did you major in?"

"Criminalistics. I guess I watched too much TV."

"You know the thing I liked the most about visiting my grandparents? What I liked the best was that it always put my father in a good mood."

"So I guess he wasn't normally?"

"He walked around like he was about to pounce on people. They used to call him the Fighting Quaker."

"He beat you?"

"Not with his hands." Then reversing the Q and A, "So, after the army, what did your father do?"

"Post office."

"Is he still alive?"

"Oh yeah. So what's it like for you?" she asked.

"What was what like for me?" Anthony thinking she was referring to his flash in the pan celebrity.

"You're with a group of white people and somebody tells a race joke or makes some crack. What do you do?"

"It depends."

"On?"

"The situation."

"What's an ok situation?"

"There isn't any." Then, "Am I on trial?"

"I'm sorry," she said, waiting for an answer.

"It depends on who else is in the room. If somebody knows me, they'll usually pull him aside and you should see some of the colors they turn. After that some come up to me and apologize, some avoid me because they're embarrassed and now and then somebody throws me the stink eye because they feel like I set them up."

"You confront them?"

"They've been confronted."

"You get mad though," Anne said, following that up with, "if it's ok for me to ask."

"Yes. I get mad. They ruined my night."

"That's it?"

"Of course that's not it," Anthony nearly snapping at her, leaving out how his suddenly being transformed from just a guest in the room to the racially insulted guest in the room invariably left him tired and deflated. The anger always came later.

"I guess I'm putting you through it," she said apologetically. "It wasn't my intention to make you feel like that."

But he wasn't finished, Anthony needing to slow himself down to get this next part right.

"The hardest for me is being around people I could see becoming friends with but if they don't know, because at some point I have to figure out a way to bring it up myself because if I don't do that, then all I'll be doing is waiting for them to say something that's going to turn everything to shit."

"Like gays needing to come out to their straight friends," she offered. "I get that."

"I just prefer to be with people who know my deal, because otherwise the whole monitoring thing is exhausting."

"I can imagine," she said, Anthony finally hearing the returning softness in her voice.

With the tentativeness of an eighth grader, he reached across the table to put his hand on top of hers and was startled to feel the tremor running through her fingers.

"I told you I was nervous," she said.

"Actually, *I* said that and you said, 'Me too.' I just want to keep the record straight for future generations."

"Funny man."

They took five to stare at each other, Anthony wanting to reach across and remove those tinted glasses but he didn't have that kind of tender license with her yet.

"You can," she said, reading his mind.

So he did, slow and careful, then laid them on the table.

"Let me tell you about these eyes of mine. When I was a kid the other kids used to call me Twilight Zone except for my father who called me Battery Eyes. Everybody sees silver but they're a super-light grey.

"I think I was in fifth grade when I saw this movie on TV, The Boy with the Green Hair. It was about a young boy with guess what color hair and how people were mean to him just because he was trying to save the world. Afterwards I wrote a little story called 'The Girl with the Silver Eyes.' I wanted to show it to my teacher but I chickened out."

"Why?"

"Because I was afraid she would like it and make me read it to the class. I couldn't handle that."

"You?"

"I don't think I ever spoke in class until I was a senior in high school. After that I never shut up. Am I talking too much now?"

"Not for me."

Anne looked down at their hands, his atop hers, but perfectly still, as if to lightly caress the other with a stray finger would shatter some kind of equilibrium.

"When I was a teenager," she said, "my mother gave me a talk about boys, not the pregnancy stuff so much but more about how to weed out the ones who're just going to wind up being a waste of my time. She said, 'If you feel that a boy isn't making enough of an effort to get to know you, if he doesn't ask you the right questions about yourself or look at you when you speak like he's really wanting to hear what you have to say, if you sense any of that coming from him then you need to move on.'"

"Move on," he said, falling hard for her all over again. "You have to, because time is precious and that right one, he's been all along looking for you just like you've been looking for him."

Anne stared at him for a long moment, Anthony unable to decode her expression.

"What do you like about being with me?" she finally said, her voice suddenly devoid of play.

"I can't break it into parts, I just do," he answered reflexively, then, as that shift in her tone started to sink in, he began to dig deeper because he knew he had to. "Because when I look at you? It takes all my willpower to look away again. Same with hearing your voice. I don't think I ever paid so much close attention to what another person had to say."

"Never?"

"Never." Anthony getting into it now. "And because whenever you ask me a question, you do this thing of slightly lowering your shoulders and tilting forward a little, looking straight into my eyes like you're daring me to give you an answer that you haven't heard from a man a hundred times before."

"I sound like a real bitch," she said dryly.

He waved that away.

"Because since we met? I talk to you when you're not even there. Because when I reached for your hand before I felt like I was thirteen. Because 'Anne' all of a sudden is the most musical name that I can imagine. And because you make me want to come at you with the best of who I am. It's a ton of small things like that and I know there'll be more and I can't wait."

"Are you slumming with me?"

"Am I what? After all I just told you?"

But the question spooked him because despite all the fireworks, maybe he was, the thought of that momentarily hollowing him out.

"What if I said I'm reverse slumming with you?"

"Anne, I don't even know what that means."

She stared at him, then stared at him some more.

"What. Just say."

"Does this, *us*, feel real to you?" It was a question, not a preamble to a statement, as if she really wanted to know.

But rather than pitching him headfirst into another desperate oratorio—*Come at her with the best of who you are*—this time the question served to calm him down.

"Honestly? Not yet. We have to get past this catch-breath stage first, then we'll find out soon enough."

She nodded in slow agreement as if she'd been waiting for him to say something sensible and thought out, because any fool can go into a swoon.

The truth. What a liberating concept. *The truth.* As far as he could take it.

One of the hells of his withholding the facts of those buried hours was that it was gradually but inexorably making him feel that his whole life previous to that had been a lie too; nothing but an extended rehearsal leading up to the big one, the game-changing one, and that in his future days he would continue to define himself by that no matter what he chose to do.

"I'm sorry for the interrogation," she said, "I just need to know who I'm with before it's too late."

"Too late . . ."

"To disconnect from you."

There wasn't much more to say after that without running everything into the ground so they simultaneously got up to leave, neither of them having even looked at the menu.

When they got inside the car, he couldn't tell who reached for who first, Anthony inhaling her breath as she cupped the back of his neck with a long-fingered hand. She was a deeply slow-motion kisser; her lips not so much pressing against his as drifting down on them and lingering there in no hurry to disengage; each soft descent a lesson on how to be with her.

They were parked on a side street but under a streetlight with people occasionally walking past, so he didn't know how welcome touching her anywhere else would be, and she wasn't reaching for any other part of him, so they settled for more of each other's mouths until she had to pull back because her lips were starting to swell. His too.

After that it took a minute or so before he felt centered enough to pull out into traffic, turning to her one last time before keying the ignition, an expression of happy disbelief on his face.

"Seatbelts," he whispered.

After pulling into the shadowed parking lot behind her building they sat in the dark listening to the tick of the cooling engine.

"I can't ask you up," she said.

"Ok."

"My son's home."

"It's too soon to meet him?"

"Something like that."

"No problem." Anthony intent on keeping their last minutes tonight easy and peaceful.

"Just so you know I'm not going to bed with you for a while."

"Ok," he said, patting himself down as if he were looking for his glasses.

"What was that?"

"My nerves making a joke." Then, "I have no idea what I meant by that."

"No, it's funny," she said, then began taking him in all over again.

"Now what?"

"Nothing." This time the word came wrapped in a small smile.

"So, when can I see . . ."

"Tomorrow's good," she said.

He moved to kiss her, and she let him but only for a second before pulling back and gesturing to the nighttime silhouettes beyond the front windshield coming and going out of the Crawfords. "We keep at it, tomorrow I'm front page news around here."

When she finally left the car, she made it halfway to her building before turning back then leaning in through the open passenger-side window.

"You ever know someone can look you in the eye and tell you a story so sad you're crying and not one word they said was true? That was my son's father."

In his kitchenette apartment, Felix started to review the footage from the funeral home. Some of it was pretty good, but other stuff was hilarious in the worst way, his favorite worst moment being Royal throwing his crown at the camera.

After eating his bodega-bought-sandwich dinner and smoking half a joint, he went back to reviewing the various takes, then got to work cutting and patching until he had put together a roughly workable flow, then smoked the other half of the joint and became cosmically inspired, downloading imagery from other sources—mostly historical—and then slipping them into his own footage in order to enhance Royal's sales pitch.

For example, on one of the takes Royal said, "New York City is home to five hundred and forty-three languages from forty-five nations and fifty-two religions and we welcome and respect all races, traditions and preferences of expression." (On an outtake, he added, "And we want to bury everybody.") So Felix dropped in footage of the United Nations on a flag-flapping windy day; a crowd of people on 125th and Lenox, another of Times Square on VE Day. In other spots he added D-Day footage of US soldiers landing on Omaha Beach—he had no idea why he chose that but rather than take it out, he followed it up with another beach, this one pristine and unoccupied with opal-tinted water and sand the color of honey, Felix, off the top of his stoned head deciding that what he was intuitively and brilliantly going after was the contrast between suffering and eternal serenity or something. Next up was footage of RFK's funeral train passing through the 125th Street station in Harlem, followed by JFK's caisson as it entered Arlington Cemetery and, lastly, why not, Nelson Mandela greeting school children in Soweto.

Juiced by what he had created, he transferred the new rough cut onto a thumb drive, then took off, still stoned, walking west towards the Royal Davis Funeral Home and Chapel. It was late, but not that late, and Royal just had to see this right now.

The buzz stayed with him until he was two blocks from the funeral home then died a sudden death when he passed by a parked car, Royal and Amina sitting upright in the back seats, both staring straight ahead as if exhausted. Amina had been crying, and her tears, caught in the reflected light of a buzzing bodega sign across the street, appeared iridescent.

Shocked, he stepped off before either of them could notice him, did a 180, and headed straight back to the brownstone, went upstairs and deleted all of his insertions.

* * *

At home after his time with Anne, Anthony attempted to put together his own show-and-tell for her, but he didn't have much. A high school track trophy. A high school chess trophy. A photo of himself and his mother. Himself and his sister. With his father. His father being arrested. With Willa and his wife who had left him, Anthony concluding at that point that there had to be some other way to reciprocate her gift to him.

* * *

Mary woke up from a dream about standing behind her father in his corner as the referee signaled for the fighters to come forward to hear the final instructions, but Teddy Burns wouldn't budge.

And when they heard the bell for the first round, he not-so-gently pushed her out towards the center of the ring.

* * *

The moment Anthony stepped into the shower, Al Green's "Love and Happiness" playing on his cell phone pulled him out.

"Good morning, I'm trying to reach Anthony Carter, is he available?"

"Who's calling?"

"My name's Royal Davis of the Royal Davis Chapel and Funeral Home and I'm looking for Anthony Carter."

"*What?*" Anthony's damp skin drying on the spot. "Who died."

"No one. I mean most likely no one you know. Sorry for the scare. Is this Anthony Carter?"

"It is."

"Great. I'm just calling to invite you to speak at a funeral for a young man."

"What young man."

"His name is Reginald White. You don't know him but his mother heard you speak at the rally yesterday and was so moved that she asked me to reach out to you in hopes that you'd say a few consoling words to the family."

"I'm sorry, how did you get my number again?"

"Our good mutual friend Calvin Ray."

"But if I don't know the kid . . ."

"Well, I imagine you didn't know any of the people at the rally either, nonetheless you pretty much got through to everybody, myself included."

"Thank you," he said automatically, the words a holding action.

"Look, what they want from you is pretty much the same talk. Life, kids, death."

"Can I think about it and get back to you?"

"Well, the funeral's pretty soon, so . . ."

"I said I'd like to think about it."

"If that's what you need then that's what you need."

"Where's the service?"

"Blessed Redeemer, it's over on . . ."

"I know where it is."

He'd been there the other day giving himself a hernia trying to infill on God. And now this request to return, as if God had taken his sweet time to answer. Coincidence or not, Anthony needed this so bad because the reality of what had really happened that day was becoming increasingly harder for him to deny while his own tale of resurrection was becoming more and more difficult for him to sustain.

"Yeah, ok, Mister Davis."

"It's Royal."

"Royal, I'll do it."

"Good man."

"Well I'm trying to be. I truly am."

When the call ended Anthony, forgetting about his shower, started to dress while imagining relating all this to Anne, especially after he had pissed and moaned last night about how maybe it's only us out here.

Just look what he's done for you—put Anne Collins in your life, offered you a return to that temple of silent despair but this time to comfort others—and for the first time in his life, he had people gravitating towards him to hear what he had to tell them and who's to say if this was all God's plan for him or just a circumstantial chain reaction of encounters and events stemming from a bizarre situation?

Well, *he* was to say, and so he chose, yet again, and with no guarantee that the conviction would stick, for today at least, to go with God.

* * *

"How are we all doing, today?" Mary addressed the brownstone crew again.

"You find him yet?" Trip asked from behind his shades.

"Not yet. So I want to ask you all again about his taxi service. Do you know where his long-distance customers came from? How he found them, or how they found him?"

"You have to ask the people who have that kind of money," Dupree said, the others nodding in agreement.

Mary took a step back to regroup, then came forward again.

"Ok, you told me that one of his side gigs was taking people's garbage to the curb on pickup days. Do know where he did that? Who he did that for?"

"All I can tell you is, around here, everybody takes care of their own garbage."

Assuming that his customers were people who at least had the money to hire him to do such a pedestrian chore and who probably lived within walking distance of his own digs and most likely lived clustered together so he could go from house to house at speed, Mary started to look for the slightly more gentrified blocks—if they could be called that—given the increasing mix and match of the poor and the better off living within a few yards of each other; brownstones cut up into kitchenettes sitting next to ones that were single-family intact; apartment houses that had gone co-op sharing an outer wall with ones where the majority of tenants received some kind of government assistance.

Since she had accidentally left her X-ray vision at home and couldn't see through brick and stone in order to find out who lived where, she decided that her best bet was the city-approved pocket gardens where many of the volunteers, Black, white, Asian had come to Harlem from all over and tended to be, if not necessarily all that much more affluent, at least to have more options and more mobility in the world.

The first two gardens she came across had padlocks on their gates, but the third was open, a handful of neighbors deadheading rosebushes and pulling weeds, a few small dogs whirling around each other at their feet.

Passing the photo around, only one of the group, a woman carrying her infant in a cloth sling across her chest, could make an ID.

"I don't know his name, but I've seen him."

"Seen him where?"

"Just now and then on the street."

"Recently?"

"Last week? Two weeks ago?"

"Was it before that building collapse? After?"

"Before, I think."

"Do you know anyone from around here that has a house upstate?"

Then repeating the question for the others.

"Where upstate?" asked a man with an accent that she couldn't even begin to identify.

"Columbia County. Chatham?"

"Where's that?" a pregnant woman asked.

"Upstate," Mary said again.

"I think Bob Young has a house in Aurora."

"Where's that?" Mary asked.

"Upstate." The pregnant woman again.

"Way up," the man with the accent said.

"You said he puts recycling out for people?" the man with the mystery accent said to the others. "Maybe we should hire him."

*, *, *,

Stepping out for breakfast, Anthony took himself to Il Fragola on 120th Street and Lenox. When he arrived, the young nose-ringed maître d' seated him at a two-top wedged into a tight row of the same next to Prophetess Irene—dressed much less theatrically this morning in white slacks and a plain blue sweater—and another older woman, their table so close to his that if he wanted to, he could reach over and fork a piece of her salmon.

"I had a dream last night that I was cooking all kind of island dishes my mother told me she liked when she was growing up," the Prophetess said, "but whatever plate I put in front of her all she did was complain about it. Complain and criticize, criticize and complain."

"She was like that when you were a kid?" the other woman asked.

"She was like that until the day she died. Last thing she said to me was, 'You need to straighten yourself out.'"

"Did you?"

"Straighten myself out? Or need to."

"Either."

"No and no," the Prophetess said. "Back then if I was any straighter I could've rented myself out as a slide rule. She just liked to say stuff like that, get you all the time second-guessing yourself."

Wanting to tell her about "the angels," Anthony tentatively leaned toward their table but then couldn't bring himself to horn in.

"My mother was kind of like that," the other woman said, "but when she started getting sick and saw how I was caring for her she softened up and started being the mother she should of been all along." Then added, "Not that I wasn't grateful for the change."

When the waitress came by to take his order, he lost track of their conversation and when he was able to tune back in, they were off on a different subject.

"He's got his issues," the Prophetess said, "but at least he has his own money."

"Does his issues have a name?"

"Rochelle."

"Wife?"

"Might as well be."

"What else?"

"He likes his oil." Tilting her head back and mimed pouring a drink down her gullet.

"I wouldn't want to be with a man who doesn't allow himself to kick it up now and then."

He took another shot at leaning in again, retreated again, the Prophetess giving him a quick slightly irritated once-over, inspiring him to at least poke at his eggs.

"I'm thinking about going to Japan," she said. "There's a church there said they could arrange a tour for me."

"That's wonderful," her friend said, reaching across to pat the back of her hand.

"Flying scares the Jesus out of me."

"I remember the last time you flew you wanted to bring your own parachute."

"Well, I'll tell you one thing, if I *do* go, I want everybody to pay for me from the minute I get in my seat until the minute I land."

"Pray for you," Anthony said before he could stop himself.

"Excuse me?" The Prophetess rearing back from his intrusion.

Thinking, *In for a penny*, Anthony dove in.

"Do you remember me? I was at your tabernacle some nights ago and you said that you saw angels hovering around my back. You said that they looked worried like there something in or on me right there that could kill me if I didn't attend to it, so I just have to tell you . . ."

The Prophetess stared sullenly at her salmon as if he were berating her, which stopped him dead, Anthony in that moment coming to understand how much of his sense of grateful well-being and blessed fortune was dependent on the validation of others and when that was withheld . . .

"Sorry, I just wanted to say thank you for your amazing vision. You're the real deal. Sorry."

Feeling cored out, he got up from his table to pay at the register, leaving most of his food still on the plate.

"I think that's that man they rescued from that building," he overheard her friend say. "I saw him on TV." Then, "You don't know him? Because he sure knows you."

"Yeah, I know who he is," the Prophetess said, "I just don't like him."

❊ ❊ ❊

Felix stood outside the Applebee's on 125th Street, waiting for Royal and Calvin to show. He had been out there now for so long that he started to wonder if he either had the wrong date or the wrong Applebee's, forty-five minutes and counting so far. At the hour mark, just as he was about to walk away, both men finally showed up simultaneously, although from opposite directions; Royal muttering something about a delayed delivery of mortuary cosmetics, Cal talking about a female assistant who did or didn't do something.

The meeting was about Reginald White's upcoming funeral, both men wanting Felix to videotape the event—Royal wanting it as a potential promotional tool; Cal wanting it to give to Tutti Speedwell as a keepsake; two separate videos, each with its own bias, doubling his fee, otherwise known as two times zero. At least they picked up his share of the tab; twelve dollars for an order of waffle fries and two Cokes.

After Royal left, Cal remained at the table lingering over his tea. Felix could have left too, but the chance to sit alone with one of his current heroes kept him in his seat even though being alone with the man left him tongue-tied. Fortunately for him, Calvin took the lead.

"Where you from, Felix?"

"Me?" Grateful for the question. "Way upstate in Oriskany, no one's ever heard of it."

"I know Oriskany."

"You do? How?"

"I did my time in Marcy Correctional, not five minutes away."

"No."

"Oh yeah."

"My uncle ran the drug treatment center there. Alvin Rosenberg."

"Rosenberg. I never met him because I didn't have any addiction issues but I remember some guys in there who did. He's your uncle huh? Small world, small world, right?"

"Cal, if I can ask . . ." Felix took a breath. "Why were you in Marcy?"

"Of course you can ask. Our stories is the message," he said.

"I was part of a dope ring that got swept up on a RICO charge. Most the other dudes, their lawyers told them to take a plea, my lawyer too, but for some reason I thought I could beat the charge and told him I wanted a trial."

"Oh no."

"Yeah, 'oh no' is right. The first couple of months inside I was a problematic individual but then I was sent to see this visiting . . . I never knew what her title was, shrink, nurse, social worker, who came into Marcy two days a week and I guess she saw something in me because after our first sit down she says, 'Calvin it's up to you whether you come back to see me again or not, but I can promise you this—if you choose *not* to come back, your time in this place is only gonna get harder—but if you *do* choose to continue with me? Not only will you make the most of your time in here, but I guarantee you . . . once you get out? You will *never* see the inside of a prison again."

"Damn," Felix said. "Do I have to go to prison to see her?"

"Oh no, she's been retired for years." Calvin once again not getting the joke. "She had me start taking classes in there, said it didn't matter in what, just go, and that's what I did, I took computers, finance, psychology, *social* psychology, world history, American history, you name it."

"That's more than I ever did," said the Monroe County Community College dropout.

"See, when I young, I hated school because I thought it was like a prison, but when I really was in prison? School was my freedom. It was my everything. I even started thinking about becoming some kind of teacher in there so I put something together with a few of the old heads, some kind of orientation class to school the younger ones just coming into the system about having the proper mentality to survive inside, all the dos and don'ts, then I went to the warden and laid it out for him and I had a reputation as a positive influence by then so he gave me the green light. And let me tell you, schooling all those young men? That's when I found my purpose in life. And then I got into teaching all these other classes, anything they'd let me. I'd go to the warden, 'I want to teach a class on how to buy and sell stocks.' He'd say, go ahead, then I'd hit up everyone who was in there for some kind of insider trading, securities fraud, running a pump and dump shop or what have you because I didn't know the first thing about stocks, two weeks later I'm teaching it. Hell, I even ran a parenting class, and I don't have any kids. But that one was pretty easy for me because it was all about how to act like a decent human being around smaller human beings, that and using your common sense."

"So you'd think," Felix said.

"In reality though, it was mainly a class on how to talk to your family on the phone or in the visitor's room because some of these guys I had? They had fifteen, twenty, thirty-year bids, so by the time they'd be getting out, their kids were gonna be parents themselves."

"But they were into it, right?" Felix asked, needing some kind of positive ending.

"Well I know a lot of them just took the class like they took any class inside, mostly to impress the parole board but another lot of them took pride in what they'd just done. You could see it in their faces when the families came to watch them get their diplomas on graduation day."

"Good for them," Felix said, bobbing his head.

"The others? They only showed up for that because with all the families being there, the food they served was going to be ten times better than the garbage they've been eating every day since they got there."

* * *

Needing to come back to himself after Il Melograno, Anthony took a walk up Lenox to 145th Street then back down to 120th and sat on a bench in front of a check-cashing business, oblivious to the Noddies on either side of him, and made a Hail Mary call to Anne.

"You picked up!"

"When my phone starts ringing that's what I tend to do," she said.

"I just wanted to hear your voice."

"Well good because I was kind of wanting to hear yours too," she said.

The man on his left turned to him and started shouting in his face. "Don't *ever* let your bulldog mouth write a check your kitty-kat body can't cash."

"Ain't that the truth," Anne said.

"Hold on." Anthony getting up to take a half-block hike uptown. "Ok, so, last night I was trying to put together a this-is-my-life kind of collage of things to show you, but all I could come up with was a lousy track trophy and a bunch of photos that I didn't want to look at."

"You ran track?"

"In high school, and some freshman JV in college."

"What was your event?"

"Hundred-meter sprints and team relays."

"Oh yeah? I ran relays myself."

"You did?"

"My junior year in high school we came in with the third best time in the state. Of course that was thirty-odd pounds ago."

"Third in the state," he said.

"Third in the state."

"Maybe tonight we should race," he said lightly.

"Beware what you wish for," she said.

*, *, *,

The bi-monthly East Harlem community meeting was held in the muster room of the 25th Precinct. Ed Murray, the high and tight no-nonsense precinct commander, was running the show from the center of a long folding dais; Mary, representing Community Outreach, seated to his left, a boss from anti-crime to his right.

Ralph Esposito stood in the back of the room and took notes.

Normally there were around twenty or so mainly senior residents at these meetings, coming in to complain about the same things, meeting after meeting; teenagers loitering in front of the buildings, the lobbies and the hallways; the ubiquitous marijuana stank coming from the elevators, the stairs, the lobbies and through the walls and from those people next door. The pop-up urinals in stairwells, the loud music, the shoddy maintenance and one or another endlessly barking dog whose owner never picked up his business when he got walked. But tonight, as Mary expected, the crowd was both bigger and younger; mothers mainly, standing up for their teenaged kids.

After Ed Murray opened it up by ticking off the latest crime stats for the area then made the usual appeal to the assembled to be more forthcoming with information, one of the mothers that Mary vaguely knew, Anne Collins, stood up and got right to it.

"You're asking us to come to you with what we might of heard or know about this or that, but if you want us be more cooperative with you? Then you better start to rein in some your people because right now it feels they're snatching up every young man in sight no matter what they're doing so why would we want to help you lock up even more? I mean you can call it proactive policing or what have you but there's a thin line between proactive and violating their rights. Just because they're young that doesn't mean they're doing something wrong."

"Look a lot of my guys are young too," Murray said evenly, "but I have no crystal ball. Police work is based on assumption but if they act inappropriately after a wrong assumption that's what I need to know."

"Consider yourself informed," an older man called out from the rear seats.

Anne was still on her feet. "I intend for my son to go to college in two years."

"Good for you, and good for him," Murray said.

"And I can't but worry that between now and then he's going get arrested because he had a certain expression on his face or because he was standing in front of the wrong building near the wrong people and it's going to make for a black mark on his applications."

The woman had a reputation in these houses for speaking her mind no matter who was on the receiving end, but Mary noticed that her hands were shaking.

"What's your son's name?" Murray asked.

"You don't need to know that right now because he's no trouble maker and I intend to keep him off your radar," she said, then, looking as if she had just spooked herself with that last statement, walked out of the room without another word to anyone.

After Anne's exit, Murray fielded a few more comments and complaints before cueing Mary to wrap it up with the reciting of the police-community calendar of forthcoming events, but before she could begin another mother rose to her feet.

"Just cause you're in a set it doesn't mean you're bangin'," she said. "You live in a certain place you got to be crewed up to not be a target. It's negotiated life."

"I understand. But still . . ." the commander said.

* * *

When the meeting finally broke Esposito walked out with Mary, the two of them being seen together in public tonight an exception to their usual down low rules because they were coming from a shared function.

"My guess?" Esposito said. "After tonight with everybody up in arms in there and this Harlem Pride parade coming up? You're going to be riding shotgun with Anti-Crime because they're gonna do what they're gonna do and somebody has to semi-apologize on the hoof."

"Great. I'm going to feel like the guy with the broom following the elephant around the circus."

As they approached the corner of Lenox they came up on a crowd in constant motion; some people running off as others ran in, so that it seemed to be pulsing, the vibe lit-up and giddy.

Stepping to the sidelines with Esposito, Mary took in the star of the show: a statuesque coffee-colored middle-aged woman sporting an African-print maxi dress and a complicated gold lamé turban, everybody looking at her like she was free ice cream as she posed for cell phone snaps with all who wanted one, her eyes oversized and electric, her voice as big as the rest of her. "Do not forget him! It's his day!"

"Every day's his day, Mami," someone shouted.

"That's right!" the woman shouted back as she took a photo with some flush-faced, grinning teenager, her arm around his neck, her long crazy-nailed fingers starfished on his thin chest.

"Who's that?" Esposito asked a teenage girl.

"Prince's mother."

"What Prince?"

"*The* Prince!"

"You mean *the* Prince?" Esposito faux-popping his eyes.

"Yes!"

"Bullshit." He side-mouthed to Mary, "The guy was five four tops, she's six feet."

"I was thinking that."

"Unless his dad was a dwarf or something," Esposito said.

Sometimes Mary was struck by the difference in how Esposito comported himself with her out in public when sex wasn't in the cards—companionable, easy to banter with, even witty—as compared to his motel persona; a special blend of chestiness and adolescent pouting.

If it weren't for genitals, she thought, people could live for hundreds of years.

"*Go*," Esposito whispered, lightly pushing her forward.

"What?"

"Come here, baby," Mrs. Prince called to Mary.

"Go ahead." Esposito nudged her.

"No."

"C'mon . . ." Esposito gave her another light shove forward until she found herself cheek to cheek with the towering woman, her meaty arm draped across her narrow shoulders; Mary looking out now at a buoyant bunch of locals—not just teenagers, but middle-aged women, curious old-timers, and young gentrifiers.

Not too many liking cops out here, Mary mostly inured to the vibe, but those beaming faces in a rough jostling horseshoe smiling at her *because* they knew she was police, this momentary moment of good will, this was really something else, and Mary, never a great emoter, was unable to keep herself from smiling.

And when she was released back into the crowd flush-faced and atingle, she looked at Esposito and it was on.

*   *   *

They met at a chain link–fenced Parks Department soccer field bright in the night beneath a brace of sodium lights and the speeding headlights of cars heading south on the nearby Harlem River Drive. Anthony, wearing jeans and sneakers, arriving first, Anne in a long-sleeved T-shirt and shorts that showcased her still muscly legs coming out of the shadows to join him with her track shoes laced together over her shoulder.

They both looked embarrassed.

"We're really doing this?"

"It was your idea," she said.

"It was, but you didn't have to take me up on it." Then scouring the field, "To the goalpost?" He had no intention of winning this.

"Ok by me."

And then they just stood there, making no move to stretch or lace up, peering at the far goal as if it were a distant land seen through fog.

And stood there.

"Ok, here's what's going to happen," she said. "I'm going to let you beat me because I don't want you to feel humiliated, but you don't *want* to win because you're afraid *I'm* going to feel humiliated. You know what that means?"

"It's going to be a race to see who's slowest."

"You know how long that's gonna take? You can clock it with a calendar."

"So . . ."

"So let's get out of here," she said, reaching for his hand as they started across the field together.

* * *

"Hey, you." The words snapping at him from behind as he was walking east on 129th.

He turned and there she was again, his personal hustler, looking pissed as she quick-stepped to catch up to him.

When she got close enough, he saw that someone had gone to work on her face, the right side of her jaw a blue-brown swollen hammock, her right cheek a knotty red.

"Jesus . . ." Felix baring his teeth in a mix of sympathy and fight/flight adrenaline.

"This is *your* fault," she hissed, her eyes popping a little with outrage.

"What are you talking about?" Felix taking a step back, *Fool me twice* . . .

"You said"—chest-poking him—"you said, that I was very talented. You said that I should be an actress. I told my boyfriend . . ."

"The cop . . ."

"I just said that. He's no cop . . . I told him I wanted to go see an acting class. He said no way. I went anyway. He found out and this is what I got for it." Finger-tracing the damage. "Plus, he kicked me out. I know I told you that the first time, and it was stone lie but this time, call me Chicken Little or whatever, it's the God's truth. So, thank you, thank you very much."

Felix, not knowing what to say, or think, went into his pocket for her because that face was for real whatever the circumstances. That and the fact that, whatever this was right here, he was happy to see her again.

"I don't want your money."

"For a doctor."

"I been to the ER, sat there eight hours waiting for my X-ray on a hard-ass bench with a lot of sick as shit people, everybody coughing and hacking their guts up all over me."

"And?"

"No broken bones, so that's good."

"You should see a real doctor."

"Fuck a real doctor. That's not the issue. The issue is I don't have a place to stay anymore." Staring at him.

His first thought regarding her being under the same roof with his Nikon was not good.

His second thought, however, had no words, just a sense memory of her hugging him that first day, the woozy mix of her raw, complicated scent, the light ripple of her percolating frame thrilling him with its honesty, its intimacy.

"Hello?" Ducking her head to get up under his eyes, then when he still wouldn't answer, "You *owe* me."

* * *

"Do you want to come up?" Anne asked him once they took a breather from each other in his car.

"What about your son?"

"He's staying at a friend's."

"Then yeah."

"Ok just let me go up by myself first, then you. 14C, ring me from the lobby and I'll buzz you in."

The first thing that struck him when he walked into her apartment were the long shelves in the hallway filled not with doodads and photos but with books, many of them self-help or popular guides for the getting of wisdom and for the getting of your shit together but also bestselling novels and mostly African American memoirs. He wanted to say something about how surprised he was, but he didn't know how without it coming off as patronizing.

The apartment layout was a carbon copy of his grandparents' place back in the day, the dinette which opened up into the living room, the tiny kitchen, the two small bedrooms at the far end of the hallway.

"What do you think?" she called from the kitchen.

"This place is immortal."

"Is that good or bad."

"Excellent."

"I wouldn't go that far."

"I feel like I lived here in another life."

"Better here than a barn in Atlantis taking care of the master's horses which is what I did before this go-around. You don't drink, right?"

"Not these days. I need to keep my head on straight."

"Not around me you don't." Coming out of the kitchen with two glasses of red wine.

"Look at you." Reaching out to cup her face just as they heard a key turning in the lock followed by her son coming into the apartment. The kid took one look at them and turned statue.

"Brian, this is my friend . . ." she said without missing a beat.

"Anthony," Anthony said.

"Ok," the kid said.

"You're not going to tell him your name?" Anne said.

"You just told it."

"What did I tell about being rude." Her voice weaker than her words; Anthony silently chanting, *Let it go, let it go, let it go.*

"Bye," the kid said turning for the door.

"Whoa, wait, what did you come back here for? Because whatever it was, you didn't get it since you're leaving the same way you came in."

Anthony got the sense that she was just bracing him out of tough-mommy habit but had no interest in an answer.

"I said nothing," he said, and left.

The moment they were alone again, she turned to him, exasperated and near tears.

"Take me someplace."

"Take . . ." Anthony momentarily turning stupid as he tried to process these last few minutes. "We could go back to my place."

"We're not there yet," she said.

"A motel?"

"No," she said. "A hotel."

* * *

Given the circumstances, Felix was nervous enough as is, but the fact that from the moment he agreed to put her up for the night and they started walking towards the brownstone, her hustle-mode manic chattiness had dissolved, replaced by an inward silence that seemed to have no access and no outlet, which made him wonder if he had a death wish.

"Last week there was an entire building there," Felix said to her, gesturing to the high wooden barrier across the street.

"That's sad," she said, not bothering to look.

Scrambling to figure out his next move he came up with, "My place is a dump," which is what more than a few dates had said to him in the past when he asked to go up to their rooms après dinner.

"You should have seen mine," she said.

"Let me go up for a minute to do a few things and I'll come back down for you."

"You're not leaving me here, right?"

"I'll be down in a minute."

Coming into the apartment, the first thing he did was stash his camera in the closet beneath a pile of shoes where she wouldn't be able to find it. Then with his eyes feeling like they were bouncing in their sockets he scanned his digs, seeing, not seeing the living room with its convertible couch, its narrow plank work desk, its bricked-up fireplace slathered in generations of paint—take a knife to it and find a rainbow—and its large shattered window, a mosaic of glass pebbles holding fast, which he had crisscrossed with blue electrician's tape. And above the other window, the unbroken one, an original decorative stained-glass clerestory panel, smutted up with a century's worth of grime.

If he stayed up here long enough maybe she'd get bored or tired and leave, or so he hoped, but when he finally looked down from the good window, there she was; walking in tight circles, still waiting for him.

"Small, right? I told you."

"It's nice," she said distantly, dropping her bag on the couch-bed. What are those, flowers?" pointing to the illustrated stained glass above the window.

"I think they're birds."

"You should clean it."

"I was just thinking about doing that."

"Where's the bathroom?" Picking up her bag again, then, "I see it," and heading down the short hallway before he could open his mouth.

*, *, *,

The color scheme of their hotel room was slate blue and slate grey, which made him think of the war between the states—not a good sign.

The moment they came through the door she headed for the minibar, made herself a gin and tonic then, bypassing the couch, sat in one of the two chairs, Anthony having to drag the other across the room so they could at least be knee to knee.

"So."

"So," she echoed, the tension in her voice making him feel like maybe coming here was a mistake.

She tossed back the G&T, got up and poured herself another one minus the tonic, finishing it off before she settled back in her chair.

"Anne . . ."

"No, I don't want to leave if that's what you're about to ask me."

The flush and rush of wanting her finally hit home, making him reach for her again.

"Not yet," she said.

"No, I just . . ."

"I'm sorry, one last one."

"Ok." Anthony understanding at that moment that Anne was a silver bell drinker, unable to relax until she heard that tinkle in her head, which meant that she was now officially not herself and therefore could relax.

When she sat back down for the third time . . .

"Anne, we don't have to . . ."

"I know we don't," she said, then leaned forward until their knees were touching and started to slip his watch off his wrist while tracking his eyes to see if he's seeing what she's doing. He was.

When she was done, she placed it carefully on the carpet then started to take out her earrings.

"Not to disappoint you in advance, but I don't have a bag of tricks," she said, rising and taking his hand.

* * *

She had been in the bathroom for so long that Felix wondered if she'd died, but when she finally emerged her mood had returned to buoyantly manic, Felix liking this better than the other because this is how he first knew her, but it also left him wondering what she had ingested or smoked in there.

"I can sleep on the floor," he said pulling out the bed for her.

"Yeah, ok," she said, as she started to strip off her clothes as unthinkingly as if she were standing in front of a gym locker, the running lights of a barreling Metro North train briefly flickering across her gaunt torso from shoulder to opposite hip.

He stood there in an odd, preoccupied dream-state of desire that wasn't exactly lust but left him aching nonetheless.

And then it came to him—he was lonely and had been so since he had come down here from upstate a very long six months ago.

"Do you need help?" she said, staring at him still fully dressed.

"I'm just self-conscious."

"*You* are?" Raising her arms high to highlight her xylophone ribs, her barely-there breasts.

"I'm kind of hairy."

"You're a man, you're supposed to be."

"I mean all over," he murmured, her flip sexuality perversely turning him at least for the moment into a prude. "In high school, they called me Cro-Magnon Man."

"What's that?"

"Cave man, ape-boy."

"Kids are mean."

Then finally taking off his shirt to prove his point, "Just don't light any matches around me."

"I don't get it."

"Never mind." Then sitting down to come out of his jeans and socks, then standing again, cupping his business.

"What are you hiding there? Is it a secret?" Reaching for it. "Let me see."

*, *, *

Lying face-to-face on their sides in the darkness, Anthony put his hand on Anne's hip then started slow tracing the swoop from there to her ribs.

"I need to lose weight," she said.

"Yeah, ok." Moving the flat of his palm from her ribs to the outer curve of her breast then up, up, until he was cupping the side of her throat, his thumb stroking her cheek like a tender pendulum.

"I guess you'd like me to take my clothes off," she said.

§ § §

"What do you like?" she asked Felix, standing belly to belly with him in the half-light of his window, her hand still cupping him.

"Like . . ."

"Sex. What do you like."

"To have it?"

Finally, finally, a real smile from her.

"What do *you* like?" he said.

"I like that when it's over, men tend to be nicer to me. For a while at least." Then, tiring of the talk, talk, talk, "Pretend that we're back in the street and all you want to do is empty your wallet on my head."

She grabbed him in the same faux-grateful rib-crushing hug that she used on him the day they had met, the familiar-unfamiliar intoxicating smells of her coming back to him but much stronger than before given the fact that they were both naked.

"Come lay down," she said.

He had slept with only two women before this night, the sex with each pretty much consisting of him humping away and them yelling, "*Jesus, slow down!*" and with that in mind, he hovered over her body, moving inside with cautious, deliberate strokes. But after a minute of this over-courtly fuckery, she had had it. "Jesus, man, I'm not a candy cane," she hissed, wrapping her arms around his lower back and bringing him down hard on top of her.

"Got it."

And then he started to let himself go, bulling her a little, then a little more.

"There you go."

And right then, he went.

"Damn . . ." Felix said blushing in the dark. "Sorry."

"Don't be."

"No, no, just give me a minute."

* * *

"You know *why* you don't know, Jordan?" Esposito yelled into his phone while Mary sat semi-patiently on the couch in their latest love nest nursing her one and only drink. "You don't know because you don't *want* to know."

If she were the type of person who instantly checked for emails whenever there was the most minute void in their day, she would have at least had something to distract her from all the ragey braying.

"No, *you're* the one who doesn't listen." The angrier Esposito became, the lower he crouched until it looked like he was shouting into a phone embedded in the carpet.

The sexy buzz she felt from being embraced by Prince's fake mother on the street that had led her to initiate this rendezvous tonight had worn off even before they entered the suite—in fact, she didn't want to be here at all, but with Esposito charging across the living room this way and that she didn't think signaling him for a time-out in the middle of his fury-fest would be a great move and so she continued to sit there waiting for him to bring his domestic drama to an end, most likely by doing some kind of violence to his phone.

No, she didn't want to be here; in fact, she didn't want to be anywhere she could think of right now, a sudden wave of loneliness coming down on her like a shroud.

"Aw hell no, I'm not going back there . . . because it's a waste of my time and a waste of my money . . . Fine, *you* go, give her my regards."

When he finally hung up on his wife he continued to argue with her complete with accessory gesticulations as if she were right in front of his face.

But when Mary finally lost patience and was about to tell him that she was going, he beat her to the punch, gathering up his shit, muttering, "Sorry," then leaving without looking back, which left her so furious with herself for WAITING when he had no trouble doing what he wanted without any thought of her.

Once she heard the elevator door groaning open and shut out in the hallway, she went to the window which overlooked the parking lot and waited for him to get in his car and drive off, which he did at speed, Mary speculating on all the possible names he was calling his wife as he took the entrance ramp to the thruway in a fishtailing rage.

Well, now that she was alone and in no rush to be anywhere, she at least had the luxury of silence and all the time in the world to freshen up that drink.

* * *

Anne lay on her back, the light outside the window silvering up her skin as Anthony ran his hand over the softening muscles of her runner's legs, the flat plane between her breasts and the plush of her belly. And then there were the places that he didn't think he had ever paid attention to or even noticed before; the half-moon curves of damp skin beneath her breasts, the smooth diagonal creases that ran from just above her hips to the insides of her thighs; the hollows slightly behind her collarbones, the skin there stretched tight.

Alternately closing her eyes and staring at the ceiling, she remained mostly still except for the times when his hand had finally moved on, her own hand taking its place, retracing his every move.

"I want to feel what you just felt," she said. "See if it's up to snuff."

"You feel like buttered silk."

"Thank you," she said, then reached out sideways to grip his stiff prick, holding on to it the way a standing passenger in a subway car would hold on to the pole, her twitchy nerves sporadically making it jerk sideways as if the train were rounding a curve.

"I just wish there was a way you could just like . . ."

"Like . . ."

"Jump into my head and be me for a minute," she said.

He didn't know what that meant but he didn't want to make her spell it out either.

"Look at you," he said.

"I don't have a mirror on me."

"I'm your mirror," he said.

Turning her back to him, she reached across herself for her bag on the night table and started to poke around inside. When she finally turned back to him, she held a small bottle. Upending it, she squeezed out some gel onto her belly, dipped her fingertips into the swirl, then brought them down between her thighs, a nut-like fragrance rising from her body.

"Ok," she said, "come in. But easy." Then wincing, a few seconds later, "Ok come out, come out."

"I'm out."

"Let's just lay here for a minute."

"Sure," Anthony said, going back to tracing her, the smooth caps of her shoulders, the bow-curve of her lips, her brows, throat, temples . . .

"I like that," she said after a while.

"Which that."

"All of it." Then, "Kiss me."

She went back to the bottle, squeezed out more gel, this time putting it on him.

"Ok, slow, slow . . ."

So, slow; at first just the head then stopping but when he tried to go a little deeper, just a little bit . . .

"Nope, no good. It's been a while. I'm sorry. I'm not what I used to be down there."

"Don't be. If it hurts it hurts," easing himself out. "Been a while for me, too."

"Yeah," she said sitting up, "but men don't go through the change. Plus, your business is on the outside, ours is on the in. And you got that blue pill while we don't have shit. Somebody should get a hold of some scientists."

No woman he'd ever been with would ever describe him as a passionate lover boy—he was too self-conscious to really let go—but with Anne, he felt so relaxed and so *interested*, sex, no sex . . .

"You're very quiet for you," she said after a while.

"I'm not quiet, I'm concentrating."

"Is that a smart word for sulking?"

"Hell no. I'm right here."

"I was thinking," she said, "have the sex, get it out of the way so we can relax." Then, "So *I* can relax."

"How about we relax anyhow."

"You want me to take care of you?"

"I'm fine."

"Fine. What does that mean, fine."

"It means I'm good. With everything."

"Really."

"Really."

"Give me your hand," she said, squeezing out a few more squibs of gel, first in his palm then on herself.

"Ok, touch me here. Easy, easy, yeah like that. Right like that. Just . . . Ok. Ok. Come in. Super slow."

* * *

"Well, I'll tell you one thing," Crystal said, digging a fingernail into Felix's bare chest. "You sure are enthusiastic."

"That's good, right?"

"Better than the opposite."

"I only ask because when it comes to sex I'm not too sharp with what the words really mean. Like, ok, this one girl I slept with? In the morning, she called me a real sexist. I said, 'Wow, thanks! And it's only my second time too!'"

"Funny," she said, not laughing. "You're pretty strong too."

"I was a wrestler in high school." Then, hearing himself, "What an idiot."

"I like strong men. I like the way they can . . ."

And in a sudden fit of euphoric heroism he blurted, "Do you want me to deal with him?"

"Who?" Then, "Deon?"

"That's his name?"

"Don't be stupid."

"Because I will."

"Fine. I'll send you his email address."

※ ※ ※

Royal got the call from the Harris Home Chapel in Mount Vernon at three in the morning to pick up a suicide from the Einstein morgue, a middle-aged woman who had put a gun under her chin and pulled the trigger.

When he came to collect her, she was still wearing the surgical cap that forensics had secured with tape around her head to contain whatever was left of her exploded skull.

He had one of the night orderlies help him transfer her remains from the gurney to the rails in the back of his limo-hearse.

"She leave a note?" Slipping the man twenty dollars.

"She did," he said. "One word. 'Liar.'"

※ ※ ※

Coming into the house well after midnight, Mary dropped her stuff on the couch and went into the kitchen to drink as much water as she could stand.

A printout of her son's homework lay face up on the table, a book report or essay about Thomas Paine, Mary taking a seat to read it but three paragraphs in, her eyelids started to flutter so she had to stop. Rising from the dining chair she said out loud, "That was really interesting, Dougie," and headed up the stairs.

When she turned on the bedroom light, she saw Jimmy's outline under the blanket.

"What are you doing here?"

"What?" Jimmy sat up; his face smeared with sleep.

"What are you doing here, Jimmy."

"It's my night." Then after a flurry of blinking, "It's not?"

Leaning against a wall, arms crossed over her chest, she waited for him to clear his head.

"Alright, give me a minute," he said, throwing off the covers, his long bare legs swinging about.

She'd seen him naked countless times, but not since they'd divvied up the house and she didn't know where to train her eyes.

"I'll be outside," she said, stepping into the hallway.

Then, through the bedroom door, "You can sleep on the couch if you don't want to drive."

"Thanks," he said vaguely.

After a few hours of dozing at best, Mary went downstairs to see if he had taken her up on her couch offer. He had not.

Going into the kitchen for more water, she got as far as turning on the faucet over the sink before being struck with a queasy premonition which made her step away, reach for her bag on the counter, take out her cell phone and check her calendar.

Tonight, as it turned out, *was* his night to be here. With her face on fire, Mary made her way back up the stairs leaving the water still running in the sink.

* * *

When Felix woke up the next morning, Crystal was gone. He got up, went to the closet, looked under that pile of shoes for his camera and discovered that it was gone too.

At first, he was furious, but it didn't last long. *Fuck it*, Felix thought to himself. *It's just a camera.*

* * *

i can still smell you

Is that supposed to be a compliment, she texted back.

Your scent I meant

Muskrat or Wet dog

He tapped out, *Spicy . . .* , then deleted it—too cornball leering, replacing it with *Ancient Evenings*—but it sounded too Come to My Casbah, so he deleted that also. He tried *dreamweaver, eau de soul, aurora, Aurora Borealis, heart pound, hearts delight,* but none of them referred to a scent or felt like much of anything. After a few minutes of stressing, he settled on *Garden*, sending it on before he could start teasing it apart because he was worried that he was taking too much time in getting back to her and how she might interpret the silence.

※ ※ ※

It was only a graze wound, but the woman who had been sitting in her aluminum folding chair playing gin with her girlfriends at one of the cement chess tables in the Duncan Houses esplanade was in her seventies, and the EMTs working on her were worried about shock and so kept talking to her.

"Lena, do you have any grandchildren? Lena, what's your favorite food? Lena, we're just going to take a quick peek at your arm, ok?" As they began to scissor off the left side of her blouse, her dazed friends reflexively formed a ring around the EMTs to protect her decency.

"I thought a bee went by," Lena said, staring straight ahead as they finally lifted her, still in the folding chair, into the back of the ambulance just as the first of the local squad and Anti-Crime/Gang Intel cops appeared on the scene.

"She good to talk?" Esposito asked one of the EMTs as he climbed into the ambo and knelt before her. "Honey? Did you see who . . ."

"I thought a bee went by."

Mary and another detective interviewed the women who were at the table, but they didn't have anything to offer, because a) they'd been either sitting with their backs to the shooter or too absorbed in their cards at the time, and b) it took a while for their friend to notice that she was bleeding which gave the shooter time enough to dematerialize.

"Whoever threw the shot, no way this lady was the target," Esposito said to a cluster of cops from his own squad, and a few others from Gang Intel and Housing.

"So, who was standing near her, behind her?"

"They're in the wind, whoever it was."

"Who's running Crawford these days?"

"They're in transition," an Anti-Crimer said.

"In chaos lies opportunity."

"Well, who last?"

"Mackhouse."

"Were they beefing with anybody?"

"Not for a while."

"How long is a while?"

"A month maybe? Some Forty Wolves got shot at in the Battles and word went around it was Mack so it could have been retaliation, but a month? That's kind of long for some fresher beef not to pop up with some other crew."

"Nonetheless," he said, "I'd start with the Wolves."

An hour later, when Mary finally began to leave the scene after interviewing a woman whose windows overlooked the esplanade, Esposito materialized by her side.

"Got a minute?"

"Sure," she said, bracing herself for his next God-knows-what.

"I just want to explain the other night. That woman's been making me batshit for months and sometimes I just go off but that's got nothing to do with you, so I just want to apologize."

"Apology accepted," she said evenly, not wanting to drag this out.

"So how can I make it up to you?"

"I'll get back to you on that."

※ ※ ※

The next morning as he left the brownstone, Felix ran into Heinrich Nagel, a two-year Swiss transplant who ran the Friends of East 116th Street block association.

Heinrich was also a master formulation chemist working for a major perfumery chain and as he approached, the riot of scents rising from his hair and person made Felix want to pass out.

"Yeah so Felix, we're having a little memorial ceremony for the people in the building," he said, gesturing to the wooden protection barrier across the street, "and if you want to be our photographer for the event that would be great, but more importantly I hear you have a connection to that buried guy Andrew Carter..."

"Anthony," Felix grudgingly corrected, Heinrich's tactless "but more importantly" getting under his skin.

"Yeah, Anthony I meant, and we'd really, really like him to speak."

※ ※ ※

"Tony, it's Clare."

"Clare!" Anthony responding too brightly to his wife's voice, his mind crackling with static.

"How are you?"

"I'm good," he said, trying to keep his voice from floating away. "And you?"

"Good. I'm in the city," she said.

"New York?"

"New York."

"Are you with Willa?"

"No, not this time."

No Willa. Anthony feeling abysmally relieved about that.

"Why not?"

"She's got school."

He knew that was bullshit.

"Why not?" asking again.

"Can we meet?"

"Wait, wait. Is she ok?"

"Yes," she said after a beat. "Tony, can we meet?"

"Sure. Do you want to come over?"

"To your parents'?" she asked, embarrassing him.

"It's a lot bigger than anything I could afford."

"I hear you," she said, then, "How about we meet at the coffee shop on 118th?"

* * *

He'd been sitting there alone for maybe twenty minutes before he finally saw her seated at another table, looking like she'd been there for a while. At least he thought it was her; the petite woman drinking coffee having the same small-featured pale-skinned face, the same light brown eyes tilting up at the outer corners and the same set to her mouth. It was the grey hair that threw him.

When he came over to her table she stood for a light embrace. "Hey there," he murmured into her hair. With his splayed hand just about covering all of her narrow delicately boned back, he inhaled her but all it evoked in him was a faint pang of regret.

She must have felt the same, briskly tapping his shoulder a few times like a referee trying to break up a clinch.

"Wow, I have to be honest," he said, touching her hair, "I almost didn't recognize you."

"This?" she said. "It's been grey for years. I just got tired of dyeing it."

"How did I not notice?" Anthony wishing he could take that last one back, the question an exercise in unwitting self-indictment.

"It looks good," he said in a rush. "*You* look good."

"Well, you do too," she said.

"Did you lose weight?"

"Gained actually," she said.

"Well, it looks good on you," he said.

How pretty she, how pretty he . . .

This was ridiculous, talking to each other like jittery flyers trying to make small talk with a passport control agent.

"When you left," he said, "which I understand why you did, although . . ."

"Although . . ." Daring him to complain.

"Although nothing. I just understood."

"So how are you feeling these days?" she asked.

"These days . . . You mean since the thing?"

"That and in general. How have you been?"

"You sound a little formal."

"Well, I'm a little nervous."

"About what?"

"I just want to know how you're holding up."

"Clare . . ."

"I've been seeing George again."

Her first husband; Anthony trying to sort out how he should feel.

"We want to start over."

"You're living together?"

"We are."

"And so you need a divorce." The words just falling out of his mouth as if he were talking in his sleep.

"But I don't want anything from you."

"I don't have anything." Then, softening, "If I did, I'd gladly give it all to you."

"Thank you," she said, reaching for his hand.

"So how does Willa feel about all this?"

"He's her father."

No, I'm her father, he wanted to say. But he wasn't, nor had he been acting like one, so he kept his mouth shut.

Reading him, she added, "To be honest? They're still trying to get used to each other."

"Understandable," he forced himself to say.

"If I can ask," she said, "has she called you recently?"

"Willa? No, why?"

"Just curious."

"I tried calling her a few times, but she never calls back."

"Did you leave a message?"

"I left a few. Is she mad at me?"

"She's mad at everybody."

After that, they sat in silence for a while, not exactly retreating from each other but mutually returning to the preoccupations of their separate situations.

"So do you have papers for me to sign?" he said.

"They're coming," she said. "I'm sorry."

"Please," he said. "You've been through hell with me, and we both know it."

When they got up to leave, she was the one who initiated the embrace, this time with a little more heart, Anthony holding her tight, thinking of Willa, thinking of Anne.

※ ※ ※

Having the day off, Mary spent it online searching city property records looking for anyone owning a house or an apartment in East or West Harlem who also owned a home in Chatham or nearby, hoping to find Diaz's passenger that way, but there was only one hit; a retired dentist having lived or still living in a condo apartment on Edgecombe Drive, but when she cross-checked the information on a property site for Columbia County she discovered that his house upstate had been demolished after a fire, and an online newspaper search for local articles covering the event informed her that the blaze had claimed two lives, the retired dentist and his late-life girlfriend.

※ ※ ※

Life, kids, death. That was the funeral man's suggested theme for his eulogy. *Life, kids, death*, as if it were a surefire routine. But Anthony didn't want to repeat himself if he could help it, didn't want to come across as an act.

Tomorrow he'd be addressing an unknown number of grieving people; among them, he assumed, would be some who couldn't possibly imagine how they would ever survive their sadness.

And so what he needed to do, if he could pull it off, was to offer them a way forward. And in order to do that, he needed to summon up that sometimes elusive flush of gratefulness for his second-chance transformation, tap the gratitude that made him capable of reaching out to people in order to deliver good news in bad times.

And in order to get that heightened spirit going what he needed was to hear Anne's voice.

But when he called, her phone went directly to message which was full up and taking no more.

First thing in the morning he tried her again with the same result. So he started texting.

A can you call me
R we on 4 tomorrow
Anne can you call me
Anne
Nothing.

On his way to the church, he tried calling her a few times then gave up because he had to focus on the eulogy he wanted to deliver. If "eulogy" was even the right word, given that he wouldn't be speaking about the dead.

Because Reginald White's death was considered gang-related, there were three police vans parked grill to bumper directly in front of the church to serve as a buffer in case of any drive-by attempts, their heavily tinted windows concealing the small army of cops inside of each, braced to jump out at the first sign of trouble.

In fact there were only three police visible to the mourners, all from Community Outreach, two on the sidewalk and Mary Roe inside.

Entering Blessed Redeemer, he couldn't believe that this was the same church that had been empty to the point of abandonment on his first visit, the former union hall now packed solid, every seat taken and two-deep standing along the walls.

Royal had suggested to Tutti Speedwell that her family dress all in white in honor of Reginald's last name and they took it to heart, the front three rows of the church a blizzard of white pantsuits, jackets, jeans, button-down shirts, T-shirts—some with his photo printed on the chest—sneakers and hats.

The only member of the clan who broke the color code was Reginald's grandmother, who wore a shimmering bottle blue dress. Tiny and trim, with eyes that glistened like wet steel, she ran in a continuous circuit from the church entrance to the front rows and back up, alternately greeting everyone like a manic hostess then abruptly stopping mid-aisle to press a fistful of tissues to her eyes, then resuming her route only to stop again to cry—lively, crying, lively, crying until Tutti's sister Rose got up to return her mother to her seat, draping her arm over the woman's shoulders, both to console her and to keep her from popping up again.

Felix, working the room for his two nonpaying employers, had briefly raised his camera to capture her distraught pacing but didn't have the heart to record it, instead turning his attention to the front of the church where the coffin rested on its high bier and started to film the three uniformed maintenance workers who were last-minute swabbing the floor. When they were done, they briefly held hands in a circle, bowed their heads in prayer then took up their mops and buckets and disappeared.

Standing by himself against a wall, Anthony watched Tutti's family in its white-on-white gloom, and felt what he needed to feel, with or without hearing Anne's voice, which was a great relief until a woman in a USPS delivery uniform, most likely coming directly from her shift, made her way down the aisle to the front rows, leaned in and started to hug whoever in the family she could reach.

Mary watched the change come over Anthony's face when the postal worker came by to console the family. And although she didn't understand why that woman's presence had torpedoed him like that, and despite whatever suspicions she had regarding his speech that day, she couldn't help but feel sorry for him.

Felix came up beside her. "Hey. Remember me?"

"Felix, right?"

"Right. How're you doing?"

"It's a funeral." Mary shrugged.

"Right," he said again, before going off again to hunt for moments.

Royal stood quietly inside the front door, watching it all starting to come together when the florist Benny David, wearing a dashiki and a vaguely religious-looking thin silk scarf, its unknotted ends coming down over his collarbones, sidled up to him, a small soft-leathered Bible in his hand. "I was shooting for something to say today floral-themed from the Bible, but nothing jumped out at me, so . . ."

"That's ok, turns out the priest here won't allow for homilies if he's not the one delivering them. On the other hand, he's letting this happen without a mass and without him officiating as long as he can be present."

"So, I came here for nothing?"

"How about you get up there and read a little scripture instead? The family would appreciate it."

Benny gave it a moment, then . . . "I always say, when in doubt, Thessalonians will bail you out."

"I'm genuinely glad to see you here," Royal said before he could stop himself. Then, "Look at that," pointing out one of Reginald's teenage cousins in a tight bandage dress fit for clubbing. "Girl doesn't have a clue."

Royal had decided to have the public viewing before the service began, so that people would file out more quickly when it was over and the cars in the funeral cortege wouldn't run the risk of getting jammed up in the Jersey-bound traffic heading for the GW Bridge and possibly getting to the cemetery when the gravediggers had already knocked off for the day. It had happened to him once and it was a genuine mess.

The line of mourners was long and full of stony grief, some of the people briefly looking down on the boy—his postmortem complexion cosmetically toned to a shade of no identifiable race—before moving on, while others paused to kiss his hands or his forehead. Tutti, the last in line, stared down at her son for so long that Royal and one of the boy's uncles had to bookend her in order to turn her around and guide her back to her chair.

Anthony, standing behind Calvin and a few of his Credible Messengers, had toddled along on that line until he arrived for his one-on-one audience, laying his hand flat on the impossibly icy forehead, thinking of it as his way of asking Reginald White for permission to speak.

He was worried about having to repeat some of the things he had already said at the rally and having to stretch and exaggerate a few others, but he felt it necessary in order to get where he wanted to go, in order *to be of service.*

Felix, still haunted by the three bodies lying silent on their gurneys in that other funeral home, had been on this line too, setting his camera aside to view this body, if for no other reason than to try and familiarize and therefore inoculate himself against what had terrified him before.

It didn't work.

There was a program in place, most of it personal and informal, the mourners in turn getting up in front of the bier to tell a story or sing or read scripture.

A young cousin of Reginald's, tall, skinny and baby-faced with his long-braided hair twisted into two mouse ears, kicked it off, singing his own anti-gun composition in a clear and rousing voice. When he was done, the family applauded him loudly, and as he walked slowly back to his seat, his eyes were ablaze with ambition.

A few of the cousins came up to reminisce, but not Reginald's brother Petey or his mother, Tutti, or his aunt Rose, who seemed a lot more subdued than she was in the apartment, and certainly not his grandmother, who was still trembling in disbelief.

And then it was the florist's turn, Benny introducing himself to the half of the room who didn't already know who he was, then reading Thessalonians 4:13–17, from Paul's epistle, the verses offering consolation to the living regarding the faithful dead, those who have "fallen asleep," and God's promise to make them whole again.

When he was done, he turned to the coffin and bowed.

"Reginald White, may flights of angels carry you to your rest." Then turned forward and bowed to the mourners. "God bless everyone in this church, and thank you for the privilege of allowing me to speak His word in this holy place."

Not dead, but "fallen asleep"—*As I was*, Anthony taking those words as a sign within the greater sign of being summoned back to this church.

A real showman, Mary thought, running her gaze across the long room scouring it for males that looked potentially problematic, zeroing in, and not for the first time, on a sour-faced young guy wearing a ridiculously inappropriate red T-shirt, *#fucyulookinat* printed across the chest—probably just some ass-clown but he hadn't taken his right hand out of his pocket since she first noticed him twenty minutes earlier and he seemed to be fixated on Petey seated in the front row so she murmured into her shoulder mike, two Black undercovers coming into the church a moment later, sidling through the crowd until they were standing on either side of him, Mary watching one cop unobtrusively yet thoroughly patting him down, while the other took his wrist and lifted his hand out of that pocket then going in himself only to come back out with half of a joint and some rolling papers, which they returned to the pocket and left, Mary shrugging it off; better safe than sorry.

An elderly gent seated in the family pews rose and took the hand of a young man who wore a white New York Rangers jersey, helped him to his feet then out to the aisle and to the front of the church.

At first, given his halting shuffle, Anthony thought he might be blind, but when the old man—who turned out to be his grandfather—turned him to face the mourners, Anthony saw that his condition was so much more grievous than that. Constantly rocking, gurgling softly, his gawping mouth revealing teeth set like a jagged row of shattered china. His grandfather held him around his hunched shoulders, pressed his forehead to the side of this man-boy's face, whispering to him all the while, then nudged him forward to stand on his own.

But balking, he immediately back shuffled to his grandfather, who patiently repeated the ritual then nudged him forward again.

"*Bring it, Dee!*" Aunt Rose called out from her seat. "*Let 'em hear it!*" And this time he stood his ground. Hunched over himself, his boggled eyes fixated on the floor and the fingers of his left hand endlessly strumming the raised team logo on his chest, he began to sing "I Believe I Can Fly," in a voice so high, sweet and clean that more than one mourner, rocked by such beauty coming out of that broken mouth, shot to their feet while others started to cry—Anthony for one; Mary, who had to swallow her tears because she was on the job, was another; and, despite having heard this kid sing before, Grandmaster Royal Davis.

"Gets me every damn time," he told Benny David.

When Dee was done singing he immediately retreated into himself, gurgling and lost until his grandfather came forward, put an arm around his shoulders again and guided him back to his seat.

An older woman standing next to Anthony gripped his hand. "God made that boy, the good and the bad, because that's how He does."

"I have been having trouble with my faith these last few years," Anthony began, "in the year past, my mother died of a heart attack and shortly after that my father plowed his car into a tree, made it to the hospital but didn't survive the surgery. Soon afterwards, I found an old cocaine habit that I thought I had discarded.

"Two months after that, I lost my job, then lost another one after that. Then I stopped even trying.

"At first my wife tried to pull me out of it, tried for months but I wasn't having it. Finally, she said that I'd changed so much that she didn't know who I was anymore, that I had become a stranger to her. So she left me and took our daughter with her without any resistance coming from me. I felt so low that I didn't even put up a fight for my own child . . . It was as if, as if, a wasp had stung me in my heart then flew away leaving his stinger still in me and in such a way that it was never going to come out for as long as I lived."

Reacting to the truth of his own words he had to pause to get himself re-centered and moving forward again.

Mary, still focused on trying to figure him out, at least had no doubt about the genuineness of his anguish, and for a moment it made her want him to be the real thing, despite all the signs and portents and poetic phrasing that whispered to her otherwise.

"I was never what you would call a religious man, but I was in such despair that I started going back to church, mostly in the afternoons when only a few people or no people were there. I'd sit in the quiet asking God for some kind of help, some kind of guidance . . . but all I ever got back from him was silence.

"The morning of the collapse I was on that street hoping to get hired as a salesman at the High and Mighty Men's shop just a few doors down the block.

"I remember stopping for a moment in front of one of those buildings to straighten the crease of my pants leg, next thing I know I'm inside a tremendous roaring cloud and then I'm in, what I thought in my mind, was my grave . . .

"In this very church and others before it I always left feeling that God either had no interest it me, or was done with me because of all my failures, and now he was literally discarding me under tons of debris.

"They say I had been buried as long as a day or maybe two, but strange as it might seem, in all that time I never felt afraid, and I never despaired.

"What I *did* feel down inside that darkness... What I did feel... was the presence of a great... *hand*, pressing down on me but also somehow, lifting me up... And I knew that that protecting hand was God finally returning all my calls.

"He wasn't discarding me, he was *preparing* me for a new life, bringing me up to a new life, a new way of being in the world. As I said before I've never been a deeply religious individual and I still don't consider myself one, but I feel guided now and my purpose in being here today is to deliver to you a message that just might make it possible to accept your aching hearts and continue to live the life that He has given you."

For a brief moment he stood there speechless, amazed at what he was about to say.

"What I have learned since that day in the rubble is that whatever befalls you in life, whatever appears to you as an impossible burden, as an unbearable weight, in the end, if you persevere, if you hold fast, will turn out to be a gift... Whatever befalls you no matter how heartbreaking or onerous will turn out to be the best thing, the perfect thing, because of what is to come out of it. In fact, it will be the best thing that could possibly happen to you."

Even though she couldn't see how that could possibly be true, Mary found herself wanting to believe it, and by extension believe in him, if that was at all possible.

When he was done speaking and started to return to his spot on the wall, some applauded but others were silent, Anthony praying that the silence had less to do with disapproval than reflection.

At the end of the service, as Royal and the custodians started to remove the flowers behind the bier, Tutti Speedwell got to her feet and went up to the open coffin to look down on her son one last time and then, slowly one by one, the entire family gradually came back up, but unlike the stony forbearance that they exhibited before, this time the first sobs provoked the next, and then the next after that, until the entire clan was weeping, not one of them showing any sign of wanting to ever step away.

"This is a nightmare," Royal said, checking the time.

* * *

At the end of the service, as Anthony headed up the central aisle with everyone else, a middle-aged Black woman stepped out from the shadows just inside the front door and took hold of his arm. "Excuse me, can I ask you something?"

"Sure," Anthony not sure at all but feeling that he had no choice as he was gently but inexorably steered back down the aisle and into a folding chair, the woman releasing his arm as she took the chair next to him.

"You said . . . You said the worst thing is the best thing that could possibly happen to you?"

"I did."

"Ok, then tell me this . . . I lost my husband last week. We were married twenty-two years and just like that he's gone. I never had a fight or a bad day with this man and our kids loved him. Now, I need to start bringing home a paycheck because his pension and life insurance can only go so far, but I can't look for a job, you understand, because three of our kids are too young and right now they need me around the clock and so does my mother who lives with us and can't do anything for herself. My guess is we're going to lose the apartment and I'm going to have to send two of my kids to live with relatives in Atlanta. As far as my mother goes, I can't think of a single thing to do with her that wouldn't speed her death . . .

"So tell me this . . . How is all what I just told you going to turn out to be the best thing that could ever happen to me?"

"I'm sorry about your husband," Anthony said numbly, not knowing what else to say.

The woman brushed that off, waiting for more.

"Maybe God . . ." Anthony began then stopped because he had no idea how to complete the sentence.

"Maybe God what."

"I don't know." His voice down to a hush, then half-heartedly added, "Nobody knows. It happens when it happens. I guess you just have to believe that it will." Hearing himself, a preening fraud, a self-aggrandizing con man.

"*You* came out of that building alive, why couldn't my husband? What's so special about you?" Then, rising out of her chair, "God has a *plan* for me?" Turning into the aisle, "Well, I don't want it."

That building . . . Anthony sitting there rocked at how he had made something of himself off the collapse without ever having given a real thought to the dead and the suffering of their survivors.

When he attempted to leave the church again, he was accosted again, Reginald White's grandmother coming out of nowhere to grab him up in her arms.

"Calvin said you were a teacher?" Looking up at him with her damp bulging eyes.

"I was."

"No '*was*,'" she said, shaking him like a tree. "You *are*."

⁂

Unable to stop thinking about Anthony, the truth/untruth of him; the effect his words and delivery had had on the people in there, or for that matter, how at least some of it had affected her, Mary decided to wait for him to come out and when he finally did, nearly the last person to leave, she was in front of the church, standing alongside her unmarked car.

"That was some speech you gave in there."

"Thanks," he said without stopping to look at her, Mary surprised by how lifeless he sounded, how down he looked.

"Are you alright?"

"What?" The question finally turning him around.

"I said . . ."

"Yeah, yes, thank you."

"Are you sure?" she pressed, asking it like a friend, then as his face slowly began to open up to her, she was struck by how undefended he seemed in this moment, how fragile.

"Mary Roe." Offering him her card.

"Thank you," he said again, either forgetting to give her his name or assuming she already knew it.

"You really have a gift."

"Can I return it to the store?" he said.

"Why would you want to do that?"

"Because people died in there," he said.

It took her a moment to pick up what "in there" referred to, because at first, she thought he meant inside the church.

"No, it was terrible," she said, holding off on adding, *You're lucky to be alive.*

"I was just passing by. I just wanted . . ."

Mary waited him out.

"It just happened. I never . . ."

And waited him out; the man wrestling with himself and losing.

When he started to walk away again, Mary opened her passenger door. "Where are you headed? I'll take you."

For the first few blocks, other than thanking her for the lift home, he was quiet, Mary letting him be, hoping he'd spontaneously come out with another of his pleading half statements, but maybe this time go all the way with it and give her something to work with.

At a stoplight, he raised his phone. "Do you mind if I make a call?"

"Go ahead."

"Hey!" he said shakily to whoever picked up.

"Hey." A woman answered, her voice flat and distracted.

Mary could hear her every breath, could hear the rustle of her grip on her cell, could even hear the tinny voices coming from a TV show playing in another room because his phone was on speaker mode; Anthony either not caring or too tense to notice.

♩ ♩ ♩

He couldn't believe she finally picked up.

"Did you get my messages?"

"No, yeah, I was going to call you."

She didn't sound like her normal self to him, more like the knotty version that needed to be liquored up at the hotel in order to regain her ease.

"Ok, so . . ."

"I can't see you tonight," she said.

"Ok, no problem. Tomorrow night?"

"Tomorrow . . ." she said, then partially covered the mouthpiece, Anthony able to pick up fragments of her talking sharply to someone, then coming back on the line. "Sorry, what?"

It was over.

"Tomorrow night," he repeated without hope.

"Tomorrow . . . No, I can't see you then either."

"Is everything ok?" Anthony wishing that she would just spell it out for him, this brutal turnabout and why.

She muffled her receiver again and gave another lecture to whoever, probably her son, then came back on, her breathing heavy with stress.

"Is everything ok?" Asking her again.

"Yeah, no. I'll call you later," she said then hung up.

His first impulse was to try and find a way to steel himself—easy come easy go—but then he remembered that first night with her when she offered him those random physical tokens of her life through the years, and the strange thrill that ran through him once he understood the raw generosity of that gesture, this woman deciding after so little time together to show him who she was because she felt that he might, just might, be the one.

* * *

Mary held off on saying anything, letting his need to talk come to a head on its own which, given how badly rattled he appeared, should come about by the next stoplight or two.

Or three; at the sluggish intersection of 125th and Lenox, the words finally coming out in a burst of despair.

"How is it that someone can come at you full force one minute then go stone cold on you the next. *How.*"

Just to keep him talking, Mary took a shot at answering that excellent question even though it was addressed more to the air than to her.

"Maybe they don't know their own minds."

"What?"

"Or maybe they have issues you don't know about."

"Everybody does."

"Or maybe they learned something about you . . ." she offered, then regretted saying it, because it was too bald a prompt, Mary quickly following it up with a softball.

"So how long were you together?"

"Not long."

"Where'd you meet?"

"At the Stop the Violence rally."

"Which one?"

"At the Crawfords."

"Just last week?"

"Yes."

"Well then, maybe she was just taking you for a test drive." Wincing at how cold that sounded. "Women do that sometimes. Men too, but they don't feel as vulnerable."

"You don't know her," he said. Mary didn't think that he did either, otherwise . . .

"What happened, she heard you talk about saving the children and—"

"No. Before that. We just looked at each other. That's all, game over."

"Because the things you said were so well expressed, so from the heart, really inspiring."

And some of it was, Mary remembering the effect they had on everyone including herself; how his sweet entreaty had inspired her to see her boys in a kinder more generous light. And he'd had that same effect today on the mourners. And again, to some extent, on her. It wasn't that what he had to say was so profound, original or verifiable: no, the key to his charisma, Mary realized, was in the absolute and irresistible conviction with which he delivered his message—it made you want to embrace his words and at least in that moment try to live by them.

"You were there?" he asked, two steps behind in the conversation.

"I mean, how you were able to compose and express all those things so soon after what you'd just been through . . . I can't even imagine how anyone could just pull themselves together so quickly to do that." Mary seeking the most minute crack in his narrative, but Anthony didn't bite, or even act like he had heard anything she said, shutting himself down before she could push any further, leaving her still wondering if he was a hoaxer who was finally confronting the deaths that he'd been dining out on, or was he just devastated by getting dumped. Or both. Or was he telling it true, having endured exactly what he described, coming up out of the earth after so much time down below to offer the gift of solace and hope to those who needed it.

When she finally pulled up in front of his apartment house, he thanked her, reached for the door handle but stayed put, Mary sitting tight, in no rush to lose him.

"What are you thinking about?" she asked after a while.

"I don't know, they asked me to talk at a memorial for the victims."

"Who did?"

"The city, the block association, I don't even know. I said yes at the time but . . ."

"But . . ."

"Now I don't think I should."

"Why not?"

"I just don't think I should," he said reaching for the door handle again.

"I don't know, Anthony, you're so good at putting people's hearts at ease. I think it would be a shame if you passed on it. I mean, for myself? I would really love to hear you speak again. In fact, I think I need to."

*, *, *,

At the grave site, as Royal feared, the cemetery manager told them they'd all have to wait for the diggers to come back from their lunch break.

"I tell you what," Calvin said, gesturing to his Credible Messengers. "How about we bury him ourselves."

"You can't. Union regs."

"Listen." Calvin going into bull-charge mode, lowering his head and raising his eyes as he stepped close enough to whisper. "These men have spent most of their adult lives in prison. God's truth, some of them were happier in there than out here. Now. They want to honor this child by burying him. Trust me. You do not want them reverting on your ass."

"Union regs," the manager said. "You can wait in your cars."

*, *, *,

"Hey, I heard you talk today," someone walking behind him that night on Lenox called out in a voice that could shave metal. Anthony stepped into the safety of a brightly lit deli window before turning to see a coal-toned overly muscled individual, his face a battlefield of wrong choices.

Coming forward, he took Anthony's hand in both of his own.

"I just want to say that all day I've been rolling over in my mind all what you said in the church this morning and now here you are again. I take that as a sign that God put us together because He wants you to hear my story, just like He wanted me to hear yours. Are you ready?"

"What's your name?" Anthony still not knowing if this guy was good news or bad and needing to personalize him.

"Russell Gifford. Russ, Gif, Russell, depends on who I am to you."

"Russell, I'm Anthony."

"Oh, you don't have to tell *me* that," he laughed. "So, if I may, here I go . . . I work in a geriatric hospital in the Bronx, Beth Sholom it's called, working around old folks as you can imagine. This one day I'm up on five in the Baruch Wing, restocking the laundry closets, there's six to a floor, I pass this old lady sitting in her wheelchair in 515, her door's wide open and we make a tiny bit of eye contact that's it, then I go along to the other supply closets on the floor, ok?

"Time goes by, this female orderly comes up to me says, 'The lady in 515 wants to see you for a minute.'

"Ok, so, I don't know why, but I go back there, she's still sitting in her wheelchair, she points to a pencil laying on the rug, says, 'Can you pick that up for me please? I want to write a letter to my sister.' Now, at first, I'm irritated, I had to come all the way back from across the ward, there must of been a dozen, twenty people passed by her room since then, but she's old, in a wheelchair and such, so I pick it up like she asked.

"Then she says, 'Is there something wrong with the soda machine?'

"I say, 'It's broke.'

"She says, 'What if you hit it on the side.'

"I say it's broke.

"She says, 'What if you . . .'

"'It's broke.'

"'Well the last time, what worked was . . .'

"'It's broke.'

"'But . . .'

"'It's broke it's broke it's broke.'

"My lady friend, who works on the same floor as me, she hears me saying all this, steps to the door and very nicely asks me to come out in the hallway for a minute.

"And when I do? She whacks me in the back of my head, says, 'Russell, are you a child of God?'

"I say, 'What are you hitting me for?'

"'I asked, Are you a child of God?'

"'Yeah, I imagine.'

"'Then go to another damn floor and get the lady her soda.'

"So, I do.

"Afterwards, in the car going home, I tell her about the pencil and me coming all the way back across the ward, got like twenty people between me and her, she says, 'And she called for you. Why would she do that?'

"'Because she thought she could get away messing with my head?'

"She says, 'Don't be an ass. She called for you because you got God's love light in you and she saw it. And, oh yeah, by the way, she's lonely.'"

Needing this, Anthony started to tear up.

"So now I come by her room a few times a day, Lilian's her name, just to talk about whatever, the news, my family, hers, and she has one hell of a life story to her, well, so do I"—lifting his chin to display the trim line of a razor slash running from jaw to jaw—"but she's always happy to see me, and, if I can say it without sounding arrogant, I believe that these little visits might be the highlight of her day. And God's truth? Seeing her puts a little pep in my step too. Like, last Monday was my birthday, right? And I still don't know how she knew that it was, maybe my lady told her . . . But when I came into her room that day she had one of those supermarket cakes with my name writ in icing on it, just waiting for me."

"Fantastic," Anthony said, seeing this man now, as he himself yearned to be, as a messenger.

"Whatever starts out in you as a burden, as an ordeal, in the end, if you persevere, will turn out to be the best thing that can happen to you," Russell announced. "That's what you said. So, just like you, I'm thankful to Him for finally having shown me my purpose and for using me like that . . . It's a gift, and I want you to know that even if I never see you again, in my heart you'll always be my brother."

And then Russell hugged him. Startled, it took Anthony a minute to return the embrace.

Who was it that spoke to this man? Who owned those words?

Russell kept his hold on Anthony's arms but otherwise pulled back. "You alright?"

"Me? I'm great," Anthony said. "You have no idea."

* * *

"So, how'd your teacher date work out?" Mary asked Jimmy on his way out the door.

"We didn't have one."

"Why the hell not?" Mary striving for perplexed.

Jimmy shrugged.

"I hope it wasn't because of that little shit fit I had."

"No, I don't think so."

He didn't sound too depressed about it, which made her bolder.

Her cell rang. Mary glanced at the number coming up, Esposito. He'd been calling her a few times a day trying to get them back on track. Mary turned off her phone.

"Who called it off, you or her?"

"Nobody, we just kind of faded on each other."

"Really."

"I don't know, the whole thing felt too weird."

"Weird for who."

"Me."

"Well, I'm sorry to hear that," she said trying to keep the merry out of her voice.

"It's fine," he said, leaving for the nesting apartment.

* * *

When his cell rang at close to two in the morning, he was deep in a dream in which his white lefty grandfather was smacking his white lefty father around in front of a crowd, Anthony caught between wanting to protect his father and cheering his grandfather on. By the time he was able to wrench himself free and find his phone it was too late.

The number showing up was unfamiliar, but it had to be Anne, maybe using another phone, because who else would reach out to him so late at night?

What to do—he wasn't absolutely sure it had been her, and to call her back at this hour on a wishful hunch, especially after she broke it off with him . . .

As soon as he put his phone down, it started to ring again, Anthony snatching it up as if he were saving it from a fire.

"Anne?"

"Who?" his daughter asked.

"Willa!"

"Hi. It's late I know but I just felt like calling you."

"Of course, honey, anytime."

"So, how are you?" she asked, striving for a casual tone and failing.

"Good!" he said, instinctually bracing himself. "I'm glad to hear your voice."

"So, how are you?" she said again.

"I'm good," he said carefully, then, "Did your mother tell you I was trying to reach you?"

"No."

"Did you get any of my messages?"

"No because I accidentally stepped on my phone."

"I'm just asking because—"

"Can you send me money?"

"Money?"

"Three hundred dollars."

"Three hundred . . ." Anthony stalling for time to reorient himself. "That's a lot. What do you need it for?"

"Atlas has a tumor in his leg, Mom says he's old and we should just put him out of his misery but it's my dog not hers and the vet says she can amputate and he can live another two years."

It all sounded rehearsed or memorized, which left Anthony berating himself: *This stranger is what you get for bailing on her, this stranger is what you deserve.*

"I don't want to go behind your mother's back. Can I talk to her about this?"

"No. Don't."

"Ok. Can I talk to the vet?"

"Why? I'm telling you everything."

"It's just . . . Ok, how about this. Give me the vet's contact information and I'll send the money to her directly."

There was a long silence on her end, Anthony sensing that she was scrambling for a way to get around his proposal.

"I thought you loved me" was all she could come up with.

"I do, you know that."

Willa hung up.

He called Clare, waking her.

"Are you going to tell me what's going on?"

"She called you?"

"Yes."

"I knew she would."

"Tell me what's going on."

"She's run away . . ."

"She's thirteen."

". . . with her boyfriend."

"What boyfriend."

"Some kid in her class. Just so you know, she's done this before. Disappears for a day or so, holing up at a friend's house then comes home."

"And you're telling me this now?" Huffing and puffing as if he had a right. "*What* boyfriend."

"Tony . . ." Clare wearily pleaded, Anthony remembering this wilted tone from the time when she had been his last-ditch caretaker.

"Maybe she can come live with me for a while," he said in a panic.

"I don't think that's a good idea." Saying that as gently as she could, then patiently waiting for him to say something but he was out of words.

"Anthony," she finally said, "it's not your fault."

After they hung up, he tried calling Willa back, tried a number of times, but she never picked up.

To avoid dealing with her pain and his own shame, he had become over time increasingly reluctant to seriously engage with her—each day's avoidance spilling over to the next and the next. But instead of pressing him to end this miserable cycle, he found himself surrendering to it, which only served to fortify his avoidance, and on and on and on.

But now he couldn't comprehend how he had allowed himself to indulge in such cowardice; to have kept up with her over the last two years should have been, if not effortless, still the natural thing to do. He saw that so clearly and was desperate to make amends.

* * *

At home late that night, Felix, looking to cull dead weight from his memorial footage and give it some momentum, kept circling back to watch Anthony Carter's address to the mourners. He was compelling, no doubt, as compelling as, if not more so than, he'd been the week before speaking at Calvin's rally, although at this event he found Carter's guarantee—that out of seemingly unendurable tragedy, eventually great and sublime rewards would come to those who persevere—utter horseshit, although many people in that church seemed struck by it, creating with hums and sighs and low *Praise God*s, a soft sea of wisdom received.

But that in itself wasn't the reason why he kept going back over the segment. Since having been hustled himself that night by Crystal, or whatever her real name was, Felix had developed a semisweet tolerance for the smooth con, so if Carter was running some kind of hustle, that by itself wouldn't really bother him. No, it was Anthony Carter himself, something about him making Felix feel he was trying and failing to hold on to a rapidly dissolving fragment of a dream.

Putting aside the memorial footage, he retrieved the film he'd made for Calvin's rally and studied what he captured of Carter in that, only to come away with the same gauzy agitation as before.

Regarding this guy, whatever Felix was searching for wasn't to be found in either film.

*, *, *,

Exhausted by the long day's funeral service and burial, Royal couldn't believe anyone would be so viciously sadistic as to call him in whatever wee hour this happened to be.

He let it ring until Amina woke up too. "Please answer it, would you please?"

It was another funeral home, this one in Peekskill, New York, calling for a pickup from an apartment in the Bronx. Taking up the phone, he left the bedroom for the kitchen, grabbed a pen and pad out of a drawer, sat down at the breakfast table and fought off sleep as the dispatcher fed him the details.

"Where in the apartment."

"Bathroom," the man said.

"Floor, tub or toilet."

"She had a heart attack on the pot, fell off and wedged herself good between that and a wall."

"How long she been there?"

"Roughly eight hours, not much more than that."

Eight hours . . . It would be like extracting a statue that had been twisted into knots and stuffed into a pigeonhole.

"Yeah I know," the man said. "We'll bump your fee to three hundred."

"What bump. That *is* my fee."

"Three twenty-five. I'd go to three fifty, but I'd have to wake up the director for that."

Royal passed.

Instead of crawling back into bed, he made himself a cup of coffee then started to wander about the Home, clocking every tatty, cramped and mismatched detail, down to and including Uncle Permafrost asleep in the cooler.

After finishing the tour he went to his office and watched Felix's promo tape shot in another man's funeral home. The kid said it was just a rough cut and that he needed a few more days to tighten it up, but really, why bother.

Royal picked up the phone and put in a call to California.

* * *

The best thing that could possibly happen to you.

He had no idea how those words had come into his head then out of his mouth almost simultaneously. But they did and not only that, he believed them to be true even if he couldn't explain it to the woman who had lost her husband. But even if those words were nothing more than an impassioned prediction without any guarantee—the best thing that *might* happen to you, the best thing that *may*, that *could* happen to you—he was still offering people a vision of brighter days to come—and that was not nothing.

Sitting on the foot of his bed, Anthony began to tally up his every defeat, every humiliation, every self-inflicted wound from the time he was thrown out of Columbia until now, imagining them as a long slow-motion procession of events that led up to his being covered in rock and wood and stone, by his own hand or God's—depending on what he needed to believe on any given day—then rising up with a widened heart that had allowed him to have Anne in his life for the brief time she was there, expanding his capacity for joy and wild surrender; and with Willa; Anthony finally able to break through the prolonged agony of his resistance and knowing, absolutely knowing, that the rift between them would be repaired.

And now this.

The earnestness of his newly found good will towards people in need of an uplift to make it through to the next day.

The best thing that could possibly happen to you.

Did it come with a guarantee? Of course not. There were no statistics and zero science to back it up, so you had to take it on faith, and in order to maintain that oftentimes fragile state of conviction you had to keep working it and working it.

Someone had sent him a list of the victims along with contact numbers for their relations.

He waited until the morning traffic became a crescendo, then started making the calls.

◆ ◆ ◆

Mary woke from a dream not knowing if she was in the apartment or at home, until the nubby pattern of the chenille under her fingers informed her she was in the so-called nest, that grey box whose euphemistic designation felt like a sick joke.

The dream.

It was about money: coins, gold, paper, someone endlessly giving it to her, immediately followed by someone else taking it from her; over and over, these endless exchanges turning her into a human turnstile.

Hours later, on the job monitoring a demonstration protesting the opening of a third drug rehab center in an area that already had two, her dream had mostly faded but some fragments of it lingering, Mary was still able to drum up the feeling of all that money passing through her—gold, paper and coins, which had her thinking once again about that never-deposited check written out to Christopher Diaz for one hundred and fifty dollars, the likely cost of a ride to Chatham.

The check-cashing spots she had already visited hadn't panned out, so when she clocked out at four, instead of heading back to that one-bedroom penalty box where she had another night to endure, she decided to canvass further out, to the far west side of Harlem, to a money transfer center whose clientele were mainly West African, the waiting area crowded with Senegalese and Côte d'Ivoirians watching a World Cup match between Cameroon and Bosnia on the ceiling-mounted TV; to another center with the transfer fees to various parts of Central America and Mexico soaped in white on its front window; and to another, smaller African money exchange which also offered cell phone and laptop repairs. The first three were busts—no surprise there—but she finally struck gold at the fourth and farthest away, GK Payout Plus, a hole-in-the-wall business sandwiched between a smoke shop with a number of AK-47 sculpted glass bongs displayed in the window and a pre-failed Jamaican seafood restaurant with wide sheets of brown paper covering the windows and a FOR LEASE/FULLY VENTED sign on the front door.

GK Payout Plus seemed deserted, no one in the minute two-chair waiting area with its faux-wood-paneled contact paper walls and no one behind the barricaded counter, Mary having to slap the heavy Lucite security glass until her palm turned red before a cashier eventually appeared, a young South Asian with a wisp of a moustache, thick glasses and a finger-width red stripe daubed down the center of his forehead. Settling himself behind the glass, he crossed his wrists on the counter and commenced bemusedly taking her in as if he were waiting for her to burst into song.

Mary produced her police ID then pressed Diaz's photo against the glass.

"Him," he said.

"He comes in here?" Trying to keep the surprise out of her voice.

"Yes."

"To cash checks . . ."

"Yes." The kid was a real chatterbox.

"As part of a missing person's investigation I need to see photocopies of the checks he's cashed in here."

"Do you have a subpoena?"

"It's coming but time is tight."

"I can't show you anything without a subpoena."

"Look. Like I just told you, this man is missing. His wife died in that building collapse, and we don't know if he died in there, too. Time is critical, so can you help me or not."

Without another word the cashier left his roost, Mary losing sight of him as he headed into the back office, leaving her to wonder if he thought that their business was concluded. But before she could start banging the Lucite again, an older silver-haired man wearing silver-framed glasses and bearing the same red marking on his forehead came to the counter, his button-down shirt untucked to accommodate his gut.

"Yes?" Another windy talker.

And then Mary recognized him.

"Weren't you the manager of Speedy Cash about two years ago?"

"Yes."

"I interviewed you after that robbery. Detective Roe, do you remember me?"

At first, looking straight at her, he didn't, but when he saw the photo on her ID—"Oh you, yes"—Mary now wondering if her face had aged that much over the last few years.

"We collared those two pretty fast after that," she said.

"Yes," he said. Then, "What do you need."

It took her a few seconds to realize the subject had circled back to the business at hand.

"As I told your cashier, I'm still waiting for the subpoena but . . ."

"What do you need."

The back office was small and cluttered, a humid ghost scent of an unidentifiable spice making it seem even more so. There were framed family photos hung on one wall, CCTV captures of bad check passers taped to another.

On the manager's desk was a large-screen computer and an old Regiscope camera used to photograph customers holding up the face-out checks that they wanted cashed.

The manager pulled up the ones featuring Christopher Diaz posing with the checks made out to his name.

There were five, all in the last half year, three of them were for the same amount, one fifty, and from the same person, Lisa Berman.

Start with her.

When Felix entered the funeral home to deliver the finished promo, Royal was in the front parlor with Amina and a man who looked a lot like Royal but slightly taller and thicker through the body.

Whatever was going on, the air was dense with tension, no one even acknowledging his presence.

He knew he should back himself out onto the street, but he was too in thrall to all the possibilities of what had just gone down before he stepped into the parlor.

When the other man finally left, Royal turned to Amina.

"Get Marquise in here." But the boy was already there, standing in the shadows, coming forward now having already heard whatever there was to hear.

"We're having a family meeting," Royal announced.

"A what?" Marquise asked.

"Just sit the hell down, ok?"

Then turning to Felix, who had been inching his way to the front door, "You too."

* * *

There were a dozen ways Mary could have gotten background on Lisa Berman, but at this point she was running out of retired detectives to hit on and tired of begging off on the required subpoenas. Besides all she really needed to know was if the woman owned a second home in the Chatham area, so she went back to the online Columbia County property site and discovered that in addition to her primary residence in the city, a brownstone, which she co-owned not with her husband but her mother, those two also owned a home in Ghent, NY, four miles from Chatham.

* * *

Anthony spent the morning talking to some of the victims' relatives; a cousin in Miami, an ex-wife in Boston, a son in Puerto Rico, a daughter in the Dominican Republic who spoke fairly good English. It had been ten days by now, but some of them still hadn't been notified about the deaths and broke down on the phone, while others barely knew the victim and were more confused than distressed. And whenever he spoke to one of them who needed some immediate consolation he tried his best which was difficult because he didn't know them or any of the people who had died but he discovered that just by staying on the line as long as they needed—it wasn't exactly Balm in Gilead but it was something.

And in between each call he tried to reach Willa, always getting a recorded message telling him her message box was full.

He decided not to phone her mother for constant updates because if there were any new developments she'd call him—that, and the fact that it was his job, not hers, to repair the relationship.

* * *

Mary called Lisa Berman and asked her for a quick meet regarding her driver for hire. This was the first Lisa had heard of Diaz's disappearance the day after he had driven her to the house upstate or that he had a wife who had died in the collapse. Shaken, she agreed to a sit-down. Mary proposed meeting at an East Harlem precinct but Lisa said that because her bullying father had been a Suffolk County detective, she was police-phobic so visiting a precinct was out of the question. Mary was about to suggest meeting somewhere neutral for coffee, when Lisa beat her to it, offering her home if Mary wanted to stop by.

She lived in a restored four-story Victorian with enormous ornate, partially desilvered mirrors set in tiger-maple frames hanging in the parlor and broad oak-carved stairs that swept down from the upper floors, ending in a graceful splayed fan on the main floor.

But there was no corresponding glamour to Lisa herself, a slight undramatic woman somewhere in her forties; sitting in the parlor across from Mary dressed in jeans and a corduroy shirt, her sober brown eyes set in an even-featured face, hair pulled back into a ponytail.

After some small talk, mainly about living in the city versus living in the country, Mary got to work.

"Lisa, can you tell me what time Chris picked you up that night?"

"About seven, maybe a little after."

"And you arrived . . ."

"About nine?"

"So, two hours? That's making good time."

"It would have been faster if we didn't stop for gas."

"And what time did he leave."

"Maybe a half-hour later. I made him some coffee for the ride back then I had some calls to make so he left."

"So roughly nine-thirty?"

"Sounds about right."

"He called his wife at ten, said he was stuck up here."

"Here?"

"In your area. Did you hear him make that call?"

"How could I?"

Mary stared at her in silence.

"Maybe he was stopped for speeding," Lisa said.

"No."

"Or had an accident."

"No."

The opening and closing of the front door made Lisa jump. Her husband, a ridiculously handsome grey-haired man, appeared in the hallway, which afforded him a clear view of the living room.

"How was the audition?" Lisa asked.

He looked at her, looked at Mary, then without a word to either, started up the stairs.

Embarrassed, Lisa turned away.

Mary recalled what a female detective, who at the time was hammered to the gills in some bar, once said to her right before she hit the floor. "I married him because he was good-looking."

When they heard a door being shut on the second floor, it should have been an all clear to resume the interview but the silence continued, Mary holding off on her questions, giving Lisa time to contemplate her unhappiness.

"Lisa let's start over."

"Ok."

"What time did he leave you again?"

"I said."

"Lisa." Mary leaned forward. "What time did Chris leave." Then lowering her voice, "That's all I want to know. I don't give a damn about anything else."

Lisa went off into herself, Mary patiently waiting her out.

"You see how he is?" she finally said in a near-whisper, nodding to the stairs.

Mary touched the back of her hand.

"What time did Chris leave."

"When I woke up at six he was getting dressed."

"At six o'clock."

"Yes."

"How soon after that did he leave?"

"A few minutes. I heard his car going over the gravel in the driveway."

Which would put him in the city around 8:30, Mary figured. That is, if he didn't head somewhere else or make stops for this or that. Mary asked her if she could identify the make and model of Diaz's car, which she couldn't, except for saying that it was a sedan not an SUV which was either black or blue, possibly foreign because what car these days wasn't.

Without having any way to track an unknown car with an unknown license plate Mary took a last stab.

"Who paid for the gas?"

"I did."

"Did you keep the receipt?"

"I think so."

"Can I see it?"

"I have to find it," she said, getting to her feet and leaving the room.

As Mary waited, the mail dropped through the door slot, which drew the husband back down the stairs to leaf through the envelopes and catalogs, still without saying a word to her.

Lisa waited for him to go back to the second floor before she returned to the room with the receipt.

"Do you mind if I take a photo?" Mary asked.

"Just take it," Lisa said.

With the receipt in hand, Mary put in a call to George Gutterman, the Chatham chief of police.

"Hey, I was just about to call you," he nearly chirped. "I'm taking my son into the city on Sunday to see *The Book of Mormon* and I was wondering afterwards if you'd like to have a drink."

"I can't. It's my husband's birthday," she said, surprising herself with her choice for a manufactured excuse. "But next time you come in, maybe?"

"Sure," Gutterman said, "I'll go for a maybe."

A good-natured guy, an easy guy—Mary enduring a brief pang of regret for not taking him up on it, but then it passed.

"Chief, can I burden you with another favor?"

"Name it."

"It's coming to you now," she said, messengering him her photo of the gas station receipt.

* * *

A few minutes after one of his fruitless calls to his daughter his phone rang.

"Willa!" near-shouting her name into the receiver.

There was a momentary silence on the other end, then, "It's Anne."

"Anne," Anthony said neutrally, not sure what tone to adapt.

"I'm calling because I owe you an explanation for my rudeness yesterday, at least as far as I can give you one."

She sounded less distracted than the last time they spoke but her flattened tone told him not to get his hopes up.

"Did you hear about that elderly woman was shot the other day?"

"I didn't, no."

"It was accidental because whoever did it was aiming at someone else. At first I was scared out of my mind that it was my son who pulled the trigger because the real target standing behind Miss Lena was an individual who put him in the ER in the recent past."

"You know that?"

"Everybody knows that. So I confronted him head-on because he can't ever lie to me. Whenever he tries it's like I'm watching him pull a rabbit out of a see-through hat and saying it's magic."

"Thank God," he said because it was an appropriate thing to say, but he wasn't really paying attention, not to the story that she was telling at least—more to her voice, Anthony trying to make out in its risings and fallings, in its pacing and pauses, whether she was talking to him as her boyfriend/lover or just some man she knew.

"But he knows who did it because he was there," she said.

"There like how?"

"Like hanging around how. Like he should have been upstairs doing his homework like he was supposed to, how. And it rips him up about Miss Lena, because he's known her since he was a baby but I won't allow him to talk to the police, not that he needs to be told that because even on the hush-hush, middle of the night in some White Castle parking lot meet-up with them it'll get out that he gave up the name and when it does, he won't be able to come out of the apartment. So, we have to move out, the problem being that I can't afford anywhere else."

"Ok," he said again, struggling to keep track.

"I have a steady income but it isn't enough. And if I go to Housing for a transfer to another project or request a Section Eight out of NYCHA altogether, the woman's going to need a 'why.' I could tell her because my son got shot, which he did, but one, these days that's not enough and B, with the investigation going on, if that ever comes out they'll take a harder look at him and knowing him as I do, he will most definitely crack. We can't live with this. We're trapped."

His first impulse was to offer her shelter in his apartment, her and her son, but then balked because he couldn't imagine how that would play out in any but a bad way.

"What if I go to the police?" Anthony thinking of Mary Roe.

"Like that won't come back on us? You think you're invisible around these houses? You think nobody knows about us in here?"

"Anonymous I meant. A phone call."

"And say what because I didn't give you a name. The only thing you can tell them is what I told you which brings us back to my son seeing it go down. My only hope? That somebody else drops the name."

"If you want to talk, I can come by."

"We're talking right now because as I said, I owe you an explanation for my behavior as far as I can give you one."

"I know, but sometimes when you're face to face . . ."

"It's a bad time," she said.

※ ※ ※

"I have good news for you but you have to act fast," Felix's mother told him over the phone.

"What." Bracing himself.

"News Eight up here? They're looking for a New York City–based video stringer. There's competition for it of course, but one of the producers was a friend of ours, Larry Post, I don't know if you remember him but I rang him up and we had a good conversation about you and the work you've been doing. All of which is to say that if you go after the job you might have the inside track."

"Do I have live up there again?"

"You're not listening Felix, the job is where you are now."

"I hear you."

"Although you didn't have to ask that like coming back here is a fate worse than death."

But it was.

"Sorry Ma, I didn't mean for it to come out that way."

He didn't think he wanted a job like that, but in case he changed his mind—because filming the same uptown playground day after day for the Parks Department wasn't exactly turning out to be much of a learning experience—he started going through his videos just to see what he would hypothetically select for his hypothetical highlight reel. The most dramatic and newsworthy of all was the jagged footage he had shot on the day of the building collapse—Felix hadn't really given it a good look since then and so now he watched it again, this time more attentively, discovering a bunch of small mostly inadvertent God-is-in-the-details captures that he hadn't realized he had trapped: ironic juxtapositions between subject and background; conflicting facial expressions caught in the same frame; gestures, outbursts, the insensate crowd flow . . .

And then, about a third of the way through, he abruptly stopped in order to slowly rewind and reexamine an interaction he'd almost blown past, returning to it again and again, raising the volume each time to hear every word being said.

*, *, *,

After having gone to the Chatham gas station where Diaz had stopped to gas up that night, Gutterman pulled the CCTV footage from their outside security cameras and sent it on to Mary along with a blowup of the license plate and two notes—one about the make and model of the car, a 2002 Chevy Impala, the other to inform her that he'd be happy to switch the date on his *Book of Mormon* tickets to any evening that was not her husband's birthday.

*, *, *,

On the day before the memorial, Clare called Anthony to tell him that Willa had finally come home.

"Can I talk to her?"

"She's in school, then she's going to her therapist."

"Can you tell her I've been trying to reach her?"

"She knows, just give her time."

"And could you please tell her to clear out some space in her message box."

※ ※ ※

According to a friend of a friend at E-ZPass, Diaz's borrowed Chevy had entered the city that morning via a toll booth in Riverdale at 8:15 a.m., fifteen minutes after the collapse that had killed his wife and five others. Mary tried to imagine what it must have felt like for him to pull up to all that chaos; what it must have felt like for him to suddenly find himself in the middle of a surging, yelling crowd while trying to make sense of what was before his eyes, and then after that, slowly coming to understand that his wife, somewhere inside that megaton ruin, was gone.

And after spending the night in someone else's bed? Who wouldn't have wanted to disappear?

※ ※ ※

Going onto the NYS DMV site, Mary tracked down the car's owner, Harold Locke, age sixty-four, a resident of the Battles.

"You calling about my car?"

"I am," she said. "Did you rent it to Christopher Diaz last week?"

"Yeah, and that's the last time I do."

"Did he return it?"

"Hell no. You find it yet?"

"No."

"Because I reported it stole days ago."

"You did?"

"What do you mean, 'You did?'"

"I didn't know that."

Harold sighed. "You people need to start coordinating your shit."

As soon as she ended the call, another call came through.

"Detective Roe, it's Felix Pearl. The photographer. You gave me your card?"

"Hey Felix, sure, what's up?"

"I have something I want to show you, can I come by?"

"There he is." Mary greeting him as he approached her in front of her precinct house.

"What do you got for me?" eyeing the laptop under his arm.

"It's too bright out here," he said. "Can we go indoors?"

Up in her office, he showed her the footage which ran for less than a minute.

When it was over, she stared at the darkened screen as if the video were still playing.

"Play it again, half-speed." Her voice abnormally even-toned, which made Felix wonder if he had made a big mistake by offering it to her.

But what was he supposed to do, keep this to himself?

* * *

A few hours after Felix had sent her a copy of the tape, Mary parked in the teachers' lot of the junior high where Jimmy was subbing yesterday but given that he was a floater, each day showing up at the school within the district where he was needed, she had the wrong one. And so, without enough time to find him before the school day ended she decided to wait for him at the house even though it wasn't her day to be there.

When he came in, he seemed mildly surprised to see her in the kitchen, but not more than that; he even slightly smiled at her although that could have been her imagination.

"I need you to watch something with me," she said.

She could have shown the video to her boss or to the precinct squad or even to Esposito but if she did that it would be taken out of her hands and there would be no way she could control what would happen next.

"Because I want your opinion about what I should do."

Jimmy watched it with her on the kitchen counter, about as surprised by it as he was when he came in and saw her there, which was not much.

"Wow," he said, straightening up, "what are you going to do?"

Big help.

Nonetheless, she stuck around for the offered coffee.

* * *

The memorial site was set up in front of the high wooden barrier that separated the remaining ruins from the open street, which, courtesy of Mary doing her job, was today closed to traffic so that sawhorse barriers and folding chairs could be set up from the north side of the block to the south, although given the surprisingly small number of people who had shown up, at least half those chairs could be folded up right now and loaded back onto the maintenance truck that brought them.

Another disappointment: the mayor was supposed to speak but at the last minute was called to the scene of a fresher building collapse down in the East Village and so sent one of his deputies to speak on his behalf. At least the borough president had made the scene, although no one seemed to know who he was.

Someone had hung six Christmas wreaths on the barrier, each dedicated to a victim of the collapse. And taped around or beneath them were small private messages that she assumed were addressed to the victims. She couldn't make out any of the writing from where she stood so she walked up and read the ones that were in English. When she was done, she turned to go back to her post and saw Christopher Diaz standing at the outer edge of the crowd.

Christopher Diaz. Just like that.

It came as no shock to her that he was still alive; the shock came from how anti-climactic, how casually unreal it felt to finally lay eyes on him after all those obsessive, fruitless days spent in trying to track him down. She had no reason and no need to approach him. He was here, her search was over, and that was that.

※ ※ ※

When Anthony got to the site, he took one look at the woman who'd confronted him in the church, the one who had lost her husband, the one who was staring at him now as if daring him to get up there and spew his bullshit platitudes to the real sorrowers, and he lost all heart.

He looked around for someone to notify that he was backing out, but no one seemed to be in charge. And then he saw Mary standing on the sidewalk scanning the still-arriving guests.

"I can't do it."

"Can't do what."

"This."

"Sure you can," she said. "Just be you and you'll be ok."

"No."

"I'm telling you, you'll be fine."

"You don't understand."

"Anthony . . ."

"I have to go," he said, turning away.

"Hold up." Taking his wrist with one hand, flipping open her phone with her other. "I want you to look at this."

And there he was, on her screen sometime after the collapse, covered in ash, shouting *Don't!* to whoever was holding the camera, then rushing forward until someone off screen stopped his progress by shooting a hard hand into his chest, making him stagger backwards.

"Don't," Anthony said again in a more subdued tone as he distractedly massaged the spot where he was struck.

"Don't what?" Felix's disembodied question coming at him as he took a further step back.

"If it's not asthma that's making you tight but something else in your lungs, if you use your puffer you could wind up spreading it to your other organs. So please don't, ok? Please."

Mary paused the film.

"Who was that?" he asked in a high scrambling voice.

Mary stared at him.

"Are you saying that's me? Because, if you're saying that's me . . . How can that be?"

Staring at him until he started to flail.

"Then how did they come to find me where they found me?"

"You tell me."

"I don't remember anything. I was in shock."

"Clearly," she said, resuming the video.

Anthony walked away, spun around and came back.

"Are you going to arrest me?" The words feathery in his mouth.

Mary took a moment before answering.

"When you spoke to people did you ever charge for your services?"

"Absolutely not."

"You never took a speaker's fee, never received a single dollar in exchange for talking to people."

"Never. Never."

"So what am I supposed to arrest you for?"

"I'm trying to do *good* for people."

"Then do it," she said.

From his window directly above the crowd, Felix zoomed in to catch his own video playing on Mary's phone screen, thinking that filming a film taken by the creator of both films should have its own genre niche, then continued shooting their encounter; Mary composed, Anthony looking like he was about to pass out.

"What are you going to do with that," he said, staring at her phone.

"It depends," she said.

"On what."

Mary looked off, something out there making her smile.

"I saw this woman the other day standing on a corner, telling everybody she was Prince's mother."

"Who?"

"Prince. *1999, Purple* . . . It doesn't matter. It was bullshit but she had this, this *knack* for lifting people's spirits up, I mean you just had to see her in action. And in these times? It was really something to see."

"What are you *talking* about?"

"And, in my mind, that's kind of what you do. I watch people when you talk to them. And I watch you: How you try to pick them up off the floor. And a lot of times you do. It's a talent you have and I think it would be a real shame to have to shut you down."

"Ok."

"So, first, you're going to go up there and do your thing because people want to hear you."

"Ok."

"And then I want you to keep at it. From now on whoever asks for you, you're going. And as long as you keep that up?" Mary held up her phone. "This stays between us."

"Ok."

Ok. Ok. Ok . . . Mary at first thrown by his off-hand briskness then thought that given the stakes, maybe "ok" was about all he could manage.

"But if I hear from anyone that you turned down their request, this might most definitely leak." Saying that just to scare him into compliance, knowing full well that even if he did bail on people, she couldn't imagine following through on her threat.

But Anthony didn't feel threatened or blackmailed; what he *did* feel, slowly at first then picking up speed, was a sensation of lightness; the ever-present burden of his story finally exposed, but instead of crushing him, it seemed to be freeing him from its weight.

"Are we understanding each other?"

"What?"

"Are we . . ."

"*Yes.* Absolutely." Anthony suddenly brimming with resolve. "All I want to do is go up there and say a little something about the people who died. That's it. No inspirational messages and nothing about me."

"Especially nothing about you because if you don't pull the plug on that Lazarus bullshit sooner than later it's going to come back and bite you on the ass."

"Absolutely."

"I mean if that lady was Prince's mother . . ." Mary laughed, walking off.

*, *, *,

After the borough president gave his more or less boilerplate speech and Father Ekubo the Malian priest from St. Rose of Lima had delivered a brief sincere homily in his near-impenetrable French-African accent, Anthony made his way to the mike, waited out a screaming ambulance flying uptown on Park Avenue, glanced at his handwritten notes, then got to it.

"Everett Martin Towne was forty-nine years old. After graduating from Aviation High School he enlisted in the Navy, where he served for five years as a radar technician then spent the next twenty-five years working for the postal service."

He stopped to find Towne's widow, the one who scoured him raw, but she was no longer there.

"In his off-hours he played the trumpet although according to his brother the minute he put it to his lips, people tended to run for the hills." Anthony paused again for a smattering of light laughter. "He was a deacon at Our Lady of Victory of St. Martin de Porres Parish in Bedford-Stuyvesant, was known as the neighborhood clothes horse, possessed a near-unreturnable serve on the handball court, a sharpshooter's eye in the pool hall and a sweet swing on the ball field.

"On that morning, he had just entered the building to deliver the mail.

"He leaves behind his wife of twenty-two years, Janine, and four children, Everett Junior, Peter, Maryanne and Giselle."

He knew that what he had served up barely skimmed the surface of a lived life, but it was better than nothing.

Back to studying the crowd, Mary noticed that Diaz seemed to be staring at her as if he knew who she was and what she'd done to find him. But how could that be?

"Robert John Cornish . . ."
"*Sweet child in a man's body*," someone called out.
"Robert John Cornish was forty years old. At birth, he contracted viral meningitis which left him permanently intellectually disabled. His mother, Felicia Hunter, a single parent, had tried to take care of him by herself but by the time he was five she couldn't anymore and had to place him in a special needs children's residence in Aurora, New York. He lived there and in other state-run institutions for the next thirteen years, until his mother passed and her sister Mildred Hunter decided to bring her nephew home."

*, *, *

"I got good news for your little mulch institute," Royal said to Benny as they stood together in the middle of their shared lot.
"Do tell," Benny said, kicking up a chip of ruptured asphalt.
"I just sold the parlor to my brothers. We'll be moving out at the end of the month."
"No."
"I know I probably just broke your heart with that, but do your crying at home."
"And here I thought we were going to start being friends," Benny said without a hint of irony.
"Yeah, well," Royal muttered, embarrassed by the florist's sincerity. "Anyways, some free advice," he said. "I think they just want it for the property value but in case they want to keep the parlor going you best

get your garden in fast because they're going to want those parking spaces."

"Good to know," Benny said. "So what are you going to do now?"

"I'm thinking a few things," Royal said. "All I know for sure is that I have to make a life that I can live with."

*   *   *

"Mildred Hunter was seventy-four years old . . ."

"*Love you Milly,*" that same person called out, Anthony waiting until the scattershot chorus of shout-outs for the woman subsided.

"Earlier in life, she was the owner and sole employee of Millie's, a women's uniform shop in the Bronx, selling mainly to nurses, aides, technicians and cafeteria workers from Westchester Square Hospital just around the corner. When the hospital was shuttered by the city, Millie's closed soon after. From what I've been told, she went to contract on another retail space close by Lincoln Hospital but when Felicia became sick"—Anthony's voice began to wobble—"she chose to break her lease and become her sister's full time caretaker which she did until the end of Felicia's life . . ."

People are so much more—Anthony having to stop for a moment to let that small epiphany sweep over him again.

"She never married or had children of her own, but a year after taking her nephew out of the state system and into her home, she adopted him outright."

*   *   *

Having left the brownstone before anyone took the stage, Felix was hanging out at the funeral home helping Amina and Marquise pack up some preliminary stuff for the coming move. When the office phone rang, Amina, up to her neck in boxes, asked him to take the call.

*   *   *

"Evelyne Sanon, born in Port-au-Prince, immigrated to the US in 2000, living first in the Liberty City section of Miami where she found employment for six years in the cafeteria of the Palmetto General Hospital before moving to the Crown Heights section of Brooklyn and started working as a visiting home aide.

"After staying overnight in the building attending to Anna Merry, early the next morning, she escorted Miss Anna to her sister's house, then returned to the apartment to retrieve her reading glasses.

"She leaves behind two children, Etienne, a US Marine warrant officer stationed in Korea, and his sister Jeanne, a dental technician living in Atlanta.

"Madame Sanon was fifty-five years old."

The call-outs for Evelyne, unknown to most of the assembled, were respectful but less than for Everett Towne, who people saw every day delivering the mail, and even lesser than for Mildred and Robert who lived in the building.

Anthony had to pause again, this time for a Metro North train moaning its way towards Grand Central.

"Kenya Henry, was forty-eight. After graduating from the High School of Art and Design she attended the New York Studio School for a year before going out on her own to see what she could make of herself as an artist but after a few years of struggle and needing to support herself, she became a permanent fixture on Lenox Avenue, as a vendor selling her own watercolor sketches of the neighborhood, portraits on demand and original greeting cards.

"I wouldn't mention this at her memorial, but her sister, Melanie Wright, asked that I do so. In her twenties, Kenya was a heroin addict for five years, then clean for one year before slipping back into the darkness for two more years, after which she finally came to grips with her disease.

"At the time of her death, she had been drug-free for twenty-one years. Melanie told me it was her sister's proudest achievement, which is why she wanted it known."

* * *

After talking to Benny then running some errands, Royal finally returned to the Home, Felix coming out of his office waving two order forms for funerals.

"You should quit the business more often," he said.

***

"Rosa Maria Diaz was forty-three years old . . ."

Mary had her eyes on Diaz; the mention of his wife's name had him pacing and talking to himself—or, Mary imagined, to her—maybe trying to explain the circumstances of that night or more likely pleading for her forgiveness.

"Born in Santo Domingo she came here as a seventeen-year-old, a skilled seamstress who worked for a number of clothing manufacturers, working her way up over the years to become the sewing shop forelady for Jeb-Mar Shirt Manufacturers in New Jersey. When Jeb-Mar began outsourcing to Asia, she took her severance and used it to start her own business, Estilos de Rosa . . ."

"Yes she did!" Diaz barked, clapping his hands then dropping into a squat, lowering his head and rocking on his haunches.

". . . which at the time of her death, had just received its first New York State Small Business Association grant."

"She leaves behind her husband of twelve years, Christopher Diaz, and a daughter from an earlier marriage, Marta Colon of Puerto Plata, D.R."

Despite having declared that he was going to stick to straight bios of the dead, Anthony, still feeling lighter than air, couldn't resist offering a small speech to those who'd been left behind, the words as always coming to him without effort.

"Pain," he announced, scanning the faces. "Pain is the chisel with which He, with which *we*, sculpt our own character. Pain, that unexpected kick in the teeth is the scalpel, the forge, the furnace, the lion's den, and how we respond to it makes us who we are. Pain is not the enemy. It is the soul's classroom. It is the soul's university. Learn from it and you learn to live . . . God bless the fallen and God bless you all."

※ ※ ※

At the end of the ceremony, Diaz came up behind Mary. "Do you know me?"

"Do I?" Startled by his sudden appearance, that was all she could manage to say.

"Because you keep staring at me like I did something."

At that moment, Mary knew that if he could, he'd arrest himself.

"Do you *know* me."

"Just from your photo."

"My photo? What photo. Why would you have my photo."

"You were missing. People were trying to find you . . . *I* was trying to find you."

"Why? I didn't do anything."

"No one said you did. But you needed to be found."

"Well you found me, ok?" he said, turning and walking away.

"I'm sorry about your wife," Mary called out, stopping him. She walked to where he stood and touched his arm. When he turned, his face was slack with anguish.

"It was like God was just waiting for me to . . ."

"He wasn't waiting for you to do anything. And what happened was not your fault," Mary said handing him her card. "I'm glad you're still with us."

※ ※ ※

When it was over, he sat on the front stoop of a brownstone directly behind the rows of folding chairs, trying to process the fact that it seemed like he always knew what to say in front of a crowd, sometimes before he could completely organize his thoughts.

The *cadaver dogs*.

Anthony remembered them now. They had come trotting over

to where he sat against a wall at the edge the rubble field, briefly inspecting him then losing interest because he didn't have that smell and moving on.

Then a memory further back.

Walking in front of the building thinking about his High and Mighty Men's job interview just a few doors down, about what he had chosen to wear that morning, when the outwards thrust of the implosion shoved him sideways, like a game piece across a board into the middle of the street.

Laying there stupid, the roar of the collapse still trumpeting in his ears.

At some point, rising to his feet from beneath a blanket of ash and seeing others lying there like Pompeii body casts; some, like himself, rising and staggering away, others trying to rise then falling back down and staying down.

Constantly being jostled and sideswiped by more *others*; half-blind ghosts feeling their way through that chalky mist.

The video showed him talking a blue streak to someone holding the camera but he had no memory of that.

Getting swept up in the rush of people racing into the wreckage in order to help search for bodies.

Finding a spot in that smoldering field to sit and take it all in, sitting for hours, fixated on the mouth of a crawlspace carved out of the collapse, no one taking note of him because he wasn't really there.

At some point there was a fire that drew everybody to the rear of the field. It was night by then and he could have left without anyone seeing him but he just didn't want to go back out there, every day putting one foot in front of the other in front of the other.

"In my mind, I was done with that."

"Done with what," Mary said, taking a seat on the step above him.

"What?" Anthony unaware that he'd been speaking out loud.

A ragged convoy of ATVs flew by on the reopened street, the high-pitched snarl of their four-stroke engines sounding like a war party of psychotic wasps.

"Just for fun," she said, "how'd you get in there?"

"In where."

"Where they found you."

"Crawled? I don't know how else. I just wanted to hole up and close my eyes for a minute."

"Did you know what you were doing? Did you have a game plan?"

She immediately regretted asking that, worried as she was that he'd confess to something that would make her renege on their arrangement.

"A *game* plan? For what? For when they pulled me out? I wasn't thinking about that happening. I wasn't anticipating that. I wasn't anticipating shit. All I wanted was to *not be* for a while. A game plan . . . You got to be kidding me, because . . . because from the minute I felt hands tugging on my leg I knew I was in trouble."

His outraged reaction, at least so far, felt honest, which helped her to relax.

"And when dragging me out turned into a story, turned into the news . . . What was I supposed to say? Who was I supposed to tell? And every day after that, every day that I held off on setting the record straight . . ." Looking away from her, "A game plan . . ."

"But Anthony," she couldn't help pushing, "you gave interviews, you gave speeches, you went on TV for Christ's sake. If you were so worried about being found out why didn't you just lay low?"

Anthony's face turned red. "Because people were rooting for me."

Rooting for me. The words making her wince.

"I just wanted to hold on to all that good will coming my way. And when I found my voice . . ."

At the top of the stairs, the front door of the brownstone swung open, Mary turning and looking up to see O-Line coming out onto the landing. Thrown by the sight of the two non-tenants sitting on his stoop, he took a few tentative steps down, then stopped.

They stood up to let him pass or find his perch, but he looked like the idea of sharing the stoop with these outsiders was a bridge too far, so he went back into the building.

One of the attendees from the memorial, a tall rangy young man with quivering fishbowl eyes that seemed to wrap around the sides of his head, eyes that projected the alertness of someone who thought of himself as a moving target, came up to Anthony and offered his hand. "My grandmother says to thank you," he said flatly, then continued on down the street.

After that, neither of them sat back down; Mary thinking, *And that's that*, but Anthony wasn't done.

"Whatever you think of me, I just want to explain to you that everything I want to say to people, all of what I believe I can offer to them, it all comes out of what they've been giving to me from day one.

"You know, I say God did this for me, God did that for me, but *they're* the ones that handed me a second life, *they're* the ones that made me new. And maybe if I wasn't such a weak person none of it would have been necessary or even happened to begin with but that's who I am, and for what they've done for me?" Shaking his head, "I mean, it's like, you say to me, *You keep this up or else.*" Smiling at her now, "Like that's supposed to be some kind of threat?"

*, *, *

"They arrested him," Anne Collins said, the first words out of her mouth.

"Arrested . . ."

"The boy."

"Thank God."

"I'm ashamed of myself for not helping out but my son's survival comes first."

"Good, good. So, you feel better now? More like yourself?"

"Not all the way. I have a sister lives in Tavares, Florida. I hate that state, every time I go down there something bad happens, but I can't take it anymore around here so we're moving. Work's no problem, the postal service can find a station for me so . . ."

"What about us?" Anthony just threw that out there without any real hope.

"Didn't you ever feel like we were a mismatch?" she said.

"No."

"I felt like we were trying each other on like new clothes but then here comes the mirror."

"Not for me."

"I don't believe you," she said, and she was right.

"I gave you my all."

"This isn't about that. You were good to me. You were patient and never made me feel like I was talking to the wall, but a lot of times I felt like something was off. First I thought that we just came from different worlds, I know that was a struggle for me but it wasn't just that. There were times when you spoke about yourself it felt like you were offering me just the tip of who you were and hoping it came off as the whole iceberg.

"And when this thing with my son happened, I just felt that if I wasn't sure of you, of who you were, then I couldn't afford the distraction."

That one stopped him short . . .

"I have to tell you something," he said, then offered his second confession of the day.

When he was done, there was a long silence on the other end which left him feeling like he had just made a grievous mistake.

"I had thought maybe it was something like that," she finally said.

"I'm sorry."

"Don't be. You felt lost, so I guess you had your motivations."

* * *

Teddy Burns kept his one-bedroom apartment in the Marion's Choice Assisted Living Center spotless to the point of antiseptic; Mary assumed her father maintained it that way because it was one of the few things he could still control in his world.

He wore the scars of his profession well; his flattened nose and scar-puffed brows were set in an otherwise firm-featured face which gave it a noble air, like that ancient pugilist cast in bronze.

At seventy-five he was still fit but only from the neck down.

These days, his short-term memory was completely shot; her father increasingly forgetting to turn things off in the kitchen—the stove, the toaster, the broiler—or he forgot to take things out when the timer went off which twice brought the fire department, including once when he had turned on the oven to preheat for a roast and forgot to remove the stack of plastic place mats that for some reason he always kept stored in there, the chemical stench invading every apartment in the building for days.

Lunch was tomato soup and toasted cheese sandwiches.

Sitting across the table from him, Mary, as always, stared at her father's hands, amazed at how small they were for all the havoc they had wreaked in the ring.

"I was thinking about that time when I was a kid when you took me to look for Danny Rivera," she said.

"Who?"

"Danny Rivera."

"Rivera . . ."

"You fought him twice. He took the first by a decision, you knocked him out in the second."

"I fought a lot of guys."

"Dad . . ."

Was he fucking with her? Or was his long-term memory going too?

"Dad, come on . . ."

"I always blamed the ref for not stopping it sooner," he said. "That last round he couldn't even defend himself. The guy's still on his feet what was I supposed to do?"

"It's ok."

"After that I said that's it for me. I'm done."

"You helped take care of him after that. Do you remember?"

"Some."

"So, do you remember that night?"

"Which."

"The night his wife called you and we went looking for him."

"We what?"

"Dad, come on." Then added, "You're killing me."

"And I blame his manager for not throwing in the towel sooner."

Mary gave up.

"You know, one thing I do remember. He had a wonderful wife, Carmen. She took care of him like an angel."

"That's great," Mary said, thinking about the traffic out there.

She was about to begin her goodbyes when suddenly her father's hands shot up in the air so fast they seemed to blur, Mary immediately thinking, *seizure*, but then they came back down to the table lightly cupped, Teddy holding them like that for a moment before slowly almost ceremoniously parting them to show her the fly he had snatched out of the air before she could even register its existence.

"Well, will you look at that," he said.

*   *   *

He had just discovered a website listing open teaching positions in the New York area when his phone rang.

"Hi," Willa said.

"Hi," Anthony echoed, bracing himself.

"Mom said I should call you to apologize."

"Mom did."

"About asking you for money. But I wanted to, anyway. Apologize."

"Ok, good. So, how are you?"

"You know."

"I miss you," he said.

"Thank you."

"Is Atlas ok?"

"Yeah. I lied about him being sick."

"We all lie now and then," Anthony said, nearly choking on his own words. "Can I ask what you were going to do with the money?"

"Stupid stuff. I'd rather not say."

Don't press.

"No matter."

"I want . . ." she said then stopped.

"What."

"Nothing."

Not nothing, but don't press.

"So how are you getting along with everybody?" he asked.

"Everybody meaning George?"

"You call him George?"

"I didn't even remember him from before."

"So how's that going?"

"He really likes Mom."

"And you?"

"He's not mean to me or anything."

"As much as I hate to say it," Anthony said, "he is your father."

"Why do you hate to say it?" her voice rising in alarm.

Anthony closed his eyes, took a moment.

"It's just a figure of speech."

In the silence that followed, he could feel her struggling.

"What's going on?" he said.

"Nothing but I have to go now," she said. Then, "We should talk more."

* * *

Mary had no real desire to hook up with Esposito anymore but he promised to have his shit together this time and to keep it just to a conversation then gave her the name of a swank hotel on Central Park South where he had booked a small suite for the evening.

She knew better than to take the bait but she took it nonetheless for reasons that might or might not have anything to do with him per se, and so, after telling herself that her curiosity had just gotten the best of her or some other flimsy nonsense, an hour later she found herself heading down a cream-colored hallway lit by small chandeliers until she came to the door of the Navarro Suite.

From the moment she stepped inside and saw the napkin-swaddled bottle of champagne chilling in a silver bucket, Mary, thinking, *Fuck, he's left his wife*, felt like punching herself in the head.

"I have some news to tell you," he said, his eyes a touch too lit as he lifted the bottle out of its ice bath.

"Oh yeah?"

"I hope it's good news," he said, gripping the cork.

"You don't know?"

Esposito turned to her. "I mean good news for you."

"What is it."

"Read my mind," he said.

"What about your kids?"

"They're my kids," he said. "They'll be fine."

He's an idiot, she thought.

"Well if that's what you want to do."

"Include you out, though, is that what you're saying?" Esposito beginning to fume now, his face darkening as he continued to wrestle with the cork.

Mary softened her tone.

"I just think you need to give yourself a little time before..."

"And you?"

"I don't need any time. I'm not going anywhere."

"In your half of the house."

"That's right."

Esposito gave up on the champagne which was fine with her.

"You think you're the only one?" he said.

"Only one what."

"For me. Doing this."

"I wouldn't know," Mary said evenly, refraining from saying, *Then ask one of them*, because at this point it was best to not to crack smart which would just keep this thing going.

※ ※ ※

Clare's call yanked him awake.

"So what do you think?" she asked.

"About what?"

"Thanksgiving."

"What about Thanksgiving?"

She took a moment before answering.

"Her staying with you."

"What?"

Another long pause. "She didn't mention it?"

"No she didn't."

"That was the whole point of calling you. She must've gotten cold feet."

"Why? Did she think I'd say no?"

"She might have."

That one stung.

"Well let me ask, how do you feel about that? Because earlier you said it wasn't a good idea."

"That was about staying with you permanently. This is just for a long weekend."

"I'll take it," he said.

*, *, *,

When Mary left the hotel and went back uptown she came up on Prince's mother again, drawing a crowd on 116th and Lenox, posing for pictures and making a scene; the only difference between this one-woman block party and the previous one was that now she was claiming to be Senator Barack Obama's sister.

In order to avoid being pulled in close for another photo op, Mary stepped to the rear, leaned against a parked car and took in the show.

*, *, *,

Leaving the house of Royal after having dinner with the family that night, Felix spotted Crystal standing in front of that same bodega as before. When she finally noticed him looking right at her, she tensed, her body coiled for takeoff.

LAZARUS MAN

Felix mimed taking her picture with an invisible camera then just waved, no harm no foul. Relieved, she blew him a kiss.

Walking on, he heard Calvin's voice coming through a bullhorn somewhere up ahead. "Now, I'm not going to be *long*, but I promise to be *strong*."

Felix followed the voice until he came on another street rally two blocks away. One of the CMs recognized him and said something to the boss.

"Just the man I was looking for," Calvin called out, coming straight at him. "You got your camera?"

"Always."

"Then here's your T-shirt"—flipping it to him—"get to it."

Felix checked the Nikon's battery—plenty of power left—then got to it.

*   *   *

Given that the boys were both away on overnights with their friends there was no rush for Mary to get home, and so without anything else to do she found herself in that same jazz bar, drinking solo at the rail. She felt like getting into a conversation with somebody—a bartender, another rail rat, male, female, didn't matter—but as she surveyed her options, the throwback blues band, Delonda and Her Boyfriends, came back from their break. Delonda, a short round shaved-headed light-skinned woman sporting hoop earrings the size of 45 records and enough ice-blue eye shadow and liner to humble Cleopatra, took a beat to adjust her mike, and backed by her group started belting out Big Maybelle's "Candy," and the possibility of Mary having any kind of conversation short of shouting or using American Sign Language was nil.

But this Delonda had some voice on her, so Mary stayed put, drinking her way through "I'd Rather Go Blind," "When My Love Comes Down," and "Lotus Blossom."

After her second vodka tonic she briefly thought about maybe giving Esposito another shot, then no, the hell with him. She stayed for one more song and one more drink then left, Erma Franklin's "Piece of My Heart" escorting her out the door.

* * *

The house was a tomb. Not even a refrigerator hum. One glass in the sink. The sound of Mary's keys dropped on a side table was an aural event. She turned on the TV just to make some noise, *Blue Hawaii* on the screen, whatever. She sat on the couch facing and fell asleep with her eyes open, waking up two hours later to *King Creole*.

She washed her face and brushed her teeth in the downstairs bathroom then climbed the stairs. Stepping into the bedroom, she saw that Jimmy was under the covers again, curled on his side, his head between two pillows.

Her first thought was that she fucked up again. Nope, no way, it was definitely her night. *He* fucked up.

She wanted to roust him, but didn't have the energy. Changing into a long nightgown that had seen better days, she got under the covers, liberated one of the pillows from his head sandwich, lay back, closed her eyes and listened to him sleep, the rhythm of his breath once so familiar to her that there had been nights when she couldn't distinguish it from her own.

After a while, she began to drift off.

They could talk about it in the morning.

PART FOUR

THE BEST THING THAT COULD POSSIBLY HAPPEN TO YOU

Over the months, people pretty much forgot about Anthony's so-called resurrection story and mainly came to hear him speak just on the strength of his reputation.

He still had his dark times, but he also had purpose.

He applied for a teaching position at an East Harlem charter school and to his surprise got the job. Not a lot of money in it, but combined with the small annuity from his grandfather's will, he got by.

Willa had come to stay with him a few times now, never for more than a week given her school and therapy schedules, but at least they were starting to get a little comfortable with each other again, even though the first day or two of any visit was always on the stiff side.

Having never made the move to Florida, Anne still lived with her son in the Crawfords. Once he found that out, he could have called her, but the fact that she never reached out to tell him as much meant that despite the crisis around her son having been resolved, now that she had voiced her deep misgivings about their relationship, there was no going back.

To be of service; Anthony unfailingly showing up whenever and wherever, even though he had come to realize that as a so-called messenger he only had one singing telegram to deliver, which with minor variations from audience to audience always boiled down to the same tune, the words coming as much from Prophetess Irene as from anyone or anywhere else—*If you have the will to stand fast long enough against the crushing blow, one day you will find that your tables have turned and your heart has healed.*

Probably as a delayed reaction—after Mary had finally set him free—to having had to contort so much of his story in the early days in order to enhance the "miracle" of his rebirth, compelling him to go on a never-ending hunt for coincidences that supposedly signified "signs," that whatever had changed in him after being liberated from the rubble was at least in part the work of His hand, these days he took the God angle down a few pegs by blending it with the message that within each of us lies the power to surprise ourselves with who we never knew we could be.

"*All you have to do is let go.*"

That was what the men's Bible group leader had said to him when he was a teenager, and now he was saying as much to his audiences, only the spirit that he wanted them to allow into their hearts was their own.

"I once heard an old guy sitting with his friends on a bench one afternoon," Anthony said, wrapping up his address to a cocaine sobriety support group in one of the conference rooms of a small hospital.

"He said, 'Last night I told God get me through this and I'll never drink again but that was just the hangover talking.'"

That one got a few laughs.

"How hard it is to keep our commitment to ourselves. And God? When things are going good, we say God is good. But when things go south? That, apparently, is on us.

"Some of you might say, 'Well, He's testing me because He wants to see what I'm made of,' or, 'Maybe He's trying to make more of me than I was.'

"If that's what you believe then you need to show Him what you got. But it's also the time when you need to show the individual in the mirror what you got.

"Show Him or Her or whatever Life Force or Higher Intelligence you believe in and you show yourself.

"'I have been here before, and I will be here again.' *Accept* that, *be at peace* with that, *use* that.

"It's not about the misfortune, it's about how we *handle* the misfortune. Because misfortune, like the common cold, is a perpetual fact of life. But when it comes again, and be you man, woman, rich, poor, white, Black, brown, Asian, it *will* come again, recall to yourself—I have been here before and somehow, I'm still standing."

When it comes again . . . Anthony briefly faltering—wondering in what way, in what *ways*—misfortune will revisit him too.

Then shaking that off—"Believe in that higher power, lean on it if that's what you need to do, but for God's sake believe in yourself. Think of where you've been, think of what you've already endured then tell yourself . . . 'And yet, and yet, here I still am.' You do that, you *keep* to that and there will come a day when you will look back and be astonished, not only by how so much of your broken heart has healed, but also by where your life has taken you since."

Then looking at each face in turn, the reachable and the shuttered, and saying that one word again: "Astonished."

ACKNOWLEDGMENTS

Lorraine Gladus Adams

Anne and Genevieve Hudson-Price

Jeremy and Margarita Price

Judge Richard Lee Price

Steve Hernandez

Richard Dillon

James Hamilton

Antonio Hendrikson

John MacCormack

Marc Henry Johnson

Nancy Chemtob

Myron Lazar

Doran Baltus

Raj Jayadev and Silicon Valley De-Bug

And with gratitude to those who, after an insanely long gestation period, helped bring this novel into being—

Jonathan Galassi

Lynn Nesbit

Katie Liptak

And Bri Panzica